GOTREK & FELIX
LOST TALES

A WARHAMMER ANTHOLOGY

EDITED BY LAURIE GOULDING

GOTREK & FELIX

LOST TALES

BLACK LIBRARY

A Black Library Publication

This edition published in Great Britain in 2013 by
Black Library,
Games Workshop Ltd.,
Willow Road,
Nottingham, NG7 2WS, UK.

10 9 8 7 6 5 4 3 2 1

Cover illustration by Phroilan Gardner.
Map by Nuala Kinrade.

See Black Library on the internet at

www.blacklibrary.com

Find out more about Games Workshop
and the world of Warhammer at

www.games-workshop.com

Printed and bound by CPI Group (UK) Ltd, Croydon, CR0 4YY

This is a dark age, a bloody age, an age of daemons
and of sorcery. It is an age of battle and death, and of the
world's ending. Amidst all of the fire, flame and fury
it is a time, too, of mighty heroes, of bold deeds
and great courage.

At the heart of the Old World sprawls the Empire, the
largest and most powerful of the human realms. Known for
its engineers, sorcerers, traders and soldiers, it is
a land of great mountains, mighty rivers, dark forests
and vast cities. And from his throne in Altdorf reigns
the Emperor Karl Franz, sacred descendant of the
founder of these lands, Sigmar, and wielder
of his magical warhammer.

But these are far from civilised times. Across the length
and breadth of the Old World, from the knightly palaces
of Bretonnia to ice-bound Kislev in the far north, come
rumblings of war. In the towering Worlds Edge Mountains,
the orc tribes are gathering for another assault. Bandits and
renegades harry the wild southern lands of
the Border Princes. There are rumours of rat-things, the
skaven, emerging from the sewers and swamps across the
land. And from the northern wildernesses there is the
ever-present threat of Chaos, of daemons and beastmen
corrupted by the foul powers of the Dark Gods.
As the time of battle draws ever near,
the Empire needs heroes
like never before.

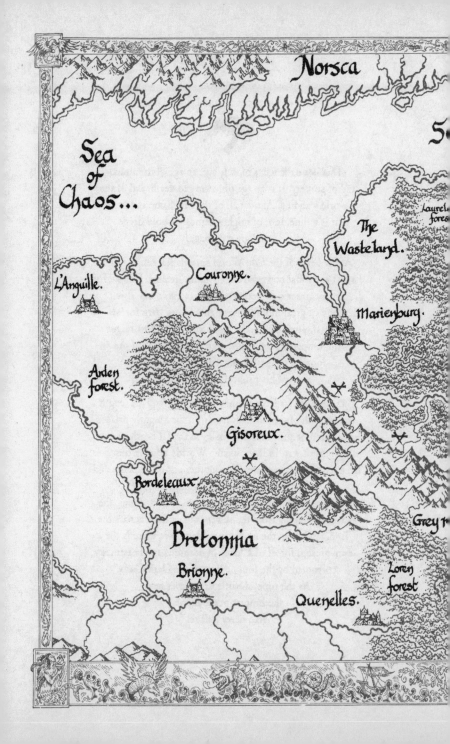

CONTENTS

CHARNEL CONGRESS

Josh Reynolds

'Sylvania. Its name stands out on a map like a pox-mark. It is a black boil that has been lanced again and again, yet never ceases to plague Sigmar's children, and it is one that I fear never will. I would journey into that sinister demesne more than once at my taciturn companion's side, though never without paying a higher toll in blood and hope than I would have liked.

Ulrika...

Sylvania, whose only export is death; Sylvania, whose serpent-fanged masters cluster in forgotten places like the great bats whose bones decorate the rude peasant shrines which line the black road! It was – and is! – a dangerous place, even for a Slayer, and more so for this all-too-human wordsmith. But as to just how dangerous, we were sorely unaware.

Luckily, or unluckily, we were soon to make the acquaintance of a tutor of some distinction...'

– From *My Travels with Gotrek, Vol. II*
By Herr Felix Jaeger (Altdorf Press, 2505)

The black water split as the pole came down. It pierced the murky depths and stirred up the dull mud below. Leaning hard against the pole, Andree Borges whistled tunelessly through stumps of rotted teeth as he forced his skiff through the water, a single torch lighting his way. The tune was half-prayer and half bawdy sonata, and had been passed down from father to son since as far back as Andree could recall. Which, he had to admit, wasn't very far. He wasn't a thinker, Andree, and he knew it. You couldn't be a thinker and survive in Hel Fenn. Instinct and faith... those were the only tools that mattered. Well, those and a good strong axe.

Eyes long since turned yellow from cheap rotgut scanned the arthritic trees that clustered on the legion of hummocks and boles of strange black earth that seemed to float on the oily water. The torch, its flame caged in an iron hood with holes punched in to let out the light, made the ugly little islands seem to dance. Andree shuddered. His grandfather had avowed as those buboes of dirt were graves, and that the Fenn was naught but a bone-garden flooded way back when.

Andree could believe it. If there was one thing that the Fenn didn't lack for, it was bones. White, yellow and brown, hiding in the tangled roots of trees or beneath the mud, there were bones everywhere, of every shape and distinction. Anatomists and articulators from as far away as Altdorf paid a pretty penny for full skeletons in good condition. Carnival men paid even more for mismatched specimens, strung together with catgut and twine, which they could pass off as mutants or daemons. And maybe some of them even were.

The dark between the trees hid many secrets, after all, and there were bowers and run-offs that Andree would not have gone into for all the karls in Stirland or all the ale in Nordland. Hel Fenn was home to more than just the dead, though they were, by far, the most visible inhabitants.

'Dead no see, spirits no hear,' Andree murmured, pitching his thin shoulder against his pole. It was an old prayer, but a good one, especially this close to the Black Road. 'Keep the Kings of Bats and Rats from smelling our fear,' he continued, listening to the whispers of the Fenn. If you had ears trained to hear, it spoke volumes, this old swamp. The flap of a heron's wings or the splash of a snake sliding into the water told you where it was safe to go. The chittering of marsh-rats spoke to the presence of the waterlogged dead that stumbled mindless through the trees, still fighting a battle long over. The rats ate the dead as they wandered, riding them like a furry cloak, squirming and heaving as they gnawed and fought over the putrid meat. That was the story, anyway, and he had seen enough to know that stories were close enough to the truth where the Fenn was concerned.

Andree felt his gorge rise and turned his thoughts to other things; namely shiny things, or even rusty things, as long as they were old things. For generation upon generation, the

Borges had ploughed the Fenn for the treasures of ancient days. And not just them – the fenmen were as numerous as the townsmen, though less apt to congregate.

The Fenn had been the sight of so many battles, of so much death, that beneath its stagnant waters was wealth enough to forge a nation. The arms and armour of human kings and lords and dwarfen thanes and elven princes were there for the taking, if you knew where to look. Aye, and more besides that; when the Blood Counts had marched to war out of the mountains and forests, they had sunk towns and villages into the mire with dark magics. Andree's ancestors had been the survivors of one such great drowning, or so his grandmother had sworn.

In a way, if you looked at it right, it was only just that he ply the swamp for his livelihood, since the swamp had taken so much in its turn. He resumed his whistling, momentarily cheered. He bent his pole forwards, digging into the mud.

The whistle died behind his lips as the skiff thumped to a halt. Mouth suddenly dry, he braced himself and probed the water with his pole. It was a root or a rock, nothing more, he thought. *But the water is skull-deep*, a small voice whimpered in the back of his head.

He jabbed down with the pole, hoping to dislodge or shift whatever he had run into. The swamp had gone silent. Andree began to tremble. He jabbed again, more forcefully.

Something grabbed the skiff. He shrieked in disbelief as the hand came out of the water and fastened on the prow of his skiff with an ugly wet sound. Bloated, dripping meat hooked the wood. Fingers like rotten sausages tightened and the skiff dipped. Andree fell onto his rear and crab-crawled backwards, trying to get away as water slopped over the sides and filled the prow. 'No, no, no…' he babbled.

A slash of orange split the water a moment later, and a strange gurgling sound filled the air. Fear gave Andree frenzied strength and he jerked the pole loose from its captor and drove it down towards the strip of orange even as it thrust upwards. The sound became words and the pole was seized scant moments from impact by a ham-sized hand. A face out of nightmare rose from the water, spitting curses.

'–on of a pox-riddled *grobi*!' the dwarf snarled, ripping the pole out of Andree's hands. A single eye blazed furiously at Andree out of a face that had seen the wrong end of too many fists, and a great orange crest of hair dipped and bobbed alarmingly over the sun-browned expanse of a shorn skull. The dwarf spun the pole and gripped it like a spear, thrusting one end down at something he was seemingly straddling below the water line. 'Die, you oversized hunk of offal! Die and be damned,' the dwarf bellowed, his massive shoulders bunching and flexing as he struck his unseen target again and again.

Whatever it was shifted beneath the water and the dwarf toppled into the skiff, still beating at it with Andree's pole. The skiff's prow sank lower, thanks to the dwarf's weight, and Andree screamed, fearing he'd be in the water with the thing in moments.

But, instead of sinking the skiff, the dwarf's opponent chose to follow him out of the dark embrace of the Fenn. Eyes like boiled eggs glared blankly out of a face-that-wasn't. The dead man's jaw champed mindlessly as the zombie reached for its prey. Andree yelped.

'You want something to chew on, maggot-belly? Have this,' the dwarf growled, clambering to his feet and letting fly with the pole. The zombie's skull exploded in a burst of black gore and stinking meat as the dwarf's blow connected.

The skiff bobbed back above water as the twitching corpse slumped back into the swamp. The dwarf watched it sink, and turned to Andree. He was big, bigger than any other of his kind the fenman had seen before. A veritable ambulatory boulder, he was bare-chested and clad only in a pair of striped trousers and thick boots. A leather patch covered one eye and a delicate chain connected one nostril to one earlobe. Vibrant blue tattoos covered the muscular frame and moved in odd ways as the dwarf breathed. 'See the other one anywhere, manling?' he rumbled, gripping the pole tight enough to cause the hard wood to creak.

Andree could only gape. The dwarf grunted in apparent exasperation. Then his one good eye narrowed and he raised the pole, as if to do to Andree what he'd done to the zombie. Andree shrieked and tried to dart past him. The dwarf shoved him aside and brought the pole down on the head of the second zombie as it pulled itself up onto the rear of the skiff. It fell forwards, revealing a large axe embedded in its back.

'There it is,' the dwarf grunted. He tossed the much-abused pole to Andree and stamped on the back of the zombie's neck. He grabbed the axe, wrenching it easily out of the squirming corpse's back, and then, almost casually, let fly with a backhanded swipe that sent the zombie's head splashing into the water some distance away.

The dwarf kicked the headless body into the water to join its head, and then turned to Andree. 'Well? What are you waiting for, manling? Get out,' he said.

'W-what?' Andree said, clutching the pole tight to his chest.

'Are you deaf? I said get out,' the dwarf said, examining the edge of his axe. In the torchlight, it seemed to glow with an eerie fire. He ran a thumb across the blade and popped it into his mouth. 'I need your skiff. I've got more maggot-men to return to their graves.'

'Look to your left,' Felix Jaeger shouted as he drove the edge of his sword through the soft neck of an ambulatory corpse. 'Damn it, Heinz! Left, I said!' As his opponent fell, still clutching for him blindly, Felix splashed towards the other man as fast as he could. It wasn't fast enough, unfortunately. Luckless Heinz gave an abortive shriek as the dead man he hadn't seen grabbed his head and gave it a brutal twist. Felix winced at the sound of bones popping and ligaments snapping, but then he was on the thing, with no more time for anything save violence.

Felix chopped through a mossy skull, dropping the zombie like a rock. He yanked Karaghul free and spun, just in time to see Heinz, with his head still the wrong way around, stagger upright. 'Heinz...' Felix said as a chill caressed his spine. They had met the man in Wurtbad, and he'd seemed a decent enough soul for a sell-sword. Now he was anything but.

Felix ducked under Heinz's groping arms and stabbed upwards. His sword cut through the corpse's chest and thrust upwards, burrowing towards the dead man's skull. Kicking Heinz's now-quiescent body into the hip-deep water, Felix whispered a silent prayer to Morr for the man's soul. As Heinz's face vanished beneath the water, he said, 'I guess you were right, Heinz. We should never have left Wurtbad.'

He looked around, blinking sweat out of his eyes. It felt like they had been fighting for hours, but he knew it had only been minutes. Minutes since they had brought their quarry to ground, only to find themselves caught in a trap.

In retrospect, it should have been an obvious ploy. They'd been fools to think the necromancer wouldn't know they were on his trail and wouldn't prepare some obstacle for them. Said obstacle had been a number of zombies hidden beneath the dark waters of the Fenn, waiting to overturn and shatter their boats. Now they were all waist-deep in the foul waters of the Fenn, fighting a seemingly innumerable horde of zombies. 'Hindsight makes seers of us all,' he grunted to himself as he waded towards the others. They had been twenty strong setting out from Wurtbad. They were now only ten.

Well, nine; Gotrek was Sigmar alone knew where. The Slayer, already at a decided disadvantage in the water, which was shoulder-deep for a dwarf, had been pulled underwater by a trio of dead men and had, as yet, not resurfaced. The thought left a bad taste in Felix's mouth. Not just because Gotrek's death would vastly increase the odds against his own survival, but because he had sworn to witness said death. Despite everything, he had come to believe that the Slayer truly did deserve a saga to celebrate his berserk death-wish.

That and he had no doubt whatsoever that the Slayer's shade would haunt him unmercifully if he failed to deliver that saga. Gotrek had pulled him from beneath the hooves of the Emperor's elite cavalry, and Felix had sworn thereafter to chronicle the dwarf's heroic doom. Alcohol had been involved, as it was in most things involving the Slayer, but Felix's sense of honour, battered as it was, held him to his newly chosen course.

A scream of pain jerked him out of his reverie. Two zombies fell on a brawny mercenary named Hugh, their jagged teeth tearing into his flesh. He howled in agony as they dragged him down beneath the water. A third fell on him and bit out his throat, reducing the number of the group to nine. As Felix passed them, he took the head off Hugh's killer. There was nothing else he could do for the man, and standing still for too long would only ensure that he joined him in death. Or undeath, as the case was for some of their companions.

He thought of Heinz and felt sick. The clutching dead were as foul as anything he'd encountered in his travels with Gotrek, even worse than mutants. At least mutants were still alive; ugly, but alive.

Nearby, Marten Holtz, a scar-faced priest of Sigmar, roared out prayers and imprecations as he swung his hammer with almost mechanical precision. Near him, Stefan Russ, a templar of the Order of Sigmar, fired one of the seemingly innumerable pistols that were holstered about his person and potted a stumbling corpse before it could close with the bellowing Holtz. The two men were the nominal leaders of this possibly doomed expedition, and though Felix had little use for either the witch hunter or his priestly companion, he had to admit that both men were giving a good account of themselves.

Maggot-riddled fingers became tangled in his red Sudenland cloak, nearly jerking him from his feet. Felix almost dropped his sword as the zombie hauled him backwards. He fumbled at the cloak's clasp as it constricted about his throat. A sword flashed and Felix stumbled forwards, off-balance. The zombie, de-limbed, turned slowly, groaning. The sword flashed again, dropping the creature to its knees.

'Eyes forward, Jaeger,' the blade's wielder said. Pale skinned and shock-headed, Andryzy Iuldvitch, a templar of Morr, was nearly as inhuman-looking as the corpses they fought.

Felix coughed his thanks and swept Karaghul out, bisecting a cadaverous thing with a cleft face. Iuldvitch joined him and they turned in a circle, dispatching the moving corpses that sought to surround them. 'Where's Olaf?' Felix said over his shoulder.

A sizzling spurt of flame nearby gave him his answer. Olaf Norheimer, bulky and bullet-headed beneath his vibrant crimson beard and wildly-spiked hair, splashed forwards, gesturing with his staff. 'Burn, you maggoty beasts, burn!' the wizard bellowed. As zombies were reduced to staggering torches, he began to laugh wildly, his eyes glittering. A sash made of clattering bronze keys dangled from his torso and a belt of the same swung about his waist. Strange tattoos covered his muscular arms and chest.

'He enjoys his work,' Iuldvitch noted dispassionately as a burning corpse toppled into the water in front of him.

'Perhaps a bit too much,' Felix muttered. The wizard had accompanied Holtz and Russ from Altdorf, though neither man appeared happy with his presence. Felix couldn't blame them. He'd met several magic-users in his time, and Olaf was by far the most disturbing. The wizards of the Bright College were, to a man, the most dangerous of their kind, as wild and uncontrollable as the flames they wielded.

That said, none of their group was what a sane man would consider to be a particularly comforting presence. A zealot priest, a witch hunter, a servant of the death god, a mad wizard, and, of course, Gotrek... A stranger crew Felix couldn't imagine.

And their quarry was even worse. Ernst Schtillman was, by all accounts, a third-rate necromancer whose sole claim to previous fame was being arrested for making dead rats dance in a restaurant that had refused his custom. Now he was accused of stealing a reliquary of some importance from the Garden of Saints beneath the Grand Temple of Sigmar in Altdorf, and murdering a number of priests and templars in the process.

The greatest heroes of the Empire were interred in the

Garden of Saints, including past emperors, high-ranking fellows of the Colleges of Magic and notable members of several templar orders, so Felix could only imagine what Schtillman had stolen. The skull of one of the Patriarchs of Magic or the preserved finger of a Grand Theogonist, perhaps... It could be anything. Neither Holtz nor Russ was saying, though Felix had tried his best to worm the answer out of them on the road from Wurtbad.

Besides the reliquary, Schtillman had also kidnapped the daughter of a semi-friendly publican who had been keeping Gotrek in ale during their stay in Wurtbad. The man was a companion from Gotrek's days as a mercenary, or so he said. That had been enough motivation for Gotrek to bully himself and Felix a berth in the hunting party.

Thinking of the girl elicited a stab of guilt. Elsa. Felix had hoped she'd share his bed, but Schtillman had put paid to that. Abruptly, a rusty sword looped towards his head and he was forced to defend himself. He pushed all thought of the girl aside. Despite Olaf's sorcery, their attackers' numbers didn't seem at all diminished. Their quarry had all the dead of Hel Fenn at his disposal, apparently, and he wasn't shy about it.

Something that might have once been an elf lurched at him from the side, moving with a crooked sort of grace. Flesh crawling, Felix parried the too-swift blow it launched at him and tried to remove its head. The zombie jerked back, blind eyes rolling in its skull. Its thin, needle-like sword darted for him, piercing his guard and tracing a line of fire across his arm. Even in death, it was faster than a human.

Cursing, Felix stumbled and fell on his rear in the foul water. The elf-thing loomed over him, raising its sword. Desperate, Felix shoved his weapon up and the zombie impaled itself on the point. With a grunt, Felix tossed the twitching body over his head and accepted a hand up from a gaunt Stirlander named Horst. 'We're going to die here,' Horst said, seemingly neither pleased nor displeased with that fact.

'Possibly,' Felix said, jerking past him to spit a zombie that had been creeping up behind the man. Kicking the corpse off his blade, he continued, 'But I don't intend to make it easy for them.'

'We may not have a choice,' Horst's equally dour cousin, Schultz, moaned, braining a long-dead orc. 'They'll overwhelm us if we don't–' he began, but whatever he'd been about to say died with him as an axe older than Felix chopped down into his head. Schultz sank to his knees, tongue protruding, eyes bulging as the dripping zombie pulled its weapon free. Horst shrieked and made to stab his cousin's killer, but two more dead things grabbed him by his arms and pulled him in half. Felix blinked in horror as blood splattered his face and then he scrambled back as more cadavers erupted from the water.

He backed away, his sword extended and his heart sinking. More corpses stepped out from between the close-set trees or rose from the water. Schultz had been right. Holtz and Russ fell back, Iuldvitch trailing them. Olaf joined Felix, his face split in a wild grin. 'Down to us, lads!' he barked, ghostly flames coruscating around his hooked fingers.

'Don't sound so happy about it,' Felix said.

'Sigmar stands with us!' Holtz snapped, getting a better grip on his two-handed hammer.

'And Morr guides our hands,' Iuldvitch said mildly. Holtz and Russ glared at him. The latter pulled two pistols from beneath his ragged cloak and cocked them. Felix readied Karaghul, the hilt slippery in his hands. He swallowed, trying not to gag on the stink of death that surrounded them. He hadn't planned on dying this way. *I hadn't planned on dying at all*, he thought desperately.

'Bugger all gods,' Olaf yelped, throwing his hands out. The water boiled and the zombies that waded through it began to cook. The wizard gesticulated and spat painful syllables and the heat grew blisteringly intense, causing the water to turn into a stinking mist and nearby trees to curl up like dead bugs.

Despite the heat, however, the dead kept coming. They had neither fear nor physical sensation to exploit. The rotting flesh sloughed off their bones, cooked into a stinking stew. Olaf cursed virulently as skeletal hands groped towards him, grabbing for his spiked beard and robes. He fell back, his bravado melting into momentary panic as he flailed backwards. Felix and the others stepped forwards to join him, stabbing and shooting.

Fingers that looked like burst sausages clutched at Felix's wrist and blade, and the flesh of his hands turned red as he stamped and cut and shoved. Felix's arms and shoulders began to cramp from exhaustion and heat, and his hands and face stung from the burns. A steaming skull thrust towards him, blackened jaws gaping. He cried out and made to swat it away, until he realised that it wasn't attached to anything.

Instead it hurtled past him, struck a tree and fell into the water with a hiss. A moment later he realised that he could hear a familiar voice bellowing imprecations in Khazalid, the tongue of the dwarfs. A shattered ribcage and a snapped femur fell into the water at his feet as the steam began to dissipate.

'Trying to kill them all yourselves, manlings?' Gotrek Gurnisson growled.

* * *

Gotrek was perched like a gargoyle on the prow of a skiff. Relief flooded Felix. Zombie parts floated around him, some still twitching, and the Slayer's muscular form was covered in spoiled blood and rotting meat. 'Where did you find this skiff?' Felix said, looking up at the Slayer.

The Slayer motioned absently towards the swamp. 'Out there,' he said. It was obvious that he had cut his way through the rear of the horde as Olaf's wall of steam had consumed them from the other side, though he wasn't even breathing hard. Gotrek looked around. 'You didn't leave me much to do, manling,' he grumbled, fixing Felix with his single glittering eye.

'You weren't around, so we had to make do,' Felix said, laughing shakily.

Gotrek sniffed. 'No fault of mine. My axe was stuck.' He looked around at the others. 'Looks like enough of you survived, at any rate,' he said dismissively.

'No thanks to you,' Russ snapped. The witch hunter was a lean man with hang-dog features and hard eyes. He was busily reloading his pistols. Felix got the feeling that the man would have been happier with a good death than he was with Gotrek's rescue.

Gotrek fixed the man with his one good eye. 'Am I expected to fight your battles for you then, burner of women?' he said. Felix swallowed, recognising the tone in Gotrek's voice. The Slayer was still worked up and killing-mad. The zombies hadn't dulled his frenzy as much as strengthened it. He could explode into violence at any time.

'I burn heretics, *Slayer*,' Russ spat. 'Be they men or women, human or otherwise.'

Gotrek flushed and bared crooked teeth in a snarl. His axe trembled in anticipation.

'An argument serves no purpose,' Felix said quickly, moving between them. 'Schtillman is still out there and likely planning to send more of his corpse-legions after us. Maybe we should get while the going is good.' Even as he said it, a twist of guilt speared through him, though he knew the likelihood of Gotrek agreeing was slim to none. He didn't like the thought of leaving Elsa to the necromancer's attentions, good reason or not. 'We could go back to Wurtbad. Rouse the militia…' he said half-heartedly.

'Run away? Flee from maggot-men and a near-sighted whelp of a necromancer?' Gotrek guffawed. Felix forced himself not to smile in relief. 'My axe thirsts for more substantial fare, manling, and I'll not deny it!'

'Aye, and Sigmar demands justice,' Holtz said. 'The necromancer's desecration of sacred ground must not stand.' Russ nodded, obviously in full agreement.

'Schtillman has been for the pyre for a long time now,' the witch hunter added.

'Not to mention the fate of the girl,' Iuldvitch said, sheathing his sword. The guilt in Felix's gut grew heavier. He glanced towards the trees and immediately wished he hadn't. 'Gotrek…' he hissed, his fingers tightening around his sword-hilt.

'Aye, I see them,' Gotrek said.

'We all see them,' Russ muttered, his fingertips dancing nervously across the butts of the pistols hanging across his narrow chest in their waterproof holsters. 'Sigmar preserve us…'

'He does,' Holtz said. He had his eyes closed, as if in prayer.

Clumsy shapes splashed through the trees. More zombies, Felix realised with a chill. 'How many dead men does this cess-pit hold?' he said.

'Thousands,' Holtz said, opening his eyes. His scarred face twisted into an expression of distaste. 'More even than fell in the Battle of Hel Fenn. They say every river in Sylvania carries corpses to the Fenn.' He patted the hammer that lay across his shoulder. 'It is a cursed place. One day we will burn it from the map.'

Olaf laughed. 'Count me in, scar-face. Let's start today!' He gestured and a spurt of flame crashed into the trees. Ranks upon ranks of zombies, both human and otherwise, were illuminated by Olaf's conjured flames. Had they been watching them all this time, Felix wondered?

Several of the creatures began to stumble forwards. Gotrek snarled. He tightened his grip on his axe and plunged off the skiff and into the water to meet the lurching dead. They closed in about him and the Slayer disappeared from view. Felix started forwards.

'What are you doing?' Russ said, grabbing his arm.

'Gotrek needs help!' Felix said, shaking his arm loose of the witch hunter's grip. There was a roar and then several rotting bodies skidded across the water like skipping stones.

'No,' Gotrek grunted, 'I don't.' The Slayer floundered through the water, dripping and sullen. 'Dead things are no challenge,' he growled, fiddling with his crest, which drooped alarmingly thanks to his plunge in the water. 'Well. Is that it?' he roared out, shaking his axe at the swamp. Silence greeted the Slayer's demand.

Then, in the darkness, someone laughed.

'Am I mistaken, or were there more of you earlier?' a thin, reedy voice said, vicious amusement evident in its tone. 'Oh, wait… There they are!'

Familiar faces stepped into the light of Olaf's fire. There

was Hugh with the gaping hole in his throat and Schultz, his bifurcated face grinning and frowning at the same time. Horst was there as well, and the others who'd fallen.

'Quite a group,' the voice continued. 'Hard men all, and dangerous, I'd say; some of you more than others.' A giggle followed. Then, a thin shape stepped out from between the trees, followed by a herd of corpses, some better preserved than others. The firelight was reflected by a cracked pair of spectacles. The face was that of a perpetual youth, spoiled and beardless. Pox scars dotted the hollow cheeks and yellow teeth surfaced from between thin lips as Schtillman the necromancer smiled at them like a boy greeting long-absent friends.

'Abomination,' Holtz roared. He smashed a low-hanging branch in his fury, his hammer reducing the inoffensive limb to splinters.

'Hello,' Schtillman said mildly. His eyes moved weasel-quick across the rest of the group. Felix felt himself shiver as the necromancer looked at him; there was nothing recognisably human in that gaze. 'Welcome gentles all, to this, my crowning moment of glory,' he continued, gesturing grandiosely. With the air of a lecturer, he bent and sat on a tree root, head bowed. 'I was not expecting an audience, it must be said, but needs must when daemons drive, eh? Eh?' He spread his hands and shrugged. 'I would ask who put you on my trail, but I know I'm quite certain, my yes, the culprit or culprits, as it were, indubitably et cetera and such...' he trailed off, head tilted. 'Still, no reason you can't bear witness to such historical proceedings.'

'Enough ranting,' Russ snapped, unlimbering a pistol and taking aim. 'Return what you have stolen, thief, and your death will be as easy as we know how to grant.'

'Death is never easy,' Schtillman said, removing his spectacles and rubbing them on his robes. 'And I am no thief, I assure you.'

'The stolen souls of our companions say otherwise,' the witch hunter said, cocking his pistol. 'Four brothers, pure and strong, stolen from the very halls of the Grand Temple in Altdorf are added to your debt, Schtillman.'

'Is that you, Stefan?' Schtillman said, putting his spectacles back on. 'I thought I recognised your voice. You, of all of these, should know me better than that, I should think. Corpse-fondler and restaurant critic I might be, yes, but thief? I have some standards, you dyspeptic clod.'

Russ's pistol sparked. A rotting heron, flying despite the condition of its bedraggled wings, intercepted the bullet and tumbled into the water, where it thrashed in an altogether hideous fashion. Russ made to draw another pistol, but more dead birds burst out of the trees and swarmed him. He screamed as cracked and broken beaks tore at him.

Olaf roared and flung out a hand. Talons of crackling flame arched towards the dead birds. Felix charged forwards and tackled the witch hunter into the water as a wave of heat and flame engulfed the squawking cloud, incinerating some of the zombie flock. As Felix rose, pulling a spluttering Russ with him, he glared at the wizard.

'Are you mad?' he snarled.

Olaf appeared not to hear him. The Bright Wizard howled with laughter as he consumed the flock in a tornado of fire. As if this were the signal he'd been waiting for, Gotrek gave a bellow and broke into a charge, his axe held over his head as he fought his way through what was shoulder-deep water far quicker than Felix thought possible.

Schtillman looked momentarily nonplussed and shot to

his feet. He spat a stream of nonsense words and Gotrek hesitated, his eye narrowing as a black cloud seemed to take shape around him. 'What's this?' he growled. Then he grunted and slapped at himself. Soon he was swatting at the air. 'Cursed insects!' he shouted, staggering. The cloud followed him, doubling in size. Gotrek howled and dived under the water. He surfaced a few feet away, but the insects followed, and something else as well... Felix called out a warning as the immense shape of a snake cut through the water towards the preoccupied Slayer. Gotrek turned as the zombie-serpent coiled around him. Roaring, arms pinned, he toppled backwards.

'Bugs, beasts and birds,' Schtillman cackled, clapping his hands. 'The dead come in all shapes and sizes, you know.'

'Send them all, we will not be deterred,' Holtz said, striding forwards, his hammer gripped tightly. Felix and Russ drew their swords and joined him as Olaf drove the end of his staff into the water. Two walls of fire rose to carve them a corridor through the gathering zombies. 'Sigmar guides us and damns you, necromancer. Return our reliquary, return the girl and return the dead to Morr's embrace!'

'No, no, and no,' Schtillman said, hopping backwards. 'Not when I'm so close! Not when I've finally found him!'

'Then die and be damned!' Holtz said, racing forwards suddenly, his scarred features alight with mad fervour. His hammer crashed down and connected with the interposed shield of a corpse clad in rotting armour. The dead man whipped out a rusty sword and nearly gutted the priest. Holtz stumbled and the corpse followed, moving with a smoothness Felix took to be a bad sign. Several more armoured cadavers followed the first, and with a start Felix, recalling the heraldry drills his status-conscious father had forced him to do, recognised the faded emblem on one's breastplate… the bat rising and the dragon rampant of the von Carstein family!

'Sigmar preserve us,' he muttered, closing with one of the dead men. Sudden suspicions as to Schtillman's purpose clustered at the edge of his mind as he blocked a surprisingly strong blow. 'It can't be!'

'Oh, but it can!' Schtillman said, apparently having heard him. 'Persistence yields success,' he said, sounding for a moment like one of Felix's old tutors. 'Study yields results and results allow extrapolation! From extrapolation, we can match variables and triangulate and thus, he rises! Unconquered! Undaunted! Undead!' The necromancer's voice rose to a shrill shriek. 'Bring forth the sacrifice!'

Two zombies stepped from around the tree, dragging an unconscious form between them. Felix immediately recognised Elsa, and he redoubled his efforts. Karaghul seemed to twist in his hands as he battered at his opponent, sending it slumping to one knee. His sword cracked the ancient helmet and spilled what was left of its brains into the water and then he was past it, moving quickly. More of the dead barred his path and his frustration boiled over into violence. He looked around for help, hoping to see Gotrek, but willing to settle for anyone. Unfortunately, all of the others were engaged in their own struggles. Exhaustion and numbers were beginning to tell, and even Olaf's flames were fading. Where was Gotrek?

On the hummock of black earth, Schtillman was ordering his zombies to position Elsa's limp form as he drew a curve-bladed dagger from within his robes. 'One thrust and the deed is done,' the necromancer said. He raised the weapon, and Felix knew that he wasn't going to be in time. All at once, everything went silent, as if the entirety of Hel Fenn were holding its breath. Time seemed to slow to a crawl.

And then Gotrek's axe took off Schtillman's hand at the wrist on its way towards embedding itself in the skull of one of the zombies gripping Elsa. Schtillman screamed and grabbed at the gushing stump. Felix turned and saw Gotrek rising from the water, his squat form covered in welts from the insect bites and the head of the snake gripped between his jaws. The dwarf spat out the head and wiped the back of his hand across his mouth. 'Insects!' he thundered as he stomped forwards. 'You try to kill me with insects and snakes? Are you stupid as well as mad, manling?'

Schtillman whined like a dog and sank to his knees, futilely trying to stem the blood spraying from his wrist. The zombies staggered and slumped as his concentration wavered. Gotrek stepped past the huddled necromancer and ripped his axe free of the zombie's head. More gently, he plucked Elsa from the slack grip of the other corpse and tossed her easily to Felix. Felix caught the woman and grunted, going to his knees.

Gotrek raised the necromancer's chin with the flat of his axe. Schtillman's whimpering changed in cadence. 'Gotrek, he's chanting!' Felix cried, shifting Elsa around and trying to get at his sword.

Schtillman's good hand shot out, clawing for Gotrek's face. Gotrek jerked back with a curse and twisted his axe around with a flick of his wrist. The edge bit upwards through Schtillman's frenzied features, obliterating them in a splash of gore. Gotrek stepped away, not wanting to get any of the writhing body's blood on him as it fell forwards. The necromancer's body twitched and jerked for several moments and then fell still. Gotrek spat on the body and turned to Felix. 'No doom here manling, grand or otherwise; just old death and maggots,' he growled.

Felix looked down at Elsa and thought that Gotrek was missing the point, as usual. No sense in saying as much, however. The Slayer would be in a foul mood as it was. Surviving made him irritable. The woman in his arms stirred, but didn't awaken.

'Mandrake root and grave mould,' Iuldvitch said, touching her cheek. Felix looked at him.

'How do you know?' he said.

'Necromancers are a bit like cooks. They all use the same basic recipes for certain things, like drugging sacrificial victims,' he said. 'She'll sleep for a few days, if Schtillman didn't misjudge the dose.'

'You look like you could use the same,' Felix said.

Iuldvitch smiled tiredly and shook his head. 'No rest for the weary.'

'Where is it?' Holtz shouted, causing them to turn. 'It has to be here!' The big priest was tearing through Schtillman's belongings, meagre as they were. Russ watched silently, as did Gotrek, though the latter's expression was anything but interested. 'It's not here!' Holtz spun around, his glare accusing.

'Maybe he was telling the truth,' Felix said.

Holtz goggled at him. 'What?'

'I said, maybe he was telling the truth when he claimed not to have stolen the reliquary.' Felix shrugged. 'Are you certain he was the thief?'

'Certain? Certain?' Holtz said, his face flushing purple. The scars on his face stood out like livid tattoos. He motioned to the floating bodies that filled the nearby waters. 'What more certainty do I need?'

'I'm not denying that he was up to something, but maybe he wasn't the man we were after,' Felix insisted, wishing he could simply shut up, but finding it impossible to do so. 'Who gave you his name? Who put us on his trail?'

'You ask a lot of questions for a sell-sword, Jaeger,' Russ said, wiping muck off his blade. 'Schtillman was our man. He must have hidden the reliquary. Perhaps in Wurtbad…'

'Perhaps,' Felix said, sharing a look with Gotrek. The Slayer looked disgusted.

'What of the fiend's body?' Olaf said, holding up a finger upon which a flicker of flame danced. 'Should we burn it?'

'Let the swamp have it,' Holtz grunted, shouldering his hammer. 'Let us go.' He started off back in the direction they had come from, Russ at his heels. Olaf shook his head and followed, Iuldvitch trailing behind. Felix looked at the body of the necromancer and shifted Elsa's weight. Gotrek held out his hands as they climbed up out of the water onto a hummock of solid, albeit soggy earth.

'Give her to me before you drop her, manling,' the Slayer said. Almost tenderly, he cradled the unconscious young woman to his barrel chest and set off after the others, moving across the patches of dry ground carefully. Felix hesitated, fingering his sword. He didn't like the idea of leaving the body as it was. But he didn't plan on sticking around to see to it by himself either.

'Curse it,' he muttered, hurrying after Gotrek.

Behind him, Schtillman's blood pooled in thick puddles in the soft ground and ran beneath the roots of a tree, first in trickles, then in rivers. The tree was black-barked and crooked, bulging with knotty tumours and sickly lichen. Its barren limbs scraped together in a sigh as the blood bubbled and dripped into the depths beneath its roots.

Drip.

Drip.

Drip.

And, after a time, something long dead, but nonetheless dreaming, opened its eyes and said, '*Ahhhhh…*'

Like pale blossoms unfurling after a rainstorm, the worm-white fingers pierced the black soil that was packed loosely amongst the tangling roots of the tree. The fingers stretched up and up, until the cat-like nails that dotted each tip hooked into one of the thicker roots. Then, with a convulsive heave, a skeletal shape swam to the surface, dirt and mud sloughing off long-buried limbs.

Flanged nostrils quivered in a death-mask face and needle teeth sprouted from bloodless gums. Pointed ears twitched above a rat's nest of grey hair, and wolfish jaws gaped, sucking in a great lungful of foetid air, tasting it in the same way a snake would. 'Ah,' it said.

It grabbed the higher roots and pulled itself up and out into the dark of Hel Fenn, bare feet scraping across the wood. Muscles that had remained rigid for a century or more pulsed and flexed. Memory, thought and instinct warred in a reptile-sluggish mind. Hunger and caution met and the former won, prompting the shape to again taste the air.

It crouched as a tantalising scent intruded. Covered in mud and soil, and remaining motionless, it blended easily with the surface of the tree. Pale pink eyes blinked slowly, watching the approach of its prey, and a colourless tongue dabbed hungrily at almost nonexistent lips.

Andree Borges cautiously made his way across the shifting hummocks, prodding the path before him with a bent stick he'd found. As he moved, he cursed the thieving dwarf under his breath. The curses burst into full flower as he saw the state of his skiff. The little boat had drifted into a nearby fire and it had been reduced to a charred ruin.

'No!' Andree wailed, rushing towards it. Sighting the floating bodies nearby, he skidded to a halt, almost falling face-first into the water. Warily he looked around, taking in the carnage. The stink of old death hung heavy on the air and his spirit quailed. There were places in the Fenn a sane man didn't go and this was one of them.

Maybe he should find the dwarf and his companions… There was safety in numbers, and it would be the least they could do for destroying his skiff. Unwillingly, but unable to do otherwise, his eyes were drawn to the bloated tree that occupied the centre of the immediate area. It was an old thing, resembling a grasping hand rising from the belly of the swamp. The fenmen told stories about that tree, about packs of shrieking ghouls dancing about it on nights when the witch-moons were full, and the strange, thready rhythm that seemed to rise from the swamp when the water was low.

Something scraped against wood, and Andree froze, sweat popping on his face despite the chill in the air. 'No, oh please no, no,' he muttered, looking around, trying to see everywhere at once. The stories his father had told him as a boy swam to the surface of his mind unbidden, filling his head with terrors.

Water splashed and he spun, jabbing out with his stick even as he clawed for the hatchet in his belt. There was nothing behind him. Branches rattled and he turned again, biting down on a scream. He needed to get out of here. He could get a new skiff. He began to back away.

There was a wet growl and Andree's limbs locked

involuntarily. His eyes bobbed in their sockets, taking in the shadows lingering between the close-set trees. Something cold brushed across the back of his neck and this time he did shriek. He lashed out with his stick and hatchet, but hit nothing but air.

He whirled again, and caught a glimpse of pale limbs as something bounded away. What was it? A ghoul? A daemon? The Fenn was full of them. His breath whistled harshly in his ears as he turned to run. He began to crash through the trees, not watching the path or the water. There was no time for caution, not any more.

He ran blind, swatting aside clutching branches and tripping over snakey roots. Something pursued him; he could hear its claws tearing up the ground and rattling the branches. Andree didn't turn around. He didn't want to see it.

Water splashed up around his thighs and his run slowed to a crawl. Heart thudding in his chest, he looked down and a strangled moan escaped from between his lips. Not water… quicksand! Tears rolled down his weathered cheeks as he thrashed about, hoping to make it to solid ground, knowing it was impossible. A shadow fell over him and he looked up.

The thing watched him from its perch, eyes shining dully from behind a curtain of stringy hair. It hissed like a kettle coming slowly to the boil. It wore the remains of strange armour and fine clothing, all reduced to mud-encrusted rags and bulges.

'Please…' Andree croaked.

It leapt. The weight drove him down into the quicksand, and his attacker sank with him, leaving behind only a stir of bubbles to mark the existence of either. Silence fell.

* * *

The quicksand bubbled, burped and split as a tall shape rose from its outer rim, striding purposefully towards firm ground. Despite the apron of blood that covered it from mouth to groin, the shape looked more human now than earlier. Sustenance-starved muscles had thickened somewhat and the white hair had filled out. The pink eyes now blazed a bright crimson.

It examined its hands and then ran them over its arms and chest. It wore ancient armour of anarchic make. Sharp edges and jutting ridges made it unlike anything worn by man, and the remains of a great cloak crafted from the fur of wolves and bats hung lankly from the shoulder plates.

'Where…' it croaked, licking blood from its teeth. It wiped a palm across its mouth and looked at the congealing blood there. 'Blood,' it said, more strongly. The animal-mind shuddered and the red fog receded. 'It' became 'he' as patchwork fragments of memory swirled about the hurricane of hunger that tried to consume him.

He shook himself and extended his hand, spreading his fingers wide. He could feel the winds of death circling him and he reached out to grab them. '*Dhar*,' he murmured, feeling the ethereal threads gather about his fingers. The winds of dark magic kissed his fingertips like excited wolf-pups, and he drew his fingers together, pulling the power towards him. He glanced at the quicksand pit.

He brought his hand to his lips and blew gently, sending the tendrils of power coursing down into the quicksand. The surface twisted and bubbled and then Andree's blood-drained corpse hauled itself out of the quicksand with slow, agonised movements. The former fenman rose into a parody of a bow and then bobbed from one foot to the next with the unsteadiness of the newly undead.

He turned away and snapped his fingers. 'Come.' The

zombie followed obediently, insects already clustering about the gaping wound where its throat had once been.

The fog in his head began to lift as the stolen blood flowed through his body. It was not enough, but it would do for now. He ran his claws through his stringy hair. Eyes closed, he marshalled his thoughts as his last waking memories threatened to overwhelm him. He could feel the heat of that accursed sword as it cut towards him. The sword had writhed in his killer's hands like a thing alive. Its blade was squirming with runes that were painful to his magically-attuned senses, even at a distance.

He had turned to face his pursuers where the Stir entered Hel Fenn, pinned by the elements and his own pride. How many had he killed? Not enough. The sword – that cursed sword! – had pierced him through and true, the heat of it burning him as it slid through his withered heart.

He staggered, clutching at his chest. He could feel a rippling scar there now, beneath his black armour; a parting gift from his murderers. A reminder of the price of arrogance, he thought bitterly. It hurt still. He leaned against a tree, eyes closed, letting the winds of death caress him and dull the pain. 'Martin,' he snarled. 'Martin!'

The name meant something. It tasted foul in his mouth. 'Weak,' he said, eyelids cracking open. The zombie, true to its nature, said nothing. The silent dead made adequate companions. He looked into the zombie's filmy eyes and then away. His last memory was of death. So, why then was he alive?

Quickly he made his way back to the tree, his eyes narrowing to slits as he scanned the area, taking in everything. Even dulled by the circumstances of his resurrection, his mind was like quicksilver. He touched a scorch-mark high on a branch and probed the edges of a zombie's cleft head. Then he caught the scent of fading magics and bounded towards one body in particular. Jerking the mauled carcass up by its sodden robes, he laughed darkly and shoved the body towards the zombie. The zombie staggered, but held the body up in a parody of an embrace.

'It stinks of dark magic,' he murmured, turning to look at the ground. There were papers and books scattered about the marshy earth. 'Ah,' he said, stooping. He snatched up a thin volume bound in tanned skin and flipped through the pages. The writing was cramped, but legible. 'Schtillman,' he hissed after a while. 'That was your name, was it? You meant to spill virgin blood on my remains, and so you did, though not precisely in the way you had intended, eh?' He grunted. 'Necromancers... all work and no sense of pleasure.'

The name was familiar, though. Where had he heard it before and in what context?

He looked back at the body, red eyes narrowed. Then he slit the robes open with a thumbnail and exposed the scrawny chest. 'Ha,' he said, tapping a curious brand scarred into the flesh above the heart. He dug his claws into the slack flesh around the mark and twisted his wrist, ripping the gobbet of flesh free. He wrung it like a rag over his upturned mouth, and then casually flensed the skin from the meat, tossing the latter aside and examining the flap of hide.

He pursed blood-stained lips and ran a thumb over the brand. 'A mark below a mark,' he said. His eyes flickered up, meeting those of the zombie. 'And both of them are familiar, though I cannot say why.' He looked past the zombie and gestured to the half-sunken remains of one of the skiffs littering the area. 'Fix it,' he said. 'I would see civilisation once more.'

* * *

Wurtbad, the capital city of Stirland, was two cities in one. The High Town sat high up on the hill that Wurtbad had been built on, while the Low Town sat on the River Stir like a toad. As places went, Felix judged that he had seen better. Everything smelled of damp and mould and the locals looked like criminals. When he said as much to Gotrek, the Slayer had given him a look that might have been considering and said, 'You're one to talk, manling.'

Felix blinked. 'Was that a joke?'

'Dwarfs are renowned for their sense of humour, manling. Ask anyone,' Gotrek said with a belch. He was as close to cheery as Felix had ever seen him, though it was likely due to the amount of ale he had put away since they'd sat down. Old Hugo, Elsa's father, had been so overjoyed to see his daughter alive and unharmed that he had re-opened Gotrek's tab. Felix thought, somewhat sourly, that Hugo's generosity was likely to burn out sooner than Gotrek's thirst. The Slayer could put away enough alcohol to drown a regiment.

There were two things that Gotrek was good at, Felix had often noted. Drinking and fighting, not always in that order. When he wasn't doing the one, he was engaged in the other. Felix thought that perhaps both were forms of forgetting; what little he knew of Slayers in general, and Gotrek in particular, suggested that whatever shame had forced Gotrek into assuming the orange crest and tattoos of the Slayer-cult could be as minor as a point of personal pride or as major as a criminal offence.

Felix, like any good poet, often speculated on that point. It nagged at him in quieter moments. What had set the dwarf on his path? What had propelled him across the width and breadth of the known world in a quest to die? And speaking of which...

'Why would Schtillman go to Hel Fenn?' Felix said, looking at Gotrek. 'Sylvania, I understand. But surely there's no lack of corpses in more comfortable climes. He could have gone north, or fled the Empire entirely.'

'Hel Fenn is a sump of death-magic,' Gotrek said. 'Always has been. Even in my father's day.'

'Your father?' Felix said, his ears perking up. It wasn't often that the Slayer spoke of his family. Indeed, not at all, to Felix's recollection.

'Aye, manling,' Gotrek said and his voice became softer than its usual rock-hard rumble. 'He was there, you know...'

'Where?' Felix said.

'Hel Fenn, on the day that dwarf and man stood shoulder-to-shoulder against the lords of unnatural creation.' The Slayer sighed wistfully. 'They say it was a dark day, that. The sky was as black as a *grobi*'s heart and the wind from the Fenn was foul. The sky was full of carrion-birds, following Mann-fred von Carstein and his rotting legion.'

Von Carstein... The name sent a chill through Felix's heart. He knew the story; every child born in the Empire did, though the implications were hidden behind a veil of myth.

'My father stood with the other Longbeards,' Gotrek con-tinued, pride evident in his voice. 'Only my people held their ground that day. When the men broke, driven to flight by fear of the dead, my people stayed firm. They gave Martin of Stirland, the elector count, time to rally his men.' Gotrek grinned, displaying his gap-teeth. 'He was a brave one, that manling. Went blade-to-blade with the arch-undead him-self, old Mannfred. Pierced him through as well, and sent the blood-sucker running.' Gotrek laughed. 'Didn't get far though, and my father was among those who brought him to bay at the edge of the Fenn.' His laughter faded. 'They say

Mannfred killed a dozen men, even dying, and that when he fell, no man dared touch him. They let him sink into the swamp, and good riddance...' He gazed at his mug sourly. 'That'd have been a doom worth singing about.' And just like that, the Slayer's good mood evaporated into melancholy.

Felix recognised the look in the Slayer's eye well enough. He'd get no more out of him tonight. He looked around. The taproom of Hugo's tavern was crowded with rivermen and travellers of all shapes and descriptions. Lumber merchants travelling the Old Dwarf Road south mingled with fruit-sellers from the Moot, who bought a round for a trio of dwarf prospectors, all of whom glared balefully at Gotrek, who pretended not to notice.

It was curious to Felix that Gotrek's reception among his own kind veered between the two extremes of relief and dismay. There was no middle ground that he had seen. He contemplated asking Gotrek about it, and then decided that his time could be better spent on other, more pleasant tasks.

'I'm going to go check on Elsa,' he said, rising to his feet.

'The templar is with her, manling,' Gotrek burped, shaking his tankard up over the table. When only a single drop dripped from the rim, he frowned thunderously. 'Hugo!' he roared.

'Does that mean I shouldn't pay my respects?' Felix said, strapping on his sword-belt.

Gotrek leered at him blearily. 'Is that all you're planning?'

'You're drunk.'

'No. What I am is thirsty! Hugo!' Gotrek bellowed again, slapping the table with one broad hand.

'Enjoy abusing Hugo's hospitality,' Felix sniffed.

'You too,' Gotrek said.

Stung, Felix headed for the stairs. Gotrek was right, of

course. It was folly of the worst sort to pant after their host's daughter. But he couldn't help himself. Felix liked to think of himself as a romantic, but in his more self-reflective moments, he had to admit that he fell in love the way Gotrek drank... stupidly and often.

'Or maybe I'm simply being too hard on myself because I'm angry,' he muttered as he climbed the stairs, leaving the cacophony of the taproom behind. *Angry with myself, angry with Holtz, angry with the situation*, he thought. It rested like a leaden ball in his gut.

The trip back to Wurtbad hadn't been pleasant. Holtz had gotten it into his head that Elsa had been involved with Schtillman, and that she knew the whereabouts of the lost reliquary. Russ had backed the priest up, leading to a number of standoffs with the others. Olaf didn't seem to care either way, but Iuldvitch had come down firmly on Felix's side. Whether that was because he agreed with Felix, or simply because he didn't like the Sigmarites very much, Felix couldn't say.

At the moment, Iuldvitch was seeing to Elsa. Once they'd arrived in Wurtbad, the templar had sent away to an alchemist for herbs and potions to treat the daze Schtillman had put her into. Felix was grateful, but at the same time ever-so-slightly jealous of the templar's ministrations. Even though he knew that his chance to garner Elsa's affections had long since passed due to circumstance, it still rankled.

He reached the landing, and the sound of raised voices reached him. Instinctively, his hand found Karaghul's hilt and he strode quickly towards the door to Elsa's room. Russ was lounging against it, his arms crossed over his chest and his fingertips stroking the brass butts of his pistols. His eyes narrowed as he saw Felix approaching. 'Keep walking, Jaeger. This doesn't concern you.'

'No?' Felix said, not stopping.

Russ pushed himself away from the door, opening his mouth to form a reply. Felix's fist shot out, catching the witch hunter in his prominent nose. Russ staggered back, both hands flying to his abused snout, and Felix shoved past him into the room.

Holtz spun around, eyes wide. 'Get out of here, sell-sword!' he snapped. The priest was in full oratory mode, the Book of Sigmar clutched to his chest, his amulet wrapped around his other fist. Iuldvitch stood between Elsa, who cringed back on her bed, and the red-faced priest.

'No, I think not,' Felix said, kicking the door shut on Russ and pressing his back to it. 'I thought we had made it clear to you earlier, Holtz. The girl had nothing to do with the theft. She was the victim, remember?'

'So you say,' Holtz spat. 'The cults of the corpse-eaters spread like leprosy. Their taint is well-hidden, unlike the marks of Chaos.' He grimaced. 'She must know something. She must have seen what he did with the–' He stopped short.

'What he did with what, Holtz?' Felix said. 'What is so cursed important that you'd chase a man from Altdorf to Stirland and threaten an innocent girl for it? I think it's time you told us.' Behind him, Russ began to beat on the door.

'What do you care, mercenary?' Holtz said, pulling himself up to his full, imposing height. 'You stink of the strange, Felix Jaeger.'

Felix's chin jerked. 'Oh?'

'Yes,' Holtz continued, stepping closer. 'A stink almost as bad as that of necromancy...' In the light of the candles strewn about the room, the priest looked decidedly sinister and Felix felt himself quail slightly. He shoved his hesitancy back and forced his shoulders to square. Travelling with

Gotrek had taught Felix more about intimidation than any puffed-up priest could manage.

'Are you making an accusation, *Herr* Holtz?' Felix said, stepping to meet the priest. Behind him, the door opened, but it was too late to worry about it.

It was Holtz's turn to hesitate. Before Felix could press his advantage, he heard the click of a pistol behind him, and felt the chill of a barrel as it dug into the back of his skull. 'Your usefulness to the Church has ended, Jaeger,' Russ said.

'Not until you've paid us, it hasn't,' Gotrek rumbled. Felix turned and saw the Slayer standing behind Russ, his axe pressed gently against the man's spine. The Slayer swayed slightly, and Felix realised that he was still drunk.

'We didn't ask for your help,' Russ said. Felix couldn't help but admire him. Not every man could mouth off with Gotrek's axe a hairsbreadth from reducing him to a red ruin.

'True enough,' Felix said, stepping aside. 'But we helped all the same. I daresay without us, you'd be quite dead.'

'True,' Iuldvitch said, speaking up. The pale man met Holtz's glare. 'And it is not their fault, nor is it the girl's, that Schtillman wasn't the thief you were after.'

'That is still to be determined,' Holtz said harshly. 'If you would let us put her to the question...'

'I think we've all had enough questions, eh?' Olaf rumbled from the hall. The red-bearded wizard stood behind Gotrek, his thumbs hooked in his belt. Beside him stood Hugo and two of his sons, as brawny as their father. Olaf sniffed and examined his fingernails. 'Hugo here was concerned, so I brought him up. Wanted to show him his daughter wasn't being bothered after everything.' The wizard grinned, showing his teeth. 'And here we find her deluged with protectors, eh?'

Felix shot a grateful glance at the wizard, whose grin grew wider. Olaf hadn't seemed overly concerned with the girl's fate on the trip back. Likely it was just his way of tweaking Holtz's nose... something the wizard seemed to enjoy.

'Is she well, templar?' Hugo asked respectfully. This close to the dark forests of Sylvania, the servants of Morr were better regarded than elsewhere in the Empire. Where the dead walked, those who made it their life's work to see such abominations back safely in their graves were figures of high esteem; much more so than officious priests or brutal witch hunters, at any rate.

'Well enough for her ordeal,' Iuldvitch said. He looked at Elsa, who shot a look at Holtz and then nodded briskly.

'Well enough to get back to work, at least,' she said, stepping towards her father.

'No! You must rest,' Hugo protested.

'And who will serve your customers, poppa? Hans? Wilhelm?' she said, jerking her chin at her brothers. 'They're more liable to give them baths than beers, considering how clumsy they are.' Her brothers protested half-heartedly, but Felix got the impression that Elsa had won that argument long ago. Hugo took his daughter in his arms and herded his children out of the room and away from the clutches of the seething Sigmarites.

Olaf rubbed his hands together. 'I hear a beer calling my name. Who's with me, eh?'

'Drink is the hobgoblin of the soul,' Holtz said mechanically. He glared at the empty bed and then turned and stalked out of the room, trailing after Olaf. Russ followed him, pausing long enough to gesture at Felix with his pistol. Felix repressed the urge to swallow.

'There will be trouble with those two, manling,' Gotrek

said, watching them go. 'Your priests aren't the most tolerant sort.'

Felix looked at him for a moment, struck by the ridiculousness of the Slayer chiding anyone for their lack of tolerance. Then he turned to Iuldvitch. 'What now?' he said.

'I'm for the Temple of Morr, myself,' the templar said. 'Schtillman has been a mark in our books for some time now and I need to report his passing.' He looked at Felix. 'That and you've gotten me curious about the object of our friends' concerns.'

'And you think the Temple of Morr will have answers?'

'We are quite knowledgeable in some areas, yes,' Iuldvitch said blandly. He shrugged. 'Besides, Holtz will almost certainly be reporting to the local prelate of Sigmar. I can do no less. Appearances must be kept up.'

'May I accompany you?' Felix said.

'Still want to know what gewgaw the priest is hunting, manling?' Gotrek said.

'Don't you?' Felix said.

'Not particularly,' Gotrek said. 'But I'm sober now, so I might as well accompany you.' He shouldered his axe and snorted. 'Besides, Hugo's ale leaves something to be desired.'

'It is free though,' Felix said.

'Aye, there is that.'

Swords sang off bleached bone, and the sky was full of the sound of wings, feathered and otherwise. Horses and men screamed and wolves howled and the carrion winds blew strong and steady. Clawed fingers scratched thin lines in the filthy surface of his cuirass, right above the point where the blade had entered him.

He lounged in the rear of the repaired skiff, his eyes

half-closed, letting his tattered memories have full rein. Hel Fenn faded in the distance, and his earlier weakness with it. Hunger still gnawed at him, but several days along he was more fully in control of his desires. The Stir would carry them further and faster than a horse, but he found himself missing his coach. Long gone now, as were his holdings and servants, he judged.

How long, though? One year or a hundred, it was all the same. His eyes flickered open and he examined his withered claw. The raw stuff of the blood he'd taken had faded, leaving him weak again. He reclined, looking up at the cold stars. The heavens had once fascinated him, he recalled. Now, above his head was simply a void... eternal, cold emptiness.

'Like the grave,' he rasped. The zombie didn't react. He reached down and picked up his sword. He'd retrieved it from where it lay beneath the tree, sleeping in its mouldering sheath. Just like him. He unsheathed it, admiring the terrible beauty of it. It was a thing of death, his sword. Larger and heavier than a normal man could wield, it felt as light as a feather in his hand.

His nostrils flared as the wind shifted and brought an influx of scents to him. He sat up, his red eyes fastening on a distant shape drawing swiftly closer thanks to the zombie's inexorable poling. Even at a distance of however much time had passed, he knew a pleasure barge when he saw one. The River Stir had always been a popular route for the moneyed traveller. Cutting through the Great Forest as it did, it was a beautiful trip if you were in no particular rush.

Swiftly, he gave orders to Andree and then slid over the side so quietly that there was nary a splash. While it was true that all of his kind suffered Nagash's Curse and thus had to avoid the glare of the sun, running water was only an obstacle to the weaker among them. He sank down slowly, and bounded up, loping across the river bottom, his unnatural eyesight easily piercing the darkness of the Stir's depths. Freshwater fish scattered at his approach, shooting in all directions. Silt billowed around his boots, and his cloak flared around him like the cap of a toadstool as he gazed up at the shadowy shape of the pleasure barge.

He pushed himself upwards, extending his hands. His claws sank into the wood of the barge and slowly, cautiously, Mannfred began to climb the slope. As the crown of his head pierced the water's surface, Mannfred caught the rough voices of the pleasure barge's crew. Stirlanders by the accents, he thought. They were calling out to Andree, who was keeping the skiff just out of the light cast by the lanterns mounted on the rail. Mannfred grinned and scuttled to the side. The barge was a side-wheeler of the type once devised by the dwarfs as war machines. Obviously, the design had been co-opted by some mercantile-minded individual.

He hopped up onto the rail, his cloak settling about him. Saliva gathered as his mouth became a sharp slash filled with needles. He inhaled softly, his spear-blade nose quivering. The crew had their backs to him, occupied as they were by Andree. He heard gasps as Andree and his skiff drifted at last into the light. A zombie, especially one in Andree's condition, was never a pleasant sight.

He rose to his feet and shrugged back the folds of his dripping cloak. 'Permission to board?' he asked, breaking the horrified silence. Men spun, their hands clawing for weapons. He laughed and dived upon them. A sword slid past him, ripping the cloak from his shoulders, and he thrust his claws into its wielder's face, crushing bone and gouging flesh. Stripping the meat from the man's skull, he flung the bloody mess into another man's face. A boat-hook swung at him and he caught it easily. Jerking it from the crewman's grip, he snapped it in two and drove the jagged end of one half into the astonished man's belly.

He lifted the dying man over his head and spread his jaws to an inhuman degree, his tongue uncoiling like that of a serpent. As he gulped down the ensuing shower of blood, he used the other half of the boat-hook to shatter the neck of another crewman. Dropping the body, he looked around. There were five men left on deck, though someone was below decks ringing an alarm bell. He spread his arms and bared crimson-stained teeth. 'Come one at a time or all at once. The music fades and I'd have this dance done,' he snarled.

He could have used his magics to sweep the life from them, he knew, and, at one time, he might have done so. It had always been his nature to take the slow path, to proceed cautiously. But he felt the urge to stretch his killing muscles; there was an undeniable pleasure in physical carnage, especially when he had for so long been denied the joys of the flesh. He didn't even need to draw his sword. Not for pitiful specimens like these. His playfulness was flushed out of his system on the instant, replaced by a sudden burst of hunger. His claws and fangs extended and his vulpine features became something horrible to behold as he pounced.

He shrieked, grabbing a man's head and ripping it in half like a soft melon. Swords and clubs rattled off his twisted armour as he tore through the sailors and the deck was awash in blood when he finished with them. The stink of fear filled his sinuses, calming him, and he turned, looking towards the upper deck. Terrified faces stared at him like mice stunned by the sudden appearance of a snake in their midst.

Slowly, savouring the fear emanating from them, he made

his way to the upper deck. 'I apologise for my most abrupt embarkation. Regrettably, I have need of your vessel.' He paused, as if thinking, and then continued, 'And yourselves.' His tongue extended in a cat-like fashion and dislodged the drying blood from his mouth. The hunger had him now. More blood, he needed more. He needed seas and messes of it.

There were half a dozen men and women on the observation deck. Two of the men stepped forwards as he came up the stairs; both drew rapiers, though only one looked as if he knew how to properly use it. He drew his own sword, relishing the way their faces went pale at the sight of it. 'W-who... who are you?' one said.

He stopped. 'Who,' he said, curiously. It wasn't a question he had thought about before. In sleep, he had had no need of a name or an identity. And in his life he had had many; dozens of them, hundreds of them and the titles to go with them. He flashed through them, trying to find the most recent. Who was he, at this time, in this place? The answer came in a flash of red and he gave a courtly bow as he said, 'Allow me to introduce myself... I am Mannfred von Carstein.' His lips skinned back from his fangs. 'And I am hungry.'

The Low Town of Wurtbad was like a different country. Thanks to the prevalence of river-traffic, Low Town was home to a wide variety of people from all over the Empire, as well as more than a few from beyond. A babble of accents and languages mingled to create a persistent background hum. Business went on in Low Town at all times. The setting of the sun was no impediment.

Felix spun as he heard the clash of steel echoing off the baked clay bricks. One hand hovered over his sword-hilt.

Gotrek chuckled unpleasantly. 'Paranoid, manling?' he said.

'Just cautious,' Felix insisted, hurrying to catch up to the Slayer and Iuldvitch. The templar walked briskly, his palm resting on the hilt of his sword.

'Wurtbad is a vibrant place,' Iuldvitch said, not sounding at all happy about that fact.

'Surprising, considering how close we are to Sylvania,' Felix said.

'In my experience, you humans never laugh louder than when you're trying to ignore the wolf at your door,' Gotrek grumbled.

'Better than the alternative, I suppose,' Felix said, shrugging. 'Strange that the temple would be in Low Town,' he went on, looking at Iuldvitch.

'Not really,' the templar said, smiling thinly. 'Morr is a necessary god, but not a loved one. And the dead are regarded more warily in these regions. Those who live in High Town have their own private mausoleums and their own pet priests, but for the rest of the population, the Garden of Bones must suffice.'

They moved across a square and then to a battered wooden footbridge that led across a narrow, brick-rimmed channel. Felix looked down into the sluggish water, marvelling at the feat of engineering that had gone into creating the web of man-made tributaries that provided water to every part of Wurtbad. Altdorf had something similar, as did Nuln, or so he'd heard. 'It's amazing, isn't it,' he said, looking down at Gotrek.

'Eh?'

'This, all of this,' Felix gestured around them.

Gotrek's reply was a wad of spittle plopping into the water. They left the bridge behind. The Bone Garden sat silent in an empty space at the end of a quiet plaza. Felix looked down and realised with a start that the face of Morr had been picked out in ivory stones in the centre of the plaza. He stooped, curious, and then straightened abruptly. They weren't stones. 'Gotrek...' he began, his mouth dry.

'Aye, it took you long enough to notice,' Gotrek said without stopping.

'Men of faith donate their bones to the temple, even as we donate our bodies to Morr's service,' Iuldvitch said, stopping before the great gate of iron that marked the boundary to the Garden of Morr. He looked at Felix. 'You disapprove?'

'I – ah – no,' Felix said hesitantly.

'Good,' Iuldvitch said, smiling. He turned back to the gate and reached for a silver bell mounted in the wall. 'The temple here is a small one. Only one priest, but then, we have never needed more...'

'Wait,' Gotrek said suddenly, raising his hand in a gesture of warning.

'What?' Felix said, his hand dropping to the hilt of his sword.

'The gate is open.'

'What?' Iuldvitch drew his blade. Gotrek, axe in hand, tapped the gate and it swung outwards with a shrill shriek. Felix flinched, the noise causing his teeth to vibrate in his gums and the soles of his feet to itch. He looked down.

'Gotrek,' he said. 'Look, footprints.' Felix gestured with his sword, showing the dark footprints that stained the white space before the gate. 'And bare feet as well; who would wander bare-footed through a cemetery?'

Iuldvitch cursed and darted through the open gate. Felix shared a look with Gotrek and then they hurried after the templar. A persistent mist curling off the river permeated the cemetery, drifting between the headstones and statuary. Felix's flesh crawled at the cold feel of the mist and he remembered suddenly that he had always hated bone-gardens. Morr was not a comforting presence, as gods went. His was the sad inevitability of oblivion, and no man liked to think of that, not with the memory of wine still on his tongue or the touch of a woman's hand on his heart.

Gotrek, of course, seemed altogether unbothered. 'Burying your dead in the dirt,' he grumbled. 'That's what causes the problems, manling. Stone is the only appropriate resting place for the dead. You never see the dead of a dwarf hold rising in revolt!'

'Give it time,' Felix muttered. Gotrek glared at him but didn't reply. They caught up to Iuldvitch just outside of the garden chapel. He waved them to silence, his pale eyes narrowed. The chapel was a squat square of brick, adorned with skulls that clustered in nooks and crannies. A peaked roof studded with weathervanes completed the image of something that was less an actual building than the merest aperture of some unseen temple.

Gotrek sniffed the air. 'Spoiled meat,' he growled low in his throat. 'And old blood as well.' Iuldvitch started forwards, his sword out. He opened the chapel door and stepped inside. Gotrek and Felix followed, one to either side of the templar.

The chapel was little more than a corridor filled with softly-burning candles and rough wooden benches. At the opposite end, beneath the light cast by a lantern held by a stone image of Morr, was the altar. And on the altar was the priest. But he was not alone.

Felix choked on a sudden rush of nausea. Gotrek snarled and hefted his axe. Iuldvitch started forwards, his face a stiff mask.

The white, hairless things that had been crouched over the priest turned, their bestial faces twisting in surprise. There were five of them, and they were skinny creatures, balloon-muscled and bloat-bellied. One of them shrieked, sounding like the largest, angriest bat that Felix had ever heard. Then, with a howl, they sprang off the altar and rushed towards the trio.

The woman squirmed in Mannfred's grip. He drank deeply of the pulsing red river of her life, but stopped short of running it dry. Contemptuously, he rolled her body off him and rose to his feet. Stepping over her, he stalked to the rail, licking blood from his claws.

The other five were attached to each other and to the lounging bench by the anchor chain. Blood encrusted the links, and they all hung limp and weak in their bonds. He had drunk from them all in the past few hours, and he would again before they reached their destination. He would drain them of every drop of noble blood that they possessed and replace it with something older and finer. He smiled, a razor slash in the dim torchlight. Mannfred leaned over the rail, the painted wood cracking in his grip. This was only the beginning.

His memories were less haphazard now. He had glutted himself, and his form, while still weak, was stronger now than it had been. Strong enough to do what came next, at any rate.

He looked down at Andree standing among the bodies of the slaughtered crew and raised his hands. The Carrion Winds caressed the edges of his mind and he spoke, the words echoing like shattering ice. On the deck, the bodies began to tremble. They twitched, squirmed and finally sat up, some still clutching the weapons that had proven so useless against their new master. In his head, Mannfred could hear the groans of horror as the bound spirits realised their predicament.

He smiled, glorying in the delicious spiritual agony. To master the dead was a fine thing indeed. To rip them from the clutches of jealous Morr filled him with a raw pleasure that was only matched by taking their lives in the first place.

'Only the beginning,' he hissed. Dominance came naturally to his kind. It was built into them to strive and conquer and rule. Even more so than in the humans they preyed upon. Vlad had taught him that; one of the few useful lessons his creator had ever given him.

Only the strongest could conquer. Only the most cunning and the canniest could rule. Instinct demanded that he return to Sylvania, to the ancient places of power. But Mannfred had ever been master of his instincts. Of them all, he had been the most cunning. While Vlad had become lost in ancient books and wasted lovers, and Konrad had raged impotently against phantom enemies, Mannfred had gone out into the wider world and supped on its delights.

He had learned things: the arts of *Dhar* and *Shyish*, the way of manipulating men and indeed, more than men. He had walked unseen in the deserts of the Land of the Dead and faced foes more terrible than any elector count armed with a bit of borrowed dwarf steel.

He frowned. That, of course, simply made his failure all the more painful. The Empire, by rights, should have been his. All of the pieces had been in place, everything was perfect, and then… what?

Mannfred reached into his belt and extracted the slice of Schtillman's flesh. He examined the brand again, his still-sluggish memories shuffling into view in his mind's eye. The brand was of old Khemri, but it had been used much more recently. Mannfred hissed in frustration as he tried to recall what it had signified. He squeezed the scrap of skin so hard that it stretched and tore in his hands.

'What are you?' he growled. He had brought the necromancer's notes with him, hoping for answers of some kind. He – all of the von Carsteins, really – had been Schtillman's life's work. The wretched creature had spent decades hunting for Mannfred's last resting place. But nothing in his interminable notes told Mannfred *why*.

Necromancers served his kind. It had always been thus. Vlad had said that it had been one of the first vampires who had passed on Nagash's ancient wisdom to the cattle, and taught them the arts of necromancy. Mannfred could see that. Some among his kind, while sorcerous in nature, had less magical aptitude than a rock. They knew the why and the how, but lacked that spark that all humans possessed that allowed them to commune with the winds of magic.

Mannfred himself had no such need for the Schtillmans of the world. He had scoured the Books of Nagash clean of knowledge and drained the Concordances of Arkhan of all that they might teach him. Granted, there was still more to be learned. There was always more. But unlike some, the knowledge he sought had a use.

He looked down at the ragged shred of flesh in his hand and traced the mark on it, noting again how it looked to have been cut up, as if someone had tried to remove it or otherwise deface the brand. He knew what it was. He had to. But he could not bring it to mind.

Mannfred snarled in frustration, and his captives whimpered in fear. His mind was still wounded, even if his body was growing stronger. It had been all he could do to raise the dead crew and set them to work getting the barge moving. He turned from the rail, stuffing the scrap of Schtillman's flesh back into his belt.

He needed more blood.

Gotrek gave a bark of joy and bounded past Felix and Iuldvitch to meet the ghouls charging towards them. 'Ho, corpse-eaters! Come to Gotrek!'

Three of the beasts pounced on the Slayer while their two fellows darted past, heading for Felix and the templar. Felix stepped back as one of the things leapt up onto a bench and launched itself towards him. It crashed into him, surprisingly heavy for its size. An unpleasantly human face thrust itself at his and bit at him wildly. Pushing it back, he drew Karaghul and made to disembowel the monster. It twisted aside and leapt at him again. Felix whirled, sweeping his cloak out to catch it. The creature shrieked as it became tangled. Felix jerked his cloak aside and stabbed the off-balance creature. It folded over his blade, weeping black blood. Disgusted, he kicked it off and turned to help Iuldvitch.

The templar needed no help, though. He fought more fiercely than Felix had seen; he literally battered the creature he faced off its feet, his normally stoic features twisted in an expression of disgust. Another of the creatures flew between Felix and Iuldvitch, trailing a tendril of dark blood. It hit the far wall and flopped down, motionless. Felix turned and saw Gotrek stamping on another's neck, even as he held the last of the grisly beasts above his head.

'Ha!' the Slayer laughed. 'My axe isn't to your tastes, eh?' He looked up at the last beast and grinned into its snarls. Then he slammed it down atop its fellow and drove his axe through the both of them in a display of strength that stunned Felix momentarily. He was even more stunned when the floor gave a groan and the boards split and fell in, carrying the bodies with them.

Gotrek disappeared into the newborn pit with a roar. The floor gave way beneath Felix's feet and he followed the Slayer with a yelp.

He hit the bottom of the pit with a thud and something clattered beneath him. Bones, he realised with horror. Gotrek was already on his feet. The Slayer had held onto his axe on the way down, but Felix's sword was still above ground. Gotrek looked at him and shook his head. 'I've never yet met a human who could hold onto his weapon,' he grunted.

Felix restrained the urge to snap at the Slayer and scrambled to his feet. The pit was full of bones, and more of them decorated the walls. 'What happened? Why did the floor collapse?' he asked.

'Shoddy human workmanship, I'd wager,' Gotrek growled, peering around. There was a foul stink rising from the pit below, and Felix wished he had a handkerchief. It was dark and a wet mist rose up, carrying the stink with it. 'The ground is soft here, manling,' Gotrek said looking more closely at the walls of the pit. 'It's been dug out as well, though not by tools.'

'It's a ghoul warren,' Iuldvitch intoned hollowly from above them.

'Ghouls,' Felix repeated, the word bringing with it a creeping sensation of dread. Even to a man with his upbringing, the word was one of horror, dredging up as it did every half-true fable of starving families eating the dead to survive a harsh winter and degenerating into inhuman scavengers as a consequence. Better a slow death by starvation than that. He prodded one of the bodies that had fallen with them with his boot, his curiosity momentarily overcoming his disgust. In death, they looked human enough, despite the slick greyness to their skin and the bestial cant to their spine. He paused as he noticed a strange brand on each of the beasts, on shoulders or haunches. It was a curious, crawling shape and it hurt his eyes to look on it.

'They cling like blowflies to the grounds of some cemeteries,' Iuldvitch said. Felix looked up at him. His flesh crawled at the thought. How long had the corpse-eaters been scurrying beneath Wurtbad and carving their foul-smelling tunnels?

'I thought it your lot's job to keep them from doing that!' he said.

'It is,' Iuldvitch said grimly. 'I'm going to go find a rope or something. Don't move.'

'Where would we go?' Felix shot back. Iuldvitch vanished without replying.

He looked at Gotrek. The Slayer was running his hand across the rough circumference of the pit. 'The templar is wrong,' he grunted.

'This looks like part of a warren to me,' Felix said.

'It's more than that. No beast can dig through stone that easily,' Gotrek said. He dug his fingers into the mud and pulled a chunk away, revealing what looked to be smooth stone.

'What is that?' Felix said.

'It's a keystone, manling,' Gotrek said, pressing his palm to the stone. He looked up, squinting. 'My people use them to identify routes and passages.' He looked down, his eye searching for something. 'This is a landing. There are stairs here, somewhere. More than one set, and dwarf-work.' Gotrek's eye narrowed. 'Wurtbad was built over an older settlement, if I recall.'

Felix heard a strange scraping sound and turned. The bones in the walls of the pit were shifting and crumbling. 'Gotrek,' he said, wishing he had his sword. The scratching grew louder, sounding like rats behind the walls of a house. The sound was echoed from the other sides of the pit. Even Gotrek had stopped to listen, his head cocked.

'Rats,' he said.

'That's not rats,' Felix said.

'Big rats,' Gotrek said.

The walls of the pit collapsed inwards, showering both of them with mud and bones. Felix found his arms pinned against his sides as the dirt swept him back. Dozens of ghouls, much larger than the others, bounded out of the holes towards them.

'Those aren't rats!' Felix yelled, trying to free himself. Gotrek had managed to get his arm free, but not his axe. As a ghoul lunged at him, the Slayer's hand shot out, his palm covering the lower half of the creature's face. With a quick push, Gotrek snapped the creature's neck.

Felix fought desperately to free himself as several ghouls moved towards him on all fours, their distorted bodies moving more like those of cats than the men they had once been. Gotrek snarled in pain as a ghoul avoided his fist and leapt onto his back, burying its teeth into his shoulder. With a powerful shrug the dwarf ripped his other arm free of the mud and reached up to grab the ghoul.

Felix jerked back as a ghoul made an almost playful snap at him. A pair of them circled him, licking their chops and chuckling. He forced his hand down, reaching for the dagger sheathed on his belt. It wasn't going to be of much use but it was better than nothing.

Gotrek forced himself up out of the mud, but was quickly

bowled over by the ghouls. The bigger beasts were far stronger than their smaller cousins. Gotrek bellowed and thrashed, driving an elbow into the jaw of one creature, knocking it backwards. He rose and grabbed another in a bear-hug. Felix heard bones snap and pop.

He got his dagger free at the last moment and jabbed it upwards into the soft spot under a lunging ghoul's jaw. It leaned into him, eyes bulging hatefully. Felix forced the blade further in, hoping to pierce the creature's brain. Its foul breath washed over him and then it sighed and slumped. Black blood washed over his hand, burning his flesh slightly.

He tried to jerk the dagger free, but he knew he wouldn't get it loose in time. Another ghoul was too close. Felix steeled himself for the bite he knew was coming.

But it didn't.

Felix's eyes cracked open. The ghoul's jaws gaped, but its eyes had rolled up in its head, as if looking towards the blade of the axe embedded in its skull. Gotrek had hurled it across the pit, killing the creature moments before it could do the same to Felix.

'Is everyone all right?' Iuldvitch called out from above.

'Oh yes, just fine,' Felix said, his voice a touch more hysterical than he would have liked. 'I'm not dead,' he said.

'No,' Gotrek said, retrieving his axe and plucking Felix out of his predicament. As he hauled Felix out of the mud, he pointed to where the ghouls had emerged. 'Stairs, manling,' he said triumphantly.

'I never doubted you,' Felix protested. There were indeed stairs there and they appeared to go down, but Felix wanted to go up and he looked away from them as Iuldvitch lowered a thick chain snagged from one tomb or another. 'Best I could find, I'm afraid,' the templar said apologetically.

'It'll do,' Felix said, as he and Gotrek climbed out quickly. 'Thank you,' Felix said, brushing mud off his sleeves. Iuldvitch didn't reply. He was staring at the body of the priest. Gently he began to arrange the dead man's outflung limbs to hide the gaping ruin of his belly and chest. 'I would have thought this place would be safer than most...' He turned and Felix noticed that his hands were trembling slightly.

'Those creatures weren't alone,' Gotrek said. 'Remember the footprints, manling?' He gestured with his axe towards the gates. 'Like as not, the rest of the pack went into Low Town. And judging by the stink, there were a lot of them.'

'You can tell that?' Felix asked.

Gotrek tapped the side of his nose. 'Of course; the stronger the stink, the more of them there were. It's the same with *grobi* and skaven.' He headed for the door. 'My axe still thirsts. We can probably catch up with them if we hurry.'

The thought of fighting more of the things caused Felix to squirm inside, but he hurried after Gotrek nonetheless. He stopped when he realised that Iuldvitch wasn't following them. The templar had drawn his sword and was kneeling in front of the altar and the priest's body.

'Iuldvitch?' Felix began.

'Leave him, manling,' Gotrek said, grabbing Felix's arm. 'He's got his own path to follow.'

'He's right,' Iuldvitch said without turning. He stood slowly, leaning on his sword. 'Where one pack rises, others are sure to follow, unless the warren is purged. This close to Sylvania, there's no telling how many packs of the creatures are lurking. I'll not have this place corrupted any further.'

Felix hesitated. 'Surely we should help,' he said, looking at Gotrek.

'We will be, manling,' Gotrek said, shoving the chapel door

aside. 'By tracking down and slaughtering the rest of this filth before they do to any others what they did to the priest.'

Iuldvitch smiled thinly at Felix. 'Go on, Jaeger. This is what I do, and I do it best alone. Besides, one of us should warn the authorities. There could be more ghouls in the city, especially if we've stumbled afoul of some deeper plan.'

'Plan?' Felix said.

'Ghouls don't do this sort of thing on their own initiative. They're scavengers. Even a pack this size...' Iuldvitch shook his head. 'Something forced them up here. Be careful.'

Felix nodded and hurried after Gotrek's swiftly stumping form.

'Wurtbad, jewel of the Stir,' Mannfred murmured, leaning across his cocked knee, his red eyes gazing at the approaching docks in barely repressed eagerness. 'It has been some time since I last tasted its delights,' he continued, more loudly, as he turned. The six newly-made vampires hissed and snarled in reply as they clustered about him, feral faces twisted in hunger.

Mannfred slapped aside a vampiress who'd gotten too close and snarled at the thirsty pack, causing them all to scramble to the opposite side of the deck. He'd drained them dry over the course of the trip, and then filled them up again, with his essence. Their thoughts, full of hunger and frustration, fluttered around the edges of his consciousness like moths around a dark flame.

Ruthlessly, he spread the tendrils of his mind and gathered their thoughts before crushing them, causing the vampires to twitch and moan. Satisfied that they would cause no trouble, he grunted and turned away to watch the zombie crew move mechanically about their duties. In truth, he'd have preferred to avoid the whole messy process of creating more of his kind. Weak-minded as they were at the moment, they were more a threat to each other than to him, but as his experiences with brother Konrad had shown, vampires were not pack animals, despite being able to assume the form of wolves.

Unfortunately, he needed servants of a more durable nature than Andree and his new fellows. Armies had to start somewhere. He extended his tongue, tasting the air. It was foul, this close to the city, smelling as it did of industry and strange spices. But below that, he could scent the far sweeter smell of death, and necromancy. It was a familiar scent, and not in the general fashion that all things derived from necromancy were familiar.

It was frustrating, that familiarity. Magic, when wielded by a particular hand, had a particular odour. It was a tang that prodded at the heightened senses of sorcerous beings like Mannfred. He could follow that tang across any ground, as his every instinct now urged him to do. To hunt was his nature and it had been too long.

He signalled his zombies to drop anchor in a bend in the river. The boat would be safe enough here, on the outskirts of Wurtbad's docklands. Abandoned jetties and outbuildings lined the shore, used only by smugglers and other rabble engaged in illicit dealings. Other than a few members of the river-watch, who were likely in the pay of those aforementioned smugglers, no one would notice. Not until morning at any rate. And he intended to be someplace else by then. Wurtbad played host to a number of secret places and lairs for one of his kind. He had set up most of them himself, in fact, during his last visit.

Planning and preparation had ever been his way. The cautious spider, rather than the rabid wolf, as Konrad had been.

He had even been more cautious than Vlad, in the end. Suddenly, he looked up, eyes widening slightly, and grunted. 'No… It couldn't be,' he muttered, pulling the scrap of Schtillman's flesh out of his belt. 'But if it is…'

He traced the brand with the tip of a claw. It had been the thought of Vlad that had done it. That was where he had seen that brand before. And a very particular brand it was. 'Would they dare?' Mannfred said, looking at his vampires as if expecting a reply. None was forthcoming, of course. Their will was his will. They could have no other.

There was a scrape of wood on wood as the crew brought them close to the jetty and he turned, stuffing the scrap back into his belt. He glanced at the vampires and pointed at them. 'Stay until I call for you, then come in all haste,' he said. Without waiting for a reply he leapt from the prow to the jetty, his shape blurring as he fell. Bone cracked and twisted and stiff hairs pierced his flesh like thousands of spear-points, causing him to be surrounded in a bloody mist as he dropped downwards. Changing shape was a pleasurable sort of pain for Mannfred. The bodies of his kind were dead and thus ultimately malleable. The more power they had, the more shapes that were theirs to assume. Weak as he still was, there was only one shape that met his current needs.

Four feet landed on the jetty, causing the wood to bow slightly, and a great black wolf bounded into the fog. Mannfred ran faster than any wolf, however, and his claws struck gouges in the wood of the jetty. Muscles pumping with stolen blood, he sprang from the jetty to the roof of an outbuilding and ran towards the city.

He went unnoticed past the trio of watchmen heading to investigate the newly-arrived barge, and gave a silent, snarling laugh at the thought of what awaited them, should they board the barge. His new followers would satiate their hunger on the unlucky men and be ready to aid Mannfred in whatever endeavour awaited him tonight.

The wolf dropped into the crooked alleys of Low Town, moving with the surety of one whose absence has not resulted in much change in old haunts. The Empire did not change, Mannfred knew. It simply persisted. It was as much a zombie as Andree, lumbering down through the centuries, its blood growing thinner and thinner with each generation.

That was reason enough to put it out of its misery. The wolf that was Mannfred growled in satisfaction, thinking of things to come. He would rebuild his forces in the secret places of the Empire, and when the time was right, when the eyes of the Empire's defenders were turned elsewhere, he would strike.

The wolf bounded up onto the awning of a vendor's stall and leapt onto a sloping roof, scrambling up and across. He ran across the rooftops of Low Town, following the skeins of dark magic he had scented in the harbour. They permeated the town, tangled up in the damp mist that seeped upwards out of the streets. Mannfred skidded to a halt as the stench of rotting meat and spoiled milk caught his attention. He loped to the edge of the roof and gave a bark of surprise as he saw the pale shapes of a dozen or more ghouls creeping towards him from the opposite direction. They swarmed up walls and across the curves of the rooftops of the city, moving like spiders, their pale gangly limbs flashing in the moonlight as they crept closer.

But not towards him; the ghouls were creeping towards the building he crouched on. Mannfred sank down, inhaling as his shape billowed back out to its human proportions. He smelled a strong wood fire and cooking meat, fermentation and human sweat. It was a tavern. Mannfred rose to his feet even as the first ghoul landed with a thump on the roof.

It shrilled at him, baring yellow teeth. Others joined it, swarming up to crouch in a semi-circle of simian malevolence around Mannfred. There were twenty of them, and he could smell more of them coming closer. One snarled and stretched out a hesitant claw. Mannfred met its dim gaze and flashed his fangs. It squeaked and shoved back, nearly dislodging several of its fellows from their perches. The brands on their flesh burned like torches to his eyes and he snarled. It was the same brand as marked the shred of Schtillman's flesh.

They had been sent on some errand, but his presence had cowed them for the moment. Deep in their tainted blood, the beasts knew who their real master was, no matter the petty magics that leashed them to hidden hands. Their kind had served his since their first degenerate antecedent had sworn fealty to the first vampires.

Curious, he stepped aside and gestured. Almost gratefully, the ghouls piled past him, whimpering and growling. They began tearing at the roof. He could hear their fellows doing the same to the closed shutters of the upper-storey windows. He watched them for a moment longer and then whispered a guttural phrase. The strings of necromantic magic that were hooked into the brands on the ghouls stretched back the way the beasts had come, across the rooftops. Mannfred gave a short, sharp laugh and set off on the trail of old friends he had thought long since gone to their well-deserved graves.

Even on two legs, his speed was preternatural, carrying him swiftly from the roof of the tavern to another overlooking a bone-coloured square that marked the entry point to the local cemetery. He caught sight of the image on the floor of the plaza and hissed, throwing up a hand instinctively.

Wincing, he hurled himself the distance from the edge of the roof to the top of the wall surrounding the Garden of Morr.

Even Mannfred, the most logical of his breed, felt some small disquiet at the thought of willingly entering an abode of the God of Death. Everything that Morr was, Mannfred and his kind made mockery of. And Morr, like any god, was a jealous entity, and prone to grudges.

Crouching on the wall, Mannfred sniffed the air cautiously. The Bone Garden reeked of dark magics. Like an apple eaten inside out by rot, it was no longer dedicated to the Final God, but instead to – what? It stank of necromancy, and the mist clung fiercely to the headstones and mausoleums. Mannfred dropped down into the cemetery and the mist coiled up around him, like striking serpents. With a gesture, he dispersed it and started towards the chapel. He could feel the tingle of the sacred there; a final holy flame.

A born conspirator, Mannfred knew a plot when he stumbled over one. It would take a sorcerer of his standing years to undermine the innate protections of a Garden even as small as this one. And the brand on the ghouls bespoke a familiar band of plotters indeed. Memories surged, bobbing to the surface of his wine-dark thoughts.

He smelled the delightful scent of newly-spilled blood emanating from the chapel. Licking his lips, he stepped inside. The mist retreated, and Mannfred himself felt an invisible pressure radiating from the altar at the other end. A figure knelt, head bowed in prayer. The syllables struck Mannfred like slaps, and he could not restrain a snarl.

The man sprang to his feet and spun around, eyes widening as he caught sight of Mannfred. 'Who–' he began.

Mannfred did not let him finish. He rushed forwards, cloak flaring out behind him, the curved ridges of his armour swallowing the light. His fangs and claws extended and he dived onto the warrior. A sword slashed up, nearly bisecting him, and Mannfred twisted in mid-air, avoiding the blow. He landed on the altar and lunged at the swordsman without pausing. Mannfred did not know him, but he was familiar nonetheless. He had faced servants of the death god before and he knew their maggoty stench.

The man's sword burned with letters of cold fire and Mannfred's flesh crawled as he ducked under a precise sweep and dug his claws into his opponent's steel gorget. The blow lifted the warrior off his feet and flung him back to crash into the closest of the benches that lined the chapel. Mannfred tossed the bent gorget aside and stalked towards the warrior, who lay in the ruins of the bench, gagging.

Mannfred scooped up the fallen sword, but tossed it aside with a yelp. His palm had blistered at the touch of the hilt and he cursed himself for being foolish. He thought of drawing his own blade, but dismissed the thought. Why sully it? The warrior was trying to get to his feet, one hand to his damaged throat. Mannfred could almost admire such determination... almost, but not quite.

Mannfred sprang forwards and grabbed the pale man by his head. He restrained the impulse to crush the man's skull like an egg and instead leaned close. There was something going on, and he wanted to know what.

'Tell me what you know,' he hissed, his eyes widening and his thoughts driving forwards to pierce the mind of his captive. The templar jerked and groaned as blood began to run from the corners of his eyes and his nostrils. Mannfred pulled him closer. 'Tell me...'

* * *

The mist seemed thicker somehow, and Felix could taste a hint of strange rot in his sinuses. The vapour was high enough now that Gotrek's crest cut through it like a shark's fin. 'Maybe we should rouse the others,' he said as they left the Bone Garden behind. Gotrek snorted.

'And what use would they be, manling?'

'Quite a bit, in Olaf's case, I think,' Felix said bluntly. He threw a hand in the direction of the Garden. 'You saw the look on his face, Gotrek. And you said yourself that there's bound to be a lot of those beasts loose in Low Town! We need to alert someone – anyone!'

'What, and spook the corpse-eaters?' Gotrek seemed aghast.

'Weren't you the one who was just talking about preventing any further deaths?' Felix snapped. He batted in annoyance at the mist as it curled around his hands. It hung off everything like a wet shroud. It made him think of Hel Fenn, something he really could have done without. Thinking of Hel Fenn made Felix think again about Schtillman and what he'd been planning. He had not voiced his suspicions as to the necromancer's intentions, seeing no need. But he wondered if that had been the correct course, considering what they had seen in the Bone Garden.

Of course, he had no proof as to what Schtillman's plan had been. He had seemingly been the only one to hear Schtillman's ranting and the thought of it was inconceivable. Resurrecting Mannfred von Carstein? The idea was laughable.

Then again... Felix shook droplets of wet off his sleeve. He looked up and tried to see the stars through the mist, but it was too thick. 'We need to get help, Gotrek,' he said. 'Especially if...' He trailed off.

'If what?' Gotrek said impatiently. The Slayer stopped so

suddenly that Felix almost ran into him. 'What's stuck in your craw, manling?'

'It's von Carstein!' Felix burst out.

'What?' Gotrek said.

'That's who Schtillman was talking about in the swamp,' Felix said. 'What if he succeeded, what if Elsa was just meant as an – an appetiser for something that was already back and hungry?'

Gotrek shook his head. 'Manling…' He turned to continue on, but by the set of his shoulders Felix could tell he was still listening. He decided to press his luck.

'What if that's what Holtz and Russ are after?' Felix insisted. 'What if the reliquary wasn't a reliquary at all, but a *body*?'

Gotrek stopped again. Felix bobbed from one foot to the other nervously. The mist seemed to press against him from all sides, like hands at an Altdorf orgy. 'Even the Sigmarites wouldn't be that stupid… to not destroy the vampire's body, if it had been found,' Gotrek said, but he sounded doubtful.

'Of course they would!' Felix said. 'It's common knowledge that they keep all manner of monsters in the Great Temple!'

'Common knowledge, eh?' Gotrek said.

'Well, rumour and innuendo, but every fiction has a kernel of truth,' Felix said. 'Gotrek, we may not be just facing ghouls, but one of the Lords of the Undead as well!'

'And?' Gotrek demanded.

'And? And?' Felix said. 'Gotrek, we have to tell someone. If Mannfred von Carstein has returned, the entire Empire is in danger!'

'All the more reason to chop the snake's head off now,' Gotrek said. 'Speaking of which…' Felix saw the Slayer's axe loop out and he threw himself to the ground. There was a scream from behind him and a ghoul crumpled to the cobbles, jerking and dying. Gotrek ripped his axe loose and flicked a blob of sticky blood from the blade. 'Looks like we found the ghouls,' he said.

Felix looked up and saw dozens of red lights shining above him in the mist. He drew his sword. Gotrek roared and cut a falling ghoul in two. A shower of gore filled the alleyway, but Gotrek didn't appear to notice. More ghouls dropped from the walls and rooftop, moving with almost reptilian grace. Several tried to dog-pile the Slayer, but Gotrek became a blur of muscle and metal, and body parts rolled into the gutters.

Felix, while not as deadly, was also not the target. The ghouls seemed less concerned with him than with bringing Gotrek down, and he couldn't blame them. Nonetheless, Karaghul darted out and a ghoul staggered, clutching its bloody throat.

Felix's former nausea was washed away in a rush of hatred. These creatures were monsters, not men. Whether of their own accord or at the behest of some monstrous master, they had dug their own grave as far as Felix was concerned. Any pity he might have felt for them was gone. He hacked and slashed at the capering figures and the world dimmed to a red tunnel.

Only when his sword scraped the brick of a wall did he come out of it, and he heard Gotrek laugh. 'Good, manling, good. But they're getting away.' Felix turned and saw black shapes scampering away. Gotrek was already charging after them.

Felix hurried after him. He could hear the sound of alarm bells ringing and the cry of horses; he couldn't see where the sounds were coming from, but it sounded like all of Wurtbad was in an uproar. The mist was literally crawling up the walls of the buildings around them. He could see barely a foot in front of his face. Indeed, he had lost sight of Gotrek entirely.

'Gotrek?' he said.

'Smell that, manling?' Gotrek said, from somewhere close to his elbow. Felix jumped, startled.

'What?'

'Smoke,' Gotrek said, waving his bloody axe through the mist. Felix sniffed and then looked. There was a dim glow in the haze.

'And where there's smoke, there's fire,' he said grimly.

'Let's go, manling,' Gotrek said. 'That's Hugo's tavern!' The Slayer took off at a run, and Felix followed. He didn't ask how the Slayer knew that it was Hugo's tavern that was on fire; the dwarf's senses were far keener than a human's. Instead, he concentrated on running. Fear for the others, especially Elsa, filled him, lending him speed. If the ghouls had attacked them as they had gone after Gotrek and him…

The mist seemed to draw back suddenly, like a curtain being twitched aside, and a two-storey inferno was revealed. Hugo's tavern was indeed burning. The street in front of it was jam-packed with people, most running in all directions, and not a few ghouls. The latter were tearing into the panicking crowd with berserk abandon. Gotrek roared and launched himself to the attack. Felix left him to it and grabbed a running figure. 'Where's Hugo?' he shouted.

'They're still inside!' the soot-stained man said. 'Let me go! Those things are everywhere!' The man jerked himself free of Felix's grip as a ghoul bounded towards them. With a start Felix realised that it was blind, its eyes boiled in its sockets, and char-marks and blisters covered its greasy hide. It leapt towards him and he jerked Karaghul up at the last moment, separating its grasping hands from its wrists. It shrieked and tumbled past him. Felix didn't bother to finish it. Instead, he rushed towards the burning tavern.

'Gotrek, Hugo and the others are still inside!' he called out to the Slayer, who was busy bashing his skull into that of an unlucky ghoul. Gotrek looked up, his face a mask of ghoul-blood.

'Then what are we waiting for, manling? Let's go get them!' the dwarf said, dropping the dead ghoul and uprooting his axe from the body of another. But even as they headed for the door, a tide of screaming, burning ghouls barrelled out of the fiery tavern and ran blindly towards them.

Gotrek shoved past Felix and his axe swung out in a savage arc, spilling frying entrails and bubbling blood across the street. Felix rammed his sword through a howling ghoul, driving it back against the smouldering door-post. It clawed at him in agony and he ripped Karaghul free and dived past it into the tavern. There was smoke everywhere and Felix pulled his cloak, still damp from the mist, up to his face, hoping it would protect him long enough to find the others.

The common room was almost entirely aflame, and comets of burning wood dripped from the ceiling. The upper floors were completely consumed, Felix knew, and anything that had been in them. In the centre of the common room, within a ring of overturned tables, stood Olaf, his arms outthrust, the flames cascading around him like an eggshell and his feet set. Blood stained the front of the wizard's robe, pouring down from under his wide beard, and even at a distance and through the smoke Felix could tell that he was weakening. Holtz knelt beside him, cradling a limp shape, and Hugo was slumped nearby, the flames licking at his boot-heels.

Ignoring the heat, Felix rushed towards them. Olaf saw him and gave a bloody smile. His legs began to buckle and his long arms stretched out. Felix felt a moment's relief from the heat. 'Olaf, you–'

'Caught me in the throat, surprised me,' Olaf gurgled, blinking blearily. 'Let it loose without thinking… stupid.' He bobbed like a drunkard, but shook his head violently as Felix reached out to steady him. 'Get 'em out, Jaeger. Get 'em…'

Felix looked down. Holtz was slumped and his robe was ripped and bloody. Felix's heart jumped to see Elsa in his arms, however. From above there came a groan and a crashing creak. He looked up. 'Grab her and lets go, manling, the ceiling is giving way,' Gotrek snarled.

Felix looked over and saw the Slayer carrying Hugo draped over his shoulders. The Slayer jerked his head and made for the door. Felix reached down to take Elsa from Holtz's slack arms. The priest didn't resist. Indeed, he toppled over as Elsa's weight was removed. Felix hesitated, wondering if he should try and get the Sigmarite out as well, but Olaf shook his head weakly. 'He's dead, the stupid bastard. All dead. Go, Jaeger. I can't… can't keep the flames at bay much longer.' He coughed and more blood spilled down his chest.

The flames pressed closer suddenly and he could hear Gotrek roaring his name. Felix held Elsa close, shrouded in his cloak, and made a lurching run towards the door. He felt more than saw Olaf topple to the floor behind him, and one of the stout timber beams of the roof gave way, smashing into the floor and hiding the wizard from sight.

With the fire clutching greedily at him, Felix hurled himself and Elsa out the doorway and into the street. Noise ripped through the smoke that filled the air. More alarm bells were being rung throughout Low Town and the sound of weapons rang through the streets. Dropping Elsa to the ground as gently as he could, he ripped off his cloak and beat out the flames that clung to it. 'Good job, manling,' Gotrek said. Felix looked over and saw the Slayer pinching out the wisps of fire that had scorched the top of his crest. Hugo sat beside him, coughing.

'What happened in there?' Felix said, helping Elsa sit up as she came around. He patted her back as she coughed. 'Was it the ghouls?' he said, looking around. Shadowy shapes lurked on the rooftops and the bodies of those they'd killed lay in the street.

'Never known the corpse-eaters to set fires,' Gotrek said. He shifted his grip on his axe as his nostrils flared. 'They're watching us,' he growled.

'It was the wizard. Olaf,' Hugo said hoarsely. 'Ghouls came in through the upper storey and attacked Holtz and the witch hunter in their room. The fight got loud and Olaf went to help. By then, there were ghouls swarming through the common room, attacking everyone. The wizard's fire got out of control...'

'They cut his throat,' Felix said, rubbing his own. 'It must have made it hard to concentrate.'

'M-my sons?' Hugo said, looking at Gotrek. The Slayer hesitated and then put a hand on the publican's shoulder. Hugo's face crumpled and he hunched over, sobbing. Elsa went to him, tears streaming freely down her cheeks. She looked up at Felix.

'They tried to help the witch hunter upstairs, but they never came down,' she said. 'I went to find them, but the priest – he stopped me – oh Felix, he was bleeding and then the ghouls came and he fought them but there was so much blood...' She trailed off, staring at nothing as she unconsciously comforted her father.

'All dead,' Felix said, echoing what Olaf had said. 'Gotrek...'

'It's as the templar said, manling,' Gotrek said, starting back towards the Garden of Morr. 'And I know where they're coming from.'

'Gotrek, we can't just leave them,' Felix said. He looked down at Elsa and her father.

Elsa looked up, her features twisting into a mask of hatred. 'Leave!' she spat. 'Go and kill them! Kill all of them!' Felix flinched, but set his face and turned to follow Gotrek, who hadn't stopped.

'Why would they attack Holtz and the others?' Felix said as they moved swiftly through the ever-thickening mist. 'Out of all the public houses in Wurtbad, why did they pick Hugo's?'

'Maybe they weren't a fan of his ale,' Gotrek said nastily. He was nothing but a dim, ape-like figure in the mist, but Felix thought he could see the glint in the Slayer's eye nonetheless. Gotrek was angry, and that did not bode well for the ghouls.

'Gotrek, something is going on!' Felix said, exasperated. 'If I can see it, surely you can as well!'

'You're a poet, manling. It's your job to see stories where there are none,' Gotrek said.

'Iuldvitch said it himself... something is driving them out of their warrens! They don't do this,' he said, gesturing to the city. Shapes ran across the mouth of an alley, and he heard a piercing shriek rise up before being abruptly silenced. More screams echoed from all over and the smell of smoke was omnipresent.

Despite that, they arrived back at the cemetery without incident. Gotrek didn't slow down as the gate rose up before them out of the mist. One broad shoulder struck the gate, slamming it open. Felix came after him, calling out 'Iuldvitch!' He hoped that the templar hadn't already gone into the warrens. If he were right and there was a vampire on the loose, then a templar of Morr would come in handy.

'Save your breath,' Gotrek growled, hurrying along. Felix

ignored him. The ground felt soft and mushy beneath his feet, and for a moment he wondered how far the ghoul warrens extended beneath the cemetery. 'He's either already down there, or he's dead. Either way, he's no help to us,' the Slayer continued.

They went inside the chapel. The smell of blood was strong, stronger than it had been before. The hole was still there, where Gotrek had put it. The Slayer looked down into the hole, his face like carved stone. 'Mannfred von Carstein is dead and gone, manling,' he said, after a moment. 'But you're right; someone has sent the ghouls out.'

'But why?' Felix said. 'And if not the vampire, then who?'

'Does it matter, manling?' Gotrek said, running his thumb along the blade of his axe. He eyed the bead of blood on his thumb for a moment, and then rubbed it out. 'They are, and that's enough for me. Are you coming?' Without waiting for a reply, the dwarf leapt easily into the pit and started down the ancient stone steps. Felix hesitated, then climbed awkwardly down the chain and followed suit.

Within moments, darkness had enveloped them. Felix was forced to trust Gotrek's sense of direction. He knew dwarfs could see in the dark to some degree. As they moved downwards, he was reminded of their trip to the City below the Eight Peaks, and another shudder wracked him. The troll-thing that they had faced there was worse than any ghoul, he knew, but it was hard to be objective in the dark. Especially when he was certain that he could hear the damn things scraping and crawling on the other side of the loose-bricked walls of the ancient stairwell.

'There are towns almost as deep as any dwarf hold in this part of your Empire,' Gotrek said, his voice echoing off the walls. 'Every time they're destroyed, you just build over the ruins, like ants.' Felix couldn't tell whether the thought pleased Gotrek or disgusted him.

'I've heard there've been three cities here, since Sigmar's time. And Low Town burns to the river bed every summer, when the wildfires on the plains get out of control,' Felix said, more for something to say than any other reason. He kept his voice low, but it echoed nonetheless.

They reached the bottom of the stairs and Gotrek paused, as if steeling himself. 'Gotrek,' Felix said.

'Did I tell you my father helped hold down the leech-king at Hel Fenn, manling?' Gotrek said, staring into the darkness of the tunnel. 'Held him in place while the Stirlanders put him down...' His axe flashed out suddenly, striking the wall of the tunnel and causing a shower of sparks to burst into being. 'I have longed to test my axe against one of his kind, manling. To meet one of the carrion-kings in combat,' Gotrek said. Then, more loudly, 'Come out, corpse-lovers! Come to Gotrek!' He roared and cursed for several minutes, spitting oaths into the darkness.

There were vague, distant shufflings in the darkness, but that was all the reply Gotrek's cries received. Felix's eyes were becoming accustomed to the dark, and he blinked as he saw that contrary to his earlier assumption, there was, in fact, some light to be had. It was a faint, surreal glow, just enough to see by, emanating from oddly-shaped patches of mould that grew on the walls and ceiling.

'Grave mould,' Gotrek said helpfully. 'They say it grows on untended graves.'

They continued on, following the sloping corridor. Felix thought that it might have been a street at one time, for the walls were less solid stone than bricks punctuated by hard-packed river-clay and soil. Vague shapes that might have been bricked-up doorways lined the tunnel, and at points in the ceiling, Felix caught sight of strange rectangles that he knew were coffin bottoms.

Gotrek's mood grew fouler as they moved further down. The sound of scuttling grew omnipresent, as did the distant hum of the River Stir, which caused the river-side wall of the tunnel to vibrate and drip incessantly.

'Where are they?' he snarled. He struck out at the walls, scoring the stone and causing the unseen scuttlers to move faster and further.

Personally, Felix was glad for the lack of enemies. His muscles ached and he was ready to call it a night, ghouls or no. 'Maybe they've all gone up. Maybe Iuldvitch was wrong, and this was just a random attack by these beasts...' he said, somewhat hopefully.

'Ghouls don't attack cities, manling,' Gotrek asserted. 'Not without encouragement.' He touched the wall and rubbed a bit of powder dribbling from the place his axe had cut between his thumb and forefinger. 'Limestone, and thin, manling; the river is right on the other side.'

'How can you be sure–' Felix began, when the sound of scuttling suddenly ceased. He looked at Gotrek, whose good eye widened slightly. Beneath Felix's feet, the stone gave a subtle shift. 'Oh no,' he said.

With a shrill crack, the stone gave way and they hurtled down into the lightless abyss below.

Mannfred, crouching in the eaves of the roof, watched the dwarf and his human companion enter the ghoul warren and grunted in satisfaction. They hadn't seen the body. The templar had resisted until the end. He had pitted his mind against Mannfred's and died in the doing.

Mannfred dropped from the eaves and, stepped to the door of the chapel, sending out a silent call, plucking the ever-strengthening strings of magic and blood that bound him to his followers.

He flexed his talon-tipped fingers and watched the play of his muscles in the light of the guttering torches. He looked up at the sky, judging that there were several hours yet until sunrise, which meant that there was plenty of time to deal with the current situation.

Mannfred shook his head. 'How the fates do conspire,' he murmured. It seemed appropriate, somehow, that the very agents of his destruction should themselves be destroyed on the eve of his resurrection.

Oh, they hadn't driven the blade into his heart, but it was they who had sown the seeds of his demise, spiteful wretches that they were. His lips skinned back from his fangs and he looked at the dead ghouls on the floor, and the familiar strange shifting brand that marked them as the property of their masters... the brand of the Charnel Congress.

The Charnel Congress, Vlad von Carstein's pet necromancers, schooled in the art of the Wind of Death by Vlad himself, whose knowledge of necromancy was greater even than Mannfred's. Mannfred snarled softly. And they were pets; loyal dogs, nipping at the heels of Vlad's heirs in the years after the first von Carstein's final death. They had scattered when mad, bad Konrad had assumed the stewardship of Sylvania, though he had hunted them mercilessly, desiring their service. Mannfred had thought them destroyed, until well into his own reign, when they had resurfaced, hungry for vengeance on him.

They had blamed him – him! – for Vlad's fall, and acted accordingly, pestering him as he fought a running battle with his other enemies. The leaping hound might not bring down the hunted bear, but it can render it vulnerable to the hunter's spear-thrust.

Granted, it had been his hand that had guided Vlad's enemies in disposing of him, but they hadn't known that. They had only suspected. It was almost insulting.

'Vlad, you chose your servants poorly,' Mannfred said aloud, tearing the flap of Schtillman's skin from his belt and ripping it in two. 'As did the Congress, apparently; was that why they removed you from their ranks, Schtillman, you petty hedge wizard? Did you fail them? Or did you succeed in something untoward?'

Such as learning the location of Mannfred's mortal remains, perhaps. No, they wouldn't want that, would they? Mannfred's return might upset whatever scheme they had going. 'Might,' he growled. There was no might, no perhaps. He would smash it. And smash them, because it pleased him to do so. Betrayal could not go unpunished, even so long after the fact, could it?

The question was, what were they planning? Ghouls slinking through the city streets, while a pleasant enough evening's diversion, were not enough to seize control of Wurtbad. No, there was something else. Something he wasn't seeing. Something, perhaps, that had to do with the dwarf and his companion; why else would they be here?

He looked back at the body of the templar, and his smile grew savage. In life, the templar had resisted him, but in death? He bounded towards the altar. Scooping up the body, he tossed it onto the altar and looked up at the statue of the death god with a snarl. 'Thus to you, god of maggots,' Mannfred said, as he tore open the templar's chest, exposing his heart and organs to the torchlight.

It was the work of a moment to sever the spinal column and pull loose the dead man's skull and brains. Mannfred lifted the head in both hands and breathed into its mouth. Red mist passed his lips and filled the head's nostrils, lips, ears and eyes. It was no small thing to do this, especially to a servant of the death god. Morr guarded the souls of his servants and protected them from the call of the Carrion Wind. But though he could not make the templar walk at his behest, he could make him talk. He forced more of his essence into the spell, shoving aside the defences around the templar's spirit by brute force. He felt his limbs, newly engorged by blood, begin to wither and shrink as he breathed more and more red mist into the head in his hands. Finally, the slack face twitched. 'Tell me what you know,' Mannfred rasped.

The lips quirked and squirmed as the word 'Theft,' dropped out. Mannfred grunted. 'What sort of theft? What was stolen?'

'Don't... know...' the head moaned.

'Who does?'

'Huh-Holtz...'

Holtz... Mannfred's jaw widened and he sucked back some of the mist, drawing images and names out of the head. Holtz was the priest of that jumped-up barbarian king-cum-god Sigmar. Vague notions and theories spread through Mannfred's mind like cobwebs. Something had been stolen from the Great Temple in Altdorf, something necromancers would want. Something–

'Ah!' he said, his eyes widening. He gave a guttural growl. 'You pathetic mongrels,' he said. Only this Holtz would know for sure, but if what Mannfred suspected was true, then this whole affair might prove to be even more amusing than he'd first thought. He drained the rest of the mist from the head, sucking it back into him, bolstering his flagging strength. Then he hurled the head from him.

He swept the body of the templar aside, off the altar, and sat in its place. With his arms spread he called to the Wind of Death, letting it sweep around him. It was easy, especially in this place, at this time. With a sharp gesture, he sent it hurtling off through the city streets, seeking the recently dead.

Perhaps unsurprisingly, there were many of those, their spirits winking like fireflies. Fires raged throughout Low Town, and High Town had sealed its entrances, the rich and powerful setting their private soldiery to the task. Come plague or peril, their response was ever the same. Vlad had been fond of saying that one could judge the season by the mood of the nobility.

The ghouls of the Congress were rampaging through the streets, attacking those that the mist – magically induced – hadn't driven indoors. Men and women died in alleyways, and Mannfred's spells curled lovingly around their corpses, dragging them to their feet. Finding one dead man would be tricky, even under the best circumstances. The simplest plan, then, was to bring all the newly dead to him. Besides, Mannfred had no doubt that he would find a use for them.

And speaking of use… he chuckled, thinking of the man and his stunted ally. He recognised the taste of the magics on the dwarf's axe, though only in a general fashion. It was a fell thing, and mighty. Mannfred himself would hesitate to face it, especially in his current state. And the sword the man – Jaeger was his name, according to the templar's shade – bore was no mere chopping blade, but something that was, in its own way, as potent as the Slayer's axe. The dwarf was implacable, and he would keep the Charnel Congress occupied while Mannfred prepared to deliver the killing blow.

Spectres and ghosts groaned in the air above him, pulled

from their rest by his manipulations. It wasn't much of an army, but it would do for Mannfred's purposes. The key would be hiding it from the Congress's own magics. If they knew of his presence, they would scatter and flee like the graveyard rats they were. Mannfred could not allow them to interfere with his second life. Hopefully the dwarf would keep them busy long enough for his forces to gather.

'Massssster…' a feminine voice purred. Mannfred smiled. His servants had arrived. The vampires hesitated at the door to the chapel, fearing to come in. Behind them, zombies hunched and shuffled, carrying makeshift weapons.

'Come,' he commanded, rising to stand on the altar. He drew his sword and felt the dark magics bound to the blade stir. With a roar, he spun and sliced through the head of the statue of Morr, sending the chunk of marble crashing to the floor. Kicking it aside, he turned as a burnt corpse stumbled into the chapel, drawn by his summons. The vampires pulled back from it, hissing. Mannfred leaned on his sword. 'Welcome, Holtz,' he said, holding out a hand to the charred carcass of the warrior-priest. 'We have much to discuss, you and I. And then we will go to war.'

The fall proved less a plummet than an ignoble slide into the darkness. Felix rolled to a stop, slamming into Gotrek's immoveable shape with a curse. Coughing, Felix let Gotrek haul him to his feet. 'Do you live, manling?' Gotrek said.

The words seemed to boom out thunderously. Felix looked around. They had fallen into what appeared to be a great cavern. The dark length of the Stir poured over the rocks through a natural channel, and the air was thick with a wet haze that settled unpleasantly on Felix's skin. More of the strange fleshy, glowing fungi Gotrek had pointed out earlier clung to the rocks and to their clothes as well. 'No thanks to our tunnel-digging foes,' Felix said. 'I'm getting tired of traps, Gotrek.'

'All the more reason to give them a taste of good steel,' Gotrek replied.

'Yes,' Felix said, looking around. He felt cold and his clothing was sodden. The ground beneath his feet was powdery and there was a strange smell on the air. Not the river, though that was part of it. 'Gotrek, do you smell something?'

Gotrek sniffed. 'Bats,' he said, looking up. Felix did the same, and immediately wished he hadn't. He had seen bats before; what native of Altdorf hadn't? But those had been minuscule things compared to the abnormalities that clung to the roof of the cavern, huddling amongst a veritable upside-down jungle of glowing fungus. They were huge, with wingspans as wide as a rich man's coach.

'Sigmar preserve us,' Felix whispered.

'Grimnir send them to us,' Gotrek snarled. Felix grabbed the Slayer's shoulder and Gotrek turned to glare at him.

'We're not after bats, Gotrek!' Felix hissed.

'The bats are after us though, right enough,' Gotrek growled, grabbing the front of Felix's shirt and yanking him forwards. Something leathery and hard brushed through Felix's hair and then the great bat was soaring away, up into the darkness. Squeals and shrieks echoed from above and Felix felt a moment of panic. 'Draw your sword, manling!' Gotrek said, shoving away from him.

The Slayer roared out an oath and something screamed a reply. Felix drew his sword and slashed wildly at the hairy shape that flopped towards him. Several bats hopped towards him on all fours, the way he'd heard that their smaller cousins in the New World did. Gotrek cut them off, slugging one in the side of the head and burying his axe in another's humped back. The cavern soon became a tornado of teeth and leathery flesh as more and more bats dropped from their roosts to launch themselves at the men who had invaded their sanctuary.

'Gotrek, we have to get out of here!' Felix shouted, trying to be heard over the shrieking of the bats. Gotrek gave no sign that he heard, however. All Felix could see of him was his brightly-coloured crest and the flash of his axe as it struck the wall.

A bat swooped low and crashed into Felix a moment later, carrying him backwards and down. Felix could feel the force of the river vibrating through his back as he struggled to get his sword up. The bat's wings folded around him like a clammy blanket, and its talons scratched at him, gashing his arms and chest. Its foul breath washed over him and Felix gagged as it snapped its knitting-needle teeth at him. 'Gotrek!' he cried out.

The only reply he got was the sound of stone cracking. The rocks beneath his back shifted, and water began to spray from the cracks. 'Gotrek!' he tried again, more insistently. The bat lunged for him, its jaws snapping closed only inches from his face. Felix took a chance and grabbed its quivering, flanged nose in one hand and twisted, eliciting a squeal that set his teeth to shivering. As the bat's weight shifted, Felix brought Karaghul up and buried it to the hilt in its furry, bloated body. The bat bucked and screamed, and there was a loud crack and then Felix found himself pushed into the waters by the dying bat. He slammed into the rocks and spun away from his thrashing opponent, carried by the irresistible current. Gasping, he fought to keep his head above water, and, more than once, his skull connected with the roof of the tunnel as the waters dragged him deeper and deeper into the darkness.

He held tight to Karaghul's hilt and tried to jam it into the rocks to halt his tumbling progress, without success. Sharp edges and fang-like stalagmites jarred him, reducing his world to one of darkness and pain until, at last, he was caught up in a swirling spout that spat him down a narrow tube of rock and, from there, into a blessedly still body of water. Felix hit the surface hard enough to wrench him out of his daze and he surfaced with a gasp and much splashing. The water glowed softly, lit from below by more of the fungi. Bones of all shapes and sizes were visible beneath the water.

The body of the bat he'd killed floated nearby, its eyes staring sightlessly at him. It wasn't alone… other bodies, of bats and other, stranger beasts, bobbed around him. With a start, he realised that the pool was yet another trap – a natural run-off, used by the ghouls to collect food from above. There was an entire world down here that no one above even suspected. These ghouls were not Sylvanian invaders, Felix knew, but native Stirlanders! They fished the Stir, even as their human cousins did, sifting the waters for food.

Swiping water out of his face, he slowly made his way towards the shore. Halfway there, waist-deep in water, he froze. Pale shapes glided out of the forest of stone, chuffing and chittering as they came to squat on the shore. 'And here come the attentive fishermen now,' Felix muttered. He raised his sword. The ghouls didn't seem bothered, however. Several had already entered the water and were dragging the dead bat onto shore.

Others started towards him, licking bestial lips with pale tongues. Felix prepared himself for the incipient charge. The gunshot, when it came, was surprising. It echoed through the cavern, and the ghouls scattered, yowling.

'Jaeger, you are just full of surprises,' a familiar voice said. Felix gaped as Stefan Russ stepped out of the darkness, his witch hunter's outfit replaced by dark leathers and a hooded doublet. He still wore his pistols, however, and as he re-holstered the one he'd just fired, he drew a replacement and cocked it. 'I laid odds that the dwarf would have made it, rather than you.'

'Russ? But Olaf said...' Felix trailed off as more men, dressed similarly to Russ, stepped out to join him.

'Olaf? I wouldn't put much stock in what a dead man says,' Russ said, smiling. Felix found the expression more disturbing than the more familiar glower. 'He is dead, isn't he? I was aiming for his head.'

'He's dead,' Felix said, feeling a sinking sensation in his stomach.

Russ nodded briskly. 'Good. I never liked him, the loud-mouth pyromaniac.' He tapped his cheek with the barrel of his pistol. 'As soon as our servants warned us of your arrival, I wondered which of you would make it to this point. I was hoping for Iuldvitch, myself.'

'He's busy alerting the watch,' Felix said. He had no idea where the templar was, but he could hope.

'Or maybe he's lying in ragged pieces in the tunnels above,' Russ said. 'Now, drop your sword, Jaeger, or you can join him.'

'I might prefer that to whatever you and this lot have planned,' Felix said. Was Iuldvitch dead? Russ had to be lying. Felix hoped for his own sake that that was the case.

'Maybe. Then, you won't find out unless you drop that sword. Now.' Russ gestured with his pistol. Several of the other men moved forwards, wading into the water towards Felix. Their faces were pale and drawn, their eyes shining with an unhealthy light. Felix gave a moment's thought to resisting, and then handed Karaghul over to one of the men.

'Fine,' Felix said. 'You've got me. Now what?'

'Now? Now you finally get the answer to that question you've been asking so incessantly,' Russ said. 'Aren't you the lucky fellow?' Strong hands grabbed Felix's arms a moment later and he was dragged to shore, not feeling particularly lucky at all.

Felix was tossed to the rough stone floor of a torch-lit cavern. It was more compact than the other, with an air of design to its smoothly-shaped walls that spoke of long use. He rolled over onto his hands and knees with a groan and pushed himself into a kneeling position. His hands had been bound in front of him. Stalactites and stalagmites decorated everything, and pillars of dripstone spiralled in all directions, giving Felix the unpleasant impression that he was in the mouth of some massive beast. Russ stood behind him with one hand tangled in Felix's hair, the black-clad men surrounding him. 'He survived,' someone said. 'You owe me a karl, Stefan.'

'Feel free to collect anytime, Utrecht,' Russ said. A heavy-set man stepped out into the light, his thumbs hooked into the broad leather belt around his waist. To Felix he looked like any other wealthy burgher, made heavy by too much good living. Utrecht sniffed as he took in Felix's bedraggled appearance.

'I think I would have preferred the dwarf. This one looks far too thin and pale.'

'He's not thin, he's… slender,' a woman said. She joined Utrecht in looking at Felix. She too was dressed finely, though inappropriately for her surroundings. Her dress swept the floor clean behind her as she stepped forwards and bent low, running her sharp fingernails across the trail-seams in Felix's face. 'Rather like a stray cat,' she continued, her tongue running across her lips.

'Thank you, Ilsa, your contribution is so noted. Someone note that please,' Utrecht said, looking around. 'Who's taking the minutes?' Felix saw several other figures behind Utrecht and Ilsa.

'I believe it falls to me, Utrecht,' a thin man said, pushing his gold-rimmed spectacles back up the bridge of his nose. 'Then, it always falls to me, doesn't it?'

'Don't be sour, Norrys,' Ilsa said, still looking at Felix. 'You like taking notes.'

'We all have our hobbies,' another woman said, stroking the fur stole that was wrapped around her shoulders. 'I knit, for instance.'

'No, you pay people to knit while you watch, Helga,' Russ said, shoving Felix forwards. 'That's different.'

'But I do know how, and that's more than some of us can say,' Helga said mildly, looking at Ilsa, who stuck out her tongue.

'At least I don't wear human hair and pretend it is real fur,' the younger woman said. She tapped her belly. 'I keep my fashion accessories subtle, thank you very much.'

'A corset made of human bone is hardly a taboo-breaker, my dear,' Norrys said. 'It's all the rage in Kislev, I understand. Then, they are a funny folk.'

'That's the problem with the younger generation… no sense of work ethic,' an older man said bitterly, with the air of one making an old argument to an audience that long ago ceased listening. 'In my day, we dug up our own materials and stitched our own soldiers.'

'In your day, you wore black rags and hid in ruined towers,' Utrecht said. 'We do things differently in Wurtbad. We have come far, since the good old days. Why, some of us are even upstanding members of the church!'

There was scattered applause and Russ bowed ironically. Felix felt sick. 'Who are you people?' he said. Russ grabbed his hair again and forced Felix to look up at him.

'The masters of your destiny, Herr Jaeger,' he said.

'Very poetic,' Utrecht said. With a grunt, he sank to his haunches and examined Felix the way a butcher might examine a cut of beef. 'You should feel honoured, Herr Jaeger. You are in the presence of history itself.' He threw out a chubby hand, indicating the walls of the cavern, which, in the light of the mounted torches, could be seen to be decorated by strange carvings and paintings, all of which made Felix uncomfortable. 'By now, you've seen the Under Town, which goes with the Low and the High. It has been abandoned for a thousand years, by everyone except our servants and us.'

Felix heard a quiet shuffling sound and saw that ghouls huddled in the corners and on the overhanging ledges of the cavern. They stayed just out of the light, as if frightened by the men and women gathered there. 'What are you people?' he said.

'We are the last faithful servants,' Utrecht said. 'The finest hour, stretched over centuries.'

'Now who's being poetic?' Russ asked. 'We're necromancers, Jaeger. From long, proud lines of the same... though some lines are longer than others,' he said to Felix. Russ seemed to be enjoying Felix's growing disgust. 'And we have been waiting a very long time for this moment. Generations of our families have been manoeuvring and searching for what would be needed to accomplish the last great task our ancestors were given by our lord and master.'

'Enough talking! Do you have it?' the older man barked, pushing past Helga and Norrys to point a shaking finger at Russ. 'Where is it, damn your eyes?'

Russ released Felix and snapped his fingers. One of the black-clad men stepped forwards, holding a small, sturdy-looking chest. 'Here, Helm, you old bone-bag... straight from the Garden of Saints in Altdorf.'

'You were the thief!' Felix said. Russ casually kicked him in the chest, knocking him backwards.

'Technically, I was allowed in there,' Russ said. 'I am a servant of the church, after all. Those foolish priests were quite surprised when I killed them.'

'Then Schtillman...' Felix began. He needed to keep them talking. The more they talked, the greater his chance of escaping. He glanced around, looking for the man who held Karaghul. He was relieved that they hadn't simply thrown the sword away.

'Was an idiot and a traitor,' Helm, the old man, snapped as he cradled the chest. 'And dangerous to boot.'

'Luckily, your friend dealt with him in a most effective manner,' Russ said. 'Two birds with one stroke, you might say.' He smiled nastily. 'Schtillman had bad habits and a dangerous obsession; one that endangered us all. But you saw to that, you and that dwarf. And now, as a reward, I think you should see just what it is you keep asking about...' He reached over and flipped open the chest that Helm held, revealing its contents.

'Behold,' Utrecht said, 'the skull of Felix Mann!'

As the echoes of his booming proclamation faded, all eyes turned expectantly towards Felix, who looked at the fractured, yellowed skull in confusion. 'Who?' he said.

'Felix Mann,' Russ said intently, gesturing. 'Mann! The thief who stole Vlad von Carstein's source of invincibility? The man who singlehandedly saved your Empire from the clutches of the Vampire Counts?'

'Felix Mann,' Helm hissed. 'The Bastard Thief! The only man who knows the location of the object we require!'

Felix frowned. 'I was never one for ancient history,' he said.

Russ, looking chagrined, cleared his throat. 'That was disappointing. Fine. We didn't save you for your limited capabilities as an audience anyway.'

'Why did you save me?' Felix said, pulling his legs up. If he could just get his feet under him…

'We are firm believers in efficiency, Herr Jaeger,' Helga said. 'Why kidnap a sacrificial victim when one handily waltzes into your lair?'

'Sacrificial?' Felix said hoarsely. 'Oh bilge.'

'Two birds, one stroke,' Russ said again, chuckling. He looked at Helm. 'Well, old man? I think we've wasted enough time, don't you? We have a god to resurrect.'

Felix was jerked to his feet by Russ's men. 'A god?' he said desperately. 'Which god?'

'Why, the creator of us all,' Ilsa purred, patting Felix's cheek. 'He is our Father in Darkness, if you will.'

'The Avatar of the Wind of Death,' Helga said reverentially.

'The king of the cats,' Utrecht said.

'Nehekhara reborn,' Norrys said, fiddling with his spectacles.

Helm lifted the skull from the chest and tossed the latter aside. 'Vlad von Carstein,' he whispered, a crooked smile creasing his features.

The name tore through Felix like the blade of a knife. It was a name that stretched across the history books like an ever-suppurating scar. Vlad von Carstein, the first of Sylvania's bloody counts, the being that had brought death to the very walls of Altdorf and shattered the armies of the Empire with an ease that the servants of the Dark Gods envied. Childhood nightmares spun through his mind's eye, bringing with them a cold, wet fear that settled about him like a cloak, strangling thought and courage in its embrace. He wanted to shout denials, to hurl curses, but no sound came out.

As Felix watched, mute, each of the six necromancers pulled a plain-looking amulet from somewhere about their person. Scratched into the surface of each was the same symbol that Felix had seen on the ghouls earlier. 'That symbol,' he said. 'What is it?'

'It's ancient Lahmian,' Norrys said, apparently happy to lecture. 'It's quite interesting, in essence it is–'

'Our master's initials,' Russ said. 'Stop talking to the sacrifice, Norrys.'

Felix fell silent. His arms were held by two of Russ's men. No one was paying attention to him, however. All eyes, even those of the ghouls, were fastened on the skull in Helm's hands. Felix's hackles bristled as a cold breeze wafted through the cavern, causing the torches to whip and dance wildly. Three of the necromancers were chanting, their voices growing louder and louder.

Ilsa sidled close to Felix. 'Can you feel it, Herr Jaeger? *Dhar*… the Wind of Darkness; it flows strongly through these tunnels, and has since Mannfred von Carstein used them to raid into the Empire centuries ago.' She stroked his hair and Felix shied away. She giggled and he shuddered. 'You'll make a fine sacrifice,' she said. 'Your blood will be the gate and the key and then he will return, even as was foretold…'

A sickly light had suffused the skull and it bobbed and shifted on Helm's upraised palms like a sack full of rats as the chant became wilder. Felix wanted to look away from it, but he was unable to. The skull rose into the air, its fleshless jaws clattering in an almost comical fashion. The necromancers raised their hands as if pushing it upwards. They strained, as if the skull were far heavier than it looked.

Helm muttered fiercely, his eyes closed, his arms thrust above his head. The other necromancers watched as the skull began to rotate faster and faster until suddenly it ceased, and bent low, as if it were attached to an overlong neck. Felix winced as something that was less a voice than a stab of cold pain flowered in his mind. It was asking a question, one he was glad wasn't directed at him.

Russ stepped forwards, his fingers dancing nervously on his pistols. 'You know who we are, Mann!' he said. 'And you know what we want! Where is the ring of the von Carsteins?'

Felix shifted slightly. His guards paid no attention, being preoccupied by the entity before them. Felix looked around, hoping to see something – anything! – that would help him out of this situation. There were plenty of weapons available, but even if he could grab one, it'd be only a matter of moments before he was overwhelmed. That was, if Russ didn't simply shoot him out of hand.

'Answer me, Mann!' Russ shouted, his face going red. 'We bind you thrice and forevermore by your bone and name! Answer us!'

A twitching, dying ghoul plummeted into the centre of the cavern, landing in a heap. Gasps of alarm and curses filled the air and men drew swords as a burly, bloody shape appeared on a high ledge. Felix looked up, his face breaking into a wild grin. 'If it's an answer you want, traitor, I'll be glad to give you one!' Gotrek shouted, gesturing with his axe.

'Gotrek, you're alive!' Felix said, relief flooding him.

'Water and stone and overgrown vermin are no death for a Slayer,' Gotrek snarled. 'Maybe you prancing fools can do better!' With a loud cry, Gotrek took a running leap off the ledge as the other ghouls closed in on him. He landed lightly for a being of his bulk, his axe unimpeded by either the skull or the torso of the guard it cut through on the way down. As the body fell in two halves, Gotrek snatched Felix's sword from the ground where it had fallen and sent it sliding towards him. 'Here, manling! Join the fun!' Then, laughing, Gotrek waded into the fray as men and ghouls moved to bring him down.

Felix lunged, wrapping his bound wrists around Ilsa's neck. The young necromancer hissed like a cat and elbowed him in the gut. Felix bent double, narrowly avoiding the blade she pulled from within her dress. She stabbed at him again and he caught the blade in his bonds. With a swift tug, the ropes frayed and parted and his hands were free. She shrieked in rage and flew at him, but he stepped aside and scooped up Karaghul. He flung aside his scabbard just in time to meet a downward stroke from one of the black-hooded men.

The man was strong, and had a wild gleam in his eye that Felix didn't like. He booted the man in the groin and leapt past him, heading for the sound of Gotrek at work. Despite all they'd been through this evening already, the Slayer didn't seem tired. Indeed, he was as energetic as Felix had ever seen him, bounding back and forth like a typhoon of destruction, tackling any opponent that either got too close or didn't scramble aside fast enough. His horrible axe looped out and spun, cleaving air, stone, steel, muscle and bone alike. The stones beneath his feet were slippery with the axe's leavings and Felix fought to keep his balance as he made his way to Gotrek's side.

'Glad to see you up and about. Had enough of a rest, then?' Gotrek said.

'I could ask the same of you,' Felix said, parrying a sword-stroke meant for Gotrek's back. 'The last I saw, you were busy with the bats!'

'Aye, devils in the air, but not so good in the water,' Gotrek said. 'Most of them drowned or flew away before I could get to them!'

'Shame,' Felix said.

'Yes,' Gotrek said, lopping off a clawed hand as it scratched at his beard. 'It is.' He looked around. 'Where's the traitor? I'd like to decorate his skull for what he's done...'

'I didn't realise you were that friendly with Olaf and the others,' Felix said.

'I wasn't,' Gotrek snarled. 'But that black-hearted bastard burned down the only decent tavern in Wurtbad!'

A gunshot sounded, echoing above the roar of voices, and Gotrek's crest wobbled as the bullet plucked a few stiffened bristles loose from his scalp. Gotrek spun and Russ danced back, his eyes wide and his mouth twisted in a snarl. 'Kill him. Kill him!' the necromancer howled.

'Yes, kill me,' Gotrek said. He leapt towards Russ. 'But first...'

Felix cracked a ghoul in the face with his elbow, knocking the beast down. He saw Russ scrambling backwards, Gotrek advancing on him implacably. The necromancer threw aside his useless pistol and raised a hand. Strange garbled syllables spewed from his lips and black lightning crackled. It spilled across the upraised edge of Gotrek's axe, lashing out at the men rushing to attack him from either side and causing them to topple in clouds of blood. Russ's expression turned comical.

In truth, Felix knew that he and Gotrek were likely only still alive because their enemies' numbers were working against them in the confined space of the cavern. As soon as the other necromancers regained their senses, they'd surely employ whatever fell magics they possessed against the Slayer, and then Felix in turn. He didn't like to think about his odds without Gotrek by his side. They needed an edge... His eyes lit on the still-hovering skull. The other necromancers were still shouting questions at it, but the spectre they had summoned seemed either unable or unwilling to answer.

'Gotrek, we need to get that skull!' he shouted. Gotrek, intent on Russ, didn't appear to hear him. The dwarf's axe thudded into the rock between the necromancer's legs and Russ scrambled up. Gotrek made to bring him down, but he was bowled under by a trio of ghouls. Felix cursed and headed for the floating skull and its questioners. If he could get his hands on it, maybe it would be enough to trade for their lives.

Before he could reach it, however, he felt the floor beneath his feet begin to tremble with the sound of booted feet, ringing on the stone. Felix's heart leapt. Perhaps someone had roused the watch. Felix cut down a gibbering ghoul and turned to face the direction of the sound, a sloping tunnel. A shape burst into the cavern, beheading a ghoul as it came.

His words of welcome turned to ash in his mouth. It wasn't the watch. The man, if it was a man, wore bloody clothes and looked as if he had undergone the tortures of the damned. Red-eyed, the being was followed by several others like it, all of them stinking of the river and slaughter, as well as a host of dead men. The zombies were of every description and condition, most of them smelling faintly of smoke.

In that moment, Felix felt as if every drop of blood in his

veins had turned to ice. The red eyes of the pack found him, examined him and dismissed him the way a hawk would a singularly unappetising mouse. Felix found himself unable to move, frozen in place by that glance.

He was not alone. Throughout the cavern, bodies stilled their motion. Even Gotrek, normally as sensitive as a stone, had paused in his rampage. Every eye was on the newcomers. The only sound was the hiss of flames and the whimper of frightened ghouls. The latter backed away from the red-eyed beings, crouching and whining like beaten dogs.

A single word burst into Felix's brain at the sight of the newcomers… *vampire*! These were the blood-drinking heirs to the wickedness of Sylvania, with far less distance between him and them than he would have wished. He had fought their kind before, but to see this many of the creatures in all their terrible glory, and so close, was terrifying. He swallowed and looked for Gotrek.

The temperature in the cavern had dropped and the torches flickered as if a dark wind had them in its clutches. The dead shifted and stumbled around the newcomers, or, in some cases, crawled. One of these struggled to a sitting position, its shattered spine sticking through its tattered back. One of the red-eyed women stroked the dead thing's head, as if it were a faithful hound.

'No,' Helm moaned, breaking the silence. The necromancer's voice was heavy with despair. He raised his crooked hands protectively.

'What is it?' Russ snapped. 'What is it? What's going on, Helm?'

'He's here…' the old necromancer groaned, his eyes bulging. 'He's here!'

'Yessss,' something hissed. Felix shuddered at the sheer

malignity evident in that voice. It seemed to come from everywhere and nowhere all at once. The torches flickered again. 'Yes, Helm, you old wretch.' The shadows cast by the torches shifted like creatures preparing to pounce. 'Did you think I was dead, Helm?' A sound like snakes slithering across the rock followed those words. Felix's nerves felt strained to breaking point. Something rustled in the darkness of the cave's ceiling. 'Did you hope that Schtillman had failed?' it purred, and Felix felt a chill caress his spine. 'Did you hope that I would remain buried in history and mud?'

The rock walls echoed with the scrape of claws. The tread of heavy, unseen boots circled them all like the pacing of an unseen animal. 'You sent assassins to kill him, to stop him from bringing me back to feel the kiss of the Carrion Winds, because... Why? Were you afraid that I would stop you, Helm?'

'No, false one,' Helm said. 'No. You are too late! We have summoned the spectre of Felix Mann and he will give us the location of that which we seek!' The other members of the Charnel Congress moved into a protective circle around the old man.

'Oh? You mean Vlad's pretty little ring, then?' the horrible voice said, its words echoing. It chuckled and Felix thought that he caught a flash of crimson in the darkness. 'I thought that might be why you stole those brittle old bones. A very good plan, or it would have been, if that skull had actually belonged to the thief...'

'What?' Utrecht said. The necromancer and his fellows all had weapons out or their hands readied for sorcerous gestures. Felix held his own sword up. The shadows seemed to be creeping closer, coiling through the fang-like stalagmites. Felix saw that Gotrek stood stock-still, his one eye moving steadily, as if following something only he could see. Could the Slayer see whatever – whoever – it was that their opponents were so terrified of?

'Did you honestly think I would allow the bones of a man who knew what Mann knew, a man who I killed precisely because of that knowledge, to fall into the hands of my enemies?' the voice hissed. 'Surely you were wondering why that dead thing hadn't answered you yet.'

'You mean–' Helga gasped.

The cavern echoed with foul laughter; the shadows seemed to ripple with the sound of it, and the ghouls set up a wail. As the laughter faded, the voice continued, 'Mann's remains are in a place known only to me, and the secret of Vlad's bauble is buried with him. And you traitors, you deceivers all, you will pay for your trespasses against Mannfred von Carstein!'

Quicker than Felix's eye could follow, the shadows solidified into a tall and cadaverous shape. It had sharp, corpse-like features and a smile like the grin of a shark. Razor-blade teeth surfaced from behind thin lips as it lunged, the fat, long blade of its sword driving through Norrys's narrow body and pinning the thin man to a dripstone like an insect to a board. The other necromancers scattered in shock and terror, scrambling for safety amongst their minions.

The creature jerked its sword free of Norrys and the stone and turned to face the others, smiling like a tiger. Its eyes narrowed to fiery slits. 'Kill them,' it snarled. The zombies jerked into motion and barrelled into the stunned ghouls and black-clad cultists, and the cavern suddenly rang again with the sounds of melee.

Mannfred stalked through it all, unconcerned. The ghouls shied back from him, and the few human servants who dared close with him were swept aside like leaves in a hurricane wind. Felix had the impression that few living things could match this creature in the physical realm. He had seen the hideous strength of the abominable warriors that served Chaos, and knew that even a champion among them would have had difficulty facing the vampire; no, not just a vampire – *the* vampire. Mannfred von Carstein was the purest incarnation of that horrible word.

The shadows seemed to cling to him as he waded through his enemies, and Felix felt the urge to flee, to run back into the darkness and throw himself into the Stir and let the river take him away from this monster. So paralysed by fear was he that he almost missed the telltale hiss of something behind him. Felix forced himself to move and threw himself aside as a female vampire lashed out at him lazily, her mouth full of fangs.

He hit the hard stone and rolled onto his back, blocking her second blow when it came. The strength of the blow left his wrists aching, and he jabbed a boot into her gut, all thought of chivalry cast aside. She snarled and grabbed at his leg and her hand vanished in a spray of blood. The vampiress shrieked and reeled as Gotrek knocked her down and separated her head from her shoulders.

'Things have gotten complicated,' Felix gasped as Gotrek hauled him to his feet.

'No,' Gotrek said, a berserk light dancing in his eye. 'The solution is still the same, manling. Kill them all and let Grungni sort them out.'

Mannfred expected the necromancers to flee. Instead, they attacked. He felt the threads of dark magic coalescing as they hurled their magics at him. He spat a word and the stabbing tendrils of black lightning clashed with his hastily-summoned defences, driving him back a step.

'You should have stayed in the grave, usurper!' one of the necromancers, the one called Ilsa, shrieked. Withering words followed and Mannfred snarled as he felt them tear at him. Their mastery of necromancy had improved since he had last faced them.

'And you should have stayed hidden,' Mannfred said, grabbing for her. She screamed as he bore her to the ground, his fangs sinking into her pale throat. He smashed her head into the floor as he tore her throat out. One of his vampires screamed as it was turned into a walking torch. It fled into the melee, setting zombies afire in its blind blundering.

Tendrils of human hair seized him, jerking him up and flinging him back. Mannfred clawed at the animated substance. Helga cursed and gestured, her stole of living hair tightening its grip on the struggling vampire. Mannfred set his feet and began to pull her towards him.

A rapier pinked him in the neck and he twisted, snarling at the fat necromancer, Utrecht, as he danced back, face red with hate and fear. 'I was satisfied to send your ancestors scrambling for rat-holes, but I'll exterminate you fools root and branch,' Mannfred said, freeing a hand and gesturing towards Utrecht, who grabbed his chest and screamed. The necromancer toppled as his internal organs began to bloat and fuse within him. 'Even at their peak, the Charnel Congress was no match for me!'

He turned back and snagged the lengths of animated hair that now sought to dig into his skin. With a roll of his shoulders, he ripped it free of Helga's grip and tore it apart. Tossing the shredded stole aside, he dived at her.

Cold flames struck at him, causing his flesh to bubble, and Mannfred winced. Forcing past the pain, he tweaked the skeins of magic, cutting off the spell at its source. Helm staggered back, eyes bulging. Mannfred slapped Helga to the ground and advanced on Helm. 'What did you fools think was going to happen here, eh? Did you think you'd simply resurrect Vlad and... What? The days of wine and roses and babies spitted over the roasting fires?'

'Vlad von Carstein is the Wind of Death made manifest,' Helm babbled, trying to beat aside Mannfred's will and resume control of the winds of magic roaring through the cavern. 'It is our duty to bring him back, we have sought his ashes scattered across the Empire...'

Mannfred lunged and caught Helm by his throat. With contemptuous ease, he tore the locket from the necromancer's neck and held it up, examining it. 'So I see... and you thought to bring him back, even as Schtillman brought me back. Tell me... did you think he'd thank you?'

'Admittedly, you weren't part of the picture,' someone said.

The pistol barked and Mannfred screeched as the bullet took him in the spine, piercing a weak place in his armour. He flopped to the ground, momentarily nonplussed. Russ, his clothing torn and bloodied, tossed aside the smoking pistol and drew two more. 'Silver bullets, usurper, in case you were wondering. I'll put you back where that fool Schtillman found you!'

Mannfred laughed and wriggled like a snake, launching himself off the floor and striking, his teeth clamping down on Russ's hand. The necromancer yelped and fired his other pistol, taking Mannfred in the shoulder. Mannfred gathered his legs under him and swatted his opponent to the ground. 'How the once-mighty have fallen,' he said, pinning Russ in place with a boot to the chest. He crushed the man's pistol and looked down at him. 'Your magics are so weak you must rely on these toys? Would you kill me with bullets and swords and scalps?'

'What about an axe then?' Gotrek said, charging towards Mannfred.

Mannfred turned and caught the axe blade between his palms with a grunt. 'I forgot about you,' he said from between clenched fangs. 'I won't make that mistake again.'

'Glad to hear it, lord of maggots,' Gotrek said, his muscles bulging as he forced the axe towards Mannfred's face. The vampire bent back for a moment and then began to meet the Slayer's strength with his own.

Mannfred caught a glimpse of Jaeger circling them and he hissed in frustration. These two were proving obstinate in their survival. They had been adequate distraction, but it was time for the finish. 'You cannot defeat me, Trollslayer. I have fought legions of your stunted kin, after all, and all of them with better reason to kill me than you.'

'Maybe, but if you knew anything about me and mine, leech, you'd know that your defeat is... a... bonus!' Gotrek roared, veins writhing on his arms and neck as he threw every bit of his strength into forcing the axe down. Mannfred blinked as the blade slid through his palms and his shape dispersed into a mist as the axe chopped down.

He screamed as whatever ancient magics had been wrought into that blade struck at him, even in his mist-shape, and he reformed a few feet away, black blood dripping from between his fingers. 'You... hurt me?' he said, hardly able to credit it. He had known the axe was a fell thing, but knowing and feeling were two different things. He staggered, shaking his head.

He looked around. The situation had deteriorated while he'd been distracted. The cavern was lit as brightly as a summer's afternoon by the burning remnants of his zombies and those that were left were being finished off by the ghouls and few remaining human servants of the Charnel Congress. As he watched, the last of his fledging vampires was pinned to the ground by several swords.

'Now, take him!' Russ shouted, pointing. Mannfred turned as a number of the surviving ghouls ploughed into him, knocking him down. Magic thrummed through their spindly limbs and he knew at once that a flesh-working had been cast. He roared and thrashed, trying to free himself, but too late.

Mannfred howled like a broken-backed wolf as the ghouls began to melt into one another, their whimpers of agony becoming a deeper, uglier sound. Even as he tore at the bubbling, pulsing flesh, it healed itself and he found himself trapped in the thing's gut.

It took an unsteady step, on a dozen feet, and groaned as the surviving necromancers approached. 'Thrash all you like, usurper,' Helm cackled, holding up his broken amulet. 'You might have thwarted our plan, but we are nothing if not adaptable, eh, Helga?'

The woman smiled and made a curling motion. The flesh-tomb split, disgorging Mannfred, his arms and legs bound by shifting ligaments and steely bones. 'Indeed, blood and the ring would have been the best, but a vampire's blood is even more potent!'

She spat in Mannfred's face. 'Besides, this way seems more fitting somehow... from out of his traitorous offspring's essence shall Vlad's resurrection be wrought!'

Felix had watched as Gotrek and Mannfred faced one another, marvelling that the Slayer could meet the creature's eyes. And when Mannfred turned into a mist, he hoped the creature would flee. Instead, the necromancers captured it, and Felix knew that while their earlier scheme was no more, the change of circumstances wasn't in his and Gotrek's favour.

The cavern was rapidly filling with smoke and the members of the Charnel Congress were fleeing through a side-tunnel, their hideous creation lumbering after them. Coughing, Felix started towards Gotrek.

The dwarf was kneeling, leaning on his axe and breathing heavily. Burning zombies stumbled around him, bereft of will at Mannfred's capture. Felix raced through them and grabbed Gotrek by the shoulder. 'Gotrek, get up,' he said, trying to pull the Slayer to his feet. Gotrek was bleeding from dozens of scrapes and bites that Felix hadn't noticed earlier.

'Where is the leech?' Gotrek muttered, pushing himself up. Felix prodded a burning zombie aside.

'They've taken him through one of the tunnels, and I think we should follow them. This whole cave is filling with smoke and I don't fancy suffocating,' Felix said, coughing. Gotrek shook his head as if to clear it.

'Then point me in the right direction, manling,' he growled.

They hurried through the crawling flames, Gotrek seeming to regain his strength with every step. The tunnel was lit by rusty lanterns, and it sloped upwards sharply. Rough steps, much like those they'd descended in the chapel, had been cut into the stone. Gotrek took them two at a time, and Felix followed. Blood and other, less pleasant, fluids dotted the stairs, marking the trail of the conjoined thing. At a curve in the stairs, a crossbow bolt narrowly missed Gotrek, skipping off the stones. The dwarf pushed Felix back flat against the wall as a second bolt followed the first.

'Looks like they don't want anyone following them, manling,' Gotrek said, frowning.

'Well, I don't intend to go back down there,' Felix said, gripping his sword more tightly.

Gotrek nodded sharply and then, with a roar, he pushed away from the wall and charged up the stairs. Felix hesitated a moment and then followed, cursing under his breath. More bolts skidded off the angles of the tunnel as they came and Felix saw a trio of black-clad forms waiting for them at the head of the tunnel. The Charnel Congress obviously didn't want to risk anyone following them up out of the Under Town. He ducked his head and charged on in Gotrek's wake.

A final bolt bounced off Gotrek's axe and then he and Felix were among them. Felix cut a crossbow in half and kicked its wielder down the stairs. Gotrek killed the other two with one sweep of his axe, spraying the stone with blood. 'I smell wine,' Gotrek said, stepping over the bodies.

'Well, we are in a wine cellar,' Felix said, poking his head out through the aperture the dead men had been guarding. 'They said that these tunnels go throughout the city. I guess it only makes sense that some of them would come up under houses.'

Gotrek grabbed a bottle off the rack and cut the neck off with his axe, then upended the broken bottle over his open mouth. Felix winced as the wine ran down the sides of Gotrek's mouth and dripped through his beard. 'That's a Tilean Burgundy, Gotrek, not a mug of ale,' he said.

'Tastes like something elves drink,' Gotrek burped, dropping the bottle and heading for the cellar stairs. As they climbed them, Felix could smell the river and hear the sound of alarm bells ringing.

Gotrek, not in the mood for niceties, bashed the door open and strode through into the corridor beyond. Distant screams echoed and the light of fires was reflected in the windows.

Felix went to the latter and looked out. 'We must be in High Town, Gotrek,' he said.

'I don't care where we are,' Gotrek growled. 'I want to know where those cowards are!'

'The city is burning,' Felix said, turning from the window.

'Maybe it's a welcoming party for the beast they were planning to bring back,' Gotrek said acidly. 'There. They went up those stairs. Follow close manling, I doubt I'll have time to save you if we get separated again.'

Felix said nothing. There was a time for argument and a time for simply following in the trollslayer's wake. They climbed the stairs, and Felix studied their surroundings. It was a fine house, reminiscent of his father's house in Altdorf. Fancy furnishings decorated the interior, though there was a sense of rot that pervaded everything. Whoever lived here had other considerations than the upkeep of their property. He wondered which of the necromancers owned this place.

Voices reached their ears, intoning strangely. Gotrek moved more quickly, reaching the landing. Felix caught up to him before he could bellow a challenge and signalled the Slayer to remain silent. Gotrek glared at him and Felix hastily drew his hand back.

'Quietly, Gotrek,' he hissed. 'For all they know, we're dead.'

'Not yet,' Gotrek said grimly.

'Let's do it carefully. After all, if I get killed, there'll be no one to tell the story of your battle with the last of the von Carsteins, will there?' Felix said desperately.

Gotrek's one eye blinked slowly, and he rubbed his eyepatch. 'Good point,' he said truculently. They crept along more slowly, following the rising murmur of voices. Gotrek stopped and raised a hand, and gestured towards a door.

The necromancers had placed no guards. Perhaps they

had no guards left. Or they felt that they would need none. Gotrek pressed himself flat against the door frame and Felix swung around to the other side. He peered around the frame. The room beyond was barren of everything, save several hastily-lit braziers and the bodies of two of the black-hooded guards. The conjoined ghoul-thing squatted in the centre of the room, drooling and wheezing. Mannfred, still held by the creaking lengths of muscle tissue, struggled and snarled at his captors, his eyes blazing as bright as the torches. A twitching hand was clamped tight over his mouth.

The three surviving necromancers were holding their amulets, as well as those of their fallen fellows, before Mannfred. Helm raised a goblet of what could only be blood taken from the two dead men on the floor and slowly shook something from his amulet into the goblet.

'Is that dust?' Felix mouthed, looking at Gotrek. Gotrek shook his head.

As if in answer to his question, Helm said, 'Behold, usurper, the very essence of our lord and master, gathered from across this damned world. The priests of Sigmar burnt him and scattered his ashes to far-flung chapels and holy places, but over the centuries, bit by bit, we gathered every fleck of ash or stub of charred bone. It took generations to convene it all, but it has been done and now, only the quickening of these cold ashes is left to do. They will gain form in the blood of our servants, but with yours, that form shall become what it once was!'

Mannfred's struggles redoubled, and his prison jerked back and forth. The vampire's strength was useless without leverage, however, though the ghoul-thing moaned in obvious strain and agony.

'All of our lives have been bent to this moment,' Helm

said. In his hands, the goblet was bubbling and frothing. Mannfred's thrashing grew more furious and his eyes glowed like lamps as he gnawed at his bonds and mumbled muffled imprecations.

'Quiet!' Russ snarled, and stabbed Mannfred in his exposed torso. The vampire screamed and then Gotrek dived around the door frame and charged towards the necromancers.

'Ho, hedge wizards! Leave him! He belongs to me!' Gotrek shouted. Russ spun and stabbed at the dwarf, but Felix slid smoothly between them, almost eager to lock swords with the necromancer.

'Surprised to see us?' Felix said. Russ's only reply was a growl of frustration and he swung wildly. Felix blocked the blow and jerked forwards, his brow cracking against Russ's. The ex-witch hunter reeled and Felix sliced his arm open. The man grunted and backed away. 'You killed good men, Russ,' Felix said, advancing. 'I didn't care for you before, but now I'll happily cut out your heart.'

'The feeling is mutual,' Russ said, twisting around and bringing his sword down on Felix's head. Felix stumbled aside and Karaghul sank into Russ's side. The necromancer gasped and fell against the wall, leaving a streak of blood as he sank down.

It was almost anticlimactic, considering the things Russ had done. Felix yearned to say something clever, to mark the traitor's passing, but nothing came to him. He turned to see Gotrek driving the other two necromancers back.

Behind him, Mannfred had begun to struggle, and his strength was such that the ghoul-thing staggered and whimpered. Helm gave a great cry as Gotrek's axe cut across his chest and the goblet went flying. The frothing substance within splattered across the floor. A moment later, Mannfred tore his arm free of the cage of living flesh with a snapping of ligaments and a cracking of bones. Distracted, the necromancers had allowed their spell to weaken. And now Mannfred was free. The ghoul-thing sank down onto its numerous knees in its death-throes. Mannfred ripped his way out of the sagging cage-creature as quick as a cat and tore out its throats with a laugh, letting the whole roiling mass collapse.

He landed in a crouch before Helga, and even as the terrified necromancer wove a defensive spell, Mannfred punched his claws through her chest and out her back, removing her heart in the process. The woman slid off his arm and he turned to Felix. 'Thank you for the distraction, Jaeger. There is one more service you can provide me, however, for I thirst,' he said, gliding towards Felix.

Gotrek's bellow caught their attention. The Slayer's axe sparked as it cut through one of Helm's spells and the flare of dispersed energy momentarily blinded Felix. When he could see again, Mannfred was almost upon him. 'Put the sword down,' the vampire hissed.

With those red eyes on him, it was all Felix could do to hold on to his sword. The urge to drop it grew overpowering and he grabbed Karaghul's hilt with both hands. Sweat rolled down his face and his muscles felt as if they would rip free of his bones, so hard was he shaking. Mannfred gave a little chuckle and lunged. He grabbed Felix by the neck, forcing him back against the wall. 'A strong will is like a fine spice,' the vampire said. 'It merely enhances the taste. First I will wring the juice from the meat of you, and then I will do the same to your stunted companion.'

Felix saw movement behind him. Mannfred, realising that Felix wasn't looking at him, turned slightly, fully expecting to see Gotrek. Instead, something snarled and sent both man and vampire staggering back in shock and horror.

The process of Vlad's resurrection had not been interrupted by the spilling of the blood-soaked ashes. Quite the reverse, in fact; the concoction had crept across the floor, seeking the sustenance it craved, the sustenance necessary to begin rebuilding the thing that had called itself Vlad von Carstein. But instead of healthy human blood, or even the charged brew of a vampire's fluids, it had found the corrupted juices of the dying ghoul-thing. What resulted both was and was not Vlad von Carstein.

The strange brew bubbled and stirred, the dark liquid emitting a thin shrill sound as a noxious smoke began to rise from it. In the smoke, a face formed and its mouth opened in a silent howl as it billowed and contracted according to the breeze. As it broke apart, something ugly surfaced from the spreading blood. Yellow fangs clashed in a bone jaw and it snarled again, despite lacking either lungs or flesh. More bones grew and clattered as the thing heaved itself up out of oblivion. The skull, up to this point vaguely human-shaped, began to sprout blossoms of cartilage as it shattered and spread, widening into a new shape. The other bones snapped and fibres of marrow grew between the tumbling halves, lengthening them to inhuman proportions.

The flesh of the ghoul-thing heaved itself free of the crumbling old bones and stretched over the new, thinning and then thickening. Coarse bristles burst through the gaping pores, spreading like a plague. The skull snapped and twisted as flesh flowed over it.

Finally, the heaving, hairy shape rose onto four twisted limbs and opened its fang-filled maw to give voice to something that was not quite the scream of a man, nor the shriek of a bat or even the howl of a wolf. The monster that crouched before them was a mingling of the worst aspect of all three creatures, with a size to match.

Felix's bowels turned to water as the great, foul eyes found him and a hungry grunt echoed through the room. 'What-what-what–' he stammered.

'*Varghulf*,' Mannfred hissed, flexing his claws.

'Looks like just another bloody vampire to me,' Gotrek said. He tossed the limp body of Helm at the abomination and it tore it from the air and stuffed the old man's corpse into its greedy maw. Still chewing, it looked around at Felix and Mannfred and shrieked again as the latter tried to sidle away. 'I think it recognises you, leech,' Gotrek said.

'Impossible,' Mannfred sputtered.

The varghulf stretched itself, its stubby wings raking the ceiling and splintering the wooden beams. It snarled and Felix thought there might have been words there, but he couldn't be sure. Mannfred, however, apparently was. He snarled something in a strange language and scooped up Russ's fallen sword.

The varghulf threw itself at the vampire, roaring. Gotrek, echoing it, stretched out a hand, grabbed a hank of the beast's mane and hauled himself up its broad back. The varghulf's talons tore up the floorboards in its haste to come to grips with Mannfred. Felix jumped aside as a flailing claw tore a section out of the wall. In its frenzy, the monster was destroying the scene of its rebirth.

Gotrek, straddling the monster, brought his axe down. It screeched and reared, reaching for him. As it did so, Mannfred rose and rammed his sword into its belly. It howled and plucked Gotrek from its back and slammed him down on Mannfred, sending them both sprawling. Gotrek's axe was dislodged from its back, and Felix saw with horror that the wounds the vampire and the dwarf had created were already healing.

Felix backed away, until his back thumped against the far wall and the great curtains that covered it. Turning, he stripped the curtains aside, revealing great bay windows that opened out onto a wooden balcony overlooking the section of the Stir that cut through the city. Felix saw movement reflected in the glass and ducked as the varghulf pawed at him, shattering the windows in the process. Felix scrambled out onto the balcony as the beast squeezed out after him, burning spittle drizzling from between its jutting fangs. It snapped at him and he dived between its legs, scrambling back into the room.

'Out of the way, manling,' Gotrek growled, running towards the balcony. He leapt at the creature, his axe biting into its face and skull. It tore at the dwarf, snatching him out of the air and smashing him into the floor hard enough to shatter several floorboards. It released the Slayer and stepped back, blood coating its claws.

And then Mannfred was there, his sword piercing the top of the varghulf's skull and exploding out through the bottom of its jaw. Hanging from the hilt, Mannfred looked into the beast's bulging, animalistic eyes and hissed, 'Have the good grace to die this time, Vlad!'

In reply, the varghulf slapped the vampire off its head and into the wall. Behind the beast, Felix saw a glimmer of light. With a start, he realised that the sun was rising.

The varghulf moaned, pawing at the sword in its head, trying to dislodge it. Felix looked at his own sword and knew that no matter what power it contained, it wasn't going to do the trick. He saw the shattered boards at the monster's feet shift. Gotrek's hand rose and Felix knew what he had to do.

He snatched up a brazier and stabbed the flaming end like a spear at the monster. It snarled and tried to grab the brazier from his hands. Steeling himself, he stabbed at it again, trying to get it out on the balcony. Instead, it lifted a wing and let the brazier slide past it as it lunged, jaws wide.

'Ha!' Gotrek cried, thrusting his axe up as the monster passed over him. The edge bit into its hairy throat, releasing a spray of foul blood. Gotrek, legs coiled beneath him, shoved upwards, using his body to force his axe's edge all the way through the monster's neck.

The varghulf's head came free of its neck and rolled across the floor, snapping mindlessly. Gotrek, covered in blood, hacked at the body, which had remained upright. 'Gotrek, get it outside!' Felix said, using the brazier to pin the snarling head in place. 'The sun is coming up!'

Gotrek seemed to have heard him and the dwarf redoubled his efforts, chopping at the stumbling shape and driving it backwards. It went blindly and ungracefully, its limbs moving independent of one another.

'You're a wise man, Herr Jaeger,' Mannfred said. Felix spun, raising the brazier. Mannfred seized it with one hand and shoved Felix down, distressingly close to the still-animated head of the varghulf. 'Nagash's Curse will see to that abomination readily enough,' Mannfred said, glancing at the varghulf's head. He frowned in distaste.

He rose, yanking Felix to his feet. In a quick movement, he reversed their positions and Felix found himself with the length of the brazier pressed against his windpipe. In his other hand, Mannfred grabbed the varghulf's head. He forced Felix towards the balcony. The sun was an orange stripe on the horizon, and Felix felt Mannfred shiver. The vampire's armour cut into his back and Felix tried to move as little as possible.

121

On the balcony, Gotrek was on all fours, clutching his chest near the unmoving body of the varghulf. He was breathing heavily, and Felix knew that the night's activities had taken their toll on the dwarf's superhuman vitality. Still, Gotrek had his axe to hand and when Mannfred stepped out onto the balcony, his one eye flashed.

'Well done, master dwarf,' Mannfred called out. He tossed the varghulf's head towards the dwarf, and Gotrek batted it aside. 'You two have helped me greatly, I must admit.' Mannfred's teeth clicked together distressingly close to Felix's ear. 'As a reward, I will let you lie in Morr's embrace undisturbed when I rebuild my forces.'

Gotrek shifted and let his axe fall with a thunk into the balcony. Beneath their feet, the wood gave a groan. Mannfred blinked. Gotrek gave a gap-toothed grin. 'Why are you smiling? Are you so welcoming of death?'

Gotrek uprooted his axe and let it fall again. The balcony trembled slightly. 'Not quite, leech. Not unless it's your death you're talking about.'

'Gotrek, what have you done?' Felix croaked, clawing at the brazier. Mannfred tightened his grip.

'Followed your advice, manling,' Gotrek said. 'You said get it out on the balcony. It's not my fault the balcony is typical shoddy human craftsmanship.' He chopped at the balcony again. There was a creak, and everything shifted suddenly towards the water. 'Rotten joists; it's the river water that does it. That's why dwarfs use stone instead of wood. Wood rots. Stone doesn't.'

'Stop it,' Mannfred said. His eyes blazed in their sockets and Gotrek stiffened. Felix could feel the vampire's black will beating against the iron of Gotrek's own just as it had beat against his own earlier. His head was filled with a purple agony that pulled the strength from his limbs.

'Even stones crumble before the tide, dwarf,' Mannfred said. He forced Felix forwards. 'Drop your axe,' he commanded. Mannfred's semi-human countenance faded as he stared at the dwarf. His flesh, marble-pale before, had gone practically translucent. Black veins spread across it like a spider's web of cracks, and his fangs had grown as long as Felix's finger. Madly, Mannfred champed at the air, his lips writhing against the force of unspoken curses. And still, the Slayer stood firm.

Gotrek's fist tightened convulsively around the haft of his axe. Veins bulged alarmingly along his arms and neck, and his teeth were bared in a frozen snarl. His eye started from his head. The head of the axe trembled and then fell, straight into the floor. Gotrek gave a satisfied grunt as the damaged joists squealed. Mannfred hissed in consternation. The vampire shot a glance at the door. Felix felt a chill and realised that the vampire was changing shape.

'Gotrek, he's trying to escape!' he said, jerking forwards and trying to drag Mannfred off balance. Gotrek jumped forwards and got between Mannfred and the door. The sun was no longer a strip of light, but a wide swath of brightness. Mannfred's shape steamed and he snarled, his body twisting and changing as he made for the door.

'Not this time!' Gotrek said, slicing through the vampire's foggy shape. Mannfred screamed and the mist turned crimson, and then he was solid once more and staggering back. Felix stretched out and the vampire tripped over him and slammed into the balcony's railing. The sudden shift in weight was followed by a snapping and tearing of wood. Felix lunged for the door and Gotrek moved past him, throwing himself at Mannfred even as the balcony gave way in a burst of brick, splinters and noise.

Felix felt the world fall away and pain flared in his chest as he caught the edge of the lintel and held on. Dangling half-in and half-out of the room, he pulled himself up and to safety. Then he turned and looked down.

Gotrek's axe had become embedded in one of the remaining support beams, which hung awkwardly, half-cracked in two from the force of the collapse. Gotrek held onto his axe – not even death would break that hold – but his skull was bloody and he looked badly dazed. And clinging to his leg was Mannfred. The vampire hissed up at Felix, his formerly aristocratic face now a bestial mask not that far removed from that of the varghulf. Claws dug into the Slayer's thigh, and Gotrek's blood ran down Mannfred's arms. Slowly, the vampire reached up, grabbing the dwarf's shoulder, obviously intending to climb up.

Felix stood and, before he could reconsider, climbed down towards the support beam. It shifted beneath his feet and he sank to all fours. 'Gotrek,' he said.

'Save your breath, Jaeger,' Mannfred snarled. 'You'll join him in death soon enough!' But even as the words left Mannfred's mouth, Gotrek's eye snapped open and he reached up, grabbing the vampire's throat. Mannfred's eyes widened and he scrabbled at Gotrek's arm. The Slayer grunted, obviously in pain, and swung Mannfred away from solid ground and held him out over the Stir, directly into the gaze of the sun.

Mannfred howled and his increasingly furious struggles caused the support beam to shift and creak alarmingly. Felix didn't stop, but instead crept closer to Gotrek.

Mannfred's features began to smoke and burn and his screams became high and thin. Gotrek jerked the vampire close and stared into his agonised eyes, as if wanting to commit to memory every moment of his death. But then Mannfred swiped his claws across Gotrek's face and the Slayer roared, releasing his hold on the vampire.

Mannfred von Carstein plummeted downwards, striking the surface of the Stir like a screaming black comet. But even as the water closed over the vampire's form, the support beam finally gave way. Felix lunged, grabbing Gotrek's wrist and nearly falling himself. 'Hold on!' he said.

'What in Grimnir's name do you think you're doing?' Gotrek said incredulously. 'He's getting away!'

'Drowning in the Stir isn't exactly a heroic doom, Gotrek!'

'Dwarfs don't drown!' Gotrek snapped. But he grabbed onto what was left of the support beam and began to pull himself up, grumbling the entire way. Felix didn't waste his breath arguing.

When they had gotten back to the doorway, Felix looked down at the river and said, 'Do you think he's dead? Again, I mean.'

Gotrek looked at him steadily. Then he hefted his axe and glared at the runes inscribed on the blade, as if they were responsible for yet another failure to die. 'I hope not,' he said finally.

THE RECKONING

Jordan Ellinger

There is nothing quite like watching the torch-lit streets of a city that wants you dead receding into the night. From where Felix stood on the stern of the *Dorabella*, he could just make out tiny orange dots moving up and down the docks as the city watch searched for them. Unfortunately for them, dozens of ships choked the busy harbour. There would be no telling which one they'd gotten on.

'You must have made many friends among di Peacocks for dem to still be chasing you dis late at night,' said Captain Di Venzo, a portly old Tilean who dressed as colourfully as he spoke. When Gotrek and Felix had dashed up his gangplank in the dead of night, he'd taken them on eagerly. The docks of Miragliano hadn't exactly been filled with men eager to make the dangerous voyage to Lustria, land of the man-eating lizardmen, and he was desperate for paying passengers. Though Gotrek wasn't much of a sailor, the rune axe strapped over his shoulder had convinced Di Venzo that he would be good for something. The Tilean hadn't cared much that the city watch had been in hot pursuit at the time. After all, half his crew were probably wanted men. 'Ne'er seen the Peacocks so upset,' he said, spitting on the deck for emphasis.

Felix sighed, remembering the drunken fight Gotrek had started at the Purple Sheep. 'Accusing a nobleman of cheating at dice likely nets you a night in jail. Cut off his hand for the same crime and they turn out the whole city watch.'

'Better you let dem catch you,' said Di Venzo with a smirk. 'Most men choose de gaol over de Dark Continent. De hangman's noose offers a cleaner death.' He smiled, revealing yellowed teeth. 'Now, signor, I go. I've got to whip dese bastards into shape.'

Felix nodded, but continued to stare back at the city as Di Venzo returned to the sterncastle. Only a moment ago he'd been glad to leave and now he was sorry to see it go.

Lustria.

After having failed to find his doom in the north, Gotrek had abruptly stated that if nothing in the Old World could kill him, he'd try the new one instead. Their travels together had taken them everywhere from the seediest brothels in the Border Princes to the skies high above the Chaos Wastes in an airship piloted by a mad engineer, but the thought of travelling to a continent where humans had a mere foothold, and that the rest of the land was ruled over by the ancient and mysterious Scaled Ones, scared Felix more than he liked to admit.

Of course, he'd had little choice in the matter. As Gotrek's Rememberer, he'd vowed to record the Slayer's death in an epic poem, and it would be pretty difficult to do that from across an ocean.

He turned away from the railing and found a nearby crate to sit on. The Slayer was ensconced in their cabin, trying to spend as little time on deck as possible. Dwarfs have no love for ocean travel, and Gotrek less than most. There was no glory in a death at sea. He'd most likely be passed out in a hammock, the tankard of ale he'd taken with them when they'd fled the Purple Sheep dangling from his fingers.

Felix envied the dwarf's ability to sleep wherever and whenever he chose. Instead of joining him, Felix decided to jot down a few notes on the day's events in his journal. Perhaps amputating Viscount von Korloff's arm over a set of loaded dice might merit a stanza or two in Gotrek's epic.

He'd just freed his journal from his pack when the *Dorabella* lurched abruptly and the sound of breaking lumber rent the air. He was thrown against a cabin wall, hitting hard enough that he dropped it. The precious book landed on its spine, then flopped open, the wind fluttering its pages.

Overhead, a scream ripped through the air as the sudden stop tore a sailor from the rigging and threw him into the ocean forty feet below. A lantern flew off its hook and smashed against the deck, spreading oil and fire in its wake. Overhead, lines snapped taut and the mast groaned. The sails were full, but the ship had stopped dead.

Still struggling to catch his breath, Felix snatched up the journal and quickly shoved it back into its pouch. He'd spent months writing in the gods-be-damned thing – he wasn't about to see it slip overboard.

More cries of alarm sounded, and then Di Venzo began roaring orders at the top of his lungs. The captain strode amongst the crew, cursing and clubbing them back into some semblance of discipline. He sent a few to help the poor bastard who'd gone into the sea, and then directed others to beat at the spreading flames from the overturned lamp with their surcoats.

Felix hesitated, wondering if he should join them. Fire was

every sailor's nightmare, but it was nothing these men hadn't fought before. Under Di Venzo's watchful eye, they formed a human chain with the man on the end lowering buckets into the ocean by means of a rope.

Instead, he decided to investigate why the ship wasn't moving. What had they struck? If it was a sandbar, they could hopefully put out one of the longboats and tow the schooner to freedom before the sun rose and they were discovered. If it was a rocky shoal, they might all have to swim for shore. He wanted to find out which before he woke the Slayer.

The ship lurched again. Wood cracked and the rigging above Felix danced madly in the torchlight. A stack of crates slid against each other and tumbled to the deck, forcing him to leap to the side to avoid them. He found himself pressed up against the ship's rail as the ocean surged and churned below him.

Near the bow, a dark shape the size of a whale rose out of the waves, forcibly lifting the front of the *Dorabella* out of the ocean. Stunned, Felix couldn't help but stare at it. Silhouetted figures dashed along its spine, stopping at a cylindrical protrusion near its bow. Metal shrieked as they swivelled it to face the ship. A flash and then a boom blossomed from it, revealing the low, sleek contours of a ship, but not one Felix had ever seen before. Made from huge plates of riveted copper, it looked like a kettle had been crossed with a fish. Could this be some infernal skaven device for travelling beneath the waves? Their cunning knew no bounds.

A spear point the size of Felix's head smashed into the side of the *Dorabella*. A cable attached to the spear grew taut and the Tilean schooner lurched again as it was drawn close to the submersible. They were being boarded!

Felix spun away from the railing, looking for Captain Di

Venzo. Despite the crew's best efforts, the fire had spread along the seams of tar between deck boards. Men still attempted to douse the flames with buckets of water, but the captain was nowhere in sight. Perhaps he'd heard the crash and gone to investigate? Felix caught the arm of Alessio, the orphan who served as Di Venzo's cabin boy, as he dashed by.

'Go below decks and awaken my travelling companion. Tell him we're being boarded. And be careful,' he said as the boy dashed off. 'He's probably drunk.'

Felix watched him go and then set off in search of the captain. He found him near the overturned crates at the rear of the ship.

'Herr Jaeger,' he called to Felix. 'Our cargo has shifted! If we don't get dese crates to de bow, we'll take on water.'

Di Venzo still thought they'd struck a sandbar! He'd been so concerned with keeping his ship afloat he hadn't even looked over the railing.

'You've got bigger problems, captain,' Felix shouted back. 'You're being boarded!'

Di Venzo's eyes widened. He set down the crate he was carrying and dashed around the sterncastle towards the bow, followed closely by Felix. Just as he arrived, a few strangled cries of alarm sounded from the sailors stationed there. Dark shapes moved across the deck, cutting men down where they stood.

'Forget the fire, men,' he roared thrusting his scimitar into the air. 'Repel de boarders!'

A short, but powerfully built, figure clumped out of the shadows towards Felix bellowing a war cry and hefting a huge maul. This was no skaven, as Felix had initially suspected, but a dwarf!

'Wait, I–,' he said, throwing his hand out. Before he could

utter another word, the maul crashed down at him. He barely drew Karaghul in time to parry and the force of the blow shook his arm down to the bone. He tried a quick riposte, and though the dwarf's strike had left him open, he was so heavily armoured that Felix's blow drew sparks. Ineffective though it was, it caused the dwarf to take a step back, wary of another strike.

Why were dwarfs attacking a Tilean schooner? They were far from their holds in the Worlds Edge Mountains. There must be some mistake...

The dwarf darted in again and swiped at him with the hammer, a huge sweep that would have taken Felix's head clean off his shoulders. Instead, Felix stepped inside the blow and brought the pommel of his blade down on the dwarf's helmet, denting the metal and provoking a grunt of pain. The dwarf's knees buckled and he began to drop, but just as Felix was about to turn in search of Gotrek, he drove his shoulder into Felix's chest. They slammed into the ship's mast and Felix slumped to the ground, crushed by the weight of a fully armoured dwarf. His vision momentarily dimmed and the enemy warrior raised his maul for the killing blow. There would be no parrying this time. Karaghul had slipped from Felix's grip and lay on the deck a few feet away. It was unarmed.

'Wait!' he yelled, throwing his hands in front of his face in a plea for mercy. 'I'm a dwarf friend,' he shouted.

The figure grunted hollowly. 'You're no friend of mine,' he said, hefting his maul. Felix quickly scanned the deck, looking for something that could help, a rope, a weapon, but his eyes alighted on his backpack. Unattended, the fire had spread across the deck towards the mast, and now licked at the leather. His journal!

Out of sheer desperation, he pushed off from the mast and launched himself at the dwarf. He caught the haft of the maul on his shoulder and felt it go numb, but he was still alive. Momentum carried him into his opponent. It was like hitting a wall of steel. Dwarfs were shorter than humans, but far stockier and this one was solid muscle. Grabbing the haft of the maul, Felix kicked out and landed a blow squarely on the dwarf's breastplate. He stumbled backwards, tripped over a coil of rope and crashed to the deck.

The maul was far too heavy for Felix to use effectively, so he cast it to the side, where it thumped onto the deck. He looked around. Men screamed in pain as a dozen enemy warriors moved through them, their heavy armour easily turning aside the sailors' cutlasses. The smell of burning tar and wood smoke hung thick in the air, making Felix's lungs burn and his skin smart.

He cast about desperately for Karaghul and spotted it lying on the deck near the railing. He hesitated. Should he go for the weapon or the book? He had a split second to make the decision and in the end he couldn't let his journal burn. The Siege of Praag was contained in that book. It could not go up in flames! Forgetting about his sword, he dashed towards the fire and snatched up the backpack, beating at the flames with his red Sudenland cloak.

The pack was ruined of course, and his quill singed beyond recognition, but the jar of ink, although hot to the touch, was whole and his journal safe within its oiled leather carrying case. He tucked them into a pouch on his cloak, and then cast about for his sword. It was nowhere to be seen. Had it slid off the deck into the ocean? The thought of losing Karaghul made his heart twinge. The blade had been at his side through so many adventures it felt like a part of him.

Losing it would be like having an arm chopped off. Worse, he thought. He had two arms, but there was only one Karaghul.

He felt, more than heard, displaced air against his cheek and dodged backwards just in time to avoid a hammer blow. The armoured dwarf he'd knocked down before stepped out of the flames.

'You just don't quit, do you?' asked Felix in frustration.

The warrior shrugged. 'I'm a dwarf,' he said, by way of explanation.

Alone and still unarmed, Felix cursed his luck. Why hadn't he gone for his sword? He looked around for help, but the battle had moved away from them and if there were any sailors still alive, he couldn't see them. He didn't stand a chance.

Just as the dwarf stepped in for the killing blow, a snarling figure emerged from the flames and hurled itself at Felix's opponent. Bare-chested and tattooed, Gotrek Gurnisson batted aside the maul with his rune axe and lashed out with a ham-hock fist. It impacted the dwarf's armoured jaw with a metallic clang that sent him crashing to the deck. Gotrek didn't even bother shaking his hand after the blow.

'Barely out of port and you decide to burn down the ship around my ears?'

'Good to see you too, Gotrek,' said Felix. The pig grease that the Slayer used to shape his hair into a crest had partially melted and smeared his skull and forehead. His skin was an angry red from the heat, almost as red as his fiery beard. He clutched his rune axe tightly in one hand. In the other… a sword?

Gotrek grunted and then held out the weapon, pommel first. It was Karaghul. 'You wouldn't be much good to me without a sword.'

Felix's heart sang as he took the blade, feeling again its

perfect balance and heft. He'd genuinely thought he'd lost it. 'Gotrek...' he said.

'Save it,' responded the dwarf gruffly. He looked down at the fallen warrior. 'Now let's see what kind of dwarf attacks an unarmed man.'

He knelt in front of the armoured warrior and ripped off his helmet with one hand, revealing a heavy set dwarf with features that looked like they'd been chiselled from stone. Dark eyes and a large, craggy nose framed a black beard bound into a warrior's braids with thick golden clips. 'Vabur Nerinson,' said Gotrek with a curse.

'You know him?' asked Felix, stunned.

'Of course I know him,' spat Gotrek. 'He's a Reckoner out of Barak Varr. If Vabur's here then that means... Norri Wolfhame! Come out and face me, you coward!'

Dark shapes stepped through the flames. Their leader wore mail and an open-faced horned helmet that flaunted a thick, white beard. He was flanked by two soldiers of identical height and build, each levelling black powder rifles. Their armour, too, was identical, except that one helmet was moulded in the shape of a lion and the other an eagle.

'Gotrek Gurnisson,' called the dwarf with the white beard – Wolfhame, Felix guessed. 'You're under arrest in the name of King Byrrnoth Grundadrakk.'

Just as he finished speaking, a burning spar above them cracked and popped, littering the group with ash and charred rigging. The Reckoner paid no attention to it. Single-minded to the point of razor-like focus, he seemed to be unaware that they were standing in the middle of an inferno.

'What's the charge?' asked Felix.

Wolfhame's gaze found his and Felix was suddenly

embarrassed to have spoken. He felt like a child who had broken the silence in one of Sigmar's temples.

'Treason,' Wolfhame answered, eyes glittering in the firelight.

Treason? The pair were guilty of a lot of crimes, but as far as Felix could remember they'd never committed treason against the King of Barak Varr. Could Wolfhame be pursuing them because of some crime Gotrek committed before he'd come upon Felix in the Window Tax Riots? But that was twenty years ago! Just how long had these dwarfs been pursuing the Slayer?

'Your king was the one who committed treason, Norri, and you know it,' growled Gotrek.

Wolfhame continued on as if Gotrek hadn't spoken. 'And – as if that wasn't enough – common thievery.'

Felix felt his jaw clench. Gotrek hunched his shoulders and took a step towards Wolfhame, prompting the twin warriors to tighten their grips on their rifles. After a visible struggle, Gotrek regained control of his temper. Felix had seen him deflect arrows before with his rune axe, but charging two dwarf warriors with rifles levelled was madness, even for him. It was the goal of every Slayer to die gloriously, not anonymously at the hands a couple of Reckoners with rifles.

'Explain yourself, Norri Wolfhame,' growled Gotrek. 'I've been called traitor before, but never a thief.'

Before the Reckoner could elaborate, a low, thumping groan came from the bow and the crack of split wood rent the air once more. Though the sturdy dwarfs were unmoved, Felix stumbled and nearly fell as the ship's deck lurched. As he regained his footing, he spotted two longboats already in the water, rowing frantically for shore. The crew had abandoned ship – and for good reason. He could see the sea pouring over the *Dorabella*'s stern as she finally began to sink.

'Can we hurry this up a little?' he asked nervously. Ocean water swept up the deck towards them, and Felix noticed with some distress that the stern of the ship was almost completely submerged. When would these blasted dwarfs get to the point? 'Do you plan to take us prisoner or carry out the sentence right here on the deck? Because if it's the latter, the sea will soon beat you to it.'

'I am not permitted to discuss the details of your crimes in front of an *umgi*,' said Norri Wolfhame to Gotrek, eying Felix suspiciously.

'The manling is my Rememberer and a dwarf friend. Anything you need to say to me can be said in front of him,' replied Gotrek.

'How do *you* merit a Rememberer?' asked one of the twin warriors in surprise. He was quickly silenced by a stern look from Wolfhame. Annoyed, the Reckoner turned back to Gotrek.

'You're already aware of why you're wanted for treason,' he said, his face stony and unreadable. 'As for the theft? The vault of Musin Balderk has been breached.'

'You lie,' sneered Gotrek with such ferociousness that the twins cocked their rifles. 'I built that vault myself. It would take a dozen dwarfs with a barrel of black powder the size of this ship more than a week to get in. If you've let that happen, then there's no help I can offer you.'

For the first time since they'd met, Norri Wolfhame lost his composure. His cheeks reddened and his beard twitched. 'Are you accusing me of incompetence?'

'Come, manling,' said Gotrek, lowering his axe and stomping towards the three Reckoners.

Felix took a few hesitant steps after Gotrek, still unsure

what had happened. One minute it looked like the Slayer was determined to go down with the ship and the next he was, well, if not surrendering, then at least agreeing to terms. 'Where are we going?'

Gotrek's single eye glittered. 'To Barak Varr. I want to see for myself how these fools let someone into my vault.'

Despite the immense amount of dwarf technology that went into the construction of a vehicle that could travel for days beneath the waves, Felix couldn't help but think they were travelling inside a floating dungeon.

Since space inside what Gotrek called a Nautilus was at a premium, everything was sized for a dwarf and Felix was forced to crouch in the narrow passageways. His back hurt the instant he set foot inside the vessel, and hurt more when he considered that it might take weeks of travel to reach the Barak.

They were led along a narrow passageway down what Felix assumed was the 'throat' of the giant copper fish. They passed rooms filled with narrow bunks and then a small infirmary where a few dwarfs were being treated for minor burns sustained in the inferno above. The entire vessel smelled like lamp oil, only heavier and more pungent. Once, Felix put his hand down on what he thought was a guardrail only to have it come away covered in grease.

They turned onto a metal gangplank made from wire mesh that allowed Felix to see into the inner workings of the vessel. It was like staring into a clock. A tangle of gears and pipes turned an enormous shaft that disappeared towards the stern of the ship. The air here smelled of oil and what the dwarfs called 'blackwater'. It was a pleasant smell, but one that Felix knew better than to inhale too deeply.

Wolfhame led them down the gangplank to a small, windowless cell in the back of the submersible. It had probably once held provisions, judging from the stink of rotten potatoes that hung in the air. A few smokeless lamps gave the room a yellowish pall, and strange copper pipes that were hot to the touch skirted the ceiling. At first these made the cramped cell unbearably hot, but as the Nautilus descended into the depths the walls grew cold and Felix began to think the ship's designers had placed them there deliberately to keep the room's occupants warm.

The Slayer had told Norri that he was coming to Barak Varr as an engineer, not a Slayer, but Felix couldn't help thinking that the vault of Musin Balderk was but the smallest part of it. His mind kept going back to the charge of treason. Dwarfs were a stubborn bunch and valued loyalty above all else. Felix had studied at the university at Altdorf and he could count the number of dwarfs accused of treason on one hand and not need the thumb. Yet, despite the seriousness of the charge, Gotrek had said nothing in all the years they'd travelled together. Felix could not keep his gaze away from the Slayer's fiery red crest and body tattoos. Could Wolfhame have been hunting Gotrek for the very crime that had caused him to take the Slayer's Oath?

Despite Felix's attempts to engage the Slayer in conversation, he would not speak of it. After a few days, he would not speak at all, merely staring darkly at a spot on the opposite wall.

With a sigh, Felix opened his journal, bit an edge into his singed quill and put ink to page. He had found precious little writing time on the road, and had not yet written of the death of Arek Daemonclaw and the events that had followed.

The days passed quickly, and he lost track of how long

they were at sea. Guards came by twice a day to empty their chamber pot and feed them a thin, but nourishing, gruel. Though Felix had no way of telling time from the confines of his cell, mealtimes were so regular he could predict them by the grumbling of his stomach.

By the time he noticed a change in the constant hum that Gotrek had explained came from the ship's engines, he'd filled forty pages. Soon afterwards, the ship lurched and a dull, metallic thump echoed through the ship's hull. The hatch's handle spun and it hissed open. Norri Wolfhame stepped over the threshold, still in full armour. Felix suspected he slept in it.

'Finally muster enough courage to face me without your two henchmen, Wolfhame?' sneered Gotrek. The pair were technically prisoners, but no one had been brave enough to relieve Gotrek of his rune axe. Wolfhame eyed it warily and fingered his hammer, but did not draw it.

'We've docked under the palace. From here we will be proceeding directly to the king's private chambers via a secret route. Though it is supposed to be reserved for the king's private use, some members of the palace staff have been known to use it on occasion and if we should encounter them, you will remain silent. Should you utter the slightest sound, my men will kill you where you stand.'

Felix rose slowly, feeling every ache and pain of the long voyage in a cramped space. He was disappointed to hear they'd already docked. Last time they'd been in Barak Varr, they'd been aboard a Bretonnian merchantman, and seen first-hand the huge sea cave in which it was situated. He'd been looking forward to seeing such a sight again. Lanterns the size of a carriage strung to the ceiling with huge chains had set fire to the perfectly still ocean and highlighted the busy harbour beyond.

It was only when he stood on the deck of the Nautilus that he realised the true magnitude of what Wolfhame had said. Unlike the harbour of Barak Varr, this was nothing more than an enclosed gorge that had been enlarged just barely enough to accommodate the Nautilus. Wolfhame's pilot must have had incredible mastery of his vessel in order to pilot it between the narrow walls. No crates or supplies lined the docks, making it obvious to Felix that the harbour only served one purpose – to bring people to and from the palace in secret. Dwarfs were such a pragmatic breed that, even though Wolfhame had just told them the dock was reserved for kingly use, it was undecorated. He glanced at Gotrek as the Slayer followed the Reckoners up a rough-cut stairway and through the secret passage. Why the need for this level of secrecy?

He wished he could ask Gotrek if he knew what was going on, but Vabur Nerinson, the black-bearded dwarf the Slayer had felled with a single punch, marched only a few feet away. His giant maul was slung over one shoulder and he carried his dented helmet under one arm. Every time he caught Felix's eye he smiled evilly and petted his weapon. Better to remain silent than to give that one an excuse to soothe his wounded pride on Felix's skull.

The walls of the passage were unmarked and the ascent so steep that Felix had to concentrate on keeping up to the hardy dwarfs. Soon he was sweating and breathing heavily. He longed to spot some kind of sign that would mark their progress, a floor number, or at the very least, another exit, but the walls were plainly cut stone and there were no doors in sight. Finally, they emerged into a wide hallway. In contrast to the corridor they'd just left, the construction here was superb. Intricate carvings graced the walls and several stone busts of past kings sat on a series of pedestals that ran the length of the hallway. Wolfhame led them deliberately to the huge oaken doors that marked the entrance to King Grundadrakk's chambers.

A half-dozen of his closest advisors were gathered around a large oaken table, upon which rested a map of the lower tunnels as large as a bed sheet. Thumb-sized stone figures dotted the map, some carved to look like Ironbreakers, while others, more crudely carved, looked like ratmen.

Felix could identify Grundadrakk immediately, despite never having met him. Completely bald with a flowing white beard that stretched nearly to his belt buckle, he towered over his advisors. Even bent over the tunnel map as he was, Felix could tell he was as large, or larger, than Gotrek – perhaps even as wide as Snorri Nosebiter. He was a giant among dwarfs.

'Your majesty,' said Wolfhame as they entered. 'I've brought you Gotrek Gurnisson, the Trollslayer.'

The king carefully picked up a stone figure, and then circled the map and placed it at a different spot. He surveyed it, checked its relationship to the other carvings, its distance, its height, and only then looked up with a frown. 'He's still got his axe.'

'Let the dwarf who wants to take it from me step forward,' said Gotrek, grinning evilly and running a thumb up its blade until he drew blood.

'I should have you executed,' said the king nonchalantly. Having placed the ratman where he wanted it, he rose and turned towards them, judging them with a glance. 'This Grim Brotherhood nonsense,' he said, waving his finger at Gotrek's tattoos and crest, 'has never impressed me. There are those – even amongst my advisors – who believe that the

Oath absolves one of all their crimes. This is false. It is just that Slayers usually have the good grace to die before their sentence can be carried out.'

'Are you saying I've been avoiding my doom?' Gotrek asked, his voice low and dangerous. Felix could sense the air in the room grow cold. Grundadrakk's advisors drew away from the king unconsciously, clearing the space between them.

Only one venerable dwarf remained at the king's side. He was stocky, sporting a belly that overhung his belt. He wore jewellery in the manner of the richest merchant-princes, one who fought wars in the marketplace rather than on the battlefield. Each finger glimmered with a jewelled ring, and he wore a thin silver band across his forehead. His forked beard was immaculately oiled and his skin free from blemishes. Though Felix admired his courage, Gotrek would cut right through him on the way to the king, unless Felix did something to defuse the situation.

'Why have you, um, summoned us, your majesty?' he asked quickly, and then gulped when all eyes turned towards him. Far from defusing the situation, he'd turned their anger on himself instead.

'Drumnok,' said the king to the oiled merchant-prince. 'Who is this umgi?'

'Unless I miss my guess, he is Felix Jaeger, your majesty,' said the merchant prince, 'Dwarf friend, and Rememberer to Gotrek Gurnisson.'

Felix was surprised that Drumnok had identified him so easily. Had news of their deeds spread so far? 'You have impressive sources, my lord.'

Drumnok shook his head. 'Just Drumnok. I'm no thane – merely an ale merchant who's done well for himself. But to answer your question, we've been pursuing Gotrek Gurnisson for more years than you've been alive. It was only prudent that we compile a list of known associates.'

Felix flushed. Of course. It would take years for news of their part in the Siege of Praag to filter down from the north, if it ever did. In most parts of the Empire, they were far from heroes. In fact, they were still wanted criminals. It was a blow to his ego to be known merely as Gotrek's accomplice, but he supposed it fit.

'Where is the book, Trollslayer?' asked the king, his attention shifting back to Gotrek like a lion picking which sheep to devour. He picked up another figurine, a crudely carved skaven, and traced its contours with his thumb.

'Book?' asked Gotrek. 'You brought me back because of a book?'

'Don't play with me, Trollslayer,' said the king. 'I've not forgotten what you did.'

Slayer and king glared at each other with hatred pure and cold. Felix felt certain that Gotrek had at last met his match – at least in stubbornness.

'The Book of Grudges.' Drumnok stepped forward, knowing, like any good merchant, when to break an impasse. 'It went missing from the vault of Musin Balderk under the very noses of my personal guard.'

'What problem is that of mine?' asked Gotrek sullenly.

'No problem at all,' said Drumnok, steepling his fingers. 'Except that the vault was untouched. Not a mark on it. My finest engineers went over it inch-by-inch and could not determine how the theft was committed. Only one dwarf could open that vault and not leave a trace–the engineer who designed it.'

Felix felt his stomach sink. All the secrecy that had shrouded their visit suddenly made sense. The Book of Grudges was one of the most sacred artefacts in a dwarf hold. In it was written every wrong that had been committed against a particular clan for thousands of years. Each new grudge was written into the book in the king's own blood, and it was considered a mark of personal triumph for a monarch to extract justice for a past grievance and cross a grudge off the list.

Without the book, the king could not show his face in public. There was no telling how the hold would react should they learn of its disappearance. Wolfhame's threat to kill them, should they utter a word to a member of the palace staff, had obviously not been idle. Grundadrakk would do anything to keep knowledge of the theft from leaking out. The only reason they were still alive was that he believed they had something to do with it.

'I've been penned in these quarters for a solid month, Trollslayer,' said the king, banging his fist on the table so hard the stone figures jumped. 'My subjects are beginning to forget what I look like. I don't care if you stole the book or your faulty design allowed it to be stolen. You owe me a book and I want it back.'

Instead of getting angry, Gotrek lapsed into silence. It was one thing to question his ability as a Slayer, but it was quite another to question his skill as an engineer. He took the former personally. He took the latter as a challenge. He was, in all likelihood, mentally reviewing plans he'd memorised decades ago, looking for any flaw.

'Did no one else have access to the vault?' asked Felix.

'No one,' said Drumnok firmly.

'No,' said Gotrek. 'There was another. My former apprentice. Malbak Drumnokson.'

'How convenient,' sneered the king. 'Malbak is the one who accused you of the theft.'

'Convenient for whom, your majesty?' Felix asked pointedly. 'Two dwarfs had access to the vault and one of them was a thousand leagues away when the crime was said to have taken place.'

Grundadrakk's eyes narrowed and he turned to Drumnok. 'Your son says he had evidence that the Trollslayer was the culprit?'

'He swears it, your majesty,' replied Drumnok firmly.

Grundadrakk considered this for a while, and then finally set the skaven carving back on the tunnel map. 'You know I've always been grateful to you for your counsel, my friend,' he said to Drumnok, 'but the umgi raises a valid point. It is difficult for even the best of thieves to commit a crime from a thousand leagues away.'

Drumnok reddened and his belly shook indignantly. 'Your majesty, I–'

'Clear every corridor from here to the vault,' said King Grundadrakk to Wolfhame who nodded smartly. 'And have Malbak Drumnokson meet us there. It is time for us to get to the bottom of this.'

They took the same hidden passage they'd used to come from the harbour. The king was large enough that his bulk nearly filled the corridor and he cursed fate richly for necessitating that he use the infernal passageway. When they'd travelled roughly halfway back to the docks, Norri Wolfhame stopped in what appeared to be the middle of an empty hallway and opened a hitherto unseen door that led down another series of corridors to the vault area. Felix wondered just how extensive this network of secret passageways was. It appeared to him that Barak Varr was riddled with them.

Malbak Drumnokson met them in front of a massive stone

door. Short, even for a dwarf, he looked nothing like his father, except for the rapidly developing paunch he tried to keep hidden behind a leather girdle. His beard was as red as the wispy hair that grew out of his ears and not on his head. He wore a thick gold chain around his neck and sparkling earrings pierced his ear. Gotrek grunted and told Felix that no member of Malbak's line could bear to be parted from the precious metal for even a day, which explained Drumnok's occupation as a merchant, and his son's as a vault engineer. Malbak was breathing heavily, as if he'd had to jog to meet them at the vault.

'Your majesty, I–' he said, beginning a bow that was arrested when he spotted Gotrek. 'You!' he said, his voice loaded with hatred. 'You should be dead.'

Gotrek grinned a toothy smile that showed the yellow stumps he called teeth. 'Gods willing.'

'Malbak!' barked Drumnok sternly. 'You forget yourself in front of the king.'

Malbak looked chastised, turning and completing the bow he'd started before he'd spotted the Slayer. 'Your majesty. It is always an honour to have you grace the vaults.'

'And it's always a pain in the neck to come down here,' grunted the king. Despite his size and relative health, Felix could tell that Byrrnoth was feeling his age. 'To think that before the skaven attacked, we used to store most of this stuff several levels down.'

'The skaven, your majesty?' asked Felix, trying to hide his disgust. The world's most prolific thieves arrive and everyone was surprised when there was a theft? There must be more to it.

'I know what you're thinking, Herr Jaeger,' said Drumnok reprovingly. 'The skaven may have attacked the lower levels, but they have come nowhere near here. In fact, much of the treasure in the lower vaults was brought here specifically because this vault was deemed impregnable. After all, it was built by one of the Barak's most capable engineers–and Gotrek Gurnisson.'

Malbak and his father exchanged satisfied looks, but if Gotrek caught the slight, he ignored it. He tapped a finger to his lips as he studied the vault door.

'Open it,' he said softly.

Grundadrakk ignored the lack of a title and simply nodded at Malbak. The younger engineer removed a golden chain from around his neck, from which dangled a large key. He moved towards the door and began to hum a deep and complex melody as he traced his finger across a string of runes. One by one the runes lit up, until their flickering blue light illuminated a keyhole. Malbak inserted his key into the lock, turned it, and then stepped back. Somewhere inside the smooth stonework, huge gears ground together and huge weights *thunked* into place as the door slid open.

Felix was amazed by the thickness of the stone. Made from solid bedrock, it must have weighed hundreds of tons and yet it was so perfectly balanced a child could have pushed it shut.

Though the inside of the vault was no large than the room in which they'd stayed at the Purple Sheep, there was more wealth inside than Felix had ever seen before. Gold ingots piled as high as a dwarf could stand, jewels the size of a clenched fist set in sterling silver necklaces, a rack of unfathomably ancient scrolls… and the empty lectern where he guessed the Book of Grudges had once rested. Felix had never felt much desire for wealth, but looking upon the contents of that vault he felt a stirring in his chest that the dwarfs might call gold lust. Karl Franz himself would weep over the treasure laid before them, and Felix guessed there were many more vaults just like it hidden in the underground expanses of Barak Varr.

Gotrek surveyed the treasure critically, as if he was mentally weighing the contents of the vault. At last, he stirred. 'I need four dwarfs to help me empty it.'

'Empty it?!' King Grundadrakk nearly popped a vein. 'It took weeks just to move it up here.'

Drumnok hurried forward, gently placing a hand on Gotrek's shoulder, then yanking it back when Gotrek glared at him. 'The vault of Musin Balderk shelters some of the Barak's most precious artefacts – not to mention a few state secrets. We can't simply store it in this antechamber.'

'Fine,' said Gotrek, crossing his arms and leaning casually against the door. 'Find the book yourselves then.'

'Wolfhame,' said the king between clenched teeth. 'Order your men to help the Slayer empty the vault.'

Six hours later, the vault was empty and the antechamber littered with untold wealth. The dwarfs stood in the hall stretching weary limbs, watching each other suspiciously to see who among them would show the first signs of fatigue, all the while trying to conceal their own tiredness.

The heaviest object by far was a large golden statue of Grimnir that Drumnok claimed was life-sized, even though it was twice as large as Gotrek himself. Much more crudely carved than the other treasures, Felix supposed the dwarfs valued it more for its sheer weight than its craftsmanship.

Though Gotrek had done the majority of the heavy lifting, he strode straight into a corner of the vault and kicked at a pile of refuse – gnawed wood, chewed bones, and droppings.

'Skaven spoor,' said Gotrek.

'Impossible,' said Drumnok, with a glance at the king. 'It must be something else.'

'Step into the vault and I'll make sure you get a closer look,' growled Gotrek with an evil grin.

'You said that some of these treasures used to reside in the lower vaults? The ones that had been attacked by the skaven?' asked Felix.

'Yes,' Drumnok answered reluctantly, 'but they were untouched when we beat back the ratmen. They could not have laid a paw on so much as a single gold piece. Even so, when we transferred their contents here for safekeeping, we had each item inspected by a runesmith. There was no trace of skaven sorcery on any of them.'

He stepped back from the vault. 'Even if they were somehow able to bypass the vault's defences with a spell, why would they take the book? We know the skaven have no love for gold, but this vault contains quite a few magical trinkets. Why would they settle for cheap parchment when they could have taken those? And how would they escape with their stolen goods? Any skaven wandering these halls would be cut down by a hundred angry dwarfs.'

'Seafaring dwarfs,' said Gotrek, spitting on the floor. To a Karak-born dwarf, ocean travel was anathema and seafaring dwarfs the victims of some collective madness. The occupants of Barak Varr, wealthy though they were, were met with scorn in some quarters.

'Tread carefully, Slayer,' growled Wolfhame, glaring at the Slayer.

Gotrek's face twisted into a snarl. 'One more word from you, Norri Wolfhame, and you'll be picking my axe out of your teeth,' he said, his finger stabbing into Wolfhame's chest. He rounded on King Grundadrakk. 'The ratmen may have your book, but they didn't get past my door. My vault did what it was supposed to do.'

The king regarded the Slayer with outright hatred. Then his eyes narrowed craftily. 'You're forgetting something, aren't you Gotrek? We have evidence of your involvement in the theft.' He beckoned Drumnok's son forward. 'Malbak?'

'Your majesty?' Malbak had been enjoying the conflict from the rear, not having offered to help the Reckoners clear the vault.

'You said you had evidence that Gotrek was involved?' said the king triumphantly. 'Show it to him.'

'Your majesty, my word as an engineer...'

'The evidence, Malbak!' Grundadrakk's triumphant tone gained a frustrated edge.

'Very well.' Malbak drew an iron chisel from a pouch and handed it to Wolfhame, who handed it to the king. 'Gotrek left this behind after he... fled.' He beckoned them over to a patch of bare stone on a corner of the vault's door. 'There,' he said, accusingly. 'I believe you'll find those marks match Gotrek's chisel exactly.'

To Felix, the stone looked like any other stone. No chisel marks were apparent. Not for the first time was he envious of the dwarfs' keen eyesight.

The king and his advisors approached the stone and studied the markings. After a moment, when the king rose, a pulsing purple vein was apparent on his forehead. 'Do you take me for a fool, Malbak?'

Malbak paled. 'Your majesty?'

'Even the umgi can see that these marks are from the vault's construction,' said the king with a dismissive wave at Felix, who could only shrug sheepishly at the others. 'And in any case, if you've been in possession of Gotrek's chisel all the while, how do you think he used it to gain entry to the vault?'

'He...' Malbak glanced nervously from the king to Drumnok and back again. 'He must have stolen it... there's no one else who could have gotten past the vault's defences!'

Grundadrakk shook his head and muttered a curse under his breath. When he turned back to Gotrek, his demeanour had completely changed. 'You may not be guilty after all, Trollslayer, but that does not change the fact that the skaven have my book.'

'So send your armies after them and leave me to find my doom!' said Gotrek petulantly.

Grundadrakk shook his head, then met the eyes of all who were present. 'Our armies have tried to dislodge the skaven and failed. They are too numerous. But a smaller expedition, consisting of no more than a dozen dwarfs, might escape their notice. Norri Wolfhame will head just such an expedition, consisting of all who know of its loss – with the exception of my faithful advisor, Drumnok.'

'Your majesty,' said Norri Wolfhame, struggling to conceal his shocked expression. 'Assuming the Slayer is right and the skaven have stolen the book, how are we to find it? We have no idea which skaven have it, or where they could have gone.'

Drumnok coughed and stepped forward. 'Our scouts know in which direction the skaven forces retreated. Surely, they will have taken such a prized artefact to the very centre of their armies. Go where the skaven forces are most numerous and you'll find the book.'

Felix's heart sank as the collected dwarfs erupted in a cacophony of objections. The skaven were present in large enough numbers to sack the lower vaults, and yet a small group of dwarfs was supposed to succeed where the army had failed? The king was sending them on a suicide mission.

At least Felix got some small satisfaction from watching the smug grin fade from Malbak's face as he realised that Grundadrakk had 'volunteered' him along with the others.

'You cannot expect...' he sputtered to the king.

'*Silence!*' roared Grundadrakk. He waited for the last objection to die in a mutter, then continued. 'If you succeed, then the book will be returned with none the wiser. If you fail, then you'll take the secret of its loss with you to your graves.'

'I'm not doing your dirty work, Byrrnoth,' said Gotrek. To emphasise his point, he crossed his arms and leaned against the corner of the vault.

'You'll go,' said Grundadrakk grimly. 'Your name was the last inscribed in the book. Bring it back and I'll make sure it's crossed off. Stay here and I'll make sure your doom isn't fit to be sung about in the seediest tavern this side of Karak Eight Peaks.'

Gotrek darkened like a storm. Tell him to do a thing and he was more than likely to do the opposite just to spite you. Felix was genuinely worried that he'd draw his rune axe and hack his way to the sea gates. If there was one thing about Gotrek, it was that he could not be bullied. Once again, it was up to Felix to defuse the situation.

'Thank you, your majesty,' he said thinking fast.

Slayer and king both blinked, and then turned and stared at him.

'What are you playing at, manling?' asked Gotrek suspiciously.

'Indeed?' said the king, arching an eyebrow.

'I am merely thanking your majesty for granting Gotrek the chance at a doom worthy of an epic,' he explained. 'A suicide mission to retrieve a valuable artefact from the clutches of an untold number of skaven warriors? That's the kind of doom Trollslayers salivate over.'

Thankfully, he was able to keep the quaver out of his voice. A suicide mission was all well and good for a Slayer... but it was far less appealing to his Rememberer.

Gotrek paused as he considered this. Then his face cracked into a toothy smile and he clapped Felix on the back. 'I like the way you think, manling!'

'Yes,' said Grundadrakk as Felix did his best to maintain his smile. 'I have a feeling the umgi is smarter than he looks.'

The need for secrecy coloured every aspect of their preparations. Supplies could only be procured through Drumnok, and he was so stingy that he treated every request as if Felix had asked for his first-born. While they waited for rations and packs, and all the other supplies one needed for a journey into hostile territory deep underground, they were confined to their quarters. Gotrek threatened to break down the door until King Grundadrakk sent him a cask of Bugman's to shut him up. Of course, that meant he was hung over the morning the expedition departed. Even so, the prospect of a grand doom gave him new energy and he quickly took the lead.

Norri Wolfhame quickly joined the Slayer at the head of the column – his Reckoner's instinct no doubt compelling him to stay close to the dwarf he'd tracked across half a continent. Gromnir and Gromnar walked just behind the Slayer as if he were their prisoner. If Gotrek noticed them at all, he didn't show it.

Malbak, furious that he'd been embarrassed in front of the king, skulked just behind the Reckoners, cursing under his breath and bemoaning his fate, while Vabur Nerinson walked nearby, still carrying his dented helmet like a mark of shame.

The king had specified that the expedition consist of all

those who knew of the book's disappearance, but Drumnok, ever the merchant, decided that that didn't mean others couldn't tag along. Wanting to afford his son the best possible chance of survival, he'd used his considerable influence and deep pockets to buy the services of Ulgar Masonsheart, a skilled runesmith, and his apprentice, Glorin. Ulgar wore a bearskin cloak and a long iron-shod staff covered in runes. His apprentice's staff was newer, but carried its own set of runes.

Labouring along at the back of the column was Tebur Tanilson, a Thunderer who had lost half his hearing in an explosion years earlier. He was by far the oddest member of the expedition. His beard was patchy with old burn scars. He stank of saltpetre and brimstone, and his fingernails were pitted and blackened by blackpowder. Though he carried a rifle, it was his pack that had gotten him banished to the rear of the column. It was as black as his fingernails and bulged in odd places. From the way the other dwarfs winced whenever he set it down for a rest, Felix guessed that he carried some kind of bomb. On those few occasions when they got an opportunity to speak, he referred to Felix as 'Herr Jogger'.

The final member of their expedition was Martinuk Ironshield, a gruff dwarf with a scarred face and ruddy red hair who wielded an axe and shield with quiet confidence. He wore a set of goggles around his neck as well as an odd mask made from a dark, rubbery material. It reminded Felix of the cone-shaped masks worn by doktors in Altdorf.

Martinuk smiled grimly when Felix asked about it. 'I saw a ratman wear something like this the day my clan was ambushed in the Lower Reaches. Many of our warriors died tearing at their throats and clawing at their eyes that day, victims to clouds of poison gas emitted from hollowed-out egg shells the skaven threw at us. I tore off one of their masks and wore it during the battle. Doing so saved my life. Later I took their design, improved upon it, and crafted this.'

Vabur Nerinson, walking nearby, barked with laughter. 'You put your face in there? Might as well kiss a skaven on the lips. You'll be dressing like them next, won't you?'

Martinuk shrugged, untroubled by the larger dwarf's jibe. 'Lungs as big as yours can hold a lot of gas, Nerinson. When the time comes, you'll beg me to let you wear it.'

'Not likely,' said Vabur. He swung his maul in a casual arc and shattered a lump of stone the size of his head that occupied the path in front of him. 'They'd have to get past my hammer first.'

'So you say,' said Martinuk, nodding his head.

Despite spending half his life in the company of a dwarf, Felix had never quite become used to travel underground. Though dwarf-built tunnels were wide and well-constructed, often they weren't especially tall, forcing him to duck his head in places. Without the sun, it was impossible to tell time and he felt like they could have been trudging for hours or even days. The dwarfs seemed to possess a sixth sense that told them when to stop for lunch and when to break camp, for which he was thankful. Night fell whenever they hooded their lanterns, which, in turn, plunged them into pitch blackness.

Though the areas close to Barak Varr were safe and well-maintained, as they proceeded further into the depths, signs of prosperity began to dwindle. The dwarfs here were sallow-cheeked with shorter, scraggly beards, and wore clothing badly in need of repair. Some were prospectors, combing over already heavily-mined veins of minerals in the hopes of finding a few nuggets the original owners had missed, while others were hermits who cared little for social comforts and had chosen a life away from the hold. Still others were simply mad.

They encountered their first threat in an ancient tunnel that ran close to a massive underground wall that kept the sea outside at bay. The rocks were slick with moisture and a small stream carved its way down the centre of the passage they followed. Even dwarf masonry did not last forever, and they'd just left behind a small crew of stonemasons who were patching a hole when a huge spider leapt out of the darkness at Felix. All eight legs extended as it flashed through the air towards him; it was brought down at the last moment by Vabur's maul. Another blow crushed it into pulp.

'Thank you, herr dwarf,' said Felix white-faced.

'I was worried about the stonemasons,' said Vabur with a shrug. He scraped spider innards off his maul with the bottom of his boot, slung the weapon over his shoulder and continued on down the corridor. After a few moments, Felix quickly joined him.

When they entered the skaven warrens, Felix longed for the comforts they'd left behind in the dwarf-built tunnels. Most passageways twisted oddly, as if the skaven had merely dug where it was easiest to dig. The walls were crudely carved rock – Felix had heard stories that the skaven often made slaves dig with their bare paws and, looking at the way the stone was furrowed he believe it to be true. It was easy to catch clothing on rocky outcroppings, or even cut a hand on a sharp piece of stone. Sometimes the tunnels became so narrow that he had to turn sideways and shuffle through an opening with a cheek pressed against the rock. He had nightmares of getting stuck and being trapped beneath hundreds of tons of rock and ore until he starved.

Despite being heavier-set, the dwarfs seemed to have no problems navigating the maze of tunnels. Even Vabur Nerinson, whose shoulder-width must have been twice as wide as Felix's, somehow managed to squeeze through openings sized for skaven.

They began to encounter a few skaven patrols, which they quickly dispatched. Despite this, there was little sign of the 'massive army' that had attacked the Barak. These skaven looked hungry and their fur was matted with filth. It looked to Felix like they'd gotten lost or cut off when the main skaven force retreated.

They'd slept three times – though whether that meant three days had passed was anybody's guess – when Felix began to hear the roar of distant water. The crude skaven tunnels soon opened up into a series of caverns. Torchlight glimmered off an underground river that churned and spat foam onto wet walls. The walls here were plain bedrock shot through with veins of granite like glittering white lightning bolts flashing amidst rolling thunderclouds. A wide ledge ran along the river's edge from where it emerged from a rounded tunnel that might once have been a lava tube to where it disappeared underneath a shelf of rock. As far as Felix could tell, they had two choices – continue through the caverns and see if they opened into more skaven tunnels, or try and follow the ledge upriver, through the lava tube, towards the unknown.

Wolfhame, marching ahead of the group to avoid having his night vision spoiled by their lanterns, raised a hand to stop them, then advanced to a spot at the edge of the river and knelt.

'Skaven spoor,' he said, lifting a ball of dirt to his nose. He dropped it in disgust, and then wiped his hand on his armour. 'They've been here recently. They could be the band we seek, or they might simply be scouts for the skaven force that attacked the vaults.' He kicked at a pile of refuse nearby, and then looked around. 'Be alert. These tunnels are unknown to us. The skaven could be anywhere.'

'Unknown?' asked Gotrek looking up towards the ceiling. 'How they can be unknown? There's dwarf construction here.'

Though Felix peered through the gloom, he could see nothing but the jagged rock the river had carved out of the bedrock.

'You have sharp eyes, Slayer,' said Vabur Nerinson, gruffly. He walked over to the tunnel wall and ran his fingers across the wall. 'The river made this tunnel, but dwarfs worked it.'

The smooth patch of stone Gotrek had spotted was a reinforcing column, so cunningly crafted that Felix would never have seen it had Vabur not pointed it out. 'Could this be a forgotten part of Barak Varr?' he asked.

'No,' said Malbak, adjusting his belt buckle around his belly. 'The tunnels under the Barak have to be carefully planned and constructed in order to keep out the sea. Besides, we're days away from the hold.'

'It's old,' said Vabur. He stepped back, his gaze following the column up to the ceiling.

Felix gulped. If a dwarf said something was old, he might very well mean it was from an era before Sigmar united the tribes of man. To a race with a lifespan several times that of the oldest man, 'old' meant 'ancient'.

'Karak Tam,' said Martinuk quietly. The name hung in the air as the mercenary eyed the other dwarfs meaningfully.

Felix felt the temperature drop two degrees. Karak Tam? He struggled to remember his geography. Barak Varr was far from the mountains in which the dwarfs typically built their holds. Surrounded by the Border Princes, the closest thing to a mountain range nearby were the Varenka Hills – if they could even be called that. A goblin could spit over them on a windy day. It would be a poor location for a dwarf hold. 'What's Karak Tam?' he asked.

'A story,' said Wolfhame scornfully. 'A fable.'

'There is some truth in those old stories,' said Ulgar. The runesmith's voice was as deep and gravelly as the sound of two rocks grinding together deep beneath the earth. He tapped his rune-covered staff against the ground, and it began to glow a violet colour that illuminated the ancient masonry. He reached out and touched the worked stone reverently, then quickly drew back.

'Karag Dron,' he said, turning to Felix, 'the volcano your race calls 'Thunder', was once mined by a clan of dwarfs who used its fires to craft the finest weapons. For many generations their forges churned, until one day the mountain erupted. Racing to outrun the lava flows, the survivors fled east, towards the sea. Legend has it that they stopped in the Varenka Hills when their king came upon a boulder that was struck through and through with gold. He proclaimed it a miracle. Unfortunately, the boulder had been brought there by fields of ice that had long ago retreated, and the surrounding regions were so poor in metals the newly founded hold was unable to support itself. In order to survive, they redoubled their efforts to become the finest weaponsmiths in the world. And they succeeded! Their weapons were without peer. It was said that a king who wielded a weapon from Karak Tam could never be defeated in battle. Many of the weapons in your race's legends were forged at Karak Tam.'

'If it was such an important hold, why is it now forgotten?' asked Felix.

'The War of Vengeance,' said Gotrek with a sneer.

'The hold could not survive without a constant supply of new metals,' Wolfhame explained. 'But with our forces committed against the pointy ears, there was no metal to spare.'

Felix found it ironic that a hold renowned for crafting weapons would be a casualty of war, but what Wolfhame said made sense. A rune blade might be invaluable to a king, but a thousand iron axes would be worth much more to an army.

'They say some of the finest weapons ever crafted by a dwarf still lie within the vaults of Karak Tam,' said Malbak, striding back towards the gear as if some of those weapons were rusting into oblivion with each passing second. 'The contents of even one of those vaults would be enough to make us all as rich as King Grundadrakk.'

'Be mindful of why we came down here,' said Wolfhame dangerously. 'It's the Book of Grudges we seek, not personal gain.' He turned to Gromnir and Gromnar, the twin Reckoners. 'Scout out the passage ahead. For all this talk of ancient riches, do not forget that skaven now infest these tunnels.'

The two saluted in unison, then turned and clumped off into the darkness. Felix shook his head. The heavy plate they wore made them the worst scouts in the history of the profession. But perhaps that was Wolfhame's plan. Those two would trigger any skaven trap long before the expedition's more vulnerable members got close–such as Malbak.

The portly engineer spoke to Ulgar's apprentice in hushed, but urgent tones. Glorin wielded a rune-covered staff, which, like his master, he had caused to glow violet. Malbak was using its light to struggle into his pack.

Felix neither liked, nor trusted, the engineer. It was obvious that he'd thought Gotrek long dead, and thus a convenient scapegoat for a break-in he could not explain. When Gotrek had actually shown up, instead of admitting his mistake he'd tried to cover it up with a hastily contrived excuse. Felix resolved that he would keep a careful eye on Malbak for the duration of their mission.

Most of the other dwarfs had finished admiring the column and were beginning to make their way after the twins, so Felix bent to retrieve his own pack, and then thanked Glorin when the apprentice held out his staff to offer more light.

It was only when Felix rose that he saw the silvery cord descend from the gloom above Malbak's head. Coiled into a loop at its end, it slipped quietly around the engineer's neck and then jerked tight. Malbak's eyes flew open and his hands went to his throat as he was hoisted silently into the air.

Felix dropped the lantern and went for Karaghul, but there was no way he could make it to the engineer in time. 'Glorin!' he yelled in alarm.

Glorin turned in surprise. He saw Malbak's feet dangling in the air and panicked, dropping his staff and leaping after the engineer. He caught Malbak's lower legs in a bear hug, their combined weight dragging them down.

Felix darted towards them, intending to cut through the cord with Karaghul, but a flash of silver in the light of the dropped torch alerted him to the presence of another noose. He ducked, but not fast enough and felt the cord settle around his shoulders. Desperately, he dropped his sword and grabbed at it. He managed to free his neck, but the noose tightened around his arm instead. The cord jerked and he felt it constrict, the material biting into his skin. It was strong like iron, but as supple as silk. Had it settled around his neck as intended, he might have asphyxiated.

The force on the cord grew and he was lifted to the tip of his toes and then into the air. The river churned beneath him, soaking him with spray. If he fell into that he might be swept miles downriver. Suddenly his struggles to get away turned into struggles to hang on.

Above him, a score of dark shapes clung to the roof of the tunnel. Humanoid rats with dark, greasy fur that reeked of blood and offal clung to the ceiling with the aid of a foul-smelling tar they'd painted onto their paws. Though dwarfs had excellent senses of vision and hearing, smell was not in high demand in their dry and dusty mountain holds and was not as well developed. Even Felix had not been able to detect the pungent aroma, masked as it was by the churning spray of the river below. The skaven had planned their ambush well.

Though each rat warrior was armed with several blades, they kept them sheathed, preferring to rely on the nooses and other, non-lethal, forms of attack.

Felix's shout of alarm had alerted the other dwarfs. Gotrek raced back towards them, axe bared, and sliced through the cord around Malbak's neck, sending both the engineer and the younger runesmith tumbling to the ground.

'Come down here and face me, you cowardly tail-biters!' he yelled, shaking a fist at the ceiling. Several more nooses descended towards him, catching him around the fist and neck. Instead of avoiding them, the Slayer let them come and then laughed evilly as he yanked down sharply. Caught off-guard, a half-dozen skaven were pulled from their moorings and tumbled to the cavern floor.

Behind the Slayer, Ulgar chanted in the harsh Khazalid tongue and a rune on the tip of his staff exploded into brilliant violet light, illuminating the skaven warriors. The roof positively seethed with skaven, more than Felix could easily count. Most clung to the ceiling with the aid of the tar he'd seen earlier, but the more massive among them hung on to ancient loops of metal that had been hammered into the rock. Most of the silver cords ran through these, back to a hidden ledge where more ratmen waited to haul in their prey. Most were dressed in black, but at least one albino rat – a grey-furred creature he recognised as one of the fearsome grey seers – was visible in their midst.

Their leader appeared to be a huge rat-ogre, half as large as their largest warrior, naked but for a ridge of red fur that ran from its sloped forehead to the tip of its tail. Strange purple whorls marked its skin in a terrifying parody of Slayer's tattoos. Even with the aid of the metallic loops and black goop, it was a wonder to Felix that it could keep that vast body suspended. The strength in those muscles must be immense! Either that or the grey seer he'd spotted earlier had used some dark skaven sorcery to enable the feat. Regardless, it paid no attention to Felix. It had eyes only for Gotrek.

At its squeaked command, several ratmen bit daggers between their teeth and dropped towards the Slayer and the young runesmith apprentice. Others followed, and soon it was raining fur and steel.

Two of the largest ratmen carried between them a metallic net that glinted in Ulgar's purple light. They landed on either side of Glorin, who was still regaining his feet, and swept him into the netting. They called up to the roof in the skaven tongue and he too was lifted towards the ceiling.

Below, Gotrek laid into the skaven with his axe, knocking aside their pitiful attempts to parry. His axe was a blur of steel and wherever he went, death followed closely. A skaven warrior lunged at him with a crude axe. Gotrek ducked aside and put his rune axe through the back of its skull, spewing blood and brain matter onto the floor. For a moment, there was a lull in the battle as the skaven skittered back from his blade, wringing their paws and clawing at their masters for mercy. In one fluid motion, Gotrek bent, picked up the skaven weapon and hurled it at the ceiling.

The axe flashed within a hair's breadth of Felix's ear and embedded itself into the chest of the skaven warrior who was hauling him to the ceiling. It stared at the axe dumbly and then vomited a torrent of blood and phlegm into the river far below. It let go of the cord around Felix's arm as its body went limp, and it would have fallen were it not for the noxious black bonding agent on its paws. A second skaven made a valiant attempt to hang onto the cord, but Felix was far too heavy for it, and it squeaked in alarm as the rope cut into its fingers.

Felix felt a brief moment of weightlessness before he plunged twenty feet into the river below. He hit the surface hard on his back and sank like a stone. Cold water stabbed into him like a knife and the shock of it almost made him gasp. For a few desperate moments, he didn't know which way was up. He opened his eyes but, this far from the lantern light, it was as dark as a grave.

Already short of breath, he struggled to free himself from the cord. He felt the knot come loose just as a stone hit him hard in the back, nearly driving out what little air he had left.

The current had him.

He was being swept along the bottom towards the unknown. His chain shirt felt like a rock tied to his back, but there wasn't time to remove it. Desperate for air, he got his feet under him and kicked for the surface. He swam as hard as he could, and then his head hit rock hard enough that he nearly blacked out. With dogged determination, he clung to consciousness. To lose it meant death.

He clawed at the rock, feeling for an air pocket, anything. His lungs were screaming and his vision was dissolving into a smear of red.

Suddenly a hand grabbed his mail and yanked him hard against the current. He broke the surface with a gasp and sucked in air sweeter than any he'd yet known as he was hauled onto the rocks. After he'd caught his breath, he looked up at his rescuer and then recoiled in fear. A rubbery black face with dark, beady eyes stared back at him.

'Gas,' a muffled voice said, and then a calloused hand removed the skaven mask, revealing the scarred face and broken nose of Martinuk the mercenary. He pushed a second mask into Felix's hand. 'Put that on. You're going to need it,' he said, hooking a thumb over his shoulder at billowing green clouds that rolled across the cavern floor.

The skaven on the roof were throwing small, egg-shaped bombs at the dwarfs. Wherever one landed it shattered, releasing more gas. Martinuk had told them he'd witnessed his friends go mad and tear at their own skin at a single whiff, but this weapon seemed to have a different purpose. On the edge of the battlefield, Vabur Nerinson was caving in a skaven brainpan with every swipe of his maul, but as the gas hit him, his movements slowed and grew clumsy. Ratmen wearing masks similar to Martinuk's retreated and let Vabur swing drunkenly around himself. When he finally sank to his knees, they advanced with a net.

'Quit dawdling! They need our help,' said Martinuk, strapping his mask back on.

Felix mimicked the dwarf's motions and strapped the rubber thing to his own skull. The pungent aroma of offal and fur hit him like a punch in the face. 'It smells like wet rat,' he said in dismay.

'You look like a wet rat,' said Martinuk pointedly. He drew a long dagger and passed it hilt-first to Felix. 'Take this.'

'Thanks,' said Felix grimly. He felt naked without Karaghul, but at least he'd dropped it on dry land and not lost it in the river. Otherwise it might be halfway to the ocean by now.

Martinuk pulled his mask tight, saluted, and said something that was too muffled for Felix to make out. Without waiting for an answer, the mercenary drew his axe and leapt into the fog, shouting a slurred battle cry. Felix reluctantly did the same, eyes watering at the smell.

The combination of mask and rolling clouds of gas deadened all sound. Visibility was restricted to vague shapes that passed into and out of view, furred creatures struggling with armoured dwarfs. Some of the dwarfs had already fallen and were being dragged away by skaven warriors. The enemy was fighting to capture, not kill – quite unlike any skaven Felix had ever fought before.

Suddenly, a furry form materialised out of the fog. Its eyes were yellow and bloodshot, the fur around its muzzle slick and oily, encrusted with dried snot. It reeled back, not expecting a fully armed and alert adversary. Felix sliced open its belly with Martinuk's dagger, then took its sword and left it to gasp out its last breaths of air on the cold rock.

More skaven appeared through the gas, each taken off guard by Felix's appearance. The battles were short and furious. The ratmen fought to take prisoners. Felix fought to kill.

Soon, he heard Gotrek shouting curses through the gas. As he turned towards the sound, he tripped over a still form. It was Ulgar, the runesmith. The dwarf was sprawled on his stomach. His bearskin cloak nearly covered him, which explained why the skaven hadn't found him yet. His staff had stopped glowing and lay nearby. Felix stared at the swirling runes on its tip. This gas was skaven magic. If only Ulgar were awake, he could find some way to dispel it!

Tentatively, Felix reached out to shake the runesmith and was rewarded with a groan. He was barely conscious. He quickly knelt and rolled Ulgar over. Holding his breath, he removed his mask and strapped it onto the runesmith. Instantly, the pungent aroma of urine and bitter almonds hit him. A terrifying thought suddenly occurred to him. Dwarfs were notoriously resistant to poison and other toxins. If the skaven had mixed their gas to render them unconscious, it might very well kill a human like Felix.

A skaven warrior bumbled out of the gas in front of him. It wore a mask, but it had been neatly sliced open, along with most of its muzzle. A few yellowed teeth stood in stark contrast to the white of shattered bone. Its eyes went wide with fear and a new aroma punctuated the gas. The musk of fear, Felix had heard the ratmen call it.

He advanced on the skaven, feeling no pity. The ratmen were brutal warriors who took slaves when food was plentiful and ate them when it wasn't. It was easy to set aside all thoughts of mercy when he knew none would be given in return.

He expected the ratman to turn and flee, but instead, in a blind panic, it rushed forward and headbutted Felix in the sternum. He felt the air *whoosh* out of his lungs and he had to twist to avoid falling. Something warm and slick coated his wrist, and he realised the crazed skaven had run straight onto his blade.

Even with no air in his lungs, Felix tried to hold his breath, but the damage was done. His head began to feel heavy and woolen, and weariness stole over him like a burial shroud. He sank to his knees and felt the dagger slip from his hands.

Gotrek could fight a few minutes without Felix at his side. He was only going to take a short nap.

Suddenly, the sound of chanting filled the air, and then the sharp rap of steel on stone, once, twice, three times. A slight wind began to stir the gas, merely twirling a few eddies at first, and then growing in power until it was a wall of wind that shoved the gas up the river tunnel like a physical thing. The dissipating clouds revealed the aftermath of an intense battle. Most of the dwarfs were down, some in the process of being tied up by stunned skaven who'd suddenly lost their cover.

Only Gotrek still stood. He was surrounded by a wall of dead skaven and hacked off limbs. The gas had slowed but not stopped him, and even a slowed Gotrek was more than a match for a few score skaven.

Close on the heels of the wall of wind was another sensation. Something reached deep into Felix's guts and infused him with energy. At first, it felt like he'd eaten too many Arabyan peppers, but soon there was a fire in his belly that suffused him with strength... and rage. He leapt to his feet and hurled himself at the nearest skaven. Still stunned, the ratman fell easily under his blade.

He was soon joined by the other dwarfs, who'd also been energised by Ulgar's runic power. Together they cleaved left and right with joyous abandon. Gromnar and Gromnir appeared and formed an iron wall, penning the skaven in while Gotrek hacked them to pieces. At some point during the battle, Felix came upon Karaghul lying on the tunnel floor. He hooked its hilt with a toe, kicked it into the air and caught it with one hand, and then stabbed an unwary skaven who'd thought to take advantage of his distraction.

With the dwarfs at full strength, the skaven stood no chance and began to flee up the river tunnel. Those without black fluid on their paws scrabbled at the walls, and then hurled themselves into the river in terror. Soon, the skaven had retreated. The battle was won.

The dwarfs were bloody, but mostly unharmed. The skaven forces, on the other hand, had been decimated.

'How did we win?' asked Felix, stunned by the sheer number of enemy corpses.

'They fought to capture, not slay, manling,' said Gotrek, kicking a skaven corpse into the river. It landed with a splash, then disappeared beneath the churning foam. 'Though for what purpose, I can't begin to guess.'

'Why did you not fall to the gas like the rest of us, Slayer?' asked Wolfhame suspiciously.

Gotrek shrugged. 'I've always preferred slaying to sleeping.'

For the first time since they'd met, Norri Wolfhame cracked a smile. He took Gotrek's hand, shook it once, and then clapped him on the back.

But not all of their members had escaped unscathed.

'Glorin?' called Ulgar. When there was no answer, the old runesmith called his apprentice's name again, a note of desperation in his voice. Alarmed, Wolfhame did a quick head count. Glorin was nowhere to be found.

'They took him,' said Tebur. The Thunderer's tone was grim, but his voice was comically loud, the result of one too many shattered eardrums. 'Netted him, but good.'

'If they've harmed a hair in his beard I'll burn every one of them to a cinder,' said the old runesmith, eyes blazing. A few of the runes atop his staff shimmered ominously. Felix felt their power prickle the back of his neck. He almost felt sorry for the ratmen. Almost.

'Can you track them?' asked Wolfhame of Gromnir, or

perhaps Gromnar. Felix was still having difficulty telling them apart.

'Don't need to,' said the Ironbreaker matter-of-factly. 'They went up the tunnel.'

Wolfhame sighed. 'After that, iron skull.'

Gromnir nodded. 'We tracked the Slayer, didn't we?'

'And it only took you twenty years to catch me,' said Gotrek with a snort.

Wolfhame put his hand on the Reckoner's chest to stop him before he could do something rash. 'Then we go. Now. There isn't a skaven alive who can outrun a dwarf underground.'

'You're joking!' Malbak's voice broke and he tried to cover his fear with a cough. 'Follow them? Have you all gone mad?'

One of Vabur Nerinson's massive hands crashed down on Malbak's shoulder. His bushy, black eyebrows were drawn low, his eyes dark and serious. 'If Glorin hadn't grabbed your feet, it would be you we're chasing after.'

'I know,' Malbak admitted. 'He's a hero. I'll remember him always. But we were nearly killed.' He looked around at the assembled dwarfs for an ally and found none. 'They'll be expecting us this time.'

An angry silence reigned that was only broken when Martinuk held up a handful of rubber masks. 'My fellow dwarfs. Might I suggest we take a few of these along? Just in case?'

They pursued the skaven for two days without rest, and by the morning of the third day Gromnir admitted that the trail had gone cold. The black liquid gave the ratmen too much of an advantage. While the skaven raced along the roof of the river tunnel, the dwarfs had to do the best they could on foot. At times the way narrowed to a crack and they had to claw their way along slick rocks as the river raged behind them.

Other times they found their way blocked entirely and had to find another route.

Exhausted, they'd stopped for a quick meal of hardtack and stale cheese and were about to resume the pursuit when Ulgar gave a cry. 'We're close! My apprentice is nearby.'

Gromnir scratched his head and looked down the tunnel. They were in the middle of another detour and the passageway was dark and crudely constructed. 'Can't be,' he said gruffly. 'We can't have gained on them that much.'

'Unless they doubled back,' offered Gromnar.

Gromnir shook his head. 'They're days ahead. Why would they double back?'

'I'm telling you, he's near,' said Ulgar, pushing himself into their midst. He held out his staff and pointed to one of the runes. It glowed a faint green. 'I've enchanted it to glow when a dawi is near.'

Felix was about to point out that several dawi were near, but thought better of it. Obviously, Ulgar had accounted for the others. If his staff was glowing, it meant that Glorin was nearby.

Exhausted though they were, the team stumbled into a trot, intent on rescuing the apprentice. Felix was relieved to see Ulgar's staff brighten as they proceeded. Could Glorin have escaped his captors and made his way back towards the group? Felix began to feel the faintest ray of hope that the apprentice might be alive after all.

As they rounded a final corner, they spotted a figure slumped against the tunnel wall.

It was indeed a dwarf.

But it was not Glorin.

* * *

The dawi they'd found was near death. He was emaciated, hovering on the edge of starvation if not firmly in its grip. His face was harsh and lined, marred by what appeared to be a permanent squint and framed by a wispy white beard he'd tucked into a battered leather belt. He wore crude rags that might once have been sturdy dwarf wool and his pants were stained by sweat and viscera. His feet were over-large, even for a dwarf. Completely bare, they were cut and scratched in a dozen different places. If he'd fled his captors, he'd done it barefoot over sharp rock.

Vabur offered the Longbeard his aleskin and the dawi took it gratefully. He sputtered and choked on the first pull, then began to drink so vigorously that Vabur had to rescue the skin before it was completely emptied.

'Not too much, ancient one. It's zharrgot,' he cautioned. He took a pull himself then looked around sheepishly at the disgusted looks on the other dwarfs' faces. Even Felix couldn't hide his loathing. Zharrgot tasted like the rutz and tended to give one the same. 'I have a weakness for pepper ales,' admitted the giant dwarf with an uncharacteristic blush.

'What are you called, ancient one?' asked Norri Wolfhame.

'Balir,' said the dwarf. 'Balir Balirson.' He blinked up at the group. 'I'd ask if I was in Grimnir's halls, except I can't imagine what an umgi would be doing there.'

'This is Felix,' said Gotrek. 'Dwarf friend and Rememberer.'

Felix ignored Balir's slight. Judging from the look of him, the Longbeard had been through a lot. They gave him food from their meagre stores and, after a quick meal, he pronounced himself if not whole, then at least passable.

He'd been the leader of a patrol sent into the lower vaults to investigate signs of skaven encroachment when that was still but a rumour. They'd run into a group of ratmen using the same tactics as the ones who'd attacked Wolfhame's crew at the river ambush, except they hadn't had Martinuk on hand to distribute skaven masks. They'd quickly fallen victim to the gas.

Balir had awoken in a nightmare.

He'd found himself in a tiny cell with a dozen other dwarfs dressed in rags, each of them so pale and thin that their ribs shaded their bellies and their skin was like parchment stretched over bone. He didn't recognise any of them and they spoke in heavily accented Khazalid that he had difficulty understanding. They were at the end of their physical strength and had little interest in communicating, so he passed the time making and then discarding plans to escape. How long he had languished there, he did not know, but the number of dwarfs in his cell dwindled daily as skaven guards dragged them screaming into the lower tunnels.

When Balir's turn came, they took him down into the bowels of what he soon realised was a dwarf hold. The masonry was ancient and crumbling, but he recognised the quality of dawi work. His guards brought him to a large central chamber. Many more black-clad skaven like the ones who'd ambushed Balir's team were stationed about the room, their tails twitching occasionally as they stood at attention.

At the far side of the room was a massive vault door that was large enough to ride a herd of mountain ponies through at once. An intricate rune was carved in the wall above it and on the floor below lay a pile of stinking corpses, many so badly rotted that it was impossible to tell what race they might once have been.

The guards threw him to the floor in front of a skaven shaman. Given Balir's limited comprehension of the ratman tongue, he could discern only that the other skaven called it 'Tazuk'.

Tazuk was a fearsome sight. He wore a dawi skull for a helmet and, Balir realised in horror, a cape made from dawi skin. A dozen golden loops pierced his muzzle ridge from his snout to his beady little eyes. Worst of all, the creature wore around his neck a necklace made from what Balir could only assume was braided beard hair. The skull, beard, and cape made Tazuk look more like a dwarf than a rat, and Balir soon guessed that that was the point.

In any other circumstance, Balir might have laughed. A skaven wanting to be a dwarf! Imagine! One look into Tazuk's eyes and the laughter died in his throat. He was indeed mad, and it was the kind of insanity would drive the grey seer to kill without mercy or remorse.

It was then that Balir knew that if he didn't escape he would end up like one of the corpses in front of the vault. While Tazuk cursed his troops in their weird, squeaking tongue, Balir seized a curved knife from the belt of one of his guards and stabbed the creature in the knee. Before it could even squeal in pain, he spun and plunged his dagger into the eye of the other guard, and then bolted for the door.

Luck was with him. He'd caught the assembled skaven by surprise. Only a single black-clad rat stood between him and the door. In a fair fight, Balir knew he could have defeated the guard, but he could not afford to waste the seconds it would take to kill it. He had only moments before the rest of the skaven came to their senses.

Instead of engaging it, he ducked his head and charged forward, hoping to bowl it over and make his escape. The skaven shrieked in alarm and try to hurl itself aside, but it was too late. They crashed together. Seconds later several distinct pops told Balir why this particular skaven had been so desperate to avoid him. The ratman had been carrying dozens of gas-filled eggs, most of which had burst open when he'd fallen.

Sweet-smelling gas filled the central room as Balir untangled himself from the skaven warrior. Dark green clouds stung his eyes and burned his throat, but he was able to push onwards and soon left the gas behind. It had done its work on the skaven though, knocking out Tazuk and much of his household guard. No pursuit was mounted for several hours.

The Longbeard finished his tale with a grunt. 'And for the first time in days I decided to take a short nap. That's when you lot showed up to interrupt it.'

Norri Wolfhame's brow wrinkled. 'A mad skaven wearing a dawi skin? A pile of corpses? What are we to make of this?'

'Who knows what foul rituals the ratmen perform away from the eyes of the dawi?' answered Malbak with a shrug. 'Perhaps they were sacrificing prisoners to their god.'

Vabur Nerinson bounced the head of his maul in the palm of one hand. 'I knew a dwarf who wore a string of skaven ears around his neck. The ratmen could be doing the same with dawi bones. We're a badge of honour to them.' He seemed to approve, despite the gruesomeness of the thought.

Felix shook his head as the others debated the meaning of the story Balir had told them. He knew far less about the ratmen than the dwarfs, but he could not imagine them leaving a pile of corpses to rot. They were rumoured to eat whatever their paws could grasp, and he'd seen with his own eyes evidence that they ate their own dead. So why stay away from the bodies? Could they be poisoned? That made no sense. Skaven were reputed to eat warpstone and other toxic brews that would fell even a dwarf. So if the corpses weren't poisoned, somehow the skaven must have been prevented from approaching them. But how? Balir had mentioned the presence of a rune nearby.

'Can you sketch the rune you saw?' he asked suddenly, interrupting the others. Quickly, he outlined his line of reasoning to the group.

'Of course I can,' said Balir gruffly. He took a dagger from Vabur and carved out its likeness in the rock-dust that coated the floor of the passageway. Ulgar grunted once when he was halfway through, then again when he was done.

'The armoury,' the old runesmith muttered to himself. 'The armoury of Karak Tam.'

'Ulgar?' asked Norri Wolfhame. 'Do you recognise the rune?'

Ulgar looked up with haunted eyes. 'We must send for the armies of Barak Varr right away.'

'You're not serious...?' asked Wolfhame hesitantly.

'When you spoke of Karak Tam I thought, as many of you did, that it was merely a legend,' admitted the runesmith. 'But the secret to crafting the rune Balir has drawn was lost to us in the War of Vengeance. It is said that the magics involved in its creation were such that it took a dozen of the finest runesmiths ever born to the dawi race over a hundred years to craft, and craft it they did. Over the entrance to the armoury of Karak Tam.'

'What does it do?' Malbak asked breathlessly.

Ulgar ignored him, instead focussing on Balir. 'You made a mistake fleeing from the skaven. The safest place for you would have been inside the armoury. The rune you speak of kills any non-dawi who crosses the threshold.'

There was a moment of silence as they digested this. A rune that kills any creature but a dwarf! If the secret to its creation hadn't been lost, who knew what the dawi nations might look like today? Felix could well imagine the dour race scrawling one over the entrance to every hold.

'If I'd have been safe inside the armoury, why did the skaven bring me there?' asked Balir.

'It wanted you to bring out whatever was inside,' offered Felix. It seemed obvious to him, but the dwarfs looked at him like he'd just suggested that Tazuk the Mad had wanted Balir to cover himself in honey and dance a jig with a cave bear. The idea that a dwarf would cooperate with the skaven was so foreign to them that they hadn't even considered it. 'That's why the skaven who attacked us strove to capture, not kill us. This "Tazuk" believes there are still powerful weapons locked inside the vault and he will need dwarfs to get them out.'

'It's possible,' admitted Balir. 'I was the last of the prisoners to be removed from my cell. Maybe they sent the others into the armoury, and they were smart enough not to come out.'

'Can Tazuk be on to something?' asked Wolfhame of Ulgar. 'Could there still be weapons inside the armoury?'

Ulgar shrugged. 'The histories do not say. But if there are, they would be among the most powerful rune weapons in existence. The dwarfs of Karak Tam were some of the finest runesmiths and weaponsmiths in the entire dawi nation. Their weapons feature prominently in many of our legends. If they were to fall into any hands but a dwarf's it would be a disaster. If a mad skaven were to get a hold of them…?'

'Grimnir's beard,' said Wolfhame, his armoured fist crashing into his palm. He stared down the tunnel towards Karak Tam, then back the way they came. 'King Grundadrakk must be alerted, but I'll not leave poor Glorin to such a fate. We'll send our strongest warrior back to Barak Varr while we continue the pursuit.'

Gotrek cursed. 'You mean your second strongest warrior.'

Felix looked back up the tunnel. They'd followed a relatively straight path upriver, but before that? He remembered the twisting tunnels carved by skaven slaves. How could anyone retrace their steps through that maze? 'Does anyone remember the way?' he asked.

They all looked at him like he was mad. 'You don't?' Malbak blurted out, before being elbowed into silence by Martinuk.

'Don't make fun of the umgi,' whispered the mercenary. Felix flushed scarlet. Of course a dwarf would remember. Navigating these kinds of tunnels was second nature to them.

'Vabur,' said Wolfhame, ignoring Felix's outburst. 'It's you. Get going.'

The giant dwarf crossed his arms stubbornly. 'I'm not fleeing to the surface like a coward. Send Malbak. He doesn't even want to be here.'

'I would dearly love to send Malbak,' said Wolfhame with a roll of his eyes, 'but I worry the message would not get through. No. It has to be you.'

Vabur puffed up, somewhat mollified by Wolfhame's confidence in his skills.

The white-bearded Reckoner knelt in front of Balir. 'I would not ask this if the situation were not dire, but the ratmen have captured one of our own and we mean to rescue him. Can you lead us back to the Karak?'

The Longbeard looked up at the other dwarfs with suspicion that quickly gave way to weary resignation. 'I can,' he said.

'Then it's settled,' said Gotrek rubbing his hands gleefully. 'My axe will feast on skaven blood tonight!'

But Gotrek's axe did not feast on skaven blood that night, nor the next.

Balir's presence in the group both helped and hindered them. He was able to lead them around skaven scouting parties but, despite his stubbornness, he was simply unable to match the pace they'd set before. Gromnir, who seemed to be the twin most versed at tracking, informed them that they were days behind the group who'd taken Glorin. Felix could only hope the skaven would keep the apprentice in a cell for a few days before they brought him before Tazuk and give them time to rescue him.

It was during one of their infrequent rest periods that Martinuk approached him.

They'd scattered up and down a narrow tunnel, each of them dropping their packs in the dust and then wearily following them to the ground. Gotrek had gone ahead to scout with one of the twins, so Felix had taken the opportunity to catch up on his writing. He'd been relieved to find that his journal had remained safe in its oiled leather pouch during his dip in the river and had just put pen to page when Martinuk sat down beside him. He cut a slice of hard cheese off a block and offered it to Felix. It was stale, but it made the hardtack go down easier, so Felix took it gratefully.

'How goes the Remembering?' asked Martinuk abruptly.

Felix studied the page, knowing that the question was probably just one of the niceties of conversation and deserved a flippant answer. 'Not well,' he admitted. 'Gotrek's adventures span many years. I find my greatest problem is deciding what parts to leave out.'

Martinuk grunted. His fingers beat against the block of cheese. Felix could tell the dwarf wanted something from him, but couldn't find the words. He closed the journal and returned it to its pouch. 'Was there something you wanted to ask me?'

'I saved your life back there,' the mercenary said gruffly.

Felix nodded solemnly. 'I owe you a great debt, herr dwarf.'

Martinuk nodded as if the matter were settled. Abruptly, he spoke again. 'Why him?'

Puzzled, Felix spoke slowly. 'I don't follow.'

'You're Gotrek's Rememberer. Why is he worthy of your services? Trollslayers take oaths to end their lives because of some great shame – often a crime they've committed,' said Martinuk. 'Gotrek's a criminal. And yet you've sworn an oath to immortalise his deeds in an epic poem.'

'I–' Felix stuttered. Though their actions during the Window Tax Riots had made them wanted men across half the Empire, he'd never consider the fact that Gotrek's own race might think of him as a criminal. 'I suppose I never thought of it that way,' he admitted. 'Gotrek speaks little of his past, and has never spoken about the events that caused him to take the Slayer's Oath.'

'And what if those events make him unworthy of an epic?' Martinuk asked softly.

Felix considered this and found he didn't have an answer. That in itself terrified him. To Felix, Gotrek's life began on that fateful day in the midst of the riots when he'd rescued Felix from the Reiksguard. But dwarfs were exceptionally long-lived, and Gotrek may have lived the equivalent of many human lifetimes before they'd met. His deeds as a Slayer formed the bulk of Felix's epic, but what if the foundation was rotten? What if Felix had spent the last twenty years of his life recording the deeds of a criminal?

King Grundadrakk's words to Gotrek echoed in Felix's ears: *Your name was the last inscribed in the book.*

Gotrek had been the engineer in charge of constructing the vault in which the Book of Grudges was housed – likely the Royal Engineer. Had he committed some crime that had gotten him banished from the Barak?

Felix looked up and down the line of dwarfs. Likely he was the only one amongst them who was in the dark about the nature of Gotrek's great shame. Although curious, he'd never pressed Gotrek on its nature, but he resolved to ask again the next time they stopped.

The Slayer himself emerged from the darkness at the end of the tunnel, followed closely by Gromnir.

'We've found a vault,' said Gromnir excitedly.

'That's not the right vault,' said Balir angrily.

The expedition had gathered on a terrace overlooking a great hall far beneath them. The twins had found places at a marble banister, evidently fearless of being seen by whatever was below, while Norri Wolfhame stood with arms folded near the Longbeard. Malbak hung far back with Ulgar and Tebur Tanilson, near a pile of wood dust that had once been a painting.

The sheer volume of the hall amazed Felix. It was nearly a hundred feet deep and several hundred across. Though it was lit only by scattered torches in iron wall braces, the dwarfs could no doubt see to its far recesses. Felix, on the other hand, had some difficulty piercing the gloom, even from their elevated vantage point.

A fine layer of rock-dust lay everywhere on the floor below them, disturbed by narrow paths of skaven tracks: paw prints followed by wide smudges where their tails occasionally dragged against the ground. The hall had once been home to a fountain, in the centre of which stood a majestic statue of Grimnir, judging from the dual axes.

A circle of raised rock surrounded the statue, forming what

might once have been a reflecting pool. Dry now, it had probably once been fed by the very same river they'd followed into the depths. It was the kind of fountain lovers in Altdorf might have cast copper pieces into as they wished for romance. Of course, thought Felix wryly, dwarfs as a race were too cheap to throw money into puddles, but it was likely that the fountain had served some similar romantic purpose.

At the far end of the hall was an enormous door – larger, even, than the vault of Musin Balderk. It lay slightly ajar, balanced on steel hinges that reflected the flickering torchlight so well that Felix judged them to be nearly free of rust – a miracle for such an ancient monument. Though Felix stood at the edge of the terrace, it was too dark to see into the next room.

'Look!' said Gromnar. 'Dwarfs!'

Several figures shambled towards the vault in single-file along the far wall. They followed one of the paths the skaven had beaten through the rock-dust. They wore thick grey cloaks stained the colour of iron ore, so that they looked like boulders come to life. They moved with a peculiar gait as if they were in constant pain, but if they'd been tortured, their torturer was nowhere to be seen.

'They're not dwarfs,' said Gotrek with a curse.

'What makes you say that?' Wolfhame rubbed his chin as he studied them. 'Those are Ironbeard cloaks, unless I miss my guess. They were a smallish clan that mined a vein of magnetite on the outskirts of Barak Varr before the skaven came. They disappeared during the war.' His eyes were grim as he met their gazes. 'We'd thought them the first victims of the ratmen, but now we know they came here instead.'

'Ironbeard cloaks or no, no dwarf would ally himself with a skaven,' said Martinuk with a curse. Gotrek nodded in agreement, but his brow creased when Martinuk averted his eyes and spat on the ground instead. It was an odd feeling for Felix to encounter someone who treated the Slayer not as a hero, but as a criminal. 'If they have joined with the ratmen,' continued Martinuk, 'then they should be dealt with in the same manner as the skaven – axe first.'

'Balir?' asked Wolfhame, turning to the Longbeard. 'What do you know of these dwarfs?'

Balir glowered into the darkness. 'Maybe the dwarfs I shared a cell with were Ironbeards, but I passed through this hall during my escape and there were no dawi to be found.'

'Something is rotten in Marienburg,' said Felix with a scowl. He shrugged when the dwarfs looked at him with puzzled expressions. 'It's a human saying. It means that there is something amiss.'

'Marienburg is indeed a cesspit then,' said Wolfhame. Felix suppressed a sigh. Dwarfs were a literal breed, and explaining a decent metaphor was often more trouble than it was worth.

Gromnar had kept his eyes trained on the column of dwarfs. If Gromnir was the tracker, then Gromnar was the scout. He had the keenest eyes of any of them. 'They've got a prisoner.'

Felix looked where the Reckoner indicated. A solitary skaven warrior walked among the ranks of the dwarfs. Smaller than average with a snub nose like an Altdorf bullhound, it clutched its tail in its paws, as if reassured by its presence. Other than this the ratman was unarmed and unarmoured, though it carried a heavy pack on its back. Felix could see no sign of restraints, or anything at all to keep the skaven from darting away from the column.

'Maybe the vault is some kind of prison?' suggested Gromnir as the column disappeared behind the door.

'What good would a skaven prisoner be to a dwarf?' asked

Ulgar. The runesmith looked disgusted by the very thought. 'What would you feed it? Other skaven?'

'They have been known to eat their own kind,' said Martinuk darkly.

'There's another one,' said Gromnar.

An enormous skaven emerged from the open door of the vault carrying a huge golden hammer embossed with runes. Half again as tall as the dwarfs, it was the same beast Felix had seen clinging to the ceiling at the river ambush. Naked, except for a red crest of fur that ran from its creased brow to the spot where its tail might once have been, its crude tattoos were clearly visible even in the dimness. It paused at the entrance, the glow from the room beyond highlighting its silhouette, and scanned the terrace where the dwarfs were hidden. Though Felix thought he felt its gaze on him, it was bright in the hall below and dark on the terrace. It must not have been able to see past the gloom. After a moment, it barked something to those inside in its crude language, and then turned around and lumbered back into the vault, leaving the door ajar behind it.

'Grimnir's beard,' barked Wolfhame loud enough that Felix worried they'd be heard, despite the distance. 'A skaven Trollslayer!'

Everyone looked at Gotrek, clearly expecting some kind of explosion. The Grim Brotherhood was often referred to as a cult, with the Slayer's Oath at its heart. Their markings were sacred. Beyond sacred – they defined all Trollslayers. This skaven mockery was sacrilege of the highest order.

Instead of storming down the stairs, axe bared, as everyone expected, Gotrek merely narrowed his eyes. 'Mine,' he said quietly.

'Caution, Slayer,' said Ulgar with his dark rumbling voice.

A set of yellow and disfigured eyes belonging to the cave bear skin he wore as a cloak glimmered just above his own. 'Unless I miss my guess, Tazuk has managed to free at least one of Karak Tam's fabled weapons from its armoury. The golden rune weapon wielded by the Ratslayer was the Flame-hammer. Though it may not work correctly for a skaven, it will retain some fraction of its power. And a powerful weapon it is.'

'I'll pit my axe against a hammer any day or night,' sneered the Slayer, unbuckling his axe and swinging it back and forth to test its weight.

'Remember our purpose, Gotrek,' cautioned Norri Wolfhame. 'We've come to rescue Glorin and to find the Book of Grudges.'

'That's not *my* purpose,' growled Gotrek. 'My doom awaits.'

'And a glorious doom it would be, wouldn't it?' asked Martinuk darkly. 'Die in battle against a few dwarfs and a painted rat, and leave an innocent boy like Glorin to fend for himself. You Slayers think of no one but yourselves.'

Gotrek reddened and glared at Martinuk with his one good eye. 'Did you say something, mercenary?'

'You heard me,' responded the dwarf, unlimbering his own axe.

Thinking quickly, Wolfhame nodded to the twins. Gromnir stepped in front of Gotrek, while Gromnar placed himself squarely in front of Martinuk, each a wall of solid metal.

'Dwarfs do not fight dwarfs when there are skaven to be killed!' Wolfhame said in a stage whisper. 'When we get back to Barak Varr you two can gut each other for all I care, but for now you'll both be silent.'

'I'll be silent when I'm dead,' said Gotrek with a growl, and such was the fury that underlay his tone that Gromnir took a nervous step back, armour or no.

'The Ratslayer is the same creature that led the ambush at the river,' Felix quickly interjected. 'I saw him when I was hoisted to the ceiling. All we have to do to find Glorin is follow him back to wherever he came from.'

'When were you going to tell me about this, Rememberer?' asked Gotrek balefully.

'My eyes aren't as good as a dwarf's,' countered Felix. 'I wasn't sure of what I'd seen.'

If there was one thing he'd learned in his years travelling with the Slayer, it was that if you ever needed to placate a dwarf, all you needed to do was appeal to his vanity. A dwarf's senses were so acute that they tended to think of humans as blind, deaf and dumb by comparison. To their way of thinking, it wasn't Felix's fault that he hadn't gotten a good look at the Ratslayer. He was only human.

'It seems you'll get your wish after all, Slayer,' said Ulgar. The runesmith had stepped to the railing and clutched it with both hands. 'If we find this mad Seer Tazuk, then we find my apprentice. And, as the manling says, that red-haired monstrosity will lead us right to him.'

They descended via an ancient stairway cut into the wall. The vault door that the Ratslayer had used was perilously close to where they stood. Even Felix could hear gentle chanting through the slightly-open door, dark words rich with eldritch meaning and pain. He'd heard rumours long ago of a race of dwarfs who'd surrendered themselves to Chaos and wondered now if these Ironbeards might not have done the same.

'I don't like it,' said Wolfhame studying the vault door. 'There could be ten dwarfs or a hundred in a vault that size.' He turned to the Longbeard. 'Is there a way around them?'

'There is,' Balir admitted. 'But it would take days to circle around to it. This is an old hold, built in times of great conflict. The founders of Karak Tam wanted to defend only one entrance and this is it. The armoury lies beyond this room,' he said.

'We could fight them,' said Gotrek, an evil gleam in his eyes.

'They'll be quickly reinforced,' said Balir with a shake of his head. He pointed at several dark side passages. 'The bulk of the skaven dwell outside the hold. Tazuk has only a small force within, perhaps to avoid sharing the loot with the entire horde.'

'We should go around,' said Malbak a little too shrilly. He blanched when the others glared at him. 'Well, it's obvious the Ironbeards don't have the book, isn't it?'

'Oh, quit dribbling on the floor, Drumnokson,' said Gotrek, unable to disguise his loathing of his former apprentice. Felix wondered if there was more to it than Gotrek's customary disdain of cowards. Could Malbak have had something to do with Grundadrakk's grudge?

Martinuk had stolen ahead and slipped into the shadows near the vault door in order to get a look inside. He returned as quietly as he could, leaving small divots in the rock-dust like a deer track across fresh snow.

'The chamber beyond is huge, and a set of… obstacles separate us from the other dwarfs,' said the mercenary hesitantly. 'If the Slayer can keep his mouth shut for more than a few minutes, we can slip around them with none the wiser.'

Gotrek swelled up like a balloon.

'What kind of obstacles?' Felix asked quickly. Silently, he cursed Martinuk for provoking the Slayer. How long before those two came to blows?

Martinuk cast a nervous eye at the rest of the group. 'Best you see for yourselves,' he said finally. Without another word, he turned and started back for the door, leaving them to follow as they chose.

Before hurrying to join Martinuk at the door, Wolfhame quietly instructed them to step in Martinuk's footprints to better disguise their numbers, and further threatened to disembowel the first man or dwarf to make a sound.

It was only when they were pressed against the wall just outside that Felix got his first look at the chamber beyond the door. It was almost as large as the one in which they now stood, and lavishly decorated by stone carvings on the walls. Once, they might have depicted heroic deeds by dwarfs of old – a dawi-version of the epic poem Felix was writing for Gotrek – except that some had been defaced by lewd carving of genitalia and scrawling glyphs that Felix guessed where curse words. A line of pillars marched down the centre of the room, each of which was carved to resemble a dawi warrior holding up the ceiling. These statues were too enormous to deface, but their feet had been chiselled away, and often been replaced by crude carvings of ratmen wielding swords. It was obvious the skaven had been here at some time in the recent past.

Piles of rubbish and possibly excrement lay about the periphery of the chamber, as if the dwarfs had been using it for a toilet before converting it to its current purpose. Though the smell assaulted Felix even from this distance, the score or so of dwarfs who surrounded a central stone slab that was placed between the massive pillars seemed unaffected. Each of them stood as if hypnotised by their leader. A hollow-eyed dwarf dressed in rags that might once have been holy robes stood over the skaven prisoner. It lay its stomach on a crude stone altar, tail outstretched. The dwarf held a rusty butcher's knife in one hand and raised it to cut off the tail at its pinkish base.

What they were up to, Felix could not begin to guess. The stink of madness lay about the place. Perhaps these dwarfs had caught whatever disease had rendered mad the grey seer, Tazuk.

The sole exit was on the other side of the chamber. Martinuk led them around the edges of the vault, keeping the piles of rubbish – the 'obstacles' to which he'd referred – between himself and the Ironbeards. Privately, Felix thought they could have simply walked straight to the opposite door, so engrossed were the dwarfs in their ritual. The whole room reeked of Chaos magic and foul, rotting things.

'Gold...' Malbak whispered behind him. The engineer had stopped in his tracks and was staring at one of the midden piles. 'It's all gold.'

Felix's eyes widened. Something deep within the pile was reflecting amber torchlight. It *was* gold! Piles of it. Coins, ingots, and who knew what else.

What kind of dwarf kept his gold in a pile of trash? A skaven might hoard gold in such a manner if it wished to hide it from its rivals, but dwarfs as a race had too much respect for the metal to treat it in such a fashion.

'Leave it,' he hissed to Malbak. The others were leaving them behind, and Felix had no wish to be in the room when the Ironbeards' ritual was complete.

'What harm could it do to take just one piece?' asked the engineer in annoyance. He reached into the midden pile and drew forth half a gold chain. The other half appeared to be caught on a bone spur deep within the pile. 'Just... need to...' he grunted, giving it a tug.

Felix eyed the shifting offal warily. 'Malbak...' he said, reaching for the dwarf.

Suddenly, the pile shifted and an avalanche of trash crashed down around their ankles, narrowly missing Felix. Malbak held the gold chain triumphantly, but the echoes of the crash still reverberated throughout the vault.

In the centre of the room, twenty dwarfs looked up, their skin sloughing away like melted wax. Felix realised to his horror that the creatures inside the vault weren't dwarfs after all. They were skaven wearing dawi skins like clothing. Amber rodent eyes, shot through and through with wormy veins, stared at the dwarfs through crudely cut eye holes. Even though their snouts were stunted and deformed compared to normal skaven, they could not quite fit them under their skin masks and their faces bulged hideously at the snout. If they had tails at all, they were small pink nubs, scarred over at the top. That was why they had been walking oddly as they entered the vault, Felix realised. None of them had tails.

The skaven-dwarfs stared at Malbak and the others with cold, dead eyes, and then drew wickedly curved blades from under their skin-cloaks. Their leader, the one who'd been about to sever the tail of their prisoner, pulled down its mask like the hood of a cloak, to better see its attackers. Its eyes were pools of blood in snowy white fur that glared at them in hatred. Felix recognised it immediately as a grey seer… not Tazuk, but no less dangerous. With a hideous squeak, it ordered the attack.

'Grungni's forge and anvil, it can't be. They're not dwarfs at all,' gasped Norri Wolfhame. The Reckoner's eyes reflected the horror they all felt. Skaven, dressed in dawi skins.

'Nobody dishonours a dawi by wearing their skin,' growled Gotrek as he freed his axe. His single eye burned with a kind of fury Felix had rarely seen before.

Martinuk glared at Malbak with undisguised disgust. 'You may be an idiot, Malbak, but at least we have a fight on our hands.' With that, he drew his axe and hurdled the offal pile, followed closely by the Reckoners.

Malbak quickly stuffed the gold chain into his shirt, and then unapologetically began rummaging through the midden pile for more gold. 'There might be weapons in here,' he said lamely.

Felix shook his head as he drew Karaghul and joined the dwarfs in battle. The skaven outnumbered them three to one, and he was certain he'd seen one or two of their number dart down the hallway towards reinforcements. Malbak's most profitable mission might end up being their last.

As usual, the fighting was thick and furious around the Slayer. Gotrek's axe wove a cage around him as he parried blows and then brought his axe around to sever a spine or amputate a wrist. A particularly powerful strike shattered a skaven blade into shrapnel that flew back into its eyes and face, provoking a shriek of dismay.

Felix took up his customary position behind and to the left of the Slayer. Even Gotrek couldn't swing his axe in every direction at once, and it was Felix's job to protect the Slayer's flank. Several skaven had circled around Gotrek, well out of reach of his flashing axe, and now leapt to the attack. Felix cut the shortened snout off one with a backhand stroke, leaving it with nothing but a shrieking mass of tongue and enamel for a face. He kicked it in the chest, sending it reeling back into its fellows. A second ratman, more agile than the rest, lunged inward before Felix had regained his balance and stabbed at him with a recurved dagger. Unable to twist again in time, he felt the rat's blade skip along his mail shirt and was once again grateful for its protection. He brought the pommel of his sword down on the skaven's skull and felt something give. It stumbled backwards, half its body limp and unresponsive. It was almost a mercy when Felix cut it down.

Elsewhere, Gromnar and Gromnir wove through the tangle of skaven reaping lives like a farmer reaps wheat at harvest. Experts at armoured fighting, they were pure offense, relying on their armour to deflect those few blows that got past them.

Though Norri Wolfhame was as heavily armoured as the Reckoners, he fought with more finesse. When a snarling skaven hurled itself out of the crowd, black fur matted in its own blood, Wolfhame merely ducked and let the creature fly overhead. It landed heavily on the ground beyond and before it could recover itself he hewed downward with his hammer, splitting its skull like kindling.

A boom echoed out from the middle of the skaven horde and fur-lined gore was hurled into the air. Felix turned with the others and spotted Tebur Tanilson giggling madly as he lit the wick of a second metal globe and hurled it at the rat-men. He hadn't even bothered to load his rifle, preferring the mayhem his charges wrought.

From atop the dais, the grey seer drew a few pellets of something that glowed a sickly green from under its skin-robe and popped them into its mouth, barely bothering to chew before swallowing them down. It shuddered, then squeaked as if in pain or ecstasy and began chanting a hideous ritual. Two points of stagnant light lit up in the vicinity of its belly, glowing beneath its skin and fur, which spread to the creature's arms and legs. With a final shriek to its Horned God, it hurled the malevolent light at the dwarfs.

Felix braced himself for the effects of the skaven magic, but at the last second the blast made a right angle turn and flew into Ulgar's staff. The runesmith watched the last of the eldritch power fade into one of the finely wrought runes at its tip, and then turned around and used it to smite a particularly brave skaven, caving in its chest.

As the combat wore on, Felix settled into a comfortable rhythm. Chop, parry, riposte. Crazed as they were, these skaven had no skill – they practically threw themselves onto his blade. Still, they had numbers. During a lull in the fighting Felix looked out into the horde and saw more warriors pouring out of the side tunnels. Worse, the grey seer had directed the majority of its troops to the entrance, cutting off their escape.

'Gotrek,' he called over his shoulder as he kicked a skaven body off his blade. The ratman collapsed and its dwarf skin settled over it with a sound that might have been a sigh of relief.

'What is it, manling?' grunted the Slayer. A rat-ogre had emerged from the crowd, tusks protruding from a distended jaw. It bellowed, drowning out Gotrek's next words. The Slayer leapt forward and, with no more effort than he'd expended on any other foe, disembowelled it and sent it tumbling into the crowd. The Slayer had already amassed a heap of corpses in front of him, and the floor was slick with their viscera.

'They've cut off our escape,' Felix yelled, pointing at the door with Karaghul. Gotrek looked over just in time to see four skaven slam it shut. The last one, quicker than the rest, attempted to dart around the door before it was fully closed and was crushed to a paste by a hundred tons of stone.

'They've cut off their own escape, manling,' said Gotrek with a chuckle. Though he bled from a dozen minor wounds, he had barely begun to sweat. 'They're trapped in here with me now.'

Felix ducked the tip of a spear wielded by a one-eared

skaven with blood on its muzzle. He grasped the shaft with his free hand and jerked it towards him. The skaven screamed as it was pulled onto the tip of his blade.

During a brief lull in the fighting, he scanned the room, looking for the others. He could see only one of the twins, and aside from Wolfhame, who stood in a circle of crushed corpses, the others were lost in the fog of war. Were any of them still alive? There must be hundreds of skaven and they could attack from all directions. If the expedition stood any chance of survival, they needed to get somewhere where they could force the skaven to come at them in small numbers.

Now that the door was closed, there was only one way out – a narrow passage that extended deeper into the hold. It wasn't perfect, but it was their only chance for survival.

'Gotrek,' he called over his shoulder. 'We've got to make for that passage.'

'Go on without me, manling,' answered Gotrek happily. 'My doom calls!'

Felix shook his head. A greater doom awaited the Slayer than death at the hands of Tazuk's insane minions. On the other hand, who was he to decide where and when Gotrek met his end? If the Slayer chose to perish here, that was his business. Unfortunately, if Gotrek fell, his Rememberer would not last long on his own. Felix looked up at the bare stone of the ceiling and felt an intense longing to see the sun again before he died. He would not perish here.

'If you die now, your epic dies with you and the only thing the world will have to remember you by is your name in Grundadrakk's Book of Grudges,' he shouted.

Stunned, Gotrek momentarily dropped his guard. He rounded angrily on Felix. 'That is an evil line of reasoning, manling,' he said accusingly. Behind him, a black-furred skaven leapt forward, hoping to take advantage of the Slayer's distraction. Its dagger descended towards Gotrek's exposed back. The Slayer blocked it without even bothering to look, shattering its dagger and leaving it panicked and weaponless. 'I won't forget this,' he threatened.

Turning back around, he swatted the black-furred skaven into the next life with the edge of his axe, then began fighting his way towards the door. Felix breathed a sigh of relief and followed. Gotrek wasn't afraid of dying – he welcomed it. But he guarded his epic jealously. It was his one concession to vanity.

They joined up with Wolfhame and Gromnir, whose lion-crested helmet was covered in gore. The four of them fought back to back in a circle that slowly spun towards the far exit. Nearby, Martinuk had formed a kind of barricade behind a pile of offal and he'd cut down so many skaven as they swarmed over it that it had begun to collapse under the weight of their bodies. As soon as he spotted them, he renewed his attack, axe-clutched in one hand. He dragged a bundle of rags with the other that turned out to be none other than Malbak.

They found Tebur at the door. The skaven had left him for dead, or perhaps set him aside to devour as soon as it was safe. A gash in his chest hissed as he breathed, revealing something ropy and grey that might have been a lung. He looked up at Felix through bushy white eyebrows and caught his gaze with eyes Felix hadn't realised were blue.

'Herr Jogger,' he wheezed, beckoning Felix down to his level. 'T-take my pack,' he said. A gout of fluid spilled out of his mouth and stained his beard. The pack he offered Felix felt lumpy and solid and dangerous.

'I can't take this, Tebur,' said Felix regretfully. It felt odd to refuse a dwarf's dying request, but there was no way he could carry it and fight the ratmen at the same time.

'No, Herr Jogger,' said Tebur with a toothy smile. He produced two of his metal globes, each casting off sparks from a burning wick. 'If ye don't take it, ye'll be blasted apart with the rest of 'em.'

Felix's eyes widened. He tore open the top of Tebur's pack. The acrid scent of blackpowder that wafted out told him everything he needed to know. Tebur was carrying more explosive powder on him than an Imperial Iron Company.

'Gotrek!' he yelled over the din of melee.

Norri Wolfhame was the first to disengage from the press of ratmen. He looked down at the explosives in Tebur's hands and cursed. 'Gromnir!' he called, grabbing the Reckoner by the pauldron. 'We're getting out of here!'

Gromnir looked down, his lion-crested helmet opened in a roar that framed his face. 'No! Gromnar is still out there!'

'He's dead,' yelled Wolfhame.

'No!'

All of a sudden, Martinuk appeared out of nowhere and clunked the back of Gromnir's helmet with the haft of his axe. Despite the metallic ringing, Gromnir did not go down, but he was off balance enough that Wolfhame and Martinuk were able to wrestle him into the passage.

Malbak stood nearby, bloody and cut. Felix shoved Tebur's bag into the engineer's hands and propelled him after the Reckoners, and then drew Karaghul and stood next to the Slayer. He wouldn't put it past Gotrek to try for his glorious death right here in the passage.

'Gotrek,' he yelled, sidestepping a skaven blade and then stabbing out an eye with the tip of his blade. 'Remember the Book of Grudges!'

The Slayer snarled and cut a ratman in half. He bent down and retrieved a spear from the ground and then sighted carefully along its length with his one good eye. With a mighty heave he hurled it across the room. The weapon shot straight over the heads of the horde and buried itself in the chest of the grey seer. The rat froze in mid-squeak. As the greenish warpstone fire died out around it, it tottered to the edge of the dais and fell into the crowd.

'One less rat,' said the Slayer, his smile revealing a mouthful of crooked yellow teeth.

Felix couldn't help but grin alongside Gotrek as he turned away.

At his feet, Tebur sighed and went still, releasing the metal balls. They bounced on the ground and then rolled towards the skaven as their sparking wicks disappeared inside their shells. Before they could go off, skaven warriors were swept aside as if by the hand of a vengeful god, and Ulgar stepped out of the crowd. 'I thought you were never going to kill that wizard,' he barked at Gotrek.

The two metal balls rolled between his legs and he recognised them instantly. Spotting Tebur's corpse, he cursed and then dashed forward with all the grace and speed that runesmiths were famous for not having.

Gotrek and Felix followed an instant before smoke and fire obliterated the passageway behind them.

They were now eight in number.

Tebur's two explosive balls had produced enough fire and flame to set off the rest of his supplies, save for the barrel Malbak now carried. The conflagration had obliterated most of the skaven horde. If not for a final burst of speed, Gotrek and Felix would be nothing more than charred corpses, crushed into jelly when the passageway had caved in behind them.

Gromnar was gone and presumed dead, though no one had seen him since the opening minutes of the fight. Gromnir's armour was so dented that he was unable to sit, and so knelt on one side of the corridor, weeping openly. It was a rare enough sight among the dwarfs that none of them seemed to know what to do about it, and now and then one attempted to awkwardly console him.

Martinuk had a deep gash in his leg that he'd sustained in his mad dash towards the corridor. He took out a noxious smelling black paste from a pouch at his belt, smeared it on the wound, and then briefly set it on fire before hissing in pain and quickly snuffing the flame with his cloak. Privately, Felix thought that the treatment was worse than the wound itself, but in a few minutes Martinuk was pacing back and forth as if he was uninjured.

Balir's arms and chest were coated with blood, but the gruff Longbeard assured them it belonged to those he'd slain. Mostly.

The skaven had left Ulgar alone while he'd fought the grey seer. Perhaps they knew better than to interfere in a magical duel, or perhaps they hoped the runesmith would kill the seer so that one of them could take its place. However, he was not unharmed. He'd sustained his wounds when he'd activated the rune to deflect Tebur's explosion. The runes at the top of his staff had heated to a searing white and then shattered, spraying shrapnel over the runesmith's shoulders and back. Thankfully, his magic had held out and they'd emerged whole from the corridor.

Wolfhame stared back into the passage. Great slabs of rock and stone blocked the way back and the smell of dust was still thick in the air. 'Skaven dressed in dawi skins,' he said. 'I would never have believed it.'

Though Wolfhame had been at the centre of it, his armour and his skill with a hammer had mostly protected him. The same could not be said of Malbak. He was bloody from a dozen different wounds, and he'd lost the tip of one ear to a skaven blade. He sat apart from the others with Tebur's keg of blackpowder, still wearing the gold chain that had started the battle.

Gromnir seemed to notice him sitting there and rose all of a sudden. Tears had carved a dusty path in his cheeks and soaked his beard. 'You! You did this!' he roared, pointing his axe at the engineer. 'You'll die for what you've done!'

He strode across the floor and swung at Malbak like a woodsman cutting kindling. If it weren't for Wolfhame's hammer catching the haft of Gromnir's weapon, the engineer would be dead.

'Calm yourself!' said Wolfhame and such was the fire in his voice that Gromnir took a step back. 'We're trapped in a hold full of skaven with no book and no way to return to the surface. We don't even know if Vabur Nerinson was able to alert King Grundadrakk to our whereabouts, which means that not only are we trapped, there might not even be a rescue coming.' He sneered down at Malbak. 'The engineer might not be much of a fighter, but we'll need every dwarf – and man,' he said, nodding at Felix, 'to work together if we want to return to our holds.'

Gromnir spat on the floor, but remained silent.

'They know we're here now,' said Malbak. 'They'll come again in greater numbers. We need to turn back.'

There was such a note of despair in his voice that Felix almost took pity on him. Coddled by his father's money and power, assigned a prestigious apprenticeship under Gotrek, and then given a cushy job guarding the vault of Musin

Balderk, he'd probably never set foot outside the Barak. Wolfhame, Gotrek, even Felix himself, were hardened to the terrors of battle. Malbak wasn't. That didn't excuse his cowardice, but it did put it in a different light.

'That way is blocked,' said Wolfhame in disgust. 'And I wouldn't turn back in any case. We're here for the Book of Grudges and I won't return to King Grundadrakk empty-handed.'

Martinuk spoke up from the edge of the group. 'Sorry to interrupt your speech-making, but I've found something at the other end of this passage that you'll want to see.'

While the others had been arguing, Martinuk had scouted ahead. He took them down the corridor to a room that might have been a twin to the one they'd just left. The ceiling was so high that it was lost to the light from their lanterns. Instead of torches in iron wall sconces, the whole room was lit by an eerie green glow that came from a set of tubular tanks that lined either wall.

Felix stared in awe at the tanks. Set in brass bases larger than carriage wheels, they reminded him of nothing more than the glass test tubes he'd sometimes seen Imperial doktors use to store medicines. The glass alone was as tall as he was and must have cost a fortune to produce. He wondered if even Emperor Karl Franz's personal glass blowers had the skill to produce something of this scale. Surely, it couldn't be skaven work. It had to be some forgotten technology left behind by the dwarfs.

Riveted copper pipes through which murky fluid flowed connected each tank to its neighbours before rising upwards and disappearing in a tangle of metal into a hole in the ceiling. A low mist clung to the floor of the room that swirled into shapes that dispersed at the slightest disturbance. He felt like he was walking between the pillars of a temple to some forgotten god, only recently awakened. The air here was charged with evil and reeked faintly of cinnamon.

'Ulgar,' said Wolfhame, his gruff tone poorly disguising his fear. 'What manner of magic are these?'

The runesmith advanced on one of the tanks and studied it. A nearby pipe gurgled as something semi-solid passed through it on its way to the ceiling. Ulgar brushed aside his cave bear hood as if to get a better look at it, and then muttered a few words under his breath. The tip of his staff began to glow a soft magenta, turning the green liquid a bluish brown. Warily, he tapped the glass with the tip of his staff. *Clunk, clunk.*

Confident that it was thick enough to resist a few blows, he advanced still further. Wiping a thin sheen of water droplets from the exterior of the tube, he cupped his hand over his brow and peered into its depths.

A sound echoed back at him from inside the tank. *Clunk, clunk.*

Ulgar looked back at the rest of them grimly. Felix wondered if anything could be living inside the tube, some horrible skaven experiment. They'd already seen ratmen wearing the skins of dwarfs. To what other depths of depravity could the skaven sink? Suddenly, he felt a wild urge to get as far away from the tank as possible.

Ulgar turned back towards it, and then reeled back with a shout as a dark face smashed up against the glass from the inside.

While the rest of them started back, Gotrek merely stood there, arms folded. 'Put away your weapons,' he said in annoyance. 'It's not getting out.'

Felix was embarrassed to find Karaghul in his hand, and he

wasn't the only one. Wolfhame had drawn his hammer, and Martinuk his axe. As they put away their weapons, the Slayer drew his and advanced on the tank. Ulgar barely had time to get out of the way as Gotrek wound up and smashed the tube with his axe.

Glass shards rode a wave of viscous liquid onto the floor. A body came with it, which Gotrek scooped up with one arm and deposited on the floor nearby. Pale as a worm and barely clad in soiled rags, it looked like a dwarf, but its face was grossly distended into a muzzle with a disturbingly humanoid nose on the end. The hair on his head and – most shamefully – his beard had been shaved, but new tufts of coarse brown hair grew from his shoulders and back and on the nape of his neck.

'Glorin!' said Ulgar, running to his apprentice's side. He knelt quickly and began to treat Glorin's wounds, muttering soothing words as he did. The apprentice gasped in short, hard breaths, as if there was so much liquid in his lungs he could not draw in enough air.

Felix could not believe his eyes. It was difficult to recognise the young apprentice. He'd heard of creatures in Sylvania who were half wolf and half man – and had even had a close brush with a mutant or two who might have looked like Glorin did now, but dwarfs were notoriously resistant to mutation. What had the skaven done to him? And to what purpose?

Ulgar's calming words had an effect on the apprentice. Glorin's breathing soon slowed.

'By Grungni's hammer and forge.' Malbak took a few tentative steps towards the pair. He looked genuinely distraught. Glorin had been the one who'd saved Malbak from a similar fate. If not for his sacrifice, it would be the engineer lying on the floor with the face of a beast.

Ulgar looked up at Malbak as he knelt beside them and quickly covered up a flash of annoyance when he saw the expression of the engineer's face.

'What's wrong with him?' asked Malbak of the master runesmith.

'He's cursed,' said Ulgar bitterly. He touched Glorin's distorted cheek then yanked his hand away as if it had been burned. 'The skaven have some foul magics at their disposal, but I've rarely seen them work on the dawi. Perhaps this foul liquid eased the transformation. For what purpose, I can't begin to guess.'

'Can you fix him?' Malbak's voice was small and loaded with guilt.

'Sometimes the best cure is a quick and merciful death, boy,' answered Ulgar, though Malbak was far from a boy.

'Did you know about this room?' asked Wolfhame of Balir, anger flaring.

'The armoury is near here and I passed through this room in my flight, but never would I have guessed its purpose,' admitted the Longbeard. 'If I had, I would never have left it intact.'

'We'll destroy these tanks and make sure that no dwarf ever again shares Glorin's fate,' said Norri Wolfhame.

'Wait,' said Felix. He ignored the dwarfs' stares as he looked down at the spot Malbak had just vacated. The engineer had left behind Tebur's great cask of black powder.

The way back was sealed, leaving only one other entrance to this room... If they could somehow lure the skaven here and then detonate the keg, they might be able to even the odds.

'Ulgar,' he said, 'you told us that the rune Balir saw above the armoury door barred entry to any but a dwarf.'

'Aye,' said the runesmith suspiciously.

'Tazuk the Mad,' said Felix to himself. His mind was racing. Skaven wearing dwarf skins, a curse designed to turn a dwarf into a skaven... it all made a twisted kind of sense. Tazuk wanted the weapons of Karak Tam so desperately he'd become unhinged. When the skaven were unable to enter the vault he'd tried to 'fool' the rune by dressing his own warriors in dawi skins. Transforming young Glorin into a skaven was merely the latest iteration of Tazuk's madness.

'What are you thinking, manling?' rumbled Gotrek, but Felix was too caught up in his thoughts to pay heed to the dangerous undercurrent in the Slayer's tone.

'How many prisoners were in your group, Ancient One?' he asked of the Longbeard.

Balir scratched his head and glared at the ceiling as if the answer could be found amongst the shadows. 'Two score? Perhaps more?'

Two score! Hadn't Balir told them earlier that it was possible that some of those dwarfs were already inside the armoury? That they'd been smart enough not to come back out?

'I need to see the armoury,' he said.

Gotrek, Felix, and Balir knelt near a stone balcony overlooking the armoury of Karak Tam. The room below them had obviously been intended for a last defence of the armoury's treasures and was littered with cunningly placed stone benches that could quickly be overturned to offer cover from archers, while leaving open a killing field in front of the massive stone door that guarded the armoury.

Tazuk stood on a central dais, holding the Book of Grudges before him, exhorting his followers with all the fanaticism of a warrior priest and all the majesty of a squeaking rat. He was the same grey seer who'd ambushed them at the river near the start of their quest – the line of piercings that ran up his snout could not be mistaken. He still wore his armour of finger bones and his skull helmet. He looked like something old, newly arisen from the grave.

The door to the armoury of Karak Tam stood nearly twenty feet high and twenty more across.

'Just as I thought,' he said. 'The door is closed.'

'What are you getting at, manling?' asked Gotrek.

'That door is sealed,' he said, indicating the vault. 'Why would the skaven do that? They want inside so badly it's driven them mad.'

He drew back away from the balcony and kept his voice low. 'The skaven have been sending dwarfs inside to retrieve Karak Tam's weapons, but like you said, no dwarf would aid a rat. I think Balir's right. I think there are dawi inside that armoury.'

'They'd be in rough shape, but if we could get word to them that we're here to help it might help to even up the odds,' said Balir thoughtfully.

'Is there any way to alert them to our presence?' asked Felix.

'Certainly, manling,' said Gotrek with a grin. 'We fight our way through fifty skaven and knock.'

Felix looked back the way they'd come. A skaven sentry lay on the floor in a pool of blood. Its head lay a few feet away. Fifty-on-three were poor odds indeed, but he could not help but think the Slayer had gone up against worse.

'We can use Grundlid,' offered Balir.

'Grundlid?'

'Hammertongue. It's a tapping language we use to convey meaning through the rocks themselves.' The Longbeard glanced at the skaven below and, seeing that most watched Tazuk with rapt attention, he stole to the rear of the balcony and selected a section of wall that appeared to be cut from solid bedrock. He tapped it quietly with the pommel of his dagger, then waited, with his hand pressed against the rock.

Though Felix listened for some response, none came. In the chamber below, Tazuk squeaked viciously and a dozen skaven warriors thrust their fists at the ceiling. How long until one of them looked up and spotted the three of them skulking about on the landing? How long until the sentry was missed? Perhaps it might be better to simply abandon the plan and retreat back to the other room.

Balir's face lit up. 'They've responded.'

Felix realised he'd been holding his breath and let it out slowly.

Balir tapped out a complex code of short and long taps, and then awaited another response. 'They're two score in number and starving to a point where they just want to slay the skaven before they die. Unfortunately, they're not able to open the door from the inside.'

'We'll have to open it from this side then,' said Gotrek with a grin that said he'd like nothing more than to leap into the skaven horde below and hack his way to the door.

'We'll have to fight our way there,' said Balir gruffly. 'That big one worries me.' He nodded at the hulking mass of rat flesh that stood next to Tazuk. The Ratslayer was not quite as tall as some of the other rat-ogres in the room, but he was twice as wide as any of them. Felix could tell that he was built like a dwarf, as if Tazuk had somehow managed to combine the best of both races. A golden hammer hung from his belt, the weapon Ulgar had called the Flamehammer.

'How do we get from here to the armoury door and then

hold it long enough for the dwarfs to open it from the inside,' Felix asked to no one in particular. They'd have to fight their way through the entire horde to reach it and, as good a fighter as Gotrek was, even he could not fight them all. If only they had some kind of disguise that would allow them to pass through the skaven unseen.

He scanned the balcony, looking for some inspiration, and his gaze alighted on the slain skaven sentry. A horrible thought occurred to him.

'I think I know how we can do it,' he said.

Felix had felt so confident in his plan on the balcony, but now, facing seven dwarfs, some of them badly injured, he almost laughed at how ludicrous it was. If any of them had suggested an alternate course of action, he probably would have taken it.

'Well, spit it out, manling,' said Gotrek.

Felix cleared his throat and adjusted his chain shirt with a roll of his shoulders. Gotrek was right. If he didn't spit it out, he would lose his nerve.

'All right. The skaven outnumber us fifty to one, and when those rats we didn't kill in the antechamber join up with Tazuk's bunch, it'll be worse than that. We need to strike now, before that happens.'

'Strike? There's only eight of us,' said Malbak. He'd lost the whine from his voice ever since he'd seen what the skaven had done to Glorin, but he wasn't stupid.

'Yes,' said Felix hastily, 'but we have Tebur's black powder bomb. A smaller amount than this killed nearly everything in the other room. If we can somehow lure the skaven here, we'll retreat down the side passage and seal it behind us. Once we're out of the blast area, we'll set off Tebur's bomb, kill the skaven, and bury the poor souls in those tanks all at the same time.'

'That's a fine plan, but it has at least one flaw,' said Wolf-hame. 'What's to stop them from simply retreating back the way they came?'

'Well, that's where Malbak comes in,' said Felix reluctantly.

'Me?' Malbak exclaimed.

'Balir used Hammertongue to communicate with the dwarfs inside the armoury. Though they're few in number, they've pledged to attack the skaven from behind. But they can't open the armoury door from the inside.' He looked to Balir for support. The Longbeard nodded for him to go on. 'Someone needs to get past the army of skaven and open the door.'

Malbak's face and cheeks reddened with indignation. 'You want me to fight through an army of crazed ratmen in order to secure the aid of a handful of starving dwarfs?'

'Sounds like a job for a Slayer,' reasoned Martinuk.

'Aye,' said Gotrek, his face splitting into a wicked smile. 'But if I took that position the skaven would die before they got to this room.'

Felix glared at the mercenary before turning back to Mal-bak. 'We'll need every available warrior to block the side passage. What good is it to close the back door if the rats can escape out the front?'

'You've seen me fight,' said Malbak in disgust. 'I won't get more than five steps before they cut me down.'

Felix felt bad bullying the engineer, but he agreed with Malbak's self-assessment. He was useless with a blade. On the other hand, the side corridor was wide enough that it would take the rest of the fighters to hold it against the skaven. Felix hated himself for what he was about to do, but the engineer was the only one they could spare.

'You... won't have to fight,' he said reluctantly.

Gotrek cast a bloody lump at Malbak's feet. The dark brown fur of the skaven sentry he'd killed was stained with gore and smelled like copper and offal. Gotrek's axe was eternally sharp but was meant for killing skaven, not skinning them. Chunks of flesh still clung to the fur.

'I got the idea from the skaven,' Felix explained. 'It's crude, but if we create enough of a distraction it should get you past them, provided you stick to the shadows.'

'What about the smell?' asked Wolfhame dubiously. The Reckoner stared at the skin morbidly and nudged it with his toe.

'You can't seriously be considering–' exclaimed Malbak in alarm.

Gotrek held up a pair of brownish sacks, criss-crossed with a web of purplish veins. 'That's what these skaven glands are for.' He seemed to be taking entirely too much pleasure in Malbak's predicament. 'They call it 'the musk of fear'. Maybe it'll cure your stink.'

Despite Malbak's protests, it had taken surprisingly little convincing to get him to wear the skaven skin. Felix had noticed a change come over the engineer ever since they'd found Glorin. Malbak was still a braggart and a coward, but it seemed that the sight of the apprentice runesmith's ruined face had aged him years.

'In poor light, and with a little luck,' said Wolfhame as he stepped away from the engineer, 'you could pass for a skaven warrior.'

'I don't see a difference,' said Gotrek with a bark of laughter. Malbak glared daggers at him, but said nothing, smouldering quietly.

Felix eyed the others. Gromnir shrugged while Gotrek merely grinned. It would take more than poor light for the most blinded of ratmen to recognise Malbak as anything but a dwarf. The skaven sentry had been rail-thin, as most skaven were, while the engineer was heavy-set even for a dwarf. Wolf-hame had done his best to cure the skin with a torch, but it still showed enough blood to make Malbak look like he'd sustained a mortal wound. They'd scooped out the ratman's brains, but its skull was too small for Malbak's head, and he wore it like an ill-fitting hat. Worst of all, he smelled like a tannery. Felix had a sneaking suspicion that the so-called 'musk of fear' was something that approximated urine. Felix mouthed a silent prayer to Sigmar that the skaven would be struck by a sudden and inexplicable plague of blindness. Otherwise, Malbak's mission would be short-lived.

Balir returned from setting up Tebur's keg, wiping his hands on a dirty white cloth. 'Your Thunderer knew his black powder. We should be well away from here when that goes off,' he said, jerking a thumb over his shoulder.

In the days before he'd taken up the hammer, he'd been something of a Thunderer himself, or at least so he told them. After watching him work, Felix began to believe. Balir's training had returned with record speed.

Tebur had been organised if nothing else, and had packed the charges and blasting caps necessary to set off the bomb in the same sack. Balir had examined it with a critical eye, pronounced it adequate and commenced to work.

While Balir tampered with the keg, Norri Wolfhame and Ulgar had done what they could to hasten Glorin's spirit into the afterlife. Interrupted mid-transformation, the apprentice had died shortly after Gotrek had broken the tank. To Felix, that was a mercy. Life in that state was too horrible to contemplate. They dared not set fire to his body with the skaven so close. Gotrek had dispatched a few sentries and soon Tazuk would begin to notice their absence. Instead, they placed him close to Tebur's keg. It was undignified, but it would do the job.

While the others made their preparations, Felix tried to pen an entry in his journal – an entry that might be his last if their plan failed. He tried putting his pen to paper but found he couldn't write. Martinuk's words rang in his ears. Was Gotrek a criminal? He had to know.

He found the Slayer leaning against a wall, chewing on some hardtack.

'Gotrek?' he asked nervously. The Slayer had never been very forthcoming about the events surrounding his shaming and Felix worried that he would once more be rebuffed. 'Why does King Grundadrakk hold a grudge against you?'

The Slayer glared up at him as he munched his hardtack. 'That is none of your concern, manling.'

Felix nodded and turned away, but after a moment he turned back. He struggled to find words to describe how he was feeling, to sum up the conflict he felt. At last, he gave up. 'I have to know,' he said simply.

Gotrek studied him. Felix could not begin to guess what was going through his mind. It was for a Slayer and a Slayer only to know his shame. Felix had violated centuries of tradition just by asking. Perhaps Gotrek read something in Felix's expression that he'd never seen before, because finally he spoke. 'You'd better have a seat.'

Felix sat and waited patiently for the Slayer to continue.

'The road to Karak Kadrin is long, and I did not travel directly to the Shrine of Grimnir after...' Gotrek trailed off, his eyes grew distant. 'Though Barak Varr was not directly in my path, it was one of the places I came before I swore the Oath. I'd run into a druchii raider in some nameless port and by the time I'd cut off his third finger he'd told me that Grundadrakk's predecessor had had a hand in my shaming.'

Gotrek cracked his knuckles one by one as his thoughts returned to the events that had taken place all those years ago. 'My wounds were still fresh and I was mad with rage. The guards recognised me from my former employment as the Royal Engineer and since I had not yet taken the Oath, they didn't realise the danger their king was in.'

His face twisted into a snarl and his fist crashed into his palm. 'He knew when he found me waiting for him in his chambers why I'd come. He didn't even call for his guards. Instead he just laughed, like it was some great joke. I left him in a pool of his own blood, but I could not wipe that grin off his face. It stayed frozen on his corpse.'

Felix's heart grew cold. Had Gotrek just confessed to murder? Had he killed the previous king of Barak Varr in cold blood? No wonder Grundadrakk had sworn a grudge against him. No wonder Norri Wolfhame had tracked him across the world for over twenty years.

'What part did he play in your shaming?' Felix asked.

Gotrek looked at him sharply. 'That is not for you to know, manling.'

'I must know,' said Felix. 'For the epic.'

Gotrek shrugged. 'Then I release you from your oath.'

Felix shook his head. 'It's not that. I just need to know if the king's death was justified.'

'I could swear an oath that it was,' said Gotrek. 'But after all our travels together you either trust me or you don't.'

With that, he rose and walked away. Felix watched him go, his emotions in turmoil. Gotrek had killed the previous king of Barak Varr in cold blood, but did that make him a murderer?

After all our travels together you either trust me or you don't.

In all those years, Gotrek had left a bloody trail across half the Empire, but he'd never killed an innocent. He was a complicated dwarf. Martinuk had called the Grim Brotherhood 'a selfish bunch', but Gotrek had time and again sacrificed a glorious death to right some wrong. His code of honour compelled it.

You either trust me or you don't.

Could he trust Gotrek? Who better to trust? Every moment the Slayer lived was evidence that he cared for causes greater than himself.

Felix felt as if a great weight had been lifted off his shoulders. Inspired, he unslung his pack and retrieved his journal from its oiled pack. He put his pen to paper and the words began to flow.

It was some of the finest prose he'd ever written.

When the preparations were complete, Norri Wolfhame called them all together in the centre of the room. 'Everyone know their places?' he asked when they were all assembled.

Felix had sought Gotrek out and, instead of explaining himself, simply read some of the passages he'd written. The Slayer seemed to approve and all was well between them again. Now Felix stood side by side with Gotrek in the small circle of dwarfs that huddled around Wolfhame.

'So the Slayer and the manling attack the skaven and draw them back to this room,' said Norri, quickly outlining the plan. 'While we hold them here, Malbak will slip into the horde and make his way back to the armoury where he will release the Ironbeards. They will, in turn, attack the horde from behind and drive them further into this room. When the skaven are massed at their thickest, Ulgar will detonate Tebur's keg from afar, killing as many as possible. After that, it should be a simple matter for the Ironbeards to aid us in mopping up the scraps.'

Even though it was his plan, Felix could not help thinking how foolish it was. Everything had to work perfectly for it to succeed. If the Slayer failed to lure enough of the skaven away from the armoury, if Malbak turned coward and ran, if the skaven managed to overwhelm the Reckoners too soon… if any part of it failed, they were all doomed.

He looked around at the others, hoping that they didn't feel the same way he did. Most wore sombre, but determined looks. Gromnir's face was especially grim. Perhaps the Reckoner was thinking of the fate that had befallen his brother. Felix thought of his own brother, Otto, in faraway Altdorf. How long had it been since they'd shared a meal? Years? He resolved to visit as soon as he could. If he survived.

The Reckoners and Ulgar took up their stations at the room's one remaining entrance while Gotrek, Felix, and Malbak proceeded towards the armoury. When they reached the tunnel, Malbak took up his position.

'Good luck, engineer,' said Felix stoically. Malbak nodded in return. Perhaps the most important part of their plan rested on his shoulders. Had that been a terrible mistake? They would soon see.

Gotrek and Felix proceeded down the tunnel towards the armoury, alone once again. They said nothing because no words needed to be spoken. They were merely two warriors about to confront their doom.

When they were near, Gotrek stopped. 'A Slayer is enough

of a distraction to get their attention,' he said. 'You can go back with the others.'

Hope flared in Felix's chest. None of them had decent odds of escaping Karak Tam alive, but Gotrek would face the worst odds of all. Half the skaven horde would descend on him. 'No,' said Felix. 'What kind of epic ends with its subject disappearing down a tunnel never to be seen again?'

'I'll try not to die before I lead them back to you,' the Slayer offered.

Felix shook his head. 'What can I say? I'm a slave to my art.'

No further words needed to be spoken between them. They'd placed their fates in the hands of the gods. One wanted to die gloriously and the other wanted to write about it from the comfort of a warm inn. This day's end would see which one got their wish.

The sound of a hundred rodents chanting a foul ritual grew louder as they passed down the corridor, until they emerged into the circular room which held the armoury. The room was packed with skaven and smelled like sweat-soaked fur and musk. Tazuk stood in front of the armoury door, dressed in his bone armour, with the Ratslayer at his right hand. They were the only skaven facing the entrance, and so far they hadn't noticed the pair.

Gotrek stood on the threshold, waiting to be seen. Slayer's honour was a peculiar thing, Felix reflected. Gotrek had killed more men than some armies and yet he was reluctant to stab an enemy in the back. Finally, he walked up to one of the taller skaven and coughed. It cast a look over its shoulder, then squeaked and spun around.

That seemed to satisfy whatever condition Gotrek's honour demanded, because in the next second it was choking on its own blood with a gaping axe wound in its chest. Before the body could hit the ground, the Slayer had ripped a dagger out of its sheath and hurled it straight at Tazuk. If a rat-ogre hadn't chosen that moment to stand upright and investigate the sound, it would have caught the Seer in the throat. Instead the rat-ogre dropped with a dagger in its eye.

Tazuk screeched in outrage, but the Slayer was already at work, hewing at the skaven like a lumberjack chopping wood. An instant after Gotrek's first kill, Felix stabbed a skaven warrior through the gut before it had even drawn its blade and then lashed out again, severing an arm and stabbing into the face behind it.

It wasn't until the Ratslayer bellowed in anger and tried to force his way through the crowd towards Gotrek that Felix realised perhaps the biggest flaw in their plan. The whole thing was predicated on Gotrek retreating and drawing the skaven after him, but the Slayer had been thirsting for a chance to bring down the Ratslayer since he'd first laid eyes on the giant rat. Instead of retreating, Gotrek hacked his way further into the crowd, bellowing challenges and threats in the direction of the crested rat-ogre.

Felix struggled to keep up. Gotrek swept his axe in wide arc that clove flesh and bone with equal alacrity, but even he could occasionally let an enemy through his guard. Once, an axe blow severed a skaven's arm and knocked the ratman to the ground. An instant later, driven by some foul magic no doubt originating with Tazuk, it leapt back to its feet, dagger in its other paw, and lunged at the Slayer's back. If Felix hadn't stabbed it at the last minute, Gotrek might have found his doom at the hands of an opponent he'd already killed.

Suddenly, a skaven spear lanced out of the crowd and caught Felix square in the chest. The air exploded out of his lungs and he was thrown backwards, tumbling to the ground.

His vision reddened at its edges and he struggled to breathe. Dark blurs that he knew were skaven warriors squealed in triumph and pressed forward, only to be stopped at the last moment by a massive metal shape.

It was Gromnir. The huge Reckoner with the lion-created helmet bull-rushed a skaven warrior that sported a mismatched tusk in its muzzle, slamming into it with full force. As it stumbled back, he lashed out with his axe, decapitating another skaven and sending its head into the crowd.

Norri Wolfhame reached down a hand and helped Felix to his feet. Surprised to find himself alive, Felix felt around on his chest for blood, but came away with only a few damaged links of chain. If he survived this battle, he'd most likely have a deep bruise on his sternum, but his chain shirt had protected him from what was probably a very dull spear.

'Aren't you supposed to be guarding the other room?' he asked Wolfhame as the latter blocked a skaven dagger.

'We've been following the Slayer for nearly twenty years. I doubted he'd do as he was told,' said the white-bearded Reckoner.

Martinuk and Balir fanned out beside him. The Longbeard wielded one of Martinuk's spare axes in one hand and a hammer in the other. Though there'd been plenty of spare armour salvaged from the skaven sentries they'd slain, he wore only the clothes they'd found him in. Felix could easily imagine him grumpily refusing to don anything previously worn by a rat.

'All right, brother dwarfs,' said Norri Wolfhame. 'We're all Slayers today. Sell your lives dearly, and try and take as many of them with you as you can.'

Ulgar looked up at where Tazuk stood on the stone dais in the centre of the room. 'That one killed my apprentice. If you can keep the ratmen off my back, I'll show him that skaven sorcery is no match for dawi rune magic.'

The dwarfs quickly formed a wall of shields around the runesmith and began to tear into their enemies. Though they were few in number, they were heavily armed and armoured, and far better trained than the skaven fighters. When Wolfhame had proclaimed a single Reckoner to be worth ten skaven lives, he was being pragmatic, not optimistic.

Still, thought Felix as he fell in beside the Reckoners, the sheer number of enemy fighters would beat them down eventually. Exhaustion would slow their reflexes or pure chance might thin their numbers. A skaven victory seemed inevitable.

Elsewhere, the tide of battle was conspiring to keep the two Slayers apart. Though both fighters shouted oaths and curses at each other, somehow they could not quite meet. Finally, the last few ranks of skaven parted and there was nothing to hold them back from each other.

Suddenly, Tazuk screeched and pointed at the small group of armoured Reckoners near the door. Reluctantly, the Ratslayer disengaged and turned towards them.

'Come back here, you filthy offal-eating flea-bitten skruglover!' Gotrek bellowed, shaking his fist at the retreating Ratslayer. A skaven warrior dared to attack him. He killed it almost indignantly, and then began hacking his way back towards the Reckoners.

Suddenly a small grey skaven shoved into Felix. In a flash, Felix had brought Karaghul around, ready to cut it down. At the last second, he realised that it was no skaven after all. It was Malbak. Frantic and terrified, the engineer disappeared into the melee, all but ignored by the other skaven.

That Ulgar's rune magic had worked was a minor miracle,

but a greater one was that Malbak was making his way towards the armoury door. Glorin's death had matured the young engineer. If he lived, he would be a better dwarf for the experience.

Martinuk fought close to Felix, assuming the same position Felix usually occupied when he fought with the Slayer. The mercenary fought quick and dirty, disembowelling his opponents more often than not and leaving them to bleed out their lives on the ground.

He'd just killed a large black ratman with red eyes when Felix noticed him drop his guard and stumble backwards as a few metal stars blossomed from his chest. A slim skaven with a whip-like body stood only a few feet away. Certain it had killed the mercenary, it turned towards Felix, fanning more throwing daggers in its hand like a gambler with a deck of cards. A moment later Martinuk's blade pierced its chest and it dropped to the ground, dead as a stone.

Mortally wounded, the mercenary could not properly defend himself. Though Felix struggled to reach him, he disappeared under a hundred skaven bodies. When they were done with him, they rose with dripping blades and came for the rest of the company.

A huge form shoved its way to the front of the press of skaven. The Ratslayer was half again as tall as Felix. Its crest stood as stiff and straight as a horse's freshly cut mane, and its pallid skin was mottled and scarred. From this distance Felix could see a thin sheen of unshaven fur that covered its tattooed body.

It had already hacked through half the skaven army to get to them, and evidence of the mayhem it had caused lay all about it. A piece of meat was draped limply over its shoulder, a long purplish vein painting blood over its chest. The other skaven drew back, much as a school of minnows part before a shark, giving the huge beast room to do as it would.

The Ratslayer picked its target carefully – the largest, most intimidating among them. Though Felix was the tallest of the lot, Gromnir easily outweighed him in muscle alone, and his mail made him almost unstoppable. The Ratslayer shifted its grip on its enormous golden hammer. The craftsmanship of the weapon was exquisite – runes covered its length in an intricate pattern that formed a dragon's head, its open jaw embossed on the hammer's face.

A circle cleared around Gromnir and the Ratslayer – no skaven was brave enough to come between them. The crested rat took a step forward, and then another, and then it rushed forward as it swept its arms downward in an overhand strike. Gromnir deflected the blow with his shield. Any other weapon would have bounced harmlessly off from the dwarf-crafted steel, but the runes on the Flamehammer flared to life and it left a furrow of melted slag across the face of Gromnir's shield. The hammer face hit the floor hard, kicking up fragments of glowing rock with the impact.

Gromnir gasped as heat seared his arm and shook the shield loose. It broke in two as it hit the ground, the halves reminding Felix of a shattered plate. Undeterred, Gromnir shifted to a two-handed grip on his axe and lashed out in a vicious sweep that would have cut the Ratslayer in two had it connected. Instead, the giant rat dexterously parried Gromnir's axe with the haft of its hammer, and then stepped forward and struck the Reckoner square in the breastplate. Though it looked to Felix that the blow had been a glancing one, Gromnir bellowed in pain and fell back, clawing at his armour. A glowing red circle had twisted the metal and Felix smelled sizzling flesh. Gromnir was essentially cooking inside his armour.

Wolfhame rushed in to try and cover for the Reckoner, but the Ratslayer shifted opponents seamlessly. Felix noticed that the runes on the Flamehammer seemed to sputter to life and then die again at random, as if the runes that lined its length would not work properly for a skaven. The Ratslayer seemed to recognise when its weapon wasn't functioning properly – parrying when the runes were dim and attacking ferociously when they flared to life. The battle raged with furious intensity while both fighters exchanged blows. Unfortunately, the white-bearded Reckoner had learned from the Ratslayer's battle with Gromnir and watched the hammer warily. The Ratslayer took advantage of this distraction, feinting with the weapon and then kicking out with a clawed foot that knocked Wolfhame to the ground.

Felix was the only one left standing, and the Ratslayer's eyes narrowed as it turned to face him. His palm was sweaty and he shifted his grip on Karaghul. The beast had just dispatched their most powerful fighters in mere seconds. What hope did he have? Though Karaghul was also a rune weapon, it was attuned to dragons and he figured that the likeness of one on the hammer's head wouldn't count for much.

The speed of the Ratslayer's attack belied its size. Felix was barely able to get Karaghul up to parry. Though he'd put all his strength into the block, the skaven was far stronger. Its strike batted aside his sword and passed close enough to his head for the wind of its passing to tug at his hair.

The spot where Karaghul had impacted the golden hammer glowed cherry red and, though it took a moment for the heat to radiate up the blade, Felix gasped in pain. Despite the searing heat, he dared not drop the blade. Instead, he lunged at the Ratslayer and cut it along its thigh. It screeched in pain, but the wound only seemed to anger it, and it struck out again, the hammer passing inches above his head. Once again Felix attacked, stabbing up at its wrist. He was rewarded with a gout of blood, but not enough to disable it.

The Ratslayer shrugged off the wound and raised the hammer overhead. Felix watched it intently, knowing that one blow would send him into Morr's embrace. Suddenly, the Ratslayer snatched at him with its other hand, catching him hard about the throat. Claws dug into his soft flesh like daggers and he was lifted into the air. He had fallen prey to the same trick that had felled Wolfhame. He'd watched the weapon and not the fighter.

With his air supply cut off, he flailed about desperately with Karaghul, but he wasn't able to do much damage while he was dangling in the air. The Ratslayer raised its hammer to end him when a voice cut through the crowd.

'Trying to steal my doom, manling?'

It was Gotrek. Small specks of blood and fur and brain matter that were spattered about his body gave him the impression of a grinning corpse. Sweat had mingled with skaven blood and he left a bloody trail as he advanced into the circle of ratmen, axe at the ready.

The Ratslayer grinned evilly and casually tossed Felix aside. He landed in a heap close to Norri Wolfhame. Air rushed back into his lungs and his vision cleared. He felt like he had a crushed windpipe and it was difficult to swallow, but as he stood a quick inventory told him that aside from a few minor scratches, he was unhurt.

In the centre of the room, Tazuk the Mad was obviously displeased that his army had ceased to fight the intruders, and screeched orders for them to attack. A few brave ratmen began to once again advance on the dwarfs, but the Ratslayer countermanded them with a bellow. He wanted no interference in this battle. Surprisingly, the skaven drew back at his command. Felix wondered who was really in charge here: Tazuk or the Ratslayer.

The two Slayers faced off and slowly began to circle one another, each testing his opponent out with a flurry of blows that was quickly parried. Each time the two weapons connected, sparks showered the floor around them, which Felix hoped were coming from the Ratslayer's hammer and not Gotrek's axe. He'd always thought that the runes on the Slayer's weapon made it invulnerable, but as he watched the metal gradually redden under the Ratslayer's onslaught he wasn't so sure. Balir had told them that Karak Tam had produced many of the dwarf race's most powerful weapons. Could the Flamehammer be a match for Gotrek's rune axe?

The Ratslayer attacked in earnest now, raining blow after blow on Gotrek, forcing him to give ground reluctantly. The Slayer was by far the strongest dwarf Felix had ever met, but the skaven beast had a dwarf's frame and an ogre's muscle. The Flamehammer flashed in golden arcs that descended again and again, each blow lethal, each barely turned aside by Gotrek's axe.

The Slayer's weapon was glowing merrily now from blade to haft, and the smell of burning flesh polluted the air. The runes on the Flamehammer occasionally sputtered out, forcing the Ratslayer to retreat, but far less often than in the battle with Norri Wolfhame. It was as if the weapon recognised the power in Gotrek's axe and was determined to match it with its own. Gotrek's hands and arms were seared and he grimaced as his weapon betrayed him, but it was a testament to his willpower that he held fast to the axe, even though it had become a burning brand. Felix could feel waves of heat coming off the rune weapon, and it left a trail as it arced through the air. No matter how tough Gotrek was, there would come a point when his hands were seared into useless lumps. After that, it was only a matter of time until the Ratslayer brought him down.

Suddenly, it looked like it was over. The Ratslayer feinted left and Gotrek could not recover in time. The hammer smashed into his right arm with a sickening thud and the sizzle of burning flesh. The Ratslayer leered and, instead of pulling the weapon back for the killing blow, it pressed it further into the wound, revelling in the pain it must be inflicting. Gotrek grimaced in agony. Any other dwarf would have dropped his weapon and collapsed, but Gotrek merely shifted the axe to his left and struck out – not for the Ratslayer, but at the hammer itself.

More sparks burst forth and the Flamehammer was knocked away, leaving Gotrek with a new mark – a brand on his right arm in the shape of a dragon's grinning mouth.

The Ratslayer roared again and struck out with its hammer. Instead of parrying, Gotrek chopped at the weapon again. Confused by this new tactic, the Ratslayer stepped back, but Gotrek pursued. Instead of targeting the beast, he went after the Flamehammer with a vengeance, chopping at it again and again. On those few occasions when the Ratslayer managed an attack, its hammer was met with full force by Gotrek's axe, and every time the two weapons met the combatants were showered with sparks. Felix could not tell which weapon was giving them off. The Slayer's axe was now glowing so ferociously that he couldn't see if the blade was notched, and the Flamehammer was so intricately carved that any crack was lost amongst the runes.

It was a daring strategy. True to his word, Gotrek was literally pitting his axe against the Flamehammer, gambling that the ancient weaponsmiths of Karak Tam could not have crafted a weapon to match its power. His grimace of pain had twisted into a mad grin as he struck with such fury that the Ratslayer was forced to its knees. Gotrek had become a berserker, crazed with pain and battle lust. He abandoned all pretence of skill and simply beat at the Ratslayer with abandon. The white-hot axe crashed down again and again on the haft of the Flamehammer until, with a flash of brilliant light, it snapped and the rune axe buried itself in the Ratslayer's skull. So mad was Gotrek with berserker fury that he didn't even realise that he'd killed his opponent until three strikes later.

He arose from that corpse like some avatar of grim violence, breathing heavily, a silver snake of saliva matting his fiery red beard. Not a creature stirred. Not a sound intruded on that place but the Slayer's tortured breath. He turned on the other skaven, madly daring them to attack, but not one of them moved. Even Tazuk stood in quiet contemplation of the massacre he'd just witnessed.

A baritone rumble broke the silence, the sound of rocks shifting deep beneath the earth. The vault door shifted behind Tazuk, and then with a gasp came open. A glittering horde emerged, dressed in shimmering gromril armour and wielding sparkling weapons. At their fore stood a pathetic-looking skaven warrior that was no skaven at all. Malbak had taken advantage of the distraction to open the vault, and the captured dwarfs poured forth, hacking into the skaven army from the rear with weapons from the days of yore.

Caught between Gotrek and the Reckoners on one side and the heavily armoured dwarfs on the other, the skaven had no choice but to fight, and the room dissolved into chaotic battle. It was every warrior for himself. Felix started to assume his customary position behind and to the left of the Slayer, but quickly realised that Gotrek was fighting left-handed now and shifted to the other side. If the fight with the Ratslayer had at all tired him out, Gotrek didn't show it. If anything he drew power from his wounds and cut through the skaven army like a scythe through wheat.

At one point, Felix saw a great cave bear rear out of the melee and strike down Tazuk with a blow from a glowing white staff. He soon realised that it was no cave bear. Ulgar stood above the downed grey seer and struck him again and again with the butt of his staff, with every blow bellowing out, 'This is for my apprentice, you vermin-loving whoreson!'

All of a sudden, the press of skaven gave way to armoured dwarfs and Felix realised that they'd met the Ironbeards in the middle. Skaven corpses lay all around them. A few survivors were fleeing for the exits as fast as their paws could carry them.

Gromnir was dead. He'd removed his melted armour and fought on bare-chested until a skaven spear had taken him in the gut. He'd killed three more ratmen before he succumbed to his wounds. They found Balir's body under a pile of skaven, a mad smile still plastered across his face. He'd demanded vengeance for what the rats had done to his clan and he'd achieved it, in the end.

After the remaining dwarfs had counted their dead, they greeted their brothers from the armoury. Though each was resplendent in some of the finest armour Felix had ever seen, when they removed their visors, he could see gaunt, half-starved faces. So weakened were they by hunger and battle that some of them could barely hold an axe.

Of the dwarfs who'd set out from Barak Varr, Norri Wolf-hame, Ulgar and Malbak had survived, and each of them had been changed by the horrors they'd witnessed. Only Gotrek, by now immune to horror, was unchanged. He'd cursed Ulgar when the runesmith had insisted on putting his broken arm in a sling and complained bitterly when he put a salve on the brand he'd gotten on his right arm.

Norri Wolfhame waited patiently for Ulgar to finish before he laid into the Slayer. 'We had a plan, didn't we? You were supposed to lure them back to the experiment room.'

Gotrek merely shrugged, then winced in pain and rubbed his shoulder. He favoured the Reckoner with a glare. 'Plans change. Seems to have worked out in the end.'

'Speaking of the experiment room,' said Felix, 'didn't we…?'

A dull *ca-rumph* echoed through the hold and the hall through which they'd entered coughed rock-dust. Tebur Tanilson's keg of black powder had gone off after all. Perhaps it had simply gone off on its own. More likely some of the fleeing skaven hadn't been able to restrain their curiosity. Either way Glorin would finally sleep in peace.

It was Norri Wolfhame who finally remembered the purpose of their quest. He found Tazuk's body and pried the Book of Grudges free from the paws that clutched it even in death.

'Grungni's hairy beard,' he exclaimed when he opened it.

'What's wrong?' asked Felix.

Instead of answering, Wolfhame passed him the book. The leather felt strange and coarse in Felix's hands. The tome was very thin, too thin to hold all the grudges of Barak Varr from now to antiquity. When he opened it, he could see why. It was filled with nothing but scrawled characters interspersed with pictures of skaven, sometimes involved in lewd acts.

'It's not the Book of Grudges,' he said simply. He passed it to Gotrek, who leafed through it himself.

'I don't believe it!' said the Slayer.

Malbak stared at the book, then at the carnage that lay all around him. 'If that's not the Book of Grudges, then where is it? We searched the vault of Musin Balderk and it wasn't there.'

Felix stared at Tazuk's corpse. It had never been a question that the skaven seer was mad. He'd dressed up his own warriors in the skins of dwarfs, and even tried to cross the dawi with his own race in a hideous experiment. He'd tried to emulate the dwarfs in every way, so why create a fake book? Why not try and steal the real one?

Felix creased his brow. Maybe he had. They'd found skaven spoor in the vault of Musin Balderk, after all. But they hadn't found any skaven. And Gotrek himself had told them that no break-in had occurred.

Suddenly, Felix remembered the huge statue of Grimnir outside the great hall where they'd first engaged the ratmen. And then there were the piles of gold in the next room… What if the ratmen had broken into the vault and not been able to get out?

'I think I know what happened to the real Book of Grudges,' he said.

'You'd better know what you're doing, manling,' said Gotrek balefully.

The trip back to the surface had been harrowing. They'd found a store of mouldy cheese and wheat that the skaven hadn't fouled, and though it wasn't much, the starving Ironbeards had fallen on it like it was a king's banquet. Though the skaven had been vanquished, the dwarfs still encountered scattered pockets of resistance as they fought their way to the surface. If not for the weaponry they'd salvaged from the armoury of Karak Tam they might not have made it. While none of the weapons they found was the equal of the Flame-hammer, put together with the gromril armour, the small group of half-starved dwarfs was a force to be reckoned with.

Halfway to the surface they'd encountered Vabur Nerinson, who led a small force of dwarf Ironbreakers. After a hearty greeting and a moment of silent contemplation for those who'd lost their lives, he'd escorted them the rest of the way back to the Barak.

Now they stood once more outside the vault of Musin Bald-erk, thinner in numbers but fatter in great deeds. Though the Ironbeards had returned to their holds after paying tribute to the king in the form of fabulous rune weapons and gromril, Norri Wolfhame, Malbak, Vabur and Ulgar had chosen to remain with Gotrek and Felix.

King Grundadrakk stood nearby, arms folded across his chest, his golden crown sitting uneasily on his bald head.

'We've searched this vault before, Herr Jaeger,' said the king angrily. 'I'll be quite displeased if we have to search it again.'

'We know exactly what we're looking for,' said Felix, nodding at Malbak.

The apprentice engineer had kept his skaven skin and wore it now like a cape – a badge of honour for one who'd had a very short supply when they'd originally left the Barak. He stepped forward and traced the opening runes, humming the correct melody to activate them, and then hauled open the door.

As Grundadrakk watched suspiciously, Felix handed Gotrek a cruder axe than the Slayer's rune weapon, one that wouldn't be mourned if it were to suffer damage from what he was about to do with it. Gotrek stepped past the engineer and hefted the weapon. Before anyone could react, he brought it down in an overhead sweep that cut the massive golden statue of Grimnir in half. Three desiccated skaven corpses tumbled out of its interior. It was obvious they'd starved to death.

He bent down and pulled a large and ornately bound book from their clutches. Without saying a word, he marched over to Grundadrakk and shoved it into his hands. They exchanged a long and dangerous look, and then the Slayer spun on his heel and stomped down the hall. Felix turned and followed.

'I haven't dismissed you yet,' bellowed Grundadrakk holding the Book of Grudges in his hands. 'Where are you going, Gurnisson?'

Gotrek answered without even turning around. 'To get myself a drink!'

INTO THE VALLEY OF DEATH

Frank Cavallo

1

Felix Jaeger ran for his life.

His feet slashed across the muddy ground with every hurried step. His muscles ached, screaming for rest. His lungs burned and his chest heaved. But he couldn't stop. He couldn't slow down, not even for a moment. Not even to catch his failing breath.

The beast was near. He could hear it, snarling and howling as it ripped through the thick forest behind him, shrinking the distance between them with each passing instant. The chase had already stretched on for almost an hour, tearing a scar across the dark forests of eastern Talabecland. It was a desperate race, a break-neck pursuit through treacherous woods and dense, overgrown brush-tangles. And it was now drawing to its inevitable, brutal end.

Each second brought the claws and the fangs closer. Every time he risked a glance backwards, Felix could see those same merciless red eyes, glowing against the cold shadows of the Great Forest. No matter how far he ran, their gaze remained locked on him. In moments the monster's furious gait would finally close the gap. Soon the beast would outlast him and Felix's exhausted sinews would become nothing more than food for the ravenous predator.

A thistle branch tore away his sleeve as he rushed through a thicket of brambles, cutting across his arm and spilling more blood in his wake. Garbed in what had once been the silken finery of a student at a prestigious university – everything he wore was now shredded and frayed – months of wandering along the fringes of civilization had left him in rags and second-hand scraps. Stains of sweat, mud and blood discoloured the expensive dyes of his ruined clothing.

When he spied a rocky clearing in the forest ahead, only a few steps away, he staggered towards it. The monster's roaring gait was growing ever louder behind him. Every step made it swell. A rushing river bounded Felix to his right, churning with white rapids, making the frothing water impossible to negotiate. Ahead, at the edge of the stone outcropping, he caught sight of the fat trunk of a great old oak, towering above the uneven ground and reaching up into the dark canopy. He clenched his fists and summoned his last ounce of strength. He charged into the open.

The beast broke through the wall of brambles behind him only an instant later, splitting the nest of thorn bushes. It was a massive, wild canine, its powerful muscles warped and swollen into a drooling grotesquery of fur and flesh. A mane of razor-sharp bristles crowned the mutant hound's fearsome head, exaggerating the heft of its enormous shoulders. Its thick body surged with hideous growth. Twisted tusks sprouted from every corner of its flea-swarmed, gore-speckled hide. Ridges of bony spines ran down the length of its arched back. Its haunches flexed over the top of scaly, claw-like paws and its scorpion tail whipped wildly through the air behind it.

Bounding in bloodthirsty fury over the last few paces towards Felix, it was on his heels in seconds. Snapping its rabid, frothing jaws, it howled at the warm scent of man-flesh that filled its slimy nose.

Felix leaped for the tree, less than a single step ahead of the hound. He stretched his arms out, as long and as hard as he could muster, straining to reach the lowest-hanging branch and ignoring the pain that rippled through his body. For a moment he was airborne, flying through the woods in a final, frantic effort to escape. His hands clamped down on an arm of grey bark, but his palms were dripping with sweat. One hand slipped from the grip a moment after, leaving him swinging in the wind, hanging on by only a single, precarious grasp.

The hound gave no quarter. It too sprang on its back legs, careening up towards the vulnerable man, suspended by his tenuous hold.

Its dagger claws swiped at his leg, tearing through his boot leather right down to the skin. The hound's snout chomped at him, gnashing its fangs within inches of Felix's midsection. He could taste the beast's hot breath, stinking with the foul odours of carrion as it bayed in maddened, mindless wrath. But the nimble young wanderer held fast. He kicked at the hound's snout, smashing its nose. Then he swung his entire body back in the other direction, somehow managing to again avoid the beast's snarling jaws.

As the mutated hound fell back to earth, Felix quickly re-established his grip, using his momentum to haul himself up from below. The snarling beast leaped a second time, but Felix draped his legs over another branch, further elevating himself until he could pull his entire body out of harm's way.

The ferocious hound remained undeterred, leaping and

growling at the base of the old tree, but for the moment, Felix had found his haven. For the moment, he was safe.

2

With the beast still circling beneath, the chase averted for at least a while, Felix reached into his pack. The tattered green travel bag was now his only worldly possession and, as he expected, it was nearly empty. Just a handful of nuts and some dry berries remained among stale crumbs. The stolen bread he'd packed away days before was long gone.

Breathing easily for the first time in a long while, his cheeks were flushed from the hunt. His chest still pounded with the rush of adrenaline as he tried to relax. Perspiration soaked his clothing, dripping from his sleeves and from the long blond locks that had fallen down over his face. He pulled back the mop of hair with a grimy hand, raising his sights to the heavens.

The wet, shoulder-length strands fell down over his collar and the top of his dirty tunic. He was a lean, lithe young man, with a hard-edged jawline and narrow eyes that always seemed to squint just a little. Despite having been on the run for many weeks, his youthful face showed only the earliest hints of a beard, no more than scattered patches of fine whiskers on his chin and a thin bit of a moustache forming above his lip.

No longer a boy, but not quite old enough to grow the beard of a man, as his father used to say.

Felix watched the hound below, licking its fangs with a serpentine red tongue. If it was hunger that motivated the vicious abomination, then he shared at least that much in common with the beast. The gurgling pain deep in his own gut, as empty as his burlap rucksack, hurt worse than any knife wound. A constant, excruciating reminder of how far he'd fallen and how much he'd lost.

It had been days now since he'd been on the run, since he'd awoken with a splitting headache to find himself alone in some of the most dangerous wild places in the Empire. Though he whispered curses to any number of gods, he also could hear his father's disapproving voice for another reason, scolding him within his head. He well knew what the old man would have said: that he could blame no one but himself for his current string of misfortunes – save perhaps the brigands who had recently knocked him unconscious and relieved him of nearly everything he owned.

He'd known, even at the time, that taking up with a band of strangers in Wurtbad was a strategy not likely to bring him good fortune. But his options had been limited.

The association had begun with the best of intentions. Seeking out a place to drown his sorrows with the last of his coins, he'd stumbled into a dingy tavern on the edge of the city and just as quickly found himself sharing tankards of ale with a motley band of other, apparently like-minded, young ruffians.

It was only after they'd become entangled in a brawl and found themselves chased out of the city that he'd begun to question the wisdom of his choice of company. The exact details, though recent, were rather sketchy in his recollection. It had all happened so fast, and after so much ale.

Someone in his drinking circle of new acquaintances had taken offence at the song being sung by another patron, praising the virtues of Reikland at the expense of all other provinces, if he remembered correctly. That of course, had led to an argument, which had led to a fight, which had turned into an all-out melee in a matter of seconds.

It was only as they fled the scene, overwhelmed by the other patrons and chased even by the city guard, that Felix discovered the identity of his new friends. But by then it was too late to excuse himself from the company of the followers of the infamous local bandit, Therkold Red-Scar.

There was no way he could have foreseen that, having made their escape to a secluded cabin along an old road north-west of the city, Therkold and his men would soon turn on their new-found friend, robbing him of all that he carried and leaving him to die in the wild forest.

Though, as he re-traced the steps in his mind, Felix realized that it all looked quite obvious in hindsight.

Returning to his present predicament, he looked down once more. The hound was still there, but was no longer pacing beneath him. Instead it had begun to look elsewhere, its interest snared by something else, out in the forest shadows beyond the clearing. Its sinister tail elevated, curling up over its body as its ears pointed in an alert posture. Whether scent or sound, Felix did not know, but as he watched, the hound began to creep away, skulking out towards some other victim.

With nothing to eat, and nothing near enough to threaten him – for the moment – Felix Jaeger laid his head back against the moss-covered bark, and closed his eyes.

He didn't rest for long.

A commotion roused him only moments later. Groggy and still aching in every part of his body, Felix was a moment in responding. But as the noises grew and his senses returned, he scrambled to make up for the lapse.

Shouting dominated the cacophony, angry calls that echoed through the darkness of the forest. They were yet too far away to make out any words, but for the occasional curse or obscenity, hollered above the rest of the calls. A band of brigands perhaps – but men at least, from the sound of distant voices. Trouble to be sure; one never could be certain what kind of rogues were likely to emerge from the shadows of the deep woodlands.

The shouting swelled as the ground shivered and trembled, sending ripples through the trees and the bushes, dislodging rocks from the riverside sediment. Then came the howls. Fierce. Feral. *Familiar.*

And getting louder – closer, with every second. The hound was returning, and this time it was not alone.

His body pressed against the trunk of the great oak, Felix felt the vibrations. They were rhythmic, not the widespread rumble of a quake, but a repetitive, powerful pounding. When he looked out from his makeshift shelter, his senses were confirmed. The raging hound charged out once more, again emerging from the deep of the woods. Every footfall of the massive beast was like a hammer-strike upon the earth. The wild monster stomped its way right up to the edge of the river, stopping and letting loose a ferocious squeal as it dug its paws into the silt.

But this time, it was not concerned with Felix at all.

It was wounded now. Blood ran in streaks and splotches across its thorny, brown haunches. A dozen arrows and just as many spears pierced its midsection from every angle, lodged beside the spiny growths that jutted out from its hide. Blade-wounds had cleaved chunks of flesh from its shoulders and underbelly, exposing raw muscle and furry flaps of torn skin.

Whatever the beast had gone forth to find, it had met with more than mere prey. It was now the hunted. Felix smiled at the apparent reversal of fortune.

Only a few moments later, after the shouting had risen to a frenzied crescendo, a party of men came up in its tracks. They appeared to be mounted hunters, just as Felix had already guessed. But they were no common trackers or woodsmen. To a man, they were garbed in matching burgundy surcoats, stitched with a gold chevron and double-eagle herald, denoting some noble livery.

Most were armed to the teeth, wielding cumbersome blunderbusses, crossbows, spears and other ranged weapons. But Felix saw that all of them were dishevelled and spattered with mud, their horses panting from their own long pursuit.

As he remained in his secluded spot, careful not to reveal his presence, the hunters dismounted and re-grouped. They fanned out in a semi-circle fashion, closing off any avenue of escape for the wounded beast, its back against the forbidding rapids of the river. Although the men were clearly no strangers to violence, hulking, burly figures all, Felix noticed that they took their orders from the smallest of their number.

His horse, the finest of the group, took up a position behind the centre, and furthest from the hound. It was a regal black stallion, well-fed, meticulously groomed and saddled with an expensive gold-trimmed bridle. Its gear hauled several large packs. The other steeds in the party, however, were equipped differently. Obviously sturdy riding horses all, their accoutrements were just as well-crafted, but lacking such elaborate flourishes, and most showed signs of wear. The leather was broken-in and the shine was worn away from the iron buckles. The animals themselves were powerful geldings and most bore the scars of old wounds etched into their hides.

The young man's head was the only part of him exposed, and to Felix, his features marked him as a youth probably not much older than himself: pale-skinned, with close-cropped sable hair and a clean-shaven face. His features were sharp, with an angular chin and nose that lent him an almost royal bearing.

Slight of build and careful to remain at a distance, he wore none of the accoutrements of a noble house or of a fighting man. Instead, he was garbed in ill-fitting, voluminous dark robes that seemed to swim around him as he moved, and he carried only a scythe atop a long, crooked staff.

Despite that, he was undoubtedly in command of the armed men who stood before him. He directed the hunters with a combination of shouted orders and deliberate gestures. The last of them was a general order to finish the hunt. With perfect obedience, the men began to move forward, closing their ranks like a vice.

First came a new round of ranged attacks, a bank of arrows fired in a single rush. Then a hail of spears hurled at the beast, as the men moved ever nearer to close quarters. The gunners took aim next, setting their wide-barrelled firearms against their shoulders and firing off the blunderbusses in an ear-splitting spasm of smoke and flame. The beast staggered with every hit. Each new wound blasted out dark, foetid blood and chunks of mutant flesh from its hide. But despite its many injuries, the battered hound stood its ground, spitting acid-mucus from its snout in utter defiance.

The man in the black and violet robes called for a change of tactics. He ordered the force arrayed before him to shift into units. Breaking off into these smaller groups, two or three at a time, the hunters followed up their distance-strikes, racing in with slashing swords held high. They alternated angles at his behest, hitting the beast from the left, then from the right, keeping it moving and bewildered as he directed their movements with shouts from afar.

But still the hound rebuffed every new attack, squealing in misery and ever-swelling wrath as it swatted down a different hunter with each attempt to subdue it. Those not cut in half by its whirling, serrated tail or gored by its upturned fangs were knocked to the side, crushed by the stomping of its claw-like paws. Others were thrown into the air, landing unconscious all over the stony ground of the riverside outcropping.

Felix watched in horror as the entire hunting party was cut down and cast aside until only two remained standing. The first was a grizzled old veteran, barrel-chested with arms like tree trunks. Streaks of black ran like tiger stripes through his bushy grey beard. Behind him, the man who directed the contingent cowered in the shrinking shadow of his lone surviving soldier. They now faced a beast with darkness surging through its blood, raging in a vicious ardour of hunger and pain.

With a fierce canine snarl, the hound charged. The lone remaining warrior heaved a half-broken spear, but the wild-eyed monster brushed it aside like a twig. The tired fighter backed up as the beast closed in on him, and his own feet betrayed him. Tripping blindly on a broken stone, he fell backwards, leaving the hound a clear path to the defenceless young man in the strange robes.

For a long, tense moment, the horrific beast paused, as though unsure of which vulnerable prey to strike first. While the veteran struggled to come to his feet, disarmed and dangerously near to the hound, he appeared careful to make no sudden movements that might provoke it into a final assault.

As he did, the man in the robes behind was not so still. Instead, he lifted his scythe, waving it as he recited some incantation that drew the beast's crimson stare. For an instant, the young man seemed emboldened as a spell wove itself around his staff in a swirl of purple fog. He then swung his scythe, casting off a blade of sparkling mist. It sliced down upon the beast, breaking like sea-waves upon its hide.

For a brief moment, Felix thought the battle won, but he soon realised that his faith was misplaced. The hound was paralysed for but an instant before it shook off the mist-attack, snarling and coughing at the fading fog, though otherwise unharmed. The young spell-caster's eyes widened at the failure. His face suddenly panicked. Again he tried to launch an attack, rushing through the complex incantation once more. But his second salvo proved even weaker than the first. This one fizzled in mid-air before the mist-wave even reached the hound.

The beast growled and then roared, its attention now focused solely on the young man. Though the pale youth raised his scythe in some feeble attempt at defence, the summoned mist seemed to dissipate from around him as the hound closed in for the kill.

Though exhausted, starving and weary, Felix could not sit idle any longer. He leaped from his seclusion, shouting with his hoarse throat to draw the beast away from the unarmed man.

It proved effective enough. The young man managed to duck aside and the hound overran him, leaving his rear flanks exposed for an instant. It was a chance Felix did not waste. Snatching a sword from the hand of a fallen hunter, he leaped towards the beast that had sought to make a meal of him, intent on having a measure of revenge for himself.

Well-schooled in the formal art of the duel, but not a hunter by training, Felix slashed across the hound from behind, slowing its recovery enough to allow him to kick a second discarded blade to the fallen soldier. The grizzled veteran clambered to his feet as his youthful master once again ducked behind. Their partnership unspoken, but sealed nonetheless in that moment, the two men pressed the attack.

Felix moved with the speed and grace of a practiced hand, slipping away from the beast's mindless charges and slicing through its already broken hide with every turn. The other man proved his mettle as well, stabbing and hacking at every vulnerable part of the hound; a trained hunter who showed no fear in the face of a ferocious enemy.

In moments, the pair had the monster broken, exploiting its existing wounds and inflicting enough fresh ones to drain what remained of its strength. Yet the hound still did not relent. Huffing and wheezing, it lumbered towards Felix in a desperate final attack. Feinting and parrying in the manner of all expert duellists, Felix opened a gash across its soft throat, spilling black blood onto the mossy rocks and sending it down, its front legs crumpling beneath it.

Before he could shift his footing, the other man leaped. He jumped atop the hound, raised his blade to the sky then plunged it through the creature's skull, cracking it open and rendering the death-blow. The lifeless carcass quickly collapsed into a heap underneath him.

His bearded face and jerkin spattered with dark blood, the man looked up in triumph. He smiled with a mouth full of crooked teeth as the foul vapours from the beast's innards bathed him in death-steam.

'Ernst Erhard,' he said, by way of introduction. 'Sergeant-at-arms for Count Otto von Halkern.'

'But you may direct your queries to me,' the other man added, stepping up from behind now that the danger was past. 'I am Draeder von Halkern. Son of the aforementioned count.'

Felix responded with the polite half-bow of a gentleman, introducing himself.

'Felix Jaeger, and I am...'

The thought occurred to him in mid-sentence that he had not had cause to speak his own name in a formal introduction since his recent disgrace and expulsion, and he stopped short of using either his father's name or that of his former university.

'At your service, my lord,' he finally concluded.

3

They only rested for a moment, catching their breath beside the steaming, rancid carcass. There was no celebration. No cheers or songs of triumph. Only a hard-earned repose.

The pause allowed Felix the chance to take a longer look at the uncommon attire of his new-found companion. It was clear to him now that Draeder was not only the son of a nobleman, but was indeed a wizard of some sort.

In contrast to his apparent youth however, the silk and velvet robes he wore looked quite old, with frayed edges and dyes faded from the passing of years. Totems and talismans of a macabre character adorned his mantle and his sashes; white skull insignia decorated his pointed sleeves and his boot-length waistcoast. The gold trim on his breechcloth and vest were stitched with human bones woven into the worn fabric. Arcane runes ran in columns down the length of his cloak, but his cowl was absent of decoration, a hood of purest black that made the man's pallid complexion seem all the more stark.

What appeared to be an hourglass hung from his belt, the timepiece dangling as another man might wear a sword.

The only thing he carried that looked like a weapon was the reaper's scythe, a wicked, curved blade affixed atop a crooked wooden staff.

Their respite lasted only a few short minutes, just long enough for Erhard to recoup his strength before Draeder ordered that he return to his duties. Despite his obvious exhaustion, the grizzled sergeant obeyed with little more than a nod.

The first order of business was to see after the remainder of the von Halkern men. In this effort, Felix joined Erhard, if for no other reason than Draeder appeared oddly uninterested in doing so himself. Instead, the young man in the fine, old robes remained beside the beast whose demise he had done so little to assist, while Felix and Erhard went about tending to the fallen.

The sergeant was a stout man, not particularly tall but very heavily built, his massive arms and broad chest evident beneath his hauberk and mail. The hair was thinning atop his pate and his tanned face had the round fullness common to men at middle age. His nose was wide and crooked. It looked to have been broken more than once. The most recent injury had healed a permanent kink across the bridge. The dappled beard he wore covered most of the lower half of his face; even his mouth was hidden beneath his thick moustache.

His gear was well-worn and his hands were callused, the signs of a life spent hard at work. Half a dozen blades and two longswords were affixed to his belt, and even with his horse nearby he carried a pack at all times that would strain the spines of most other men. Though all appearances suggested him to be far more experienced and capable than Draeder, he nonetheless went about his work following the younger man's orders with never a complaint, even as his master appeared to sit idly by.

· Some of the men they were able to rouse without much effort, merely knocked unconscious by the force of the hound's blows but otherwise unharmed. Of the dozen who had entered the fray, they found four in reasonably good condition.

Three more of the men were still alive, but wounded and requiring aid. The best that could be offered was river water to wash out their lacerations and bandages from Erhard's pack to bind them. Felix could already tell that one of the men was hurt too badly to survive without more expert care. In its absence, he'd be dead within a day.

The other five men lay dead, their bloody, savaged bodies bearing witness to the brutality with which their lives had been taken: throats torn out, flesh ripped from their bones, disembowelled or bled nearly dry from too many wounds to count.

At Erhard's direction, the able-bodied four and Felix joined him in the task of corralling the horses and then interring their lost comrades in shallow, muddy graves along the edge of the treeline. As they finished that grim work, Felix accompanied the bearded old sergeant back to the river's edge, where Draeder remained beside his peculiar prize.

Erhard made a round of introductions once the group was re-gathered.

'Young Felix, these are some of the most trusted servants of House von Halkern,' Erhard said, presenting them as they stood, in a kind of informal muster. 'These first two dangerous looking men are Reinhard and Volker.'

The two acknowledged him with polite head nods. The hunters were obviously veterans, not as experienced as Erhard, but men who bore the scars of battle across their skin and their similarly well-worn gear. The first was thick-armed and compact, the second taller but no less hearty.

Erhard came next to the most fearsome looking of them all, a dark figure with a craggy face and a patch over one eye. He stared out from under a brooding mass of long, black hair and a forked beard. His brigandine and surcoat were stained with both blood and soot, and his gauntlets and pauldrons were studded with dozens of iron spikes.

The man beside him however, standing almost in the other's shadow, looked to be even younger than Felix. His hair was dark, but clipped much shorter than the others, and like Felix his beard had not yet grown in fully. His eyes were brighter and wider than the man next to him, although the two had very similar, narrow faces and resembled one another in a certain respect.

'These two are my twin attack dogs,' Erhard joked. 'The brothers, Strang and Torsten. Thick as thieves and utterly inseparable, try as we might. Strang is one of my most experienced men, and Torsten is the youngest of the company, but we expect great things from him given that he's learning from a sibling with such distinguished service.'

The smallest of the hunters, Torsten's frame was thinner than the rest and his armour bore none of the dents and stains that soiled that of his fellows. While his elder brother said nothing, his greeting was the most enthusiastic of them all.

'Good to have another hand at the ready,' he said, although the others grumbled a little at his eagerness.

A newly-built fire centered their makeshift camp, some distance from the festering hound carcass, in the relative safety of a larger stone outcropping along the riverside. The beast seemed like something akin to a trophy to the young wizard, and he at first appeared reluctant to leave its side. Indeed, he seemed enrapt by the fallen monster, admiring every warped corner of its flesh as a cultured patron might study a painting or sculpture.

Finally, having concluded his examination, Draeder von Halkern left the dead creature and joined his men around the fire, seating himself atop the highest rock in sight, as if assuming the mantle of a conquering hero. The sun had crept lower on the horizon by then, bringing a dour dusk to the party of men that was now halved in strength. As the brothers assumed sentry duty, Erhard retrieved a flagon from the pack he kept on his horse, and he proposed a solemn toast to those of their number who now lay beneath the ground.

When it was done, Draeder announced what they all suspected. They would make their camp there for the night, in the relative safety of the clearing among the rocky outcropping along the river.

'You're quite good with a blade,' Draeder said, as Felix sat down. 'Had you not joined our cause, we all might have fallen victim to this vile creature.'

Erhard passed the flagon to Felix, who took a long drink of the wine inside it, despite its spoiled, vinegary taste.

'I should be thanking *you*,' Felix answered. 'That beast nearly made a meal of me, before you came upon it.'

Draeder smiled.

'Indeed, that abomination has been rampaging throughout these lands for some time now, often straying into my father's estates nearby. Many folk living on my father's grounds found themselves facing the same difficulty as you. The rest were not so fortunate in the end, however,' he said.

'We've been chasing this hound for days, tracking it deep into the haunted woods,' Erhard added.

The old sergeant lit an ivory pipe and began puffing a sweet-smelling smoke.

'So it seems this was indeed something of a common cause for us both,' Felix replied.

'Well then, on behalf of House von Halkern, we are happy to have been of assistance to you,' Draeder said. 'That does beg the question however, of how you came to be all the way out here at all. These dark woods are haunted by many dangers. Monstrous beasts are not even the worst of them. It's no place for wandering alone, even for one so skilled with a sword as you appear to be.'

Felix grimaced, and he took a second, longer draught from the flagon.

'Let's simply say I have no one but myself to blame, and leave it at that,' he replied.

Draeder laughed.

'Forgive me, good sir,' Felix continued. 'But I must tell you, though I am not native to these lands, I recognise the name of your noble house. Yet something troubles me.'

'And what is that?'

Felix paused for a moment, unsure if his next words would bring offence. Given the circumstances, he finally decided the chances were unlikely.

'The fierce reputation of Count von Halkern is known even in my home in the north of the Empire,' he said. 'Yet I must ask, I know of only two sons born to the man. One is said to have been killed in battle, and of the other they say his combat prowess is the equal of his sire.'

Draeder smiled, flashing his teeth in a knowing, almost clever grin. He did not seem offended at all by Felix's insinuation.

'Forgiveness is not required, but you've not actually asked a question,' he said.

Felix nodded, grimaced a little as he took another drink, then put his manners aside entirely.

'You do not appear to be either a ghost... or a warrior,' he said.

Draeder laughed.

'Still not quite a question, but diplomatic nonetheless,' he said. 'You clearly come from a refined background.'

'My father is a merchant, fairly well off indeed,' Felix replied. 'Though we are somewhat... estranged at the moment.'

'Ah, then perhaps we have even more in common than either of us has yet realised,' Draeder replied. 'But you have been patient with me, and I have not yet answered your query. I am indeed the son of Count Otto von Halkern, and you are correct as to the identity of his first two sons.'

'His *first* two?'

'I am the *much less well known* third son of House von Halkern,' Draeder said. 'The one my father has never been proud to speak of, and so the one you – and most people – have never heard of.'

'And why is that?'

Draeder laughed.

'You've seen me facing a beast, would you ever mistake me for the son of a renowned warrior?'

'He disowned you because you couldn't fight?' Felix asked, making no attempt to disguise his amazement.

'Oh, I never said I have been disowned. At least not formally,' Draeder answered with a sly smirk.

Felix noticed Erhard grumbling a little at the suggestion. Felix downed more of the lousy wine.

'No, the situation that brings me to this place is quite a bit more complicated than that,' Draeder continued. 'But it is true, my father and I are not on the best of terms, and our falling out did indeed begin with my failure to take to the ways of swords and armour.

'I was always more given to the study of books than to blades, you see. That alone made me the least of my brothers in my father's eyes, as you can well imagine. Eventually I left his estates, looking for a way to regain my lost favour through other avenues. That led me to Altdorf, and to the Colleges of Magic.'

'So you *are* a wizard, then?' Felix asked. 'I had thought as much, given your attire. But I must admit, I have rarely been acquainted with users of magic. And your spell against the hound was somewhat…'

Erhard muttered something under his breath, which Felix couldn't quite make out. Draeder did seem to hear it though, and his face tensed. Felix thought he sensed a slightly defensive turn in his voice as he glanced over at his sergeant with a disapproving eye.

'There is quite a reasonable explanation for my *apparent* lapse against that beast,' he finally replied. 'Controlling the winds of magic is a complex and difficult endeavour, and one not easily understood by common folk. The hound was clearly more powerful than I expected. Had I known the extent of the dark influence upon it, of course I would have chosen a different approach.'

Draeder seemed to be very nearly boasting, despite what had seemed to Felix an obvious failure. Again, Felix noticed Erhard bristle in the dim, though the sergeant said nothing more.

'Should I face such a beast again,' Draeder continued, 'I promise you the correct spell would dispatch it with little effort. My studies with the Amethyst Order have taught me many ways of dealing with such abominations.'

Felix's face went blank. Without thinking, he recoiled, edging away from his new companions. He looked again at Draeder's attire, as if for the first time. The skulls. The bones woven through aged fabric. The sinister black runes.

'The Amethyst Order?' he said. 'You're a student of… death magic?'

Draeder nodded. He took a reassuring tone, clearly seeking to put Felix's trepidation to rest.

'Do not be frightened by that, my friend,' he said. 'Whatever you may have heard, the Amethyst Order is not a cabal of necromancers. The study of death is the study of change. Of endings and beginnings. Consider, for a moment, how can one truly understand life, if one does not also comprehend the mysteries of death?'

The explanation seemed to satisfy Felix. He reflected on the notion with a furrowed brow – and yet more wine.

'I had never viewed it in such a fashion, but there does seem to be some sense in that, I grant you,' he finally said. 'Did your father not see the wisdom in that philosophy?'

Draeder laughed.

'He might, if I ever actually converse with him over it. But as yet I have not done so. You see, I have only just recently returned from the Order after several years spent cloistered away, deep in study. Shortly after my return to my father's castle we heard tell of this hound terrorising the local villages.'

'The count dispatched us to see after the threat,' Erhard said. 'He ordered Draeder to lead the expedition. Though I had not laid eyes on him in several years, I knew him at first sight.'

'A challenge, no doubt. For that is the kind of man my father has always been. And so I joined my old comrades on the hunt, to perhaps prove to him that my training has been worth something after all,' Draeder said. 'In my father's estimation it is no source of pride to have a son studying something as cowardly as magic. But, now I can return to him having led the expedition that has slain a threat to his people. My sincere hope is that such a feat might erase some of the disappointment he feels at my course in life.'

Felix's face changed. His eyes brightened, and he lifted his head.

'Disappointment? You feel like you're an embarrassment to him?' he said. 'I know *exactly* how that feels, as it happens.'

Draeder von Halkern put down his flagon.

'Do you now?' he said, a curious and rather serious glint in his eye, despite the effects of the drink.

'As well as any man in the Empire, I'd bet,' Felix answered, rising to his feet. The wine was affecting him now, and he began to speak as though giving a half-drunken speech in a tavern. 'I know how it feels to do precisely what he says, just what he tells you that you have to do to satisfy honour and tradition. I know how it feels to try to do everything you can to live up to his exalted name – and to be kicked in the face for the effort.'

Draeder extended Felix a hand.

'You must tell me of this,' he said.

That was all the incentive Felix required.

'Three years ago he sent me off to study at university. I remember how his face beamed when I left, so proud of having a son enrolled at such an esteemed institution. We have had our disagreements since then, of course. My passion for poetry was not to his liking, for example. But we remained on good terms, until the events of this spring.'

'What was that?'

'Another student and I became embroiled in a dispute. The details are rather unimportant now; that it involved a woman and too much wine is all you need to know. This fellow crossed a line, widening the dispute to offer insult to my family and my heritage. It was an affront I could not tolerate. My entire life, I had been striving to earn the respect of my family, and this spoiled aristocrat spat upon my very name! I could not stand for it.'

His voice fell still for a moment. His eyes looked out to the shadows of the darkening woods, as if seeing the events unfold against that black tableau. His hand drifted to the hilt of his sword.

Draeder guessed what came next.

'You duelled,' he said. 'And given the skills I have witnessed you employ this day, I'd imagine this other man stood very little chance.'

'I've never been one to run from a fight. I gave him just what he deserved. I ran him through like a pig, in the main square, in sight of all,' Felix answered.

'And for that, they expelled you,' Draeder replied.

Felix nodded.

'Word made it to my father before my belongings were even collected. He cared nothing for the circumstances, nothing for our honour. He cared only that I was expelled. I had besmirched our good name, he wrote to me. And I am thus forbidden to return home.'

'Then we are kindred souls indeed,' Draeder said.

'You appear to have fared better in your exile than I,' Felix answered. 'Since my dismissal I have done nothing but wander. I have taken up with brigands and outlaws and many a wench, but most nights my aimless journeys have left me with without so much as a roof over my head. At this moment, I cannot even say with authority where in the Empire I am.'

'Then you are in luck, on both accounts,' Draeder replied.

'What do you mean?'

'For one, I can not only tell you exactly where you are, I can show you.'

He began to reach behind him, putting a hand into one of his travel bags. Erhard reached across to clutch at the young wizard's arm, lowering his voice to a whisper that Felix could not quite hear. But Draeder waved off his sergeant's hushed concerns with a dismissive gesture.

'This man saved your life, as well as mine,' he said. 'What else could he do to earn your trust?'

Erhard nodded, and returned to smoking his pipe.

From within a leather saddlebag that he had placed behind him, Draeder pulled out a thick scroll of parchment, brittle from age. He untied the scarlet bands holding the scroll closed, and then unfurled it very slowly, holding it with care, as one might handle a most treasured heirloom. The edges were uneven, ragged and frayed and charred in spots from some long-ago fire.

The inside surface of the vellum was stained with splotches and discolorations of every sort: blemishes from wine, soot and possibly even blood, all of which bespoke the document's great antiquity. The centre of it was covered in faded lines, sketching out a design in old black ink that Felix recognised as some kind of ancient cartography. Unlike the modern maps with which he was familiar though, this scroll was etched in a highly stylised script, with artfully drawn mountains and rivers alongside images of serpents and horrific daemons.

The map quite literally reeked of age. When Draeder rolled it open, a musty odour spilled out, along with hints of dust and mould.

The young wizard held it out for Felix to see. He pointed at a section near the bottom, just north of where two great rivers separated, near where a smaller third tributary split off from the eastern stream.

'The river that runs beside us is the Stir,' he said, then touching his finger to a single spot. 'We are roughly here, in southern Talabecland, on the edge of some of the deepest woods in the Great Forest.'

Felix studied the map. The geography looked vaguely familiar, but the notations and script were of a sort he had never seen before.

'That settles one question, then. What of the other?' he asked.

'As it happens, my journey back to Castle von Halkern was not quite a direct route. Instead, the mission upon which I was engaged when I returned to my father's house was only half-finished when this beast intruded upon our lands.'

'I don't understand,' Felix said.

'Quite simple, really,' Draeder answered. 'I was recently dispatched from the Amethyst Order on an official, albeit rather secret, errand, to seek an item of great value that my superiors believe is to be found to the north-west of here. That is the purpose of this map, in fact, for it is our guide through these most perilous of lands. I had at first intended to purchase the services of some hired swords to assist me in the effort, but having secured this contingent of my father's men, that soon became unnecessary.'

Draeder rolled the map scroll back up, returning it to his pack before clasping his hands, bringing them together under the wide sleeves of his wizard's robes. His eyes narrowed.

'However, you do seem to be just the sort I was looking for,' he continued. 'In fact, I'd say you more than passed the audition.'

Felix lifted his eyes at the suggestion.

'Are you offering me a job?' he asked. 'Doing what, exactly? My most recent attempts at employment have not gone as well as I would have hoped.'

Draeder smiled.

'We have just this evening buried five of my men, and three more nurse deep wounds. This quite obviously leaves my party rather short on manpower. I could use someone with your kind of skills. I have been promised by my superiors in Altdorf a chest of gold to be split among the mercenaries who accompany me. Quite a decent haul for a young man such as yourself,' he said.

'And just what is this mission that you're on?' Felix asked.

Draeder looked to his comrades, then leaned in closer, bringing his face so near to the campfire that his pale skin was cast in a deep, blood-red shade. His voice fell to a deliberate stage whisper.

'I'm searching for something that even my fellow wizards of the Amethyst Order have never seen, though they have sought it for centuries: a book that holds the key to unlocking the deepest mysteries of life and death,' he said.

'I must confess, I do not know much of magic at all, whether contained in books or otherwise,' Felix answered.

Again, Draeder took a measured tone in response.

'I assure you, Felix, my intentions are only the purest. What I told you of the College of Amethyst guides everything we do. The book I seek is a very old and very important text. It was compiled ages ago and it contains many of the oldest spells known, as well as some of the most powerful methods to harness even the most obscure currents of magic.'

'Unschooled as I am in such things, I will admit that it sounds like quite an important volume,' Felix said.

Draeder laughed.

'An uncommon gift for understatement! That could only come from a poet,' he joked. 'Indeed, my new friend, anyone who possesses a book such as the one we seek, if they also command a sufficient knowledge of the lore of death, would be the greatest of assets to the Empire.'

'How is that?'

'While many wizards do fight alongside the armies of the Empire, I am quite obviously unsuited for combat. But what if I were to stand with them in command of forces that could shield the armies from death itself? Imagine if all those who did take up arms in the Emperor's name were protected from the cold touch of mortality. Our warriors would never fall to the swords of the enemy. Our homeland would be made stronger than ever. Invincible, perhaps.'

Felix, whether because of the drink or the persuasive tone of Draeder von Halkern, could find no fault with the man's reasoning. The sound of adventure seemed to brighten his eyes and lift his already brimming spirits.

'Well then, consider me among your party,' he said. 'Never let it be said that I shy away from action.'

Erhard laughed, taking the flagon from him.

'Awfully quick to rush into things, aren't you?' the old sergeant said, his voice raspy and rough from a lifetime of pipe smoke.

Felix almost took offence at the suggestion, but elected to find humour in it.

'I suppose that's one of the reasons I'm here, come to think of it,' he replied.

'Well, you'd best be careful. One of these days, you might rush into something you can't get out of so easily,' Erhard said.

The eager young wizard, shrugged off his sergeant's worries.

'Don't listen to him, Felix. He's an old timer, his best days are behind him. The future belongs to men like us, men willing to venture into the unknown, to take risks. And even if the gold were not enough to persuade you, consider this… It could mean even more to you than money,' Draeder said.

'How do you reckon?' Felix asked.

'Think of how you would be viewed by your family if you were to assist me,' he continued. 'If you were to return not as a disgraced student, but as the hero who helped bring such power to the armies of the Empire? How could your family refuse a son celebrated by the Emperor himself?'

Felix pondered again, his mind now awash with suggestions, a flicker of lost hope and the thrill of both money and adventure quickening his pulse. He looked over to Erhard, then back to Draeder, before answering with the kind of certainty only known to the young – or the foolish.

'Like I said before, count me in,' he said.

4

The gloaming of dusk had faded, followed by the roaring scarlet of the campfire. So too had the conversation. Eventually the flagons had run dry, and the old familiar numbness had crept into every corner of his exhausted limbs. Then Felix Jaeger put aside the horrors and the mundane triumphs of his day. He found a spot to rest his tingling head, grabbed a ratty old cloak to wrap himself in, closed his eyes and finally slept.

What awakened him this time, many hours later in the darkest still of the night, was neither violence nor carnage. It was something far stranger, at once more wondrous and troubling than anything he could have imagined.

It was a voice. A hissing sort of call that seemed to cry out from a distance, as though half-buried in the whistling of the cold night wind. At first its silky, spectral whispers soothed him, rousing Felix gently from sleep. Just enough to announce their presence, without disturbing the peace of the evening.

He didn't even lift his head, merely listening to the strange echoes as they rose and fell in a soft and slinking symphony; the peculiar music of the haunted shadows.

But the echoes in the dim did not remain tranquil. What had been one voice soon doubled, and then doubled again, until the single tone had swelled into a ghostly chorus, bringing a multitude of eerie, rasping voices. Somehow, they all seemed to shout and whisper at once.

The change roused Felix ever more slightly. The numbing effect of the wine combined with the utter exhaustion in his bones had sent him into the deepest of slumbers, and he came around to no more than a muddled, groggy haze. The gauze of a deep repose veiled his eyes like a curtain of mist.

When he looked out, he saw only gloom. Black skies over dark woods. The fire was all but dead. Gone were the crimson and golden glimmers of the camp hearth. Only the milky shine of moonglows now lit the river banks.

The rest of the men huddled in their cloaks, nestled in every crevice and nook of the rocky outcropping. Most snored in a similarly deep slumber. Even Ernst Erhard lay still, wrapped in his woollen shroud beneath the great oak tree.

Draeder von Halkern, alone among them all, was not at rest.

Dressed in his capacious robes, black and violet and emblazoned with the grisly designs of the Amethyst Order, Draeder was outside of the camp. He'd hiked down-river, just barely in sight. He looked to be standing over the carcass of the hound, ministering like a priest over a coffin. The old leather-bound volume was open in front of him again, set upon the flank of the hound like a lectern. He seemed to be reading from the pages, as though speaking to an invisible congregation at an altar that stank of death. He chanted and made blessings, and each of them found its echo in those ghostly whispers that somehow carried on the wind itself.

Neither Draeder's words nor the answers spoken from the deep recesses of the night were in a language Felix understood. It wasn't even one he had ever heard spoken. The words were utterly foreign, almost serpentine in their rhythm, in the elegant way each syllable wove its way into the next. To the ear of a poet, attuned to the subtleties of tempo and meter, Draeder's recitations wove an intricate tapestry of voice, made all the more exotic by its inherently incomprehensible character.

For a long while, Felix watched. And he listened, unsure even if what he was witnessing in the hazy pre-dawn hours was real or merely a dream. He dared not disturb the strange rite, fearful of making so much as a whimper lest he draw the attention of the spirits spilling forth from the darkness. So he continued to watch, quiet and still – until, inexplicably, everything stopped.

After a long and twisted incantation, Draeder paused. He looked down over the length of the beast, as though studying it yet again. Its wounds already festered with pus and the first stages of decay, a process of putrefaction only accelerated by the dark forces that had corrupted its form.

Once his eye settled on a section of the beast-corpse, near the mane of thorny bristles that framed the hound's great head, he reached a hand into the folds of his mantle. From within the dark robes he drew a single-edged sword, more like a woodsman's machete than a fighting weapon. Draeder then knelt down above the hound carcass, and proceeded to hack the largest of the beast's tusks from its hide.

The carving was not easy, the tusk rooted deep in the hound's thick skin. Draeder chopped and sawed at it with more effort than Felix had witnessed him employ at any other task. When he finally managed to cut it free, he returned to his feet, clutching the severed tusk like a precious gem. Dark, congealed blood clung to his hands like clumps of black jelly and oil. It dripped down on to his sleeves and splattered across his pale face.

The student of the Amethyst College then picked up his scythe, which had rested next to him as he worked. Caring little for the stains on his hands, he wrapped a leather thong around the base of the tusk, then lashed it to the very crest of his reaper.

'And now the blood,' he announced, speaking to the winds again, but now in common Reikspiel. Once more he consulted the pages of the aged book in front of him. 'I summon the purple winds of Shyish. May the blood of the living and the blood of the dead now come together within its cold embrace.'

Draeder turned his blade. Slicing open the palm of his own hand, he let blood leak out from the slit in his pale flesh. It fell on the tusk, staining the ivory dark red and slathering the wild beast's horn atop his staff.

Another incantation followed. Once again, the winds answered. But this time, they did more than echo his inscrutable verses. Descending from the clouds, a column of mist centred around the blood-bathed tusk. Every word from Draeder's lips spurred the winds, turning them around the scythe.

As the air churned, the blood-speckled wind seemed to ignite, first spinning the red-purple tusk at the centre of its vortex, then sparking flames that soon overwhelmed the entire crest of the scythe-staff. Soon the glows merged into a single column of flickering purple flame, a ghostly violet fire that burned atop the tusk-crowned reaper.

The violet fire gave off no smoke. It made no sound. Its light was unreal, cold and unforgiving and unlike true fire.

Draeder lifted the flaming scythe into the sky, piercing the swirl of ghostly, whispering winds. The fire climbed, as though fuelled by the ghostly congress of purple wind. It grew and grew until the violet flame rose up into the clouds, roiling with dark lightning.

It all built to a crescendo, until the flame could ascend no more. Then the churning winds collapsed back down on the violet flame, sending a wave of phantom light surging across the outcropping. The whispering voices screamed in that moment, their ghostly calls fading away just as the flash of flame.

When it was done, all that remained was Draeder von Halkern, standing beside the hound corpse, holding his scythe in the air as he bathed beneath the purple flame. His eyes glowed with the same foul fire.

Felix clenched his muscles, too frightened to move. He squeezed his eyes shut, but despite his exhaustion, he barely slept at all the rest of the night.

5

When the men began to stir just after dawn, Felix remained in his place. He waited until all the others had arisen before getting himself up. When he saw Draeder standing upon the edge of the river with his scythe in hand, he couldn't help but stare. He puzzled over the events of the past night, questioning his own perceptions.

If it had been a dream, then it was the most vivid of his life. If it had been real, then Draeder von Halkern was indeed something more than the ineffectual young wizard he'd saved from the jaws of a rabid hound.

In the light of day, there was no hint of the purple flame, and the winds were calm. But when Felix looked closer, he noticed that atop Draeder's reaper-blade there was indeed a single bloody tusk affixed to the staff. When the wizard turned in his direction, and for an instant caught him staring, Felix quickly looked away.

A chill ran through him.

For close to an hour the men gathered up their things in near silence, struck camp and prepared to move out. None of them even seemed to know of it, unless all of them held their tongues out of some measure of fear, as Felix himself did. He was not inclined to broach the subject, either way.

Two of the wounded had died over the night, and the matter of their final rites brought the first real discussion of the day. Draeder appeared anxious to move on, and initially ordered them left where they lay. When that met with some protest from Erhard, he further suggested dumping their bodies in the river. Again, Erhard argued with his master, until he finally relented.

As the others assisted the last surviving wounded man, Walder, to make ready for travel, Felix helped to bury the dead once again. He and Erhard carried one of the bodies out to the edge of the woods, digging a shallow grave in the wet ground just as they'd done the day before. But this time, when Felix put down his spade and lifted the body to lower it into the dirt, Erhard stopped him. Instead, the old sergeant knelt down before his fallen comrade.

Felix at first assumed it was a moment of solemnity, a final farewell to a lost friend. He bowed his head in a show of sympathy, but Erhard soon disabused him of such sentimental notions.

The veteran began pulling off the dead soldier's regalia, first his hooded cloak, surcoat and belt, before unstrapping his iron gauntlets and studded leather jerkin. He looked up at Felix with a wry grin.

'Perhaps you'd be willing to lend a hand,' he said, 'Given that this is for your benefit.'

Felix knelt down too, and Erhard passed him the gauntlets and sword belt from the dead man.

'Put on as much as you can, whatever fits is now yours.'

'I'm not sure I feel right taking your dead friend's gear,' Felix said.

'Where we're going, you'll need every bit of it. Trust me, it does him no good to hold on to anything now.'

Erhard made sure to take every bit of useful material, including a fine pair of woodsman's boots, several knives, some armour and a chainmail shirt. Felix found that most of it did fit him, and the rest required only a few adjustments.

'I admire what you did back there,' he said, as he donned the dead man's attire.

Erhard seemed confused by the comment.

'What's that, exactly?'

'You challenged Draeder, in front of the men, no less,' Felix said. 'He is your lord, is he not?'

Erhard nodded, but with a shifting smile that hinted at sarcasm, if not outright resentment.

'He is the son of my lord,' he said. 'I indulge him as part of my service to his father, and because I have always done as much for him.'

'So you've known the man a long while?'

'Since he was a boy,' Erhard replied. 'I've served in his father's livery for more than twenty years now.'

'You watched him grow up then?'

Erhard scoffed a bit. He looked up from the dour task of grave-digging to cast an eye at Draeder, standing at a distance with his head held high along the riverside.

'I watched him get older, let me say that,' he answered. 'None of us were certain if he would ever *grow up*.'

'He seems to have done quite well for himself though,' Felix answered. 'Sent forth on this official mission by one of the Colleges of Magic.'

Erhard came to his feet, stuck his shovel into the mud and rested his hands atop the shaft.

'Just between you and I,' he continued, in a lower voice. 'We were all more than a little surprised when he returned to these lands recently, fully attired in the mantle of the Amethyst wizards.'

Felix was intrigued, if not a bit indignant.

'Just like his father, you expected him to fail as well?'

Erhard shook his head.

'I've probably said too much already.'

Felix put a hand on his shoulder.

'If I'm to travel with your party into these haunted woods, and to take up arms with you again, do I not deserve to know at least a little of what you do?'

Erhard agreed.

'There's nothing to tell, really,' he said. 'I'll only say that... Draeder was simply never the type to follow through with anything. If there was an easy road, you could always count on him to take it.'

'He cheated?'

'He did whatever he needed to do, whatever the situation required to accomplish what he wanted – usually with the least amount of effort. So you can understand that it came as a bit of a shock to me when, after vanishing with no word for several years, he returned not as an acolyte or an apprentice, but having claimed the hard-earned title of wizard.'

'He does indeed appear to command the winds of magic, does he not?' Felix said.

Erhard grimaced.

'Just barely, at times,' he said, though he seemed to think better of his insult only a moment later. 'But who am I to judge? I've never been fond of mages.'

'Nor I,' Felix said. 'At least thus far.'

They didn't set off on the trail until mid-morning. But their path soon took them from the banks of the river to the perfectly-fitted masonry of an ancient road. Felix recognized it, for it was the very same road his companions from Wurtbad had taken on their exit from the city. The weathered paving stones seemed to have endured for ages, scarred with the ruts and grooves worn down by centuries of wagon traffic. While choked with weeds and overgrowth, it remained as a silent echo of days past, fading yet defiant of the wilderness into which it led.

'This road goes all the way to Talabheim,' Draeder said, reading from the map, though he seemed to have memorised the details. 'We'll follow it as far as the third marker – that's as near to the Barren Hills as most ever go. After that, we've only this map to guide our way.'

Felix looked out over the massive expanse that lay ahead of them from the high ground where the old road crested atop a hill. The forest stretched out as far as he could see, a vast expanse of dense, old trees clustered so thick that the vista blended into an ocean of leaves and shadows. He breathed a little deeper as he surveyed the massive, perilous wilds. He felt his heart begin to pound.

The Great Forest was notorious. Felix couldn't help but wonder what horrors lurked beneath that dark canopy. It was said to harbour all manner of beasts and rogues, unspeakable and unimaginable.

Draeder charted their course, following landmarks etched in faded markings on the parchment map and using the ancient road as a reference. His companions acted as something of a guard, two riding on each side of him and with Ernst Erhard bringing up the rear on his old spotted gelding.

Just before midday, Draeder fell back from the lead, to ride beside Felix, who had also taken the horse of one of the fallen men. He was now rid of his ruined university attire, garbed more like a woodland tracker or huntsman. He wore a heavy woollen cloak, the hood lowered for travel and clasped at the neck with a brass amulet. A new sword hung at his side, a bandolier of daggers was slung over his iron-studded leather jerkin, and he wore a knife on the side of each boot. Everything stank of sweat and grime, but after a short while, he found the foul odours no longer bothered him, for he was as filthy and unwashed as the dead man whose clothes he now wore anyway.

He had not taken the fallen soldier's livery-emblazoned coat however, setting him apart from the other men in the party. It was this decision that he expected Draeder to mention when the wizard came up beside him, looking him over in his new attire. Instead, he asked something completely unexpected.

'So you're a poet?' Draeder asked, very much out of the blue.

'I'm a student of verse, yes,' Felix answered.

'You recite it, but you don't create it?'

'Oh I do, believe me. It's just that my own efforts at composition have yet to find the audience they deserve,' Felix answered. 'But that is why we study the works of those who have gone before, is it not? To build upon their art and to take it somewhere it has not yet been?'

'Indeed it is,' Draeder answered. 'I happen to know precisely how it feels to be unappreciated in one's true calling. And I am something of a student of the written word myself, in a manner of speaking.'

'How so?'

'The incantations and rites of my schooling are very much like your poems, I imagine,' Draeder said. 'In fact, many of them possess a quality not unlike the rhythm of good verse. That is how one commits so many of them to memory, after all.'

Felix looked over at him, and found Draeder staring back at him with a knowing, almost suspect glare. He suddenly realised that the young wizard might be referring to the ritual he had witnessed the night before, though he was still quite unsure if that was something he was not supposed to have seen. He elected to remain stoic.

'I had never thought to make such a comparison,' Felix said. 'Though I must confess, I am rather unfamiliar with any rites of magic or spell-craft, having never seen them employed for myself.'

He looked back at Draeder with those words, and the

wizard's face changed the moment he said them. His glare softened. He nodded once to Felix; an acknowledgement perhaps of some greater level of trust just now established, or else suspicion erased. It put Felix at ease, at least for a while.

They came to a peculiar landmark on their third day trekking along the ancient road, a huge rocky spire that rose up from the undergrowth with three points of smooth granite. It looked vaguely like a dragon, stretching its wings as it took flight.

Draeder brought their party to a halt. He flashed the map so that Felix could see it, pointing to an inscription. Though Felix could not read the runes, he recognised the drawing that accompanied them – a dragon taking flight.

The men gathered round in a circle of horses at his behest.

'Men of House von Halkern,' he began. 'Here we leave the road behind, and we begin our true journey. Beyond this point no woodsmen dare venture. No trails set down by men penetrate this most thickly-grown wilderness. And so it is time to tell you what lies ahead.

'My colleagues of the Amethyst Order have long laboured in the study of reams of ancient manuscripts. They've spent years searching for clues to a quest that has lasted generations. Recent discoveries have led my superiors to one inescapable conclusion: the lost volume called the Book of Ashur rests in a secluded tower deep in the hidden mists of this very forest, north-west of our present location, in a lost valley of the Barren Hills,' Draeder said.

'The Barren Hills?' Felix asked. 'Is that land not cursed?'

'According to some, but the rumours and stories of it are mostly wild tales and outright myth,' Draeder said, appearing more confident than his comrades.

'That depends on who you ask,' Erhard added, echoing the palpable unease that had come over the rest of the men. 'There are those who live amongst these woods who would tell you that the Chaos moon spat upon these lands many years ago, and its noxious spittle turned the once-green hills foul. Most everything alive was killed in a single night, and what little did survive *was changed*.'

'Changed how?' Felix asked, though he suspected he knew the answer.

'It was said that everything touched by that poison moon's light grew warped and twisted, plants and animals alike, bent and perverted in ways too horrible to relate,' Erhard said.

'But I had always heard that the elector count's men swept through the ruined hill country, seeking to eradicate the vile mutants. Did they not?' Torsten asked.

'Indeed they tried, but no force of men could ever hope to clear an area this large of so many horrors. No doubt many escaped their blades, and others lurk in the caves and shadowed thickets of the deep woods to this very day,' Erhard replied.

'That's comforting,' Felix added.

'How, may I ask, did this book of yours come to be in such a cursed place to begin with?' Erhard asked, turning back to Draeder.

The young wizard seemed perturbed by the question. He answered with a sour expression that hinted he was losing his patience.

'The valley we seek, deep in the Barren Hills, was once the home of a reclusive necromancer,' he said.

The men stammered, muttering to each other in hushed tones. The suggestion alone appeared to make them all plainly uncomfortable, agitated in a way uncommon among such imperturbable fighting men.

Even Erhard, as stalwart a soldier as Felix had ever met, seemed suddenly apprehensive. He furrowed his brow and shook his head, stepping back a pace in unconscious solidarity with his nervous men.

'A necromancer?' Felix asked, his voice lowered as though the word itself was a curse to even utter. 'You told us this was about the "nobility of death magic", not the work of some evil sorcerer.'

The men echoed his complaint, their muffled protests breaking out into open grumbling. Draeder lifted his arms in response, waving at his soldiers in a gesture of reassurance. The hard-edged lines of his face softened, as if to stress his own, more decent motives. But Felix sensed something else in that instant, a look in the young nobleman's eyes that, while indeed more gentle, still betrayed a kind of arrogance. He looked for a moment as if he were about to speak to children, pitying them for their naïve folly and proud of his own superior wisdom.

'My friends,' he began. 'You are wise to be concerned, of course. These are dangerous lands into which we venture, and I would never proceed if I did not have the greatest of faith in the determination and the strength of the men accompanying me.'

'Admirable, young master,' Erhard replied. 'But such qualities will take us only so far in the face of a rogue of the kind you describe.'

'You must permit me to finish, for while the mission upon which we act is fraught with peril, I can bring you the greatest of assurances from the Amethyst Order itself that the corrupt conjurer has long since perished. My colleagues in Altdorf are convinced he wasted away years ago, withered into nothing at the end of a vain and failed quest to achieve eternal life.'

'That may be, but it does not change the fact that you have set us on a course in pursuit of an item that was once employed by an evil magician, to the foulest of purposes, I can only imagine,' Felix said.

Draeder again looked at him with a condescending gaze.

'My friend, do not fall into the trap of judging the object by the character of the man who wields it,' he said. Then he pointed at the sword resting by Felix's side. 'Should your blade fall into the hands of an evil man, it would no doubt be put to evil ends. That would not render your sword an instrument to be loathed in and of itself.'

Felix nodded, forced to admit that he agreed.

'The book we seek is no different,' Draeder continued. 'It is true, it was stolen ages ago and set to foul purposes by a cruel and wicked man, but it need not be so. The wisdom it contains is just as capable of serving the Empire as harming it.'

'I see the wisdom in that,' Felix conceded.

Erhard stepped up again, clearing his throat as if to draw all attention to himself.

'That may all be the case,' he said, signalling at least a vestige of incredulity. 'But should my men be asked to ride out into the lands of a sinister villain, even one long dead, we must know precisely what it is we are about to face.'

'Your men?' Draeder replied. 'These are servants of House von Halkern all, including yourself, as if I needed to remind you.'

Erhard growled.

'We entered this forest as servants of your father, it's true. And we continued on at your behest for that reason, but the moment you purchased our further services with the promise of gold, you took us beyond the limits of our fealty,' the old sergeant said. 'Make no mistake, these boys may serve your house, but they serve *with me*. Servants to your noble name they are, but these men are like my own family. I will not see them ride off unaware of exactly what they face.'

Draeder lowered his hands. He sighed as if exasperated, but seemed persuaded nonetheless. The tone of his voice changed from that of a noble rallying his troops to a man merely telling a story.

'The man's name was Skethris, and he was a master of dark magic so powerful his like has rarely been seen beyond the tombs of distant Khemri,' he said. 'No one living today knows from whence he came or for how long he walked the earth, all we can say is that the rumours were many and varied.'

'What *do* you know?' Felix asked.

'The best of the tales are sketchy and of questionable provenance, but I believe this much about him: he began as we are, a simple man, who set about searching for the secrets of this world. Only his path led him astray.

'Some say he was a rogue magic user even then, a hedge wizard in the days before the founding of the Colleges of Magic. He pursued the study of the mystical winds in secret, travelling from city to city, following whispers and legends of secluded masters. He learned from them all, taking whatever elements they could offer and adding them to a growing repertoire of spells and incantations.

'But always he sought more. More knowledge, more skill and more power. Eventually, he grew obsessed with seeking the one thing that no amount of fortune or facility can bring – more time. Thus did he embark on a quest to prolong his life, to continue learning and accumulating knowledge. It is possible that he began with the best of intentions; we will never know now. But in the end, it corrupted him.'

'How so?' Felix asked.

'Some say he ventured to the distant, sun-scorched Land of the Dead to steal the secrets of the Tomb Kings, others that he murdered wizards in an attempt to take by force the secrets they refused to teach him. It was even reported that he sought out the tutelage of the living dead, a vampire lord, to reveal to him the mysteries of controlling death – and ultimately defying it.

'Perhaps all of those legends are true, perhaps none. What we do know, however, is that he extended his reach deep into the realms of shadow, and the foul things he drew forth prolonged his life for centuries, in the least.'

'They say such men are driven mad by the darkness,' Erhard said, a haunted look falling over his eyes.

'And so it must have been for Skethris,' Draeder answered. 'He would have peered longer and deeper into the haunted places than almost any other man I've heard of. No one can do so without suffering ill effects. Whatever power he obtained would have been enormous, but the cost even greater.'

Draeder stepped away from them, staring off into the sky with an almost dream-like gaze.

'I can see it now... Currents of dark magic filled his body, flowing through his blood like the most terrible, *wonderful* poison,' he said, raising his arms for effect.

Felix looked to Erhard then, for they both saw a change in Draeder as he continued. The more hypnotic his words became, the less frightened his voice grew, until the young wizard almost sounded admiring – even envious. It began to seem as though he was doing more than simply relating a history, more than merely telling a story. He seemed to be enjoying it. His voice lowered and his pace quickened, as if he were seeing the macabre events he could not possibly have witnessed.

'The dark magic corroded his body, forcing him to delve deeper and into ever more foul reaches to preserve his flesh, to stave off the decay that only grew worse with every passing year,' he continued, stretching out his own arms either to give effect to his words, or else imagining himself performing the acts he described with such careful, intimate detail.

'Just as his body failed him then, so too did his mind. The things he witnessed beyond the veil haunted him, driving him past the brink of madness until he fell into a permanent nightmare from which he could never awaken.'

Felix and Erhard looked to each other, and then back to Draeder, momentarily lost in his own rambling story-telling. He did not seem inclined to continue.

'And then what?' Felix prodded.

Draeder was a moment in responding, staring off into the distance a while longer. When he did finally turn back, his cadence had returned to normal.

'Eventually, I imagine he could not sustain himself any longer, and that was how he passed finally out of existence, fading into the shadows he had so long struggled to master,' he said. 'No one really knows, truth be told.'

'How do you know the book is still there, if the necromancer himself has indeed passed away?' Torsten asked.

'There can be no doubt that Skethris had the book. No one has seen or heard from him in decades. He is surely long dead by now,' he answered. 'It is rumoured that other expeditions have ventured into these wilds before, seeking the same thing we do. But the book has never been seen anywhere else in all that time, even though possessing it would bestow enormous power upon whoever owned it. The only conclusion is that none of them returned.

'Thus, the reasonable place to look is where the trail ends. The book is there, of that I have no doubt,' Draeder said.

'If no one has *returned* alive, then that means others have ventured into this cursed land and failed in the same endeavour you have now set us upon,' Felix said. 'How exactly do you propose to spare us the same fate?'

Draeder smiled. He lifted his glowing, flaming scythe overhead. Its peculiar purple light fell on them like cold rain.

'I have here fused the dark energy that pervaded the flesh of that mutant hound with the winds of Shyish, the source of all Amethyst magic. In so doing, I have woven this veil of violet light, whose source is the wild energy of the forest itself. It will help protect us from the savage horrors that lurk in the deep of the cursed land.'

All of them stepped closer together, drenched in the light of the magical purple flame. Draeder rolled up the map and handed it to Erhard. Then he held up his scythe and announced what they all knew.

'Now we are prepared to approach the Valley of Death.'

Excerpt, Journal of Felix Jaeger – Unpublished, undated

Our journey has been long, these past several months. Beset by dangers and hazards each and every day, I fear I have not had the occasion to make entry in this journal as often as I might otherwise have done. Having now come upon the best shelter we've found in weeks, I finally have the opportunity to once again open these pages that I might chronicle at least some of the perils we have survived of late.

Since we left behind the ancient road, the path charted upon Draeder von Halkern's map has led us on a winding route, ever deeper into the dim reaches of the Great Forest, a dark and thickly grown wilderness where a foul mist lies upon the land at every hour and currents of polluted air move with every shifting of the wind.

Unspeakable vermin have been our constant companions, creeping out from infested groves of twisted, unnatural trees and swooping down to sting at us from above. The pestilent under-growth swarms with carnivorous plants that slither thorny vines through the mud, reaching out to strike at every turn.

On occasion, the light of the purple flame has indeed protected us from a cruel and grisly fate, just as Draeder promised. The eerie fire hid us from both a horde of immense spiders and two marauding packs of rabid tuskgors. But more often than not, the conjured flame was no guarantee of safe passage. On more than one occasion over these trying, difficult months, we have been forced to fight for our very survival amidst this fierce and terrible wilderness.

A vicious tribe of forest goblins nearly overwhelmed us a while back, after we charted what now appears to have been an unwise shortcut around a smouldering crater. Erhard and I both took the heads of more than a dozen each, while the brothers Strang and Torsten proved their worth as well, battling bravely alongside one another in a long and desperate fight, a struggle that claimed the lives of two of our number: both Reinhard and Volker.

Less than a week later we were forced into a similarly narrow escape upon trespassing over the sacred burial lands of a troll clan. That misstep had us all imprisoned for days in a deep pit of the trolls' camp, and had brought one more of our men to the premature end of his journey, Walder having been roasted upon a spit and eaten by the barbaric creatures. We could hear his horrific screams for hours as the contemptible creatures burned him alive, and I must truly confess that it was perhaps both the longest and the worst single night of my entire life.

I managed to trick the dullest of the trolls into releasing me from the vile pit the following morning. That was a mistake that Strang and Torsten made the troll pay for with his life, as the rest of us regained our horses and rode away.

I fear the dreams of gold are fading in the minds of my companions as our trek begins to keep us in this horrid realm far longer than any of us expected. The brothers have already started to grumble. Strang, as laconic a soldier as there is, yet confines his complaints to his superior, Erhard. Torsten, however, less experienced and disciplined than his elder sibling, has begun to talk openly of abandoning the adventure altogether.

As dusk fell yesterday evening, we could detect a change in the terrain. The ground has grown hilly and rocky. Draeder now seems moved by some new urgency.

I await the sunrise yet again. Of what horrors may yet lurk ahead, I cannot even begin to guess.

6

For several days they trekked uphill, their horses slowed by the increasingly difficult ground they were forced to negotiate as the Great Forest became even more rolling and strewn with rocks. A deeper chill seemed to fill the air as they moved higher in elevation, condensing into a thick mist as they continued under the ever-present shadows of tall, ancient trees and vermin-haunted thickets.

The treeline seemed to falter however, when they came to the sight of a long ridge above them. The dense growth that had long surrounded them faded into scattered copses of oaks and lonely pines across the length of the long slope that led up to the bare, stony rise.

Beyond it, the forest came to an abrupt end. What lay ahead was an altogether different landscape, unlike anything they'd witnessed on their journey. A bleak expanse of scrub brush and exposed rock.

'Finally… the Barren Hills,' Draeder announced, as they all came over the ridge to survey the lands before them.

Slate grey and the pale yellow of withered grass dominated the vista in every direction. The terrain was fractured and uneven, dented by deep swales and scattered with jagged, stony outcroppings that reached up into a fog of low-hanging clouds. A cruel stink hung over the empty wasteland, the odour of stagnant marsh water and hints of sulphur fumes.

Draeder alone among them seemed encouraged by the frightful vista, and it spurred him forward with a renewed purpose, his eyes alternating between the map and the seemingly forsaken lands. He rode out ahead of the party, taking his horse down a precarious slope and then up along the edge of a barrel-shaped rock mound. For a moment, he looked out in each direction, searching for a landmark or some other point of reference on his map.

When the rest of the riders caught up to him, he turned and pointed towards another hillock half-shrouded in the mist. They once again followed, only to repeat the same routine yet again, and then a third and fourth time until their passage through the foggy barrens seemed to stretch on for hours.

Overhead, massive carrion birds appeared out of the haze. The unnaturally large crows squealed and circled, five or ten at a time. For a long while, the foul scavengers stalked the party from the air, keeping pace with them as they went, always present, but never close enough to reach.

Paying the birds little attention, Draeder once again rode out ahead of them, his eyes snared by some formation in the hazy distance. At Erhard's direction, Strang and Torsten took to the gallop behind him, leaving Felix with him, behind at the rearguard.

'Would it be impertinent to suggest that we may be lost?' Felix asked, as they watched the trio charge into the fog beyond.

Erhard grunted.

'It would be,' he said. Then his gruff, craggy face widened in a broad smile as he continued. 'But that wouldn't make you wrong.'

Felix laughed. As rough a man as he was, Erhard had become something of a mentor to him over the long months of their journey. The old sergeant may not have been of high birth, but it was clear that he had earned his position as a leader of men.

'You don't trust him, do you?' Felix said. 'I wouldn't mention it in general company, but given our present circumstances, I may not have another opportunity.'

Erhard looked out, first to Draeder galloping out once again in the distance, then back to Felix. Again, he answered in the simple, direct manner to which Felix had become accustomed.

'I do not,' he said.

Although it confirmed his suspicions, hearing the old sergeant speak them so plainly struck Felix.

'I'm not certain I ever have, truth be told,' Erhard continued. 'But even less so now.'

'Why is that?'

'Perhaps it would be better that I speak no more of this,' Erhard said. 'I know that you look up to him, that you see something of yourself in Draeder, in your shared background.'

Felix agreed, but pressed the conversation regardless.

'I do respect what he's done, given his circumstances,' Felix said. 'I understand what it's like to be cast aside by a prominent family. But I've also seen how you carry yourself these past months. You care about your men and you're as fine a solider as I've ever known.'

Erhard nodded.

'Thank you, young sir,' he said.

'So then you must tell me, as we're moving ever deeper into this strange wilderness at Draeder's behest – you have known the man far longer than I – what troubles you?'

'You've seen what I've seen, have you not?' Erhard replied. 'I trust a man I can count on. A man who can handle a sword, as you can. Some of Draeder's spell-casting works, some of it does not. Would you call that reliable?'

'His magic does seem rather... erratic,' Felix said, relieved that he was able to express his own concerns openly for the first time.

'That's charitable,' Erhard replied. 'At times his conjuring has been quite useless indeed. I don't trust wizards as a rule, but one who cannot be counted on in battle is one I will never put my faith in.'

'It is strange, as you say. He wears the weathered robes of an old, wise wizard,' Felix replied. 'I know very little of the Colleges of Magic, but I had always heard that mages of that sort engaged in long study, for decades sometimes, before they attained the mantle of a fully-fledged wizard.'

'So had I,' Erhard answered. 'But Draeder was gone from his father's estate for no more than three years before he returned, clothed in the way you see him now, in the age-worn regalia of an old adept.'

'And dispatched on a mission of some importance by his superiors, no less,' Felix said. 'Do you suspect he's lying?'

The question seemed to make Erhard uncomfortable. He winced as he answered, clearly reluctant to continue the exchange.

'I can't say I suspect anything in particular,' Erhard said. 'Though in my experience, I've found it better to suspect *everything*. That's the reason I've lived this long.'

Felix smiled. He was about to reply, when a scream interrupted.

Both men arched up in their saddles. The rest of their party had just vanished in the mist ahead of them, obscured by a bank of dense fog that had settled over a low swale. Another followed. The first was a cry of pain. The second was a call of battle.

Felix noticed the crows were gone from overhead. Neither man said a word. They simply charged.

Galloping headlong into the low terrain, they soon found themselves swallowed up by the cold, heavy mist. The hooves of their horses splashed through a boggy flat of stagnant, muddy water. The fog was so thick at the bottom of the marshy vale that Felix and Erhard could barely see an arm's length in front of them.

That was when they heard the terrible squeals close in from above.

The black birds strafed them, diving down out of the thick clouds and then retreating back into the grey. Talons clutched at them, tearing at their horses and ripping across their shoulders. Wings flapped and soared in every direction as the screeching swelled into a rage.

Felix swung his sword wildly overhead, trying to fight through the haze to see what he was striking as he struggled to beat back the attackers from above. Blood splattered into his eyes. Black feathers, wet with slime and stinking of carrion, fell in every direction.

Their forward gallop brought Felix and Erhard together with the others, all of them swarmed by the vicious birds.

'Ride hard, men!' Erhard shouted through the mist. 'Climb the slopes out of this blasted marsh or we'll never see the sun again!'

Felix kicked his boots into the side of his mount, joining the others in a hard, blind gallop forward. The raven swarm did not relent. Even as they urged their horses on, the birds continued their onslaught.

But with the forced ride, the horses quickly found a slope on the far end of the swale, bringing them all up to a crest where the fog cleared. Out of the mist and finally able to see again, the men swatted down the ravens who remained, slashing and chopping any who swept low enough to reach.

When it was over, the remains of the bird swarm lay scattered in every direction, leaving them at the centre of a field of blood and butchered ravens.

'I thought those were supposed to be scavengers, just carrion birds,' Felix said, panting as he fought to catch his breath.

Draeder, however, regarded the carnage with an almost solemn eye, looking over the messy, scattered remains of the slain animals with a kind of reverence.

'In the Barren Hills, you'll find that very little is what you would expect,' he said.

7

Draeder once again studied the vista before them. He scanned the map, looked at the fields of seemingly featureless stone and scrub weeds, and pointed them towards a rounded barrow hill just a short ride off. Once they arrived at the tumulus, a low and unremarkable mound, he quite unexpectedly issued an order that none of them wanted to hear.

'We'll set up camp here for the evening,' he declared.

The men bristled, and Erhard spoke up for them.

'We have several hours of daylight left, and given what we've just gone through, we're all restless to get on with this journey. Let us press on at least 'til nightfall,' the old sergeant said.

Draeder shook his head, flashing his hand with the same dismissive wave he had so often used to silence his long-serving aide-de-camp. This time, however, he found the gesture met with some resistance.

'We should keep moving ahead,' Erhard said, edging his horse near enough to grab Draeder by the arm. 'Unless you have lost your way.'

The affront to his authority drew a cold stare from the young wizard.

'We have not gone astray and I have never taken orders from you, old man,' he said. 'I certainly have no intention of starting now.'

Erhard would not relent.

'We've all sacrificed for this mission of yours,' he said. 'Most of my men have been lost already, every one of them claimed by a death I would not wish upon my enemies. Yet we have seen nothing to make us believe we are any closer to our goal.'

'Is this some rebellion you've concocted?' Draeder replied. 'Are you now to mutiny against me like traitorous sailors upon a lost ship – and after my magic has protected you for this entire way?'

Felix could feel the tension. It had been simmering between them all for weeks. While Draeder's claim of magical prowess was rather an exaggeration and Erhard was now verging on outright breach of his oath of fealty, Felix nonetheless tried to manoeuvre his horse between the two in an effort to defuse the situation.

'An explanation might go further than you think,' he said to Draeder, attempting to mediate. 'Perhaps Ernst is out of line, but even still, he is right. We've all suffered on this trek and in so doing we have all demonstrated our loyalty as well. I'm sure I speak for every one of us in saying that if we are indeed finally close to the end, then you must tell us *why* we do not proceed.'

Draeder edged his mount back. He straightened his robes and lifted his chin.

'I do not *need* to answer to anyone,' he said. 'But if it will placate you, then I will indeed choose to tell you what I know that you do not.'

Felix nodded, though he could see that Erhard remained unconvinced. Draeder, however, was a moment in answering, as though he actually had no explanation at the ready, despite his boasting. Finally, after a long and uncomfortable pause, he replied with a rambling narration.

'We are in fact very close to our goal. Next we must seek out a single hill, one unlike any other across these barren fields, for it is crowned by a distinctive marker, an ancient gateway of three great standing stones. There will we find the passage into the Valley of Skethris. The map outlines the trail we have thus far followed, and I believe we will find the location soon. But we must be fully prepared when we arrive.'

'Prepared for what?' Felix asked.

'The dolmen stones are watched over by an unliving guardian.'

'A ghost?' Felix asked.

'More than that,' Draeder replied. 'But the texts do not make clear the nature of the sentinel. They say only that this guardian is bound to the portal itself, and that it never sleeps. It is forever on watch. By the time we see the hill-tower, that-which-dwells-within will already have seen us.'

'Then how do we hope to pass through it?' Erhard asked.

'The secret to entering and safely crossing through such portals is a matter of magic, and thus it is my concern. You need not consider it except to know that if we are to succeed, I must be quite ready before we arrive.'

He held out the vellum, but only so that Felix could see it, pointing to a series of runes stencilled beside the representation of a dolmen. Felix studied it for a moment, puzzling at what he saw.

'There appear to be two markers there, are there not?' he asked, pointing at the dolmen and something beside it.

'Which one is the right one?' he asked.

Draeder sneered. He yanked the map away.

'That is my concern. I was not asking for help,' he said.

'Why wait then?' Erhard questioned. 'If you know the path, and you have the rite at hand, then lead us there. What more must you prepare?'

Draeder scoffed at him, as though he were but an ignorant child.

'Here indeed is written the oath that must be recited upon these hills, the incantation that can open the gateway. But it is more than a mere matter of recitation,' he said. 'The tower must only be approached by moonlight. To attempt to cross the path any other time would be disastrous. Even a perfectly done incantation would fail if not performed at the right time.'

Erhard groaned and bade his horse to edge backwards. He fell in with Strang and Torsten, whose haggard eyes bespoke their shared frustration.

'We've come this far,' Felix said.

'Listen to Felix. Let me do what only I can do, and soon I will… *we* will have the Book of Ashur within our grasp,' Draeder said, half by request, but spoken more as a command.

Felix looked over to the men and then back to Draeder. Erhard finally nodded, and the others agreed.

'Do what you must,' Felix said. 'We will camp here while you prepare. Summon us when you've made ready and this journey can finally come to an end.'

Draeder nodded.

'Indeed. Make your camp and I will consult my volumes. Once I have the incantation prepared, we can proceed.'

As the men turned away, satisfied for the moment to merely circle their horses in preparation for setting up camp, Draeder put his hand on Felix's shoulder. He drew the young man aside, sidling their horses close and lowering his voice so none of the others could hear.

'Keep your eye on them, Felix,' he warned. 'They're not like us. They're not men of education. Only you and I can truly understand our purpose here. *You and I, Felix*. We must watch out for one another as this mission goes forward. I know I can count on you.'

Felix nodded, but as Draeder dismounted and collected his volumes, he cursed under his breath, realising that the two men he most depended upon did not trust one another, and that both might soon ask him to turn upon the other.

Several hours passed in near silence. Draeder sat with his back turned, perched atop the barrow itself. He was frozen in a pose of perfect concentration, all sign of him lost beneath his huge shroud. The entire time, neither Felix nor Erhard detected so much as a hint of movement from the mage.

The men huddled together in a small circle at the base of the hill. Having no wood with which to build a fire, they wrapped themselves in their cloaks to guard against the damp cold that prevailed over the misty barrens. For a long while they clustered there, some trying to steal a few moments of sleep while the others patrolled the area, keeping a watchful eye for whatever might come out of the wastelands as the sun set upon the Barren Hills, lowering a veil of darkness over them once again.

They were not looking for a threat from within. But only moments after the fall of night, a terrible, blood-curdling scream alerted them to their error.

It came from behind them, from the barrow itself. The shrieking was vile and it reverberated with many voices – high-pitched and deep-throated in unison. It roused them all at once, scrambling to their feet, but covering their ears in some small effort to blunt the awful noise.

Yet that was hardly the worst of it. Still down on his knees and straining as the horrible wailing pounded in his head, Felix managed to look up. He saw a column of mist and shadow emerging from the heart of the barrow. At first merely a shapeless mass, the currents of darkness and fog began to coalesce and, as he watched, they took up a human-like form.

The figure assembled itself into a kind of translucent female, as dreadful and horrific as an animated corpse. Her stare was ghastly, a face frozen in an anguished grimace, with sunken cheeks and eyes that glowed pure white. Black currents of twisted, moving shadow crowned her with a mane of ghostly hair. The gown of mist that trailed behind her was a shredded mantle that rippled with every scream from her pale lips.

Her voice shrieked with abominable fragments of sound. As she moved towards them, she raised her thin, bone-like hands, pointing long white fingers at them as she wailed.

Felix leaped from the ground, slashing his long sword at the ghostly maiden. The blade passed through her with no effect. When he pulled back his sword the steel was cold and covered in frost.

Erhard did the same, but again to no avail. The banshee ignored the attack altogether. Unperturbed by any strike or flail, she merely pointed her long, ethereal fingers, and continued her screeching cry.

Draeder came running down the hill, drawn by the sight and the sound of the ghost maiden. As Felix moved for yet another attack, the wizard shouted at him to hold his position.

'Our weapons have no effect!' Felix shouted. 'Is there nothing you can do?'

Draeder came to the base of the hill, falling in beside Felix and his men. He pointed his scythe at the banshee, but that too seemed to accomplish nothing.

For a long, terrible moment the translucent figure merely hovered over them, screaming.

Then, just as suddenly as she had appeared, the ghostly woman backed away. In the same fashion as she had come, the wraith drew herself off, floating backwards towards the haunted barrow. The shadows of the hill seemed to reach out to reclaim her as her spectral form began to fade, disappearing like little more than candle-smoke.

As she vanished, the last thing that remained of her was her skull-like face. It turned from a ferocious visage into a devious, evil smile before it too faded away.

'We drove it off!' Torsten said.

'We did no such thing,' Erhard replied. 'That cursed spirit left of its own accord.'

'Why?' Felix asked. 'But for a fright, it did us no harm at all.'

'It wasn't *trying* to harm us,' Draeder said. 'It was issuing a warning.'

'What was it warning us about?' Felix asked.

'Not us,' the wizard replied, looking out towards the misty, dark horizon. 'It was warning the guardian. Night has fallen, and now it knows that we're coming.'

8

Moonlight touched the Barren Hills with an eerie, ghostly glow. The pale shining of Mannslieb reflected off every surface, glinting from steep slopes and at odd, oblique angles. A haze of cold shimmers and ever-shifting shadows filled the air. Deep and sombre quiet reigned across the barrens by night, a stillness that sent a shiver through Felix. No howling or shriek-ing he had heard in all his travels bothered him quite so much as the spooky, flawless still of that deathly silence.

They'd made haste after the banshee's departure, having no time to lose with their presence now known across the barrens. After a short while trekking through yet another stretch of bad-lands, a larger formation grew up out of the foggy distance. A single rocky hill rose high over the bleak sea of stone, its rise dominating the terrain for miles around. The path of a wind-ing trail had been cut into its face, snaking up along the front slope. Upon its crest there stood a lonely, half-crumbled stone triptych. The ancient, free-standing granite blocks sparkled in the weird moonlight, like a beacon across the misty barrens.

Again, Draeder halted the party. He studied his map, com-pared it to what he saw and puzzled for a moment.

'That is the hill,' he said. 'There we will find the entrance to the Valley of Skethris. We must be on guard now.'

As if in answer to his announcement, the ground rumbled underfoot. An eerie call sounded in the distance, a guttural roar that echoed through the cold mist.

'There can be no doubt. It knows we're here,' the wizard said.

They rode ahead with swords drawn, Draeder still at the lead but now with Strang and Torsten never more than a pace behind him.

As they proceeded, the dead silence began to give way. At first the still was broken only in isolated bursts, a screech in the distance or a muffled howl somewhere in the shadows. But it soon became more and Felix began to wish for the uncomfortable quiet he'd so dreaded only hours earlier.

When they reached the crest of the hill and dismounted, they found the great dolmen standing alone. It appeared to be a large doorway of rock leading down into the earth. Composed of three great standing stones, two were anchored into the ground while a thinner, flat capstone lay atop them, tilted at a slight angle.

'I've never seen such a thing,' Felix whispered.

'The ancient tribes who once ruled these lands laid their kings and chieftains to rest beneath monuments such as this. They were believed to mark portals to the land of the dead,' Draeder replied.

Although he realised he should have been inured to such a notion already, the suggestion sent a fright through Felix.

'What must we do?' Erhard asked.

'Just as it was for the ancients, the dolmen is the entrance for us as well. Beneath that stone triptych is the portal into the necromancer's realm,' Draeder said.

'We can just enter it?' Felix asked.

Draeder shook his head.

'I'm afraid it is not nearly that simple. I must perform the proper rite in order to open the way. And you must distract the guardian for long enough for me to do so.'

Felix stammered, looking around across the barren, lonely hill.

'But I see no guardian,' he said.

Draeder stepped back, leaving Felix and the men nearest to the dolmen.

'Look again,' he advised, even as he receded.

Just as the wizard spoke, the moon-shadows beneath the capstone began to stir. Once more the eerie howls echoed, and as the wind began to blow they were joined by a sort of sinister laughter.

Clanking and shuffling and the hard grinding of stone against stone accompanied the movement beneath the dolmen. A figure crept up from beneath, as if spawned from the foetid earth. It reached out with pale hands until it emerged fully from the grave, standing before them in a display of evil majesty.

The wight was massive. He wore finely-crafted armour of an archaic sort, the antiquated gear of an ancient barbarian warlord. His breastplate was age-tarnished bronze, the edges and the faded inlay infested with green verdigris. His black iron pauldrons and gauntlets had been dulled by centuries of dust. A mail undercoat fell to his knees, the links rusted out in places, leaving gaping holes.

His great, old helmet was crowned with a single spike and a pair of ragged eagle's wings. Beneath the visor his haunted eyes gleamed bright crimson, stark against his cadaverous, decayed face. He wielded a massive broadsword, the flat of the blade inscribed with black runes that pulsed with dark magic.

'That is no mere watcher,' Felix whispered.

Draeder was already a pace behind him.

'No doubt the warrior-king interred beneath this grave,' he said. 'Raised from death and bound to this place long ago by the black hand of Skethris himself.'

The undead warrior king still retained a shadow of his human form. What remained of his skin was desiccated and discoloured. Swathes of his bare, dry flesh were the greenish-grey shade of a corpse, while other places bulged with black and purple splotches where congealed blood had settled and hardened long ago.

'Welcome, travellers,' the wight said, its deep thundering voice making the ground tremble again. 'It has been so long since anyone has come. So long indeed that I've nearly forgotten the pleasures of company.'

Felix looked to Erhard. He raised his hands in a gesture of peace.

'We come with no ill will,' Felix said. 'We wish only to pass.'

The wight laughed.

'Why, that is the very pleasure I have so missed,' the wight replied. 'Killing those who wish to pass this way.'

Felix lowered his hands. They all lifted their swords. Draeder, standing further from the menacing figure, looked up and centred his eye on the full moons rising behind the hill.

'The rite must be employed now, while the light shines down. The glow of the Chaos moon will show us the way. I'll require time to recite the entire incantation.'

'It does not appear we have much!' Erhard shouted.

'You do not need to defeat the wight, merely hold him while I perform the rite that will open the portal,' Draeder said.

'That'll be harder than it looks,' Felix said. 'And it doesn't look easy.'

Felix charged at the undead warrior-king, slashing at him with an expert cut from his blade. The wight merely brushed it aside with little effort, and Felix was forced to quickly duck down from the return blow of the wight's great rune-blade. Even then, he was nearly cut in two by the undead warrior's next swipe, two blows rendered faster than any living man could have placed one. The enchanted sword sliced across his jerkin but luckily did not go any deeper. He whirled, and cut through the arm of the unliving guardian, but the strike seemed to have no effect against the hulking, unfeeling attacker.

As the warrior-king swung around, his ardour undiminished, Felix dodged yet another slash of the massive broadsword.

This time he leaped up the moment the blade was past him and plunged his own sword directly into the wight's throat. The blade penetrated and came right back out, pulling with it nothing more than foul-smelling dust.

The wight simply cackled, returning the favour with another blow that Felix only barely managed to block. The sheer force of it sent him tumbling.

Erhard raced into the fray just as Felix fell. He struck at the wight, cutting across rusted mail and severing a rotted leather belt. Yet none of his attacks weakened the guardian either. In moments, he too was thrown aside, landing in a heap beside the dolmen itself.

'This is madness!' Torsten exclaimed, his eyes wide with a kind of panicked terror that bordered on insanity. 'We can't defeat such an enemy!'

Strang grabbed his brother by the collar, yanking him back to a measure of sense.

'Then we die here, brother,' the one-eyed man growled.

The encouragement held them all together as they backed up, keeping close as they fought off every new attack from the undead warrior-king. Felix looked back to Draeder, ministering with his Amethyst scythe.

The wizard stood before the dolmen, reciting a long and complex chant, lifting and gesturing with his staff as if trying to focus for the magic he was attempting to channel. But for all his incantations and summoning, nothing appeared to happen.

Only a moment later, Strang met with disaster.

The veteran warrior stabbed at the wight and struck it dead on in the chest, but found his blade lodged in the old armour and dry flesh of his attacker. He struggled to pry it loose, but a defenceless moment was all that the undead warrior required. The shambling monstrosity reached over Strang's trapped sword, slashed his great blade through the man's throat and tore his head from his neck in a fountain of blood.

Torsten shrieked as he watched his brother die, felled by as horrible an end as could be imagined. He shivered and wailed, swinging his blade wildly as a mad frenzy overcame him, erasing all reason and sense.

The wight laughed with a deep, maddened chortle, somehow enlivened by the pain and suffering he had inflicted. Torsten leaped at him, raising his sword high, but the wight merely caught it with his bare hand, wresting the blade from his grasp. His own massive rune sword whirled in a terrible arc, slicing down upon Torsten. It cleaved clear through his cloak and mail, splitting his neck from his shoulder in a bloody, vicious gash that opened up half his chest.

Felix and Erhard hurried backwards, the powerful wight still bearing down as he cast the young soldier's mangled body aside. They fell in beside Draeder, standing before the dolmen in confusion, puzzling over the failure of his rite to accomplish anything.

'I performed it exactly as it is written,' he muttered. 'Each rune, each verse. Every turn of the staff exactly correct.'

'Try it again!' Felix shouted, seeing the wight close in.

'What good will that do?' he replied. 'I've done it all exactly right, it was supposed to work. It should have worked. The moonlight should show the...'

A moment later, Draeder saw something that stopped him. Behind the dolmen, on the far side of the hill, he caught sight of something. A pile of stones rested over an indentation in the earth, where one flat rock lay atop the rest. It was glowing. The stone was illuminated, gleaming in the moonlight. Runes sparkled milky white and bright red across its surface.

'Of course!' he shouted. 'The second stone marker! The dolmen is not the gateway! That is!'

Felix readied for another attack. He looked over to Draeder, pointing frantically in the direction of the glowing rune-stone.

'But you said the dolmen was–' Felix began.

'I was mistaken,' Draeder replied. 'You were more correct than you realised, Felix. The rune stones there are the second marker on the map! That is the meaning of the inscription. The portal rests *behind* the dolmen, not within it! We must get past the wight!'

'It's impossible!' Erhard shouted back. 'Have you seen nothing here? It can't be slowed, or even wounded. It is relentless. There's no way to get by.'

Draeder snarled and he reached for Erhard, grabbing his subordinate by his cloak like a master would assail an unruly child.

'I cannot abandon this venture now!' he shouted in the older man's face. 'I refuse to accept that. There must be a way! You must find a way!'

Erhard finally lost his temper. Seething in a rage of suppressed anger, he reached up with his thick arms and seized Draeder. He stared into the younger man's face.

'I am done taking orders from you, boy!' he shouted.

Then he lifted Draeder off his feet and heaved him backwards, throwing the young wizard against the dolmen. He landed so hard his back edged the upper stone of the triptych, grinding it against the stones beneath.

He groaned and wheezed as he fell, but Felix noticed something else in that instant – the guardian staggered as well.

As Draeder tried to come to his feet, the mix of pain and wrath across his face making clear that he intended on a second run at his sergeant, Felix jumped between the two.

Erhard turned his back on the wizard, returning his attention to the wight.

'You'll pay for that!' Draeder shouted.

'I doubt any of us will live long enough,' the sergeant answered.

He lifted his sword once more, and again he charged the wight, its armour dripping with Strang and Torsten's blood.

Draeder grabbed his scythe and started to follow, but Felix stopped him.

'This creature is bound to this spot, you told us,' he said.

The wizard seemed uninterested in answering. Felix grabbed him and shook him.

'Tell me!' he demanded. 'How is this undead thing held here?'

'As I said,' Draeder replied, angrily. 'The dark magic of Skethris binds him to his eternal resting place.'

'This dolmen,' Felix replied.

'Indeed, he is bound to this place for…'

Felix ignored the rest of his answer, turning to the dolmen itself. He dropped his sword, bared both hands and pushed against the capstone. For all his strength, he managed to shift it only a tiny bit.

The moment it moved however, even just a small distance, he heard a peal of agony from across the hilltop. Turning his head, he saw the wight stagger again, though Erhard had not landed a blow.

'Help me!' Felix shouted, grabbing Draeder and turning him towards the dolmen. 'Push with everything you've got!'

The two men joined forces, heaving their full weight into the capstone until they felt it edge away, grinding pebbles and dust under it as it scraped across the standing stones beneath it. The effort took all of their might.

The wight howled, stumbling for a moment. Erhard stood

against it still, his twin swords meeting the undead warrior's next blow.

'Again!' Felix shouted.

Once more the two men pushed, and a second time they managed to shove the dolmen's top stone until it was teetering. The wight staggered again, weakened but not defeated. It raged, striking a blow that sent Erhard careening across the hill. The old sergeant fell with a painful thud.

Felix knelt down next to him, helping him back to his feet.

'Give a hand to Draeder,' he said. 'When I call back to you, follow his lead.'

The sergeant nodded, fighting to regain his balance as he fell in beside the young wizard, both men poised beside the dolmen with the precarious capstone.

Once again lumbering towards them, Felix intercepted the cackling wight. Drawing his sword, he bounded and leaped towards the grisly guardian.

'Now!' he shouted back to the others.

Draeder and Erhard threw their combined weight at the dolmen. They pushed hard against it with everything their arms could muster, until the capstone slid off of its perch between the two supports, collapsing down in a heap of broken stone.

Felix's blade crashed against the barbarian king's rune sword the instant the dolmen crumbled. The two razor edges slid down against one another until the pommels met, wedging the cross-guards together with a clang and a spark.

The wight squealed in agony as the ancient monument broke apart. He shrieked and shook, but Felix held fast. He wrestled with the weakened guardian, forcing the undead sentinel backwards. They moved to and fro, the wight's strength failing with Felix's every move. Then, as the dead king staggered, Felix shouted back to Draeder and Erhard a second time.

The two answered the call, joining Felix in jumping upon the wight with sword and scythe. As Felix held the undead watcher, Erhard stabbed at the creature and Draeder slashed. This time, their blades wreaked havoc, cutting and chopping the pale flesh of the watcher until his body mirrored the ruin of his grave marker. His severed arms dropped down at his sides, followed by his legs as they collapsed under him.

Finally, Felix swung his sword in an arc, slicing through the wight's throat. His head tumbled down from his neck, dropping the winged helmet as his body crumpled into a heap of dust and ancient armour.

Draeder fell back against the fractured dolmen, relieved and out of breath for the moment. When he did recover, he ignored Erhard and looked to Felix only.

'Good thinking all around, Felix,' he said. 'Truly, I could not have asked for a more able assistant on this endeavour.'

Erhard looked over to Felix, his face dour and his brow furrowed. Felix sighed and turned his head, for he found that he could not muster anything to say.

9

It was not much of a memorial, but Felix and Erhard took the savaged bodies of the fallen brothers and carried them both to the dolmen. There, in the centre of the ancient burial site, collapsed though it was, they laid the two brave warriors to rest.

Though they gave some thought to keeping Strang and Torsten's horses, they chose instead to leave them behind, freeing the animals to run wild. By the time the moon was fully overhead, they were re-packed and ready to move on.

No sooner had they observed a silent moment than Draeder demanded they resume. He had already studied the portal entrance, the stones above it still gleaming with inscrutable runes. Where there had once been little more than a marker of several stones embedded over a hole in the earth, his incantation had magically opened it into a wide stone gate. Behind lay a tunnel, deep enough to ride a horse down into it with room to spare.

Draeder led the way again, the first to enter the portal. Felix and Erhard formed up in his wake, leaving behind the moonlight and following only the eerie glow of Draeder's violet scythe flame.

'I seem to think I might have once considered something like this rather unwise,' Felix said, as his horse carried him down into the tunnel. 'But now I suppose I can't complain.'

The descent through the tunnel seemed to carry them deep into the earth. No hint of the outside world remained as they moved down a long and dark path. On the far side they found that it opened upon a slope at the edge of a long and deep valley – but of the dolmen or the Barren Hills, there was no sign at all.

The grade was steep and the ground was rocky. They could not see the floor of the valley, blanketed by a thick carpet of fog. Strangely, the mist did not rise to the higher elevations, obscuring only the distance but leaving the near terrain untouched.

Jagged boulders lay strewn about, massive broken hunks of stone that looked more like the rubble of giants than natural formations. The fractured rock jutted out from the dirt, forcing them to follow a narrow path that snaked for miles in every direction before it finally brought them down to the edge of the mist.

A vile reek filled their nostrils before they reached the fog, and it only grew deeper as they penetrated it. There was no wind down there. The air was cold and stagnant, and filled with a dense curtain of grey mist that hung all about in a dim murk. It stank of corpses, the musty reek of old tombs and decay.

While Felix and Erhard recoiled at the stench, Draeder took the opposite approach. He inhaled the rotten scent with a peculiar relish.

The sun had just gone down, their winding descent having consumed the entire day. Though they found themselves now on the floor of the valley, the fog robbed them of all but the faintest hints of moonlight to guide their way, leaving the forest ahead cloaked in a deep shadow.

'Should we not pause here and attempt to continue once the safety of daylight has returned?' Felix asked.

Draeder shook his head.

'Daylight may guide our eyes, but we now follow the path of the scythe. The violet flame is strongest at night. Death magic is weakest at midday, and nowhere is the odour of death stronger than here. We must proceed now.'

'It might be wise to leave the horses,' Erhard said. 'If we're to approach this place with some stealth.'

'Indeed,' Draeder replied, as if it had been his own idea. 'I believe we should proceed on foot from here.'

They dismounted, tethering the horses to a tree and following behind him on foot as they entered into the lower valley. The realm of the necromancer quickly revealed a more ghastly character than the monster-addled lands they'd left behind. The forest had been cleared in every direction, leaving only scattered groves of winter-bare trees. What stood in its place was an immense landscape of blight and ruin.

Hints of faded grandeur stood all around, age-worn and battered, yet clinging to a shadow of opulence, a vast plantation of death.

Crumbled walls lined the edges of what might have once been gardens. The stone work was incredible, chiselled with such care that the granite seemed as thin as a veil of lace, petrified for all the ages. Everything was mouldered and decrepit, a ghost of its former splendour.

Rows of broken columns flanked the grim estates. The pillars were solid marble, but cut with such exquisite artistry as to resemble flowers in spring bloom, vine-covered and delicate as rose petals. The once-fine white stone was now stained with swarms of black lichen. The perfect masonry was pockmarked and charred from some long-ago violence.

Felix ran his hand over the faces of some, almost in disbelief at both the richness and the decay alike. He found that the stone had been eaten away in places, as if gnawed upon. The thought sent a shiver through him.

Water remained in artificial ponds, brown and foetid with oily slicks that lingered across the weed-clogged surface. The detritus of some long-forgotten battle left its mark in the broken spears and rusted helmets that lay abandoned throughout, grisly monuments to the fall of an entire realm.

The complex and beautiful designs of ancient courtyards survived as mere outlines etched into the scrub-brush and the dirt. Dry canals choked with debris traced the lines of once-flowing streams and captive waterfalls, the rushing rivers reduced to mere trickles of sludge.

The viscous grey mist floated beside them everywhere they went, seething up from the rotten earth, stinking of decomposition. After more than an hour pressing onwards, strange noises began to echo in the dim. Footsteps sounded in the misty shadows. Creaking and clanking followed, joined by muffled screams in the distance.

The men penetrated ever deeper into the ruins, and with every moment the noises grew louder. Still they moved forward, further into the gloom, until figures began to emerge from the haze and the darkness ahead.

At first, only their outlines could be discerned, and they were unlike any sentinels the three men had ever seen. Thin and nearly stick-like in silhouette, their movements were likewise inhuman. Awkward, herky-jerky steps brought them closer until the front ranks paraded into the moonlight, revealing their horrific nature.

They appeared from the mist as though marching forth from a nightmare. None were truly men, nothing more than bones animated beyond the grave. All of them stared ahead with cold, soulless eyes, every face exactly the same – a bare skull.

'The watchers of the valley,' Draeder said. 'Long-dead warriors forever bound to this place by the will of the necromancer.'

Erhard pointed just behind them to their left, where a wall of ancient stone ran along the edge of a decrepit garden.

'I don't think they've seen us yet,' he whispered. 'If we circle back, taking cover behind the wall, we might be able to side-step them and find another way forward.'

Felix looked at Draeder. Both nodded.

'No argument,' Felix said.

Stepping away with utmost care and proceeding on as stealthily as they could, the party ducked behind the wall and re-traced their steps back, looking to chart a path around the advancing skeletal host.

But their efforts soon proved futile.

Coming up from behind the length of the wall, they found their path once again blocked by yet more of the foul walkers.

These emerged not only from the mist, but from the foetid ground as well, creeping up from the rotten earth in fits and starts to stand among their undead brethren.

Of the dozen or so who now mustered before them, some still clung to fading vestiges of life. Scraps of dried flesh or stringy hair hung from a few. The tattered, yellowed remains of tunics and cloaks dangled from others. Their evil, hollow black eyes scanned in every direction, holding their mouldered shields and waving their antique swords before them.

'What a vile sight,' Felix gasped. 'Of all that we've encountered so far, what could be more horrific than bare skeletons that still walk as living men? Please tell me the magic of your scythe holds sway over these things.'

Draeder didn't answer. Instead he slowed, taken aback by the lumbering undead that now approached.

Felix sensed his trepidation.

'You may wish to draw your swords now,' Draeder whispered.

Erhard grumbled, unsheathing his twin blades. He sneered at the wizard.

'I hope your courage is stronger than your magic.'

Draeder scoffed at the insult, but beads of sweat had started to form on his forehead, despite the chill.

'It is no failing of mine,' he said. 'My scythe flame draws its power from the wilds of the forest and the winds of Shyish. Though it follows the currents of the purple wind, it has no power to control those who walk beyond death.'

Felix snarled, as he drew his own longsword and prepared to meet the dreadful sentinels. Erhard fell in beside him, though Draeder attempted to edge his way back, shuffling in the opposite direction. The old sergeant extended his arm, blocking his path.

'Not this time,' he said. 'If you're planning to conjure some spell you'd best get to it, because you're about to stand and fight right alongside us.'

Felix girded himself for the fight, nodding at Erhard as the two men prepared to enter battle beside one another yet again. The undead came at them in a surge of unliving warriors staring at them with dead eyes.

Erhard crossed swords with two skull-faced sentinels at once. Withered though they were, they wielded their blades with relentless furore. It took all of Erhard's might to force two of them back. Even then, they parried his return strokes, dodging and blocking several times without a hint of fatigue.

Though the veteran sergeant managed to dispatch them both, smashing the skull of one with a pommel strike from above and chopping the other to pieces, he took a slash across his shoulder. Blood began to stain the edges of his jerkin, soaking through his undercoat.

Felix struggled in similar fashion beside him, matching every feint and counter-strike before he was able to cleave his undead attacker's mandible from its jaw. Though it betrayed no hint of pain, Felix nonetheless pressed his advantage and cut down the ghastly guardian with two more cuts that shattered its vertebrae. Once its skull came away, the bones collapsed at once into a heap.

'The heads,' Felix shouted. 'Cut off their heads.'

Erhard saw it, and despite his injury he immediately began striking at the bony necks of the sentinels. Even Draeder took the advice to heart, whirling his scythe in wild fashion, decapitating skeletal warriors one after another.

Drawing on some of his old fencing tutor's more obscure lessons, Felix dropped down to his knees and sliced the legs out from under three of the skeletal warriors with one single swipe. As they crumpled to the dust, he seized a spear from one, and using his full weight, he drove it through the shield of a warrior nearby, pinning it to four others behind and knocking down an entire row of the undead guardians.

Once the undead warriors were knocked to the ground, Erhard and Felix swooped in. They stomped on the fallen skeletons, chopping the skulls from each one until the entire patrol had been reduced to nothing but a pile of bones.

When it was done, once all hint of movement and every last twitch among the animated bones had quelled, Felix dropped down to one knee. He held out his sword to prop himself up. Erhard too permitted himself a rare moment's rest, taking a seat on an empty helmet as he felt under his shirt, gauging the depth of his wound.

'I don't know how much more of that I could have taken,' Felix said, out of breath as the sweat dripped from his hair.

'Nor I,' Erhard wheezed. 'I'm not a young man any more. If we don't find our destination soon, I'm likely to end up just like one of these old boys here soon enough.'

Felix laughed.

'Nonsense, old man,' he said. 'You're not done yet.'

Draeder, breathing heavily himself, though he had taken down the fewest of the assailants, was the first to return to his feet.

'We must keep moving,' he said.

'Not yet. At least permit Erhard a moment,' Felix said.

'We know there are more of these creatures lurking beyond. The longer we remain in one place, the greater the chance that more of these things will find us,' Draeder replied.

Felix was about to argue, but Erhard stopped him as he began to get up, having already tied a torn piece of cloak around his upper arm as a makeshift bandage.

'He's right, Felix,' the sergeant said, as he took up beside Draeder to continue on ahead. 'Don't worry about me, young man. I'll be just fine.'

10

They passed through the remainder of the outer precincts quickly after that, but always on guard for more undead sentries. Feeling the effects of their long struggle, each one of them haggard and pushed nearly to the limit, they now preferred discretion to valour. Careful in their every movement, they skirted the edges of ruined gardens and kept off anything that looked like a pathway. In so doing they managed to avoid two more such patrols as they charted a winding course deeper into the heart of the valley.

Finally, they came to the ruins of a large stone wall, which seemed to mark a border of sorts, to what had once been some kind of inner realm. Beyond it stood more elements of ancient architecture, but they quickly saw that these sections were somehow better preserved than the faded, crumbling ruins scattered through the remainder of the valley. While the columns and courtyards that lay ahead had also fallen into disrepair, overgrown with weeds and black lichen, their condition suggested that they had been abandoned much more recently, hundreds of years past perhaps, rather than thousands.

The style of the carvings and stonework differed in another respect as well, and it was one Felix took note of straightaway. Where the age-worn, dilapidated ruins of the outer valley hinted at a kind of lost elegance, a sort of finery rarely seen in the Empire, what they gazed upon now were grim, dour monuments.

Skulls replaced floral motifs atop the columns. Sigils depicting fangs and crossed swords glared in faded tones across the flagstones and the archways. From atop the broken stone embankment, Felix caught a hint of what lay even further out, behind the gruesome landscape, still half-shrouded in the mist.

He could barely discern the outline of a tall tower, cast in silhouette by the fog and the moonlight, looming in the distance directly ahead of them. He pointed it out to the others.

'The tower of Skethris,' Draeder said. 'We're nearly there.'

They pushed on, risking a final approach without benefit of cover. But the moment they moved out into open ground, they realised that they weren't alone.

Directly before them stood a portal that opened with three archways. Beneath each one stood what at first appeared to be great statues of magnificently armoured warriors holding large, curved swords before them. When the massive warriors began to move however, marching out in unison towards them, it was clear that they faced yet another, even greater set of guardians.

Though only three, matching them man-for-man, it was obvious that these warriors were of a different, more dangerous sort. While the guardians were skull-faced, just as their brethren in the outer valley, these tall warriors were well-armoured from head to toe. Mail hoods and full length hauberks covered their bones, overlaid with bronze plate. They carried massive round shields and huge broadswords.

Their hollow eyes glowed with a foul green light.

'Skeletons they may be, but it'll be much tougher to take *their* heads from their necks,' Felix said. 'And I don't honestly know how much strength I have left.'

Erhard grimaced, his wound clearly bothering him more than he wished to let on.

'We cannot fight through such a force again,' he complained.

'Agreed,' Felix said, turning to Draeder. 'Have you truly no spells to combat such a scourge? I can't believe the winds of death are no help against warriors who are themselves undead!'

Erhard sneered.

'I wouldn't look there for assistance,' he said, lifting his blades once more for what now seemed the most desperate of fights.

This time the insult appeared to motivate Draeder, and he stepped nearer to Felix, leaving Erhard apart and closest to the ghastly sentinels.

'Dead or not, if I cannot *stop* them, I may be able to draw up a spell that will hold them – for a while, at least,' he said. 'But I'll require time to summon the winds of Shyish.'

Felix acknowledged him with a hard pat on the shoulder. Then he closed ranks with Erhard, coming shoulder-to-shoulder with the sergeant.

'Let him fall back to work his magic,' Felix said. 'It's the only chance we have.'

Erhard refused.

'He'll do nothing of the sort!' he said. 'He's not capable of it!'

Felix looked back to the wizard.

'*Can* you do it?' he asked.

Draeder looked to the attackers, marching forward and nearly upon them. Then he gazed back to Felix.

'Of course, I can,' Draeder replied, as if it were not even a question. 'But you must hold them at bay for long enough for me to perform the rite, or I will not be able to loose it upon them.'

Felix took Erhard by the arm.

'What other choice do we have?' he asked.

The sergeant grudgingly acknowledged. Felix looked back to Draeder.

'Stay behind us,' he said. 'We'll hold them here for as long as we can, but waste no time. The moment you are able, cast your spell!'

Draeder assented with a nod. Felix and Erhard rallied. They shouted curses and battle cries and met the charge of the guardians head-on. Hacking and chopping for every inch of ground, the exhausted swordsmen parried every blow of the undead warriors, listening to the archaic verses that Draeder chanted behind them. Bones and blades and broken shields scattered in every direction. Dust choked the staid, foul air.

Struggling for every foothold, Felix slashed his way forward. For a brief moment he managed to push back the onrushing skeleton sentinels, cutting ancient armour and brittle bones with every stroke. But the offensive lasted only an instant. Beside him, Erhard howled as he took another blow. Blood spilled out from a fresh wound in his leg, hobbling him.

'We can't hold them, Draeder! Let loose your spell, by Sigmar!' Felix shouted.

The wizard stepped forward, raising his scythe and calling out the final words to summon the magic he sought. Felix and Erhard continued to battle at close-quarters, in brutal hand-to-hand combat, holding off the skeletal guardians in an increasingly failing effort.

When Draeder's incantation seemed to accomplish nothing, leaving him standing behind them with no magic summoned to his call, Erhard only renewed his jeering.

'Damn you!' he cursed. 'I knew this was folly. We're doomed because of you!'

Felix however, remained resolute. He turned to Draeder

again, who now looked sheepish and terrified at the onrushing attack he seemed powerless to stop.

'Try again!' Felix shouted.

Draeder wiped the sweat from his brow, his hands trembling. He lifted his staff and once more began the spell. But Erhard's strength had already run out. He screamed, swinging his arms in a wild fury as one of the guardians drove its blade deep into his gut.

Felix held his ground, but as soon as he heard the old sergeant's terrible scream he knew what had happened. Even as he fought on, he peered out of the corner of his eye, watching as Erhard beat back the skeletal warrior who had impaled him, until his blade managed to cut through the undead walker's spine, reducing it to a crumpled heap of bones.

Now there were only two guardians remaining, but Erhard couldn't stand for much longer. With blood drooling from his lips, the grizzled sergeant dropped to his knees. Felix abandoned all caution, fighting his way over to the old soldier, knocking the remaining two guardians back a pace with his sudden, bold counter-attack.

When Felix turned, he saw something he did not expect. Draeder had stepped up in his place, standing alone against the two remaining skeletal warriors. With a swing of his scythe, a pale ring of purple mist did finally spread out across them. It seized the pair, holding them fast and quelling their attack.

Safe for at least a moment, Felix helped Erhard to the ground. Blood was spilling out from the wound in his stomach, gurgling in his throat. The old sergeant clutched at Felix's cloak as he came to rest in the dirt.

'Easy, old timer,' Felix said, trying to comfort his companion, though he knew very well that the wound was mortal.

Erhard pulled him close, near enough to whisper with his last bit of breath.

'Trust your instincts...' he wheezed. 'He's not what you think... Not what he says...'

Felix, puzzled, again tried to comfort the dying warrior.

'You must listen,' Erhard managed. 'You're a good man. You're *not* like him.'

Felix tried to encourage the grizzled veteran, but the man had nothing left. His eyes froze and his chest stopped moving. Then Ernst Erhard, sergeant-at-arms for House von Halkern, died in Felix Jaeger's arms.

Felix cradled the body of his fallen friend, holding him tight for a long, quiet moment. Tears choked his eyes, running down through the grime on his cheeks.

When he finally wiped them away to look out at the stilled scene of battle, he saw Draeder standing over the frozen sentinels. The young wizard wore a gleaming, triumphant look upon his face, all-but ignoring the death of his loyal, longtime servant.

Felix looked back at the dead man resting in his embrace. Despite Draeder's obvious success, or perhaps because of it, Erhard's last words repeated in his mind. He felt a chill run through his blood, making him shiver down to his bones.

11

Draeder and Felix pushed ahead. They had no choice now. It was not long before the fog cleared out, and a space opened before them that evoked both awe and terror in equal measure.

The tower they had glimpsed in the distance was even more fearsome up close. Skull-topped flag poles crowned with bronze wings flanked a long avenue leading to its gates. They lined the narrow path from the outer grounds into the very centre of the cursed estate. The standards themselves were worn. The fabric was faded, the ends tattered and frayed. But the sigils remained evident: skulls, blades and the bony wings of bats.

Twin statues stood at the terminus of the death-walk. The figures each guarded an obelisk of pure obsidian glass that reflected their shapes in the weak moonlight. Both were carved from a single slab of alabaster five times the height of a man. Garbed in archaic armour, with scythes and oval shields, their faces were skulls.

'Fantastic,' Draeder whispered. 'He made this a monument to the worship of death itself.'

Still reeling from the death of Erhard, Felix could say nothing, merely taking in the evil vista. The tower of Skethris loomed beyond. It was not at all what Felix had expected it to be. It was much worse.

No common citadel lorded over the centre of the wicked grounds. Stout defensive turrets crowned with bastions and crenulated walls formed the core of it. The base and the sides of the structure were solid, old stone: great, hewn mega-blocks of basalt and black marble locked together in perfect order. But there was something gruesome about it as well. The steep outer walls were interlaced with something else, and that was neither stone nor mortar.

Felix stared at the massive, eerie tower, and he shuddered when the dreadful realisation came to him, peering ever closer. The remainder of the structure was the dirty yellow shade of old bones, as though the entire keep had been somehow *fortified* with the remains of the unliving.

The skeletal conglomeration seemed welded to the stone keep in a twisted, parasitic fashion, as though not built or fused to the original structure by ordinary means, but rather something that had grown into place; like the gnarled, fractured trunk of a long-dead tree or some great, thorny weed that threatened to swallow the host upon which it climbed. Outcroppings extended from the whole ghastly length of it, bony arms reaching out to the darkness. Some were interwoven amongst themselves, creating a frightful skeletal latticework all around the structure.

Dark stains befouled the whole of it, dry rivulets of deep red that hinted at something unimaginable, a downpour of blood or the proceeds of some immense slaughter draining away from the misty heights, the site of such atrocities now hidden behind the clouds.

Felix couldn't help but pause, standing in grim awe of such dark and evil splendour. But Draeder was unmoved. Holding his scythe high, he yanked Felix by the shoulder and pulled him into the musty shadows of the necromancer's tower.

'We're close now,' he said. 'Very close indeed.'

They forced open the tall, rusted-out iron gate, raising a gritty, high-pitched creak from the old hinges. It required the strength of both men to edge it apart wide enough for them to pass, the joints nearly frozen in place after ages of disuse. Behind it was a small antechamber under a vaulted arch. A gauze of cobwebs hung down, blocking the way. Felix cut them apart, spilling a cloud of dust into the staid air. He coughed as they moved forward, Draeder doing the same as he followed.

Behind the entranceway, the inner tower opened into a round chamber. It too was suffering the effects of age and neglect. A thick carpet of dust and old webs coated everything. It smelled rotten, musty and decrepit like an old tomb opened after centuries under seal.

'The Book of Ashur should be with the altar,' Draeder said. 'That would be at the highest point of the tower.'

Felix pointed to the spiral staircase that wound its way up along the far side of the chamber, leading up to the entrance of a second level. It was rusted and swathed in grey, but it made for the only path they could follow.

Though Felix took the first steps on the old stairs, testing if the iron was any sturdier than it appeared, Draeder quickly pushed past him, taking the lead as they proceeded into the upper reaches of the tower.

Above, they found nothing more than a second chamber of the same sort. The entire place seemed to have been unused for quite some time. Finding nothing of note, Draeder wasted no time, following the stairs ever higher.

They fought through several rounds of spider webs and rotten stenches stirred up by their arrival, climbing nine such levels without any hint of an end. Already exhausted from the constant fighting and now nearly out of breath, Felix finally paused at the base of the next level before continuing their seemingly endless ascent.

'From the outside, this tower looked no taller than five, maybe six storeys, at most. Yet we've already scaled nearly twice that and seem no nearer to the top,' he said, gasping a bit. 'How can this be?'

'The winds of magic can be turned to many purposes,' Draeder replied enigmatically.

The strangeness did not appear to disturb him, and his answer seemed to Felix like nothing more than an after-thought. Instead, he merely continued to chart the path forward, looking up to yet another level.

Coming up through the tenth level, they met with an obstacle – a wall of broken stone. The rubble of some ancient collapse, blocks of shattered stone from the level above had fallen in, piled to the ceiling, clogging the stairwell that was their only path further up.

Felix looked around. There were only a few small windows and no corridors leading off the main chamber. For a few minutes, he and Draeder tried to peel away the fallen roof, but the effort left them no closer. Behind each stone lay more rubble, and the largest of the blocks were too big for twenty men to budge.

'It's no use,' Felix finally said, wheezing and out of breath. 'We have no idea how high up this goes. All we know is that we are no closer to a way through it, and half of these stones will not move no matter what we do.'

'So close,' Draeder whispered. 'Again, so close. And again, we face a barrier we could not have foreseen.'

'On that, finally, we agree,' Felix said.

He picked up one of the smaller stones. Grunting with frustration, he heaved it across the hall. It smashed against the old wood of the nearest shuttered-up window. The stone broke through the aged timber, opening a portal to the sky beyond. Mist from outside drifted in through it, breaking the staid air of the tower.

Draeder jeered at the seemingly pointless act, turning to once again study the stone blockade. Felix, however, fixed his eye on the window. Something had caught his attention.

He went over to it, tested the heft of the remaining shutters and then stepped back. With a snarl that drew Draeder's eye back to him, he drew his sword, reared back and broke out the rotted wood of the shutters, opening the entire window to the outside.

Beyond was not a flat wall, but a ledge. He scanned the side of the tower, looking over the walls. The entire structure was composed of irregular blocks overlaid by the grisly bone-lattice that encircled the whole of the tower.

'I have an idea,' Felix said.

'We cannot go back down,' Draeder replied, guessing at his comrade's notion without even bothering to inquire further.

'I'm not suggesting that we do,' Felix said. 'Quite the opposite, in fact. Come here. Look out upon the walls.'

Draeder rather reluctantly came to Felix's side, and peered out from the broken window frame.

'That ledge is more than wide enough for a foothold,' Felix said. 'And the bones above it offer plenty of places to grip.'

Draeder stepped back.

'What are you saying?' he asked. 'That we should *climb* up?'

Felix answered by sheathing his sword, jumping up on the ledge and straddling the window.

'Exactly,' he replied.

'That's madness,' Draeder said.

Felix stepped out fully onto the outer ledge, leaving only his head and his arms inside the tower.

'It's not madness. Given our predicament, it is, I believe, the only sensible course.'

The two men climbed for a long while, realising as they proceeded that the tower was somehow even taller than they had already imagined. Fog obscured the ground beneath them, and above them the parapets remained hidden behind a thick bank of clouds.

Using the latticework of bones to scale the wall, they managed to ascend for a few moments without incident. No skeletal warriors troubled them out in the mist, but even high up on that most remote of places, they soon found that they were not alone.

Ghostly voices hissed at them with nearly every foothold, taunting them or cursing the pair in some attempt to distract them. Several times, the phantoms nearly succeeded. Draeder and Felix each slipped on more than one occasion, both grabbing the other whenever a false step made a fast hand necessary.

Spectral faces appeared from the fog, glaring at them with sinister eyes and haranguing them with high-pitched, wraith-like screams.

Finally, with their arms aching and the skin on their hands rubbed bloody and raw, they recognised a change in the wall. Just above them, the bone lattice tapered off. Beyond that there arose a final ring of giant blocks that crowned the tower. The stones were obsidian black, three times the height of a man and utterly smooth.

'There's no place to grab,' Felix said. 'Nothing to hold.'

Draeder scanned the heights. Though Felix expected a rebuke for setting them on a futile course, none came. Instead, Draeder began to kick at the bones nearest him, breaking several free from the superstructure.

'What are you doing, robbing us of what little we have to stand on?' Felix asked.

Draeder did not reply. Instead, he took several of the bones in hand, recited a chant-like invocation and then tossed the bones up into the air. Instead of falling, the bones aligned themselves in a magical row, forming a sort of makeshift ladder suspended in the fog. It stretched all along the un-scalable section of the wall.

Draeder turned back to Felix with a smirk.

'What was that you were saying?'

'Lead the way,' Felix replied.

* * *

As they climbed higher, the ghostly minions only grew more numerous. Every step closer to the tower summit seemed to bring more of them streaming down from the clouds, their faces ghastly and skull-like despite their phantom forms.

They swooped all around the two men, weaving and diving on currents of frost-choked wind. They shouted and taunted from afar, then crept closer, whispering obscene curses in their ears.

After a while, one chorus rose up above the rest. The spectres all seemed to join in uttering the same phrase, one after another as they passed by.

'Draeder...' the ghostly voices whispered. 'Draeder von Halkern...'

They repeated the same thing over and over, as if the wizard's very name were an accusation. Felix heard it, and though he struggled to keep climbing through the pain and the fatigue in his bones, he managed to call out to his companion above.

'These phantoms... They seem to know you,' he said. 'How can that be?'

Draeder tried to ignore it. He pressed onwards, shouting down to Felix to do the same. But the voices only grew louder, and more numerous.

Among the myriad phantoms dancing about in the mist, one figure finally veered closer. Its spectral form grew more substantial, drawing in fog and shadow until its features were well-defined. No mere phantom, Felix could see that the hovering ghost had taken the form of an old man.

It swooped down, apart from the cadre of spectral familiars, to pass right by Felix and then past Draeder above him.

'Betrayer!' it said, in a raspy, eerie voice.

The phantom turned, moving through the sky for another pass. Its eyes were black and its translucent hands tried to clutch in vain at Draeder as it flew along.

'I gave you shelter. I took you in,' it continued. 'You repaid me with treachery… deceit… and murder.'

'What does that mean, Draeder?' Felix shouted. 'What is it saying?'

'Pay them no mind, Felix,' Draeder shouted back. 'The dead who dwell here are jealous of the living and wish to deprive us of our lives. They will do or say anything to make us like them. Deceivers and liars, all.'

'But how could they…?'

Draeder pre-empted him, looking up at the bastions rising atop the tower, finally in view, almost near enough to reach.

'Keep moving, Felix,' he yelled down. 'Do not allow them to lead you astray. We're nearly there. Just keep climbing!'

Felix looked out at the swirling spectral familiars, hovering and cavorting in the haunted mist. He caught sight of one. The ghostly old man stared him in the eye as he paused on the bone ladder. Something about its gaze gave him pause. Though frightful and ghastly, a far greater horror occurred to him as he looked into the phantom's eyes.

He somehow knew that every word it said was true.

12

Felix and Draeder both collapsed upon reaching the top of the tower.

Exhausted from the climb, their eyes were red-sore and haunted by the ghostly terrors that had assailed them. They were at first relieved to find the rooftop quite empty, though Felix blanched at the stench. A foul stink pervaded the place with odours of rotting carrion and mouldered, decaying flesh.

For a moment, they merely listened as they huddled, doing their best to catch their breath and recover whatever strength they had left. The tower crest was eerily silent. No banshee screams or ghostly howls could be heard atop it. Everything was still and deathly cold. Not even a gust of wind disturbed the peculiar, sinister serenity that reigned atop the necromancer's black tower.

Pillars crafted of bleached human skulls framed the perimeter of the rooftop. Tattered banners hung limp beneath them. The crest was bare in every direction, crowned only by a single altar, elevated at the centre of a crimson star etched into the roof stones. The red pentacle sparkled against the granite, gleaming in the cloud-diffused moonlight.

It was a massive piece of ceremonial statuary, set upon a huge pile of discarded human bones. The ritual dais was itself a single mighty slab, gilded and bejewelled in a ghastly fashion. The face of it was cut to the likeness of a horned skull. On each side there stood familiar skeletal guardians, their bony limbs garbed in gold armour and their gauntlets resting upon massive swords.

Skeletal vultures cast in pure gold flanked the flat-top central platform, their bony wings rising up like serrated daggers on each side of it. Dark, oily smears of blood and muck stained the whole of it with old spatter and thick streaks. Beneath it lay dry pools of maroon and purple that reeked of death.

Draeder was the first to get up. He staggered across the summit, approaching the altar with a kind of reverence Felix had never seen him employ before. Despite that, he quickly began searching all around the platform. He cast aside bones and refuse, digging and reaching all around the altar.

'It's not here,' he muttered. 'It should be here.'

Felix came up behind him, straining just to walk.

'You have to explain,' he said.

Draeder looked around.

'It should be here,' he said. 'Everything I read, everything I learned tells me it should be near the altar.'

'That's not what I mean,' Felix replied. 'And you know it.'

Draeder didn't seem to hear him, or to care.

'Those phantoms knew you. They knew *about you*,' Felix continued. 'What did they mean… murder?'

'I told you, ignore them, it was nothing,' Draeder said.

He came around the far side of the altar, posing as if he were the necromancer himself, lifting his hands in a mock ritual, guiding himself through a silent rite.

'What are you up to?' Felix asked.

Draeder didn't reply. He kept looking, scanning the back of the altar until his eyes widened. He reached down, grabbed hold of something and pulled it. The slow groan of rusted hinges once again rose up, just as tired and creaky as the tower gate far below. With the sounds, the altar itself began to move, sliding forward to reveal a chamber directly beneath.

Felix came around to see what Draeder had discovered.

'Of course,' the wizard said. 'The necromancer's lair was beneath the summit. It must be there. *It must be.*'

Descending yet another winding, cobwebbed staircase, the two men entered a chamber of the macabre. The room beneath the rooftop was a shrine to the study of darkness. It was at once a vast library of foul knowledge and a repository of tools devoted to the most sinister of conjuring.

A round room not unlike the many lower levels of the black tower, this one was crammed full of every grim accoutrement imaginable. Shelves lined the entire room, floor to ceiling. Every bit of space was crammed with texts. Rows upon rows of bound volumes circled the chamber, mismatched and arranged in chaotic fashion. Their spines bore all manner of varied inscriptions, hieroglyphs, runes and twisted elven characters. Dozens of racks beside them were packed full of weathered, crumbling scrolls.

Baubles and gemstones affixed atop white skulls rested upon gruesome pedestals draped in chains. Candelabra cobbled together from human bones stood at intervals throughout, holding the remains of old black candles, the cold wax frozen in ancient drippings.

At the centre of it all though, resting upon a bone-carved stand all its own, was the prize they had so long sought. A single book.

Draeder approached it slowly, creeping towards the tome with the lightest of footsteps. When he came close enough, he reached out and scooped up the dusty volume in his arms as a father might cradle a newborn child. Tears welled in his eyes.

'It is true. It is here,' he whispered. 'The Book of Ashur.'

It was a volume unlike any other Felix had ever set eyes upon, or any other in the grim library itself. A grisly monument to unspeakable horrors, the very spine of the tome appeared to be made of human vertebrae, the white bones stitched together with strands of woven gold. The leather cover was blackened from age and centuries of exposure to the foul winds its pages conjured from the depths.

Draeder held the book with the awed reverence of a true believer. When he opened it, leafing through the pages, he inhaled the rotten scent of old papyrus, every inch of its surface scrawled with bright crimson runes.

'Written in the very blood of the ancient mages themselves,' he whispered. 'This will make me the most powerful wizard alive.'

Felix turned at the statement.

'So *it is* true,' he said.

'What is that?'

'You have no intention of helping the armies of the Empire. You never did. This was about you all along.'

Draeder looked up from his precious volume. His eyes were narrowed, and sinister. The grin on his lips was merciless. A terrible feeling crept over Felix in that moment. The last words of Erhard echoed in his head.

'And what of all the good men we lost on this journey, the sacrifices and the hardships we suffered?' Felix continued.

Draeder peered back at him with a familiar, condescending gaze.

'Those men served their purpose. Do not fret over them. As I told you before, they were beneath us, Felix,' he answered.

'You were out for yourself all along.'

'We're all out for ourselves, Felix,' Draeder replied. 'A lesson I'm surprised it took you this long to learn.'

Felix stammered.

'In any case,' Draeder continued. 'That is all in the past now. You should be pleased, my friend. Soon I will take my rightful place as the most powerful wizard of this age, and for your assistance on this journey you will continue to enjoy my favour – as my loyal assistant.'

But Felix refused to let the matter go.

'All your talk of the nobility of death magic, was that a lie as well?'

'No, that was quite accurate,' Draeder replied. 'The Amethyst Order believes precisely what I told you.'

'But you do not,' Felix realised.

'The true power in death magic is the ability to control it, to move through it. To live beyond its cold touch,' he continued. 'I admit, I seek that power for myself, in these lost secrets of Skethris that I have now obtained.'

'And *that* was why they threw you out of their order,' Felix said.

Before Draeder could reply, a third voice answered instead. It was weirdly familiar as its tones reverberated through the chamber.

'This man was never *in* the Amethyst Order,' the strange, ghostly voice declared.

As the words echoed, a figure took shape out of the mist. When the fog came together, Felix recognized the face. It was a tired, old man.

'The ghost beside the tower,' he said.

The figure took on a more complete form then, spectral but garbed in the full regalia of an Amethyst adept.

'You know him, this ghostly wizard,' Felix said. 'Tell me how.'

Draeder sneered. He clasped the book and turned towards the stairwell. The voice called out to him nonetheless.

'You were turned away by the Amethyst Order, adjudged unfit for the study of magic,' the ghostly figure said, pointing an accusing finger at Draeder.

Felix looked over to Draeder.

'The erratic casting. The failed spells,' he said. 'You were never a true wizard. Erhard saw through it, but not until it was too late. That was what he was trying to warn me about.'

'They refused to listen to me!' Draeder protested. 'My talents were obvious. My natural facility with the winds of magic was greater than any of them. I would have been the greatest of their Order! My gifts frightened them.'

'But you were not one to fade into the shadows,' the ghost wizard taunted.

'I spent years honing my skills, learning from anyone who would teach me,' Draeder said, now arguing with the ghost.

'You're nothing but a hedge wizard,' Felix replied. 'That's why your spells were so inconsistent.'

'Strong enough to save your life on more than one occasion,' Draeder rebuked.

'But weak enough to fail us on many more,' Felix replied. 'We all watched out for one another on the trail. Every one of us saved the others' necks more times than I can count. But that changes nothing. Everything you said, everything you did was a lie. And many good men died because of it.'

'As I said, they were of little consequence. Those men died so that I might take what I deserve to have,' Draeder answered.

'What you deserve?' the ghostly wizard continued, his voice rising as his spectral face twisted with wrath. 'You've earned nothing. You came to me as a weary traveller, pretending to beg assistance. I took pity upon you, and the moment my guard was down you murdered me. You stole everything I had: my book, my scythe and even those robes you wear – my very identity!'

Felix stood stunned. Now, when he gazed upon the man who had been his travel companion, the only other survivor of their long ordeal, he had only contempt. He looked at everything again. The age-worn robes. The great scythe. The spell book.

Draeder remained indignant. He continued on his way, ascending the stairwell back to the tower summit. But Felix followed close behind, clambering to the top of the steps and clutching at Draeder from behind. The imposter wizard turned, anger simmering in his eyes.

'Ignore that ghostly wretch, Felix,' Draeder said. 'It matters little now.'

'But it is all true,' Felix replied. 'You lied, you cheated and you murdered your way to this place.'

Draeder clutched the book but looked back to Felix with an expression not of shame, but filled with a strange pride.

'Indeed,' he finally said. 'I did all of those terrible things, and many more, if you wish to know.'

Felix stepped back, his hand reaching for his sword.

'And do you know what it all means?' Draeder said. 'Nothing. It means nothing now. For I have the Book of Ashur. The power long denied to me is finally mine to wield. There is no one who can stand against me now.'

Felix drew his sword, pointing it at the wizard.

'I can't let you leave here with that,' he said.

Draeder sighed, shaking his head.

'You're making a mistake, Felix,' he warned. 'You and I are very much alike. I saw it in you the moment we met. We're men of culture and wisdom. We deserve to take what is rightfully ours. We are the men who should rule this land, and this book gives me the power to do so. Now put aside this nonsense and take your place beside me.'

Felix kept his blade raised.

'I want no part of this.'

'Step aside, Felix,' Draeder said. 'Lower your sword and permit me to pass. I could have struck you down already, if I wished to.'

Felix clenched his teeth and gripped his blade.

'You're going to have to,' he said.

Draeder smirked back at him, lifting his scythe and pointing it at Felix. He began to chant, and his great staff started to glow with violet flame, ready to strike. Felix shifted into a fighting stance, prepared to launch his own attack.

Neither one got the chance. A booming crash of thunder split the skies overhead, quaking the very floor of the tower. With it came a flash of crimson lightning. It blinded them both, casting their armaments aside and sending them reeling.

A terrible, ghostly voice followed. It seemed to call out from the dying echoes of thunder across the summit.

'Blood will be shed here only by my hand,' the voice proclaimed.

It was possessed of an ethereal quality, deep-throated and raspy, yet mellifluous as a winter wind. The words were enunciated with an antiquated, formalistic diction, in the manner of a man to whom the common tongue was quite foreign. His accent was unrecognisable, blending words together with an eerie, slithering lilt.

'Who goes there?' Felix demanded, turning his sword from Draeder and raising it against the shadows. 'Reveal yourself!'

A swirling smog of red mist and black flames answered him, a sudden cyclone that swirled out of dark clouds above. Ghastly faces, claws and vile phantasms roiled within the foul tempest. The wrenching cries of weeping maidens, suffering and wailing in some unknown sorrow, sang a foul serenade to the coming of the storm. Bloodcurdling, sinister laughter echoed from the dim, sending ripples through the rancid mist.

Draeder seemed to recognize the signs. His confidence melted into a look of utter terror.

'By the gods,' he muttered. 'It cannot be.'

The unliving fog was a mere harbinger. From its heart, a centre of raging darkness and howling winds, a figure began to grow. At first no more than the outline of a being, a silhouette against a tableau of shadow and flame, its full aspect soon came into view. Draeder turned to look upon it, and his face went pale.

Even as he said the name, he couldn't believe his eyes.

'Skethris.'

* * *

His was a visage of utter terror – something that only barely resembled a living man. He was so gaunt as to be skeletal, though not shorn of flesh like the undead guardians beyond the tower. Desiccated, grey skin covered his ghoulish face. It was deathly pallid and emaciated, hints and outlines of skull showing through the leathery skin that was drawn thin across it. The barest hint of beard whiskers, wispy and long, clung to his pointed chin. A twisted rune was branded into his forehead.

His deep-set eyes peered out from under a set of bony brows, glowering like two crimson flames.

The robes he wore were ancient and ragged, deep sable and the maroon shade of old blood. The folds of his mantle were almost ethereal, as though woven of nothing more than mist and shadow. Ghostly faces shimmered in and out of view within the many creases of the voluminous sheath; the tortured faces of the undead screaming out for a rest they could never know.

Skulls and cryptic death-runes ran along the edges of his midnight-black cloak, glistening red. A spiny cowl rose up like a series of evil horns behind his baleful head. Stringy, matted locks of long, white hair hung all about his crown, framing his face and further suggesting his great age.

Felix's eyes burned and his lungs revolted. He choked on the icy frost and the sulphur fumes that flooded the tower summit. He looked upon Skethris in frightened disbelief. For a moment the ghastly figure merely menaced them in silence. Then he spoke again.

'How foolish of you to attempt to steal what has long been mine,' he said. 'Your punishment for that will be unimaginable, an everlasting agony the likes of which you cannot yet even conceive.'

Felix edged back from the roiling, haunted mist. He came nearer to Draeder, though even that seemed unwise.

'You said he was long dead,' Felix said, trying to keep his voice low, as if to hide his words from the necromancer.

'Everyone I consulted told *me* that he was,' Draeder replied, though his gaze could not turn away from the dreadful sight of the necromancer. 'They lied to me!'

Skethris snickered, a deep and disturbing laughter that echoed like his booming, ghastly voice.

'Just as I gather you have lied to all those you have met, ever since,' the necromancer replied. 'Rather fitting, is it not?'

Felix and Draeder came together, united again for the moment in the face of a much more terrible enemy. But the necromancer permitted them no quarter. Not even a moment's respite.

'Now you will pay for your crimes,' Skethris declared.

The necromancer raised his bony arms, bringing the horrid swirl around him to a boil. Incomprehensible incantations followed, sparking blood-red lightning across his pointed fingertips. The wailing souls that flanked him raged as he cast down his cold vengeance, raking the crest of his tower with jagged bolts of black flame.

The summit erupted in a paroxysm of dark fire. One twisted tangle crashed into the floor only inches in front of Draeder. He tried to dodge, to make a leap for some kind of safety, but a second whirl of death magic sent him into a tumble across the rooftop. Felix rushed to his side. But he never made it. Yet another blast of cold flame sent them hurtling apart.

As he staggered to his feet, Draeder was hit by a final

explosion of lightning. He lost his grip on both the book and his scythe-staff as he fell backwards, sending them sliding across the floor of the tower. In no more than a moment, he and Felix lay exposed. Skethris cackled at the sight of the two interlopers, howling in delight as though merely playing with them before exacting his true vengeance.

Felix regained his footing first, seeing Draeder coming to his feet slower, weakened by the attacks he'd already endured. The force of the blow had opened a gulf between them, separated by a stretch that seemed so very far under the watch of the necromancer and his minions. The Book of Ashur now lay across the tower summit.

Felix didn't waste a moment. Risking another attack, he dodged a column of ghostly fire and leaped towards Draeder, sliding through the foetid dust until he reached the hedge wizard.

'We have to stay together,' he said. 'It's our only chance.'

Draeder shook his head.

'We can't fight him, he's too powerful,' he replied.

'We may not need to,' Felix said. 'If we charge for the edge of the tower, right through the centre of the ghostly horde, we might be able to get over the side fast enough to make it down.'

'And if we can't?'

Felix lifted his sword, turning towards the horror they were about to launch themselves upon.

'Then we'll die, just as we surely will if we stay where we are,' he said.

Draeder hesitated. He looked back at the menacing, horrid form of Skethris, the master of the undead looming in the heart of the storm. Then he turned to the book. It lay just out of reach. He couldn't draw his sight from it, despite the danger.

'All that power, so very near,' Draeder whispered. 'If I could only reach it…'

The ghostly figures closed in around them.

'We must go, 'Felix shouted. 'Now!'

Felix struggled to his feet. He lifted his sword one more time, whispered a final prayer to Sigmar and pressed the attack. Though he could not see who or what his blade struck, he plunged headlong into the mist, his own sight robbed from him as he dove into the putrid miasma of ghosts and fumes. He whirled and slashed, shouting and raging in his last stand against the darkness. But he soon realized that his blade cut only mist. His steel met nothing but smoke and shadow.

It was a moment before he realized that Draeder was not beside him. The young wizard had made his own charge – but not with Felix.

He turned, and tried to see through the mist and the black haze. When he finally saw the nobleman, he was across the rooftop. Though Draeder had managed to once again take hold of the Book of Ashur, he was surrounded by the ghastly minions of Skethris.

'Draeder!' Felix shouted. 'You must leave it behind!'

It was already too late.

As Felix watched in horror, Skethris turned his full fury upon Draeder, not attacking directly but rather swarming him with his spectral followers. Claws and cold hands grasped at him from every direction. Vaporous tentacles coiled like serpents around his legs, rooting him into the floor of the tower. Phantom chains sprang up from the stone. They encircled him, plunging barbed hooks and spears into every corner of his flesh.

'Though your feeble magic was enough to bring you here,' Skethris taunted, 'you are nothing compared to me. My hands command the winds of death itself. Even with the Book of

Ashur, you stand no chance against my power.'

The foul necromancer hovered before Draeder. He towered above the frightened young hedge wizard in a column of mist and dark fire. When he lifted his bony, gnarled hand Draeder's entire body rose up. Skethris reached out with his other hand, his long fingers stretched like talon claws aimed at Draeder's face.

'But you are… *interesting*,' the necromancer said.

His eyes grew brighter, burning with scarlet flame as he studied the man he held in thrall before him.

'The stench of death surrounds you,' Skethris continued. 'The tortured spirits of your many victims trail behind you, in an ever-present wake of suffering and ruin.'

'Please, I only wished to learn,' Draeder pleaded. 'To see what you see. To know what you know.'

Skethris smiled as he clenched his fingers into a fist. Draeder cried out in pain the moment he did so, howling with a scream of such agony that it turned Felix's blood cold.

Felix readied himself to face the same fate, holding his sword high in a last measure of defiance, though he knew it was no use. The necromancer seemed unconcerned with him however, all of his attention focused on Draeder.

'You wish to learn the deepest mysteries of the dark?' Skethris said.

Draeder trembled, squinting and squealing in absolute misery as the necromancer delighted in tormenting him.

He could manage little more than a feeble response.

'Yes…'

Again Skethris turned his fingers, sending jolts of pain rippling through every inch of Draeder's flesh, laughing at the spectacle of suffering.

Felix edged backwards, finding that the phantoms still

did not impede him. All eyes upon the summit were now drawn to Draeder von Halkern, suspended above the tower, tortured and pilloried for his hubris, the dire consequence of his abject failure.

'You wish to know death itself?' the necromancer asked.

Draeder could barely acknowledge.

'I *am* death,' Skethris said. 'And you belong to me now.'

A dark energy pulsed through Draeder. It surged in his bones, filling his eyes with a blood-red glow.

'I am yours… master,' he said.

Skethris smiled, laughing along with his chorus of lost souls.

'Then as your first act of servitude, renounce the world of the living and rid this place of the defiler who remains,' the necromancer announced.

Draeder's head turned, moving slowly until his glowering crimson eyes came to stare upon Felix.

Across the summit, Felix gripped his sword. He now realized what had not occurred to him before – Draeder *had not* failed. He had found exactly what he sought.

The rogue wizard leaped from the embrace of the necromancer, trailing mist and flame as he charged upon Felix. His scythe swung high over his head, the long, wicked blade slashing down as he came.

'You should have joined me when you had the chance, Felix,' he hissed. 'Now your choice has doomed you.'

Felix met the attack, and though his muscles ached with exhaustion, his sword clanged against the wizard's staff in a clash of steel and splinters. Draeder's face was crazed, his eyes seething with dark magic. He wheeled, and struck again, but this time Felix was faster. He parried, knocking Draeder's scythe aside.

Then he whirled around, slicing back at Draeder. His sword

tore a bloody gash across his chest. A second cut ripped open the flesh of his leg in a blur of red. The wizard howled and clutched at his wounds, staggering through the flames and the blood.

'You're wrong,' Felix whispered. 'This was always your choice. Your path. It was never mine. *I'm not like you.*'

Draeder swung his scythe again in a last-ditch effort, flailing it towards Felix. But Felix dodged, cutting the staff to pieces with a slash that ripped through Draeder's arm, sending him crumpling down in a heap.

Then Felix turned and ran, and though Draeder wailed in agony behind him, calling out his name as he crossed over to the edge of the wall, Felix never looked back. He jumped over the parapet, sliding down until he reached a ledge, where he climbed the rest of the way to the floor of the valley.

For a moment, as he passed the tower gates towards the avenue of death, Felix could still hear the awful, chilling screams. He could make out the last dying echoes of Draeder von Halkern; cries of desperate anguish, fading somewhere in the distance, cursing him through unspeakable tortures.

Then it was gone. The mist and the shadows and any hint of the undead menace that he now knew lurked behind him in the shadows. With nothing but his sword at his side, thankful for the very life in his bones, Felix turned his back on the darkness and began the long journey away from the Valley of Death.

CURSE OF THE EVERLIVING

David Guymer

Felix angled his face from the wind and narrowed his eyes, holding up a hand to shield himself from the grapeshot hail and sleet. The snow was falling thick and hard, whipped up into swirling eddies by the howling gale before lashing spitefully back at his face.

'Gotrek!' he cried, straining to be heard over the storm.

He blinked hard, spitting ice water as a fresh gust blasted his cheeks. The Trollslayer had been *right* there, not ten paces ahead, but the moment the blizzard had struck it was as if the dwarf had simply vanished. Felix had screamed until his throat burned, for all the good it had done him. He tried again anyway, shouting his companion's name into the storm.

'Gotrek! Where are you?'

He turned on the spot, feeling panic rise. It was like a directionless maze of formless white and it would be easy for him to lose his bearings. Quickly, he spun around, stooping into the wind as he staggered on.

His eyes focused on a dark shape as it emerged from the snowstorm. 'Thank Sigmar,' he mumbled, stumbling towards it. 'We need shelter, Gotrek,' he yelled as he drew near. 'We can't stay out here in this.'

The shape remained motionless. Its stillness was unnatural, its body becoming steadily buried in snow. It was not the Slayer, that much was clear. It was the statue of a man, kneeling in the snow with its face lifted to the sky in prayer. Something in its aspect chilled Felix even more than the harsh winds, but he tried to set the feeling aside. Not even in the desolate wilds of Kislev did statues appear in the middle of nowhere. It meant people and, hopefully, shelter.

He placed a hand on the statue's icy shoulder, using its support to rest his legs as he cast his eyes about for the Slayer once again. He snatched his hand from the statue, staring at it as he tried to make sense of what he had just felt.

That had not been the touch of stone.

With a grim sense of foreboding, he reached out and worked to brush away the snow from the shape's forehead. Even half prepared, he couldn't hold back a cry of horror as he swept away a layer of frost to reveal a pair of dull green eyes staring out from that upturned face.

He shook his head at the sorry sight. A frozen corpse. The whites of the eyes were cracked and dry, faded with the departure of the man's soul.

'There's another one over here, manling.'

Felix bit down on his lip to swallow a curse. 'Don't sneak up on me like that,' he muttered tersely. 'Where have you been anyway? You said the map pointed in this direction.'

The dwarf didn't respond, forging through the snow like a barge through pack ice. Small icicles sprouted from the frosted gold of his nose chain and the blizzard had left his bright crest of hair flattened and sodden, running orange dye smearing the swirling tattoos on his forehead. His immense battle axe

rested lightly across one hugely muscled shoulder; the glowing runes of its silver-blue blade painted the falling snow like
a bloody halo. The Slayer's bare torso was goose-bumped – a
thick, squirrel-skin scarf wrapped beneath the beard his one
concession to the harsh demands of a Kislevite winter.

Gotrek paused to examine the frozen figure. 'Same clothes,'
he mumbled, seemingly to himself.

Felix craned forward to see for himself. By the look of his
attire, the man might have been some kind of knight or warrior priest. He was garbed in crimson robes cinched at the
waist with a silver chain and worn over an armoured suit of
interlocking white scales. His most striking feature, however,
had to be his age. He was old, very old, deep lines frozen for
eternity into hard flesh, arms and chest withered by time.

Gotrek stepped away, clapping snow from his ham-like fists.
'I don't like this, manling. I don't like this one bit.'

Felix thought long and hard before answering. It had been
too long since he had seen something he *had* liked. A sudden
rush of wind tore the reply from his lips, sodden shanks of
filthy blond hair slapping at his cheeks as he hunched low. He
choked as his cloak snatched and fought at his collar.

As the wind subsided, he straightened and grinned.

The sudden gale had parted the snow to grant them a
momentary glimpse of a squat, black-walled castle crouched
atop a nearby hill, before the blizzard swept over them again.

'Gotrek! We're saved!'

Gotrek turned and peered through the flurry with his one
good eye, as if the wall of snow were no barrier to his dwarf
vision. He shrugged. 'If you say so, manling.'

Felix edged along the dark-stoned corridor, his footsteps
echoing eerily along the length of the abandoned hallway. It

seemed Gotrek had been justified in his misgivings. The gate had been unbarred, but they had found dozens more frozen guards inside. Felix wished he had turned around right there, but his bones ached with the cold and whatever else this place was, at least it was out of the wind.

They pressed on, past faded, peeling canvases and beneath high arched windows that rattled angrily in the snow-laden wind. The hallway continued until it met with another, stretching into frigid darkness to left and right.

'Hold up there, manling,' rumbled Gotrek, just as Felix had begun to move.

The dwarf stepped past him and got down to his knees, setting his axe reverently on the flagstones by his side. As the dwarf brushed aside the frost that clung to the dark stones, his damaged face was suddenly bathed in a soft, bluish light.

'What is that?' whispered Felix, peering over him.

'Ice runes. For warding or protection, I think.' Gotrek stood up with a shrug. 'Poorly rendered. I can't read it.'

Felix looked about nervously, his fingertips feeling for the dragonhead hilt of his runesword Karaghul. 'Protection from what, I wonder?'

Gotrek smiled grimly, recovering his axe. 'Let's just hope we don't freeze to death before we find out.'

Felix turned away with a scowl. Trust the Slayer to be thrilled by the prospect of a minion of Chaos close by. All he craved was somewhere warm to sleep.

'Come on, let's–'

'Silence,' Gotrek hissed, cutting him off with a raised hand. 'Listen.'

Felix froze. At first he heard nothing, except the buffeting of the wind against glass. He was ready to say as much when another sound reached his ears. From the shadows of the left-hand passage there came the sickly sound of shallow, rasping breaths; something approaching with the shambling gait of useless limbs dragged across stone.

Felix struggled to draw his sword in the narrow hallway, holding it tight to his own chest, its point almost against his chin.

Gotrek pressed him forward, bristling with unbridled aggression. 'Out of my way, manling!'

Felix would have loved nothing better, but the dwarf was far too broad to squeeze past him, and the realisation dawned that he was trapped between an agitated Slayer and the dark silhouette just beginning to rise from the gloom.

'Hold!' he yelled, as the apparition came near.

The shuffling form halted.

'*Are you... real?*' rasped the voice from the darkness.

Gotrek shoved Felix aside. 'Real we may be,' he barked, 'but what is it that asks?'

An awkward moment passed. Felix hardly dared to take a breath.

'A *dwarf*,' observed the voice. 'I don't remember ever seeing a dwarf before. I suppose you must be real.'

The figure that dragged itself free of the shadows was as near to a corpse as a living man could be. His skin was drawn and callow, hair clinging to his head in clumps of silver. The only features that looked alive were his eyes, with pupils of the most striking gold, but even those were hung with heavy bags like bruises.

The old man shambled closer, his feet sliding to a halt as they neared the frostily glowing ice runes. 'You'll forgive me. It has been so long since I last had visitors.' He extended a pallid, blue-veined hand that seemed almost transparent in the rune's light. 'Viktor. Last of the Bilenkov line.'

Felix took the old man's hand, trying not to show how its tinder-dry touch made his skin crawl.

Gotrek pointed back down the corridor. 'Your home is filled with frozen corpses,' he said, showing his usual amount of tact. 'Are they the rest of your lot?'

The old man's gap-toothed smile faltered, and it took him a moment to answer.

'They are... *were*, sworn to me, after a fashion. It comforts me to see them here still.'

Gotrek turned and muttered to himself. 'Mad as a coot.'

Felix frowned but didn't contradict him. Viktor seemed not to hear.

'You will want food and warmth. Come! I have food enough for a hundred, and spiced vodka from Erengrad, untouched for two centuries. Come!'

The strange old man shuffled off the way he had come. Felix made to follow as Gotrek appeared at his side, a brawny fist pinning his arm at the elbow. The dwarf sniffed the air. 'Smell that, manling?' He sniffed again, his ugly face cracking apart into a leering grin. 'Chaos taint.'

'Oh really, this far north? I imagine you can spit on the Chaos Wastes from the battlements, on a clear day.'

Gotrek laughed grimly. 'Interesting thought, manling, but mark my word. There's something in this castle. Something powerful and old. When have I been wrong?'

Felix suffered his opinions in silence. There was really no right answer to that.

He hurried on after the old man, trying to ignore his sudden trepidation. Viktor waited for them before a dark, iron-banded door at the hall's end. Felix struggled to keep his teeth from chattering and even Gotrek – sturdy though his dwarfish constitution was – hugged his thick arms close to his chest. How did a feeble old man survive out here on his own?

A prickling sense of disquiet wormed its way into his belly as Viktor reached for the latch. 'Herr Viktor, wait. Perhaps you should let us check that all is as it should be.'

Viktor treated him to a wide grin as he unlatched the door and pushed it inwards. 'Such courage. Yes, you will do nicely.'

A fresh blast of icy wind drove through the open doorway. Felix shivered as he felt it pass straight through him.

'Come,' said Viktor. He turned and passed through the open doorway before calling back. 'Let me warm you.'

Felix caught Gotrek's look. The runes of the dwarf's axe underlit his scarred and battered face with a baleful glow. 'Do you smell it now?'

Felix nodded reluctantly, and raised his sword. 'Sigmar's mercy!' he exclaimed. 'The old man.' With the Slayer in tow, he rushed headlong into the open chamber.

The room was circular with high walls surrounding an inner ring of limestone columns. The pillars stood bereft of purpose amidst the rubble of a fallen ceiling, sinking into the snow that billowed through the cracked roof.

'Viktor!' Felix yelled into the darkness.

'Be still, manling. I think we're about to learn what those runes were for.'

Muttering a curse, Felix attempted to peer through the swirling snow. It was hopeless. He couldn't see ten strides. 'Is he a cultist? A sorcerer?'

'I reckon there's more to him than that.'

Adopting a fighting stance, Felix held his sword before him as he crept towards the nearest pillar, studying each of the stone columns in turn. Where was the old man hiding? He tried listening for any sign of movement, but all he could hear was the crunch of fresh snow beneath Gotrek's boots as he made his way towards the centre of the room.

'Gotrek,' he hissed. 'I think that's possibly the last place we want to be.'

'Are you suggesting there's anything here I should be afraid of, manling? Hah!' Gotrek swung his axe through a lazy circle, making the starmetal sing. 'Come out, fiend,' he bellowed. 'My axe thirsts!'

Felix hurried to the Slayer's side, the echoes of the challenge fading away into the falling snow. His short breaths came in clouds of rapidly cooling fog; his arms were trembling. At last he could endure no more. 'You heard him, Viktor! Where are you?'

A cold laugh reverberated between the circle of standing stones. 'Dead, Herr Jaeger, long dead. Merely a single link in a neverending chain.'

'Hold fast, manling. He hopes to weaken your guard,' Gotrek snorted. Hot air blasted from his flattened nose as if he were a maddened bull. There was something about the Slayer's presence that was always profoundly reassuring. Felix doubted the crazed old man would laugh so hard once Gotrek was done with him.

But again, wicked laughter echoed through the whiteout. 'And what is it that you fear, dwarf?'

'I fear nothing, in this world or the next!'

'Bold words from someone so small.'

Felix shuffled backwards as the insane tittering engulfed him. 'And as for your human companion – he is *filled* with fear.'

Felix felt his fingers tremble on the grip of his sword. The old man's words circled some animal part of his brain like wolves. Inarguable instinct commanded him to run and–

'–Oww!'

Thick fingers pressed into his bicep like bands of steel. He looked down into the steady gaze of the Slayer.

'Take so much as one step back, manling, and you'll find my axe in your spine. How's *that* for fear?'

His lips parted to form an answer. Suddenly his eyes widened as a shape emerged from the snow like some daemon of shadow. Gotrek's back was turned and he was blind to the danger as the entity closed with impossible speed. Without time for fear, Felix dropped his shoulder and slammed into the dwarf's stomach. Gotrek bellowed in surprise as Felix bore him over, something angry whisking past as they rolled together through the snow.

Gotrek swore in Khazalid, no doubt to curse Felix for the clumsy get of goblins and simpletons that he was, and he came up straddling Felix's chest. The Slayer's thighs pressed down on his chainmail shirt like a vice, his eye glinting madly. '*Thank you*, manling.'

'You're welcome,' he wheezed though the dwarf's crushing grip.

With a roar, Gotrek spun to his feet, swinging his axe in an upward arc. The clang of metal on metal rang in Felix's ears. He looked up to see Gotrek's straining features, every massive muscle bulging and taut as the wiry old man forced a slender-bladed rapier onto his axe. Steam rose from Viktor's skin, his flesh bubbling like hot oil and his eyes blazing gold. The daemonic thing noticed his regard and opened his mouth into a lopsided grin. The open maw was empty but for bleeding gums.

Gotrek gave a strangled roar, forcing every sinew against whatever daemonic might lent strength to Viktor's withered arms. The runes of his axe glowed brighter and brighter as Gotrek struggled, bathing the contest in a bloody light.

All of a sudden, one of the ancient runes of power flickered and died, followed by another, and then another. Felix had never seen anything like it.

'What in all the gods...' he murmured.

Viktor cackled, oblivious to the blood that ran freely from his mouth, as the Slayer's axe turned dark. The old man raised one hand from his sword, showing no difficulty restraining the spitting and cursing Slayer one-handed as he grabbed the dwarf by the dyed and crusted roots of his beard. In one moment of impossible strength, he hauled Gotrek from his feet, spinning him around and around like a hammer before letting go. The Slayer flailed his arms madly, before crashing through one of the limestone columns. The massive pillar crumpled, crashing to earth at the old man's back, but Viktor didn't even flinch.

Felix cried out. 'Gotrek!'

Viktor vanished into the billowing whiteout, but Felix knew he couldn't be far. His heart thumped. He knew of only one thing that could gift such power – daemonic possession. His hand groped for his sword but he had lost it somewhere in that initial roll with Gotrek.

He spotted it some way off in the deepening snow, buried halfway to the hilt. He dived, his fingers tightening around its grip as he dropped into a roll that carried him back to his knees, steadying himself upon the icy stones.

He flicked a strand of hair from his eyes, squinting into the glittering haze.

Where *was* the cursed creature?

A kick struck him under the jaw before he even registered the movement. His head snapped back, reflex jerking the sword from his grip. A hand, soft and sticky with blood, but stronger than a troll, gripped his throat. Helpless as a child, Felix was hauled upright.

He stared into the demented eyes of his attacker, just as one golden orb burst into flames. The eye burned like balefire in its socket but the thing that had been Viktor didn't seem to notice or care. Its face sloughed away to reveal bleeding muscles, and its toothless mouth opened to speak, its voice bubbling as though its lungs drowned in blood.

'Sentinels die and wards fade, but *I* am Everliving. Your body is strong, for a mortal, and still youthful. It will last me for many years still to come.'

Felix tried to speak but could not. He felt sick. He had always suspected that it would end like this.

Viktor opened his bleeding mouth and began to chant, sickly brutal words flowing from his lips like blood from a severed artery. Felix felt his vision swim, a wave of dizziness passing through him. He looked up at the leering daemonic thing, but its face seemed to warp and twist before his very eyes. Pain seared his skull, echoing with the daemon's voice.

'In you I will live anew...'

For an instant, their minds touched. He saw a flurry of images, like a blood-soaked picture book of horrors and brutality perpetrated over uncounted centuries. Faces raced by. Men. Women. Children. Some, he recognised from the portraits in the hall, but there were more, so many more. All in pain, all in terror, all dying in unspeakable violence. And he heard a name.

Ghrizzhtadt... Ghrizzhtadt the Bloody. Death is not the end. Not for the Everliving...

Just as his own consciousness began to flounder under the weight of untold atrocities, Felix felt the daemon's presence dragged away. He opened his eyes, sights and sounds flooding back in a rush.

He came up like a drowning man, finding his face dripping with blood.

Viktor's grip still held, but the lower half of his jaw had vanished and taken his chanting with it. A defiant artery spurted blood into Felix's face, and he glanced aside to see Gotrek's thrown axe embedded in the stone of the nearest column.

'Hold, Chaos spawn!' bellowed Gotrek. 'My axe is not yet done with you!' The bruised and bloodied Slayer stood atop a rock pile, his arm still extended from the throw that had saved Felix's soul. He leapt down, shaking dust and snow from his muscular frame.

Felix's fists beat against the daemon's arm. Flesh fell from the limb in greasy globs, until he scratched at naked muscle, but still the grip was like hell-forged iron.

Robbed of his daemonic voice, Viktor gargled from his splayed mouth, his tongue flopping around the unpronounceable words.

Gotrek ignored his protests, hurtling forwards unarmed, but Viktor's grip gave and he dropped Felix to the floor, molten fat dribbling from his fingers. Viktor howled in frustration as a punch from Gotrek smashed his ribs like brittle clay. He gasped, his melting body flopping to the bloodstained snow like a jellyfish. The old man tried to laugh, a sickly dying sound, blood splattering from his throat in seemingly endless supply.

Shaking off his disgust, Felix retrieved his sword from the snow, holding it point down above the daemon's dissolving chest. The thing met his eyes.

'Death is not the end,' Felix muttered. 'Not for the Everliving.'

The creature shuddered, a red mist rising from its body like a bloody shroud. Felix plunged his sword through the daemon's heart – so little of the beast remained that the blade passed through it as if it were not there at all. Felix's cry of triumph was cut short by a yelp of pain as the point struck hard stone.

The old man rocked from side to side as though in silent agony. Felix stepped back, leaving his sword standing as the man's body decayed around it. The collapsing husk continued to vent the strange mist which, if Felix squinted just right, seemed to coalesce into some kind of brooding shape, a golden pinprick glimmering like a single malevolent eye within the roiling haze.

Gotrek waved his axe angrily through the cloud, eliciting a terrible shriek that made Felix wince. The dimmed runes on the Slayer's axe flared once with blinding brilliance, before returning to a normal glow that slowly faded as the evil mist dispersed.

'You see? Daemon taint,' said Gotrek, spitting on the thing's corpse even as it continued to dissolve. 'Firmly back in the claws of its master now, I'd wager, and good riddance to it!'

Felix shivered and then sneezed. He felt clammy under his mail and he dreaded the thought of the sweat freezing against his skin. He gathered up his cloak and wrapped his hands, pressing the bundle to his face as he huffed warm clouds of air. 'Come on,' he mumbled. 'Let's find somewhere to start a fire while I still have the fingers to pen your epic.'

It was finished, he told himself. He let the dwarf lead him away, trying to dismiss the malicious laughter ringing between his thoughts.

Black smoke choked the small antechamber, summoning tears to Felix's eyes. He dared not open the door, not even a fraction. Even sat this close to the fire he could feel the ice in his bones.

And some instinct told him he should not. Some whispered fear implored him to stay down, stay hidden. Shivering, he tore more pages from an ancient book and tossed them into the flames. Watching the paper bundles disappear in crispy flares, he tried to convince himself that all was well. It didn't work.

He glanced over the fire at his silent companion. Felix frowned. Gotrek had probably retreated into one of his more morose moods. His failure to meet the glorious death he craved weighed heavily upon him at times.

Gotrek brooded over a yellowed parchment, the corners curling inwards from where it had been rolled. Felix was distrustful of any map that confused Middenheim with Marienburg, but the dwarf had been immediately convinced by its authenticity. Or perhaps it had been the promise of gold that had convinced his companion to part with two coppers to possess it?

He shivered again, blowing his nose on the hem of his cloak before presenting his open palms to the fire. 'The tomb of Okedai Khan, Gotrek?' He forced a smile in an attempt to quell his unease, but he felt about as cheerful as the frozen guardians they had encountered in the castle grounds. 'It seems unlikely that hobgoblins would bury their leaders with gold, even if the man who sold you that map was truthful about having already seen it.'

Still the dwarf said nothing, simply staring down, his one eye glinting red with reflected flames. Felix scratched his stubbled chin in concern. He had honestly thought the mention of gold would spark some life into the dwarf's heart.

He shuffled around the fire's edge until he was sitting at his companion's side. 'Gotrek. Are you asleep?'

The dwarf remained unresponsive, staring blankly down. Felix saw clearly now: the red fire was no reflection. Gotrek's eye glowed with its own light, the daemonic lustre of some inner horror!

He fell back with a cry, and the dwarf's eyelid flickered.

'Quiet, manling. I'm trying to think. It's hard enough in this damned cold without you carrying on like some hysterical elf woman.'

Felix gasped with relief. 'I thought... I thought...'

He trailed off. He'd thought what? That Gotrek was possessed by a daemon? What was he, a child that saw dark shapes in firelight and ran to his mother for protection from wicked spirits? He laid a palm on his forehead. He had a fever.

'What's the matter with you anyway?' Gotrek grunted, stretching his massive arms before the fire.

Felix's eyes widened. The Slayer's huge, broad chest was stained with barely dried blood, and the swirling blue tattoos seemed to writhe in the firelight as though quickened by some dark magic. The runes of his axe glowed with a dull red light, piercing Felix's soul like the eyes of a daemon.

'I'm... I'm sorry. Never mind.'

'Get some rest. You look bloody awful.'

Felix lay down, but sleep wouldn't come. The shadows had eyes. He felt them prickling at the nape of his neck. Gotrek had assured him more than once that the daemon was gone, banished by his axe to the Realm of Chaos.

Felix opened his eyes to glance suspiciously at the dwarf.

But of course, he *would* say that.

He cursed himself for a fool and, fighting down the sense of foreboding, tried to sleep. Fragments of memories swirled through his fevered mind. Not all of them were of events he recognised. There were unknown faces and cold, foreign lands. There was battle. There was death. He saw himself towering above it all, his blood-drenched sword gleaming in his hand, a mountain of bodies strewn before a throne of skulls.

He tossed and turned on the hard floor. A voice spoke in his mind, nothing more than the shadow of a whisper, ever present when he wasn't thinking of it, conspicuous by its absence when he did.

'*Sleep, Felix*,' it whispered, over and over with a tortuous monotony. '*Sleep*.'

'No...' he mumbled through dried lips, his eyes half closed.

Suddenly, filled with uncertain dread, he snapped awake. His heart raced from some half-remembered terror. The fire had sunk to glowing embers and he could hear the Slayer's vigorous snores from across the chamber. He worked his way into a corner and hugged his knees to his chin, staring fearfully at the darkened room. Gotrek's axe loomed large. It seemed to have grown massive, throwing dim shapes against the walls that flickered and writhed with shadow claws. At its black core, runes pulsed with a cold, rhythmic heartbeat.

'It's just a fever,' he repeated, over and over like a prayer. With his eyes scrunched tight, he tried to block out the fear, listening instead to the insistent voices inside his mind.

Felix's leather boots crunched into knee-deep snow. The sound of them carried unnervingly. The sun rose late in this strange northern sky and, despite the lateness of the morning, the forest remained dark, stars peering down from a clear sky. His scalp itched under their unwelcome scrutiny. He fancied that he could hear their cold, hard, whispering voices on the north wind.

A panicked squawk split the air. Felix shot his head around as a flock of waxwings took noisily to flight. He let out a long breath as he unclawed his fingers from the hilt of his sword.

Some way back, Gotrek waded through the drifts with his usual aggressive fervour. Lacking Felix's longer legs, the dwarf struggled in stubborn silence. Felix pinched the bridge of his nose as the dwarf caught up with him. Gotrek hadn't acted in any way he could call abnormal, but still the poet's stomach clenched every time the dwarf came near, with the strangest sensation of *otherness* that made his heart skip a beat.

Gotrek panted heavily. He planted his axe shaft into the frozen earth, crossing his powerful arms over the butt of the blade as he fought for breath. 'Trees and snow,' he said, staring at the spindly, snow-capped forms with a disapproving eye. Felix knew what was coming. 'Nothing but trees and snow. There's only one thing I despise more than trees and snow, and that's–'

'*Elves!*' screamed Felix. 'Yes, I understand – you hate elves! Shallya's mercy, you say nothing for hours on end and when you do speak I have to suffer this interminable nonsense!'

Neither of them spoke for a long moment. Felix trembled, his disquiet finally having bettered him. Gotrek merely glowered.

'I don't care much for your tone, manling. If it weren't for the oaths of friendship we swore, your corpse might now be decorating those damnable trees.'

'Oh yes, the oath!' cried Felix, close to tears. Since the day he had made the oath, Gotrek had dragged him to every foul place in the Old World and beyond. He had promised to follow the Slayer and record his mighty doom. It had been the naive promise of a drunken young fool.

A strange anger stoked his blood, filling his veins with bitterness and bile, bringing all of the hurt and pain bubbling back to the surface. 'Curse you! And curse your oath! I have a father who is old and frail, and a family that needs me. What of that?'

'Have a care, manling. There's naught in this world lower...' He paused for a moment before spitting out the words as though they were poison. '...than an *oathbreaker*.'

Felix tried to calm himself but couldn't. It was as if he were no longer in control of his own tongue. Rage filled him, a burning hatred that was only partly his own. He was doomed. Doomed to follow this mad dwarf until they were both dead. Suddenly it all became clear. It was so obvious he couldn't believe it had never occurred to him before.

Gotrek had to die.

His sword slithered from its scabbard almost with a will of its own.

Gotrek studied the blade with interest. His face split into a grin as his own ham-like fist slid ominously down the haft of his axe. 'And what do you plan to do with that, manling?'

Felix gave no answer, but something did – amused laughter whispered between his ears. *'Now you will rest, Felix. Rest, and live anew...'*

Whatever strange madness had driven him slipped away. He felt cold and empty. What had he done?

Something rustled amidst the trees, some animal, he assumed, startled by his little outburst. Gotrek heard the noise too, and something about it made his expression change, softening it into a crooked grin. He winked.

Felix's mouth dropped open.

The Slayer laughed and shoved a brawny fist into Felix's chest. He swayed back, arms windmilling in an unsuccessful attempt to stay upright as he plunged backwards into deep snow.

Spluttering on a mouthful of ice, Felix saw Gotrek turn away to face the forest.

'Come out, you filthy lurker!' he shouted. 'We know you're there.'

Felix rose, shivering uncontrollably as a shape detached

from one of the nearest trees. It was a tall, barrel-chested man, almost invisible against the snow in white fur britches and coat. The flaps of a mink ushanka hid his face such that only a short blond beard and pinched red cheeks peeked out below a pair of icy blue eyes. He carried a short yew bow unstrung in his hands like a staff.

'An excellent distraction, manling,' said Gotrek. 'I'll admit, you had me going there until I heard his breathing for myself.'

The fur-clad man held up his hands as Gotrek strode over to him. 'I mean no harm, I swear. My name is Tamascz and I was just gathering berries when I heard raised voices.' He looked downwards, clearly embarrassed. 'I hid.'

'Berries particularly vicious up here, are they?' grumbled Gotrek, prodding the man's bow with his axe.

'This is not your Empire,' said Tamacsz. 'In Kislev, everyone must be prepared to fight, be they man, woman, or child.'

Felix grunted in something that might have been amusement had his fraught nerves allowed it. He knew a thing or two about the... *ferocity* of Kislevite women, even before his former lover had been lost to darkness.

'Be gone, woodling. Run back to your berries,' Gotrek jeered.

'Wait, please,' said Felix, turning to Tamascz. 'We're a little lost. Maybe you can help us.'

'Say nothing, manling. You thought to venture into that castle against my advice. I don't trust this fellow, and I'll certainly not be sharing my gold with him.'

The woodsman backed away with a look of horror. 'You come from Castle Bilenkov?'

Felix shrugged. 'Perhaps. What of it?'

'Then goodbye!' Tamascz hurried away, almost slipping in the snow in his haste. 'Whatever fate awaits you is one you've earned. That house is cursed!'

'Bah!' scoffed Gotrek, waving his hand after the fleeing figure. 'Good riddance to him.'

Felix wasn't listening. His attention had been wholly claimed by Gotrek's axe, which seemed to be glowing brighter and brighter in the dwarf's hands. At last, the Slayer noticed, staring as though his timeless heirloom had been switched for some cheap replica. Vicious daemonic syllables seemed to drip from its edge in an unholy chant. It was Viktor's voice.

Or that of the daemon that had inhabited his form.

The axe glowed red hot now and, as Felix watched, a red mist bled from the ancient starmetal, streaming off after the running woodsman. A wispy umbilical hung in its wake, fastening to the blade like a tether.

'What has it done to my axe?' bellowed Gotrek, charging after its departing shape, swinging his weapon madly through the ethereal cloud.

Tamascz turned to look over his shoulder just as the daemon cloud struck, his face twisted in horror as the red mist descended. Battling through the snow in pursuit, Felix saw the man disappear into the cloud, evident only in an arm or leg that thrashed within the enshrouding mist.

'Don't attack it,' yelled Felix, hoping that the maddened Slayer would hear. 'You'll only hurt him.'

Bellowing a war cry, the dwarf swung back his axe to strike, the mere proximity of the Slayer seeming to affect the daemon cloud like a sacred icon of Sigmar might repel the undead. It lifted from the ground, relinquishing the gasping woodsman as Gotrek barrelled into its roiling mass, laying about with his axe like a madman. The red fog enshrouded the Slayer completely, and Felix could only vaguely hear muffled shouts from within.

The shape shuddered, a wave of what Felix imagined to be

pain rippling across its nebulous face. It shrank back, seeming to draw in on itself until Felix noticed it was being pulled back into Gotrek's axe.

The Slayer roared as the fog withdrew into his beloved weapon, slamming the axe again and again into the bole of a nearby tree as though it might shake the daemon loose. Gradually, he calmed down and sank into the snow beside the splintered trunk. He stared glumly at his axe.

'It would appear you're right, manling. This Ghrizzhtadt does not die so readily.'

Felix extended his hand to the cowering woodsman. Tamascz stared at it for a moment as though it might grow teeth and bite him. Eventually he took it and allowed Felix to help him to his feet.

'The Everliving should be trapped in its castle,' he muttered. 'There are wards, there are guards!'

'What, exactly, is the Everliving?' asked Felix.

Tamascz gave him an odd look.

'A daemon, but not any daemon. It is said that during the Great War, Voivode Bilenkov refused to abandon his home and retreat to Erengrad. He denounced his rulers and appealed to the gods for strength to fight alone.'

'And then what?' asked Felix.

'What do you think? He got it! But somehow the daemon remained after Bilenkov passed, claiming the souls of his family one by one. That was when the Knights of the Silent Shield were founded. It was they who warded the castle, and who stand sentry to this day.'

'Tell us about these knights,' said Gotrek.

'The Silent Shields are sworn to destroy the daemon. Deafness is the one defence against the Everliving, and initiates take needles to their ears to thwart its curse.'

Felix winced, but Gotrek only snorted. 'It seems your Ever-living has outlived its gaolers,' he said. 'They should have killed it while they were still able.'

'It can't be killed, don't you see?' said Tamascz, on the brink of tears. 'And it's out now, thanks to you!'

'Well it's not staying in my axe!'

'But Gotrek, if it's bound to your axe maybe we can just take it back and bury it.'

Gotrek glared at him, his voice low and threatening. 'I'd sooner bury you, manling.'

'We have time to think of something. It's trapped in the axe, so long as its magic protects us.'

The three of them stared at it. As if the imprisoned daemon had selected that precise moment to act, one of the glowing runes blinked out with a metallic chime, the potent ward fading like a dead star.

Gotrek snorted with black humour. 'Not as much time as you might wish for, manling.'

'H-how many of those wards do you have?' murmured Tamascz.

'Enough,' grunted Gotrek, testily.

'Then what do we do?' asked Felix.

Gotrek ran his thumb down the blade of his axe. He grinned as though someone had just offered him a tzarina's ransom in gold. 'We find it a new host. Something I *can* kill!'

Felix buried his face in his hands. He should have known.

'Not for me,' said Tamascz firmly. 'You set this horror loose. I have a wife and two girls at home.'

'You can't leave, Tamascz,' said Felix, gently. 'If you venture too far the daemon will try to claim you again. I'm afraid you're stuck with us.'

Rolling his eyes, Gotrek turned to walk away. 'Fine, he can

stay. But he's sharing your half of the gold.'

Felix couldn't help a disbelieving smile. He didn't know what was stranger, the dwarf's hunger to face the Everliving one last time or his conviction, even now, that they might still locate the barrow of Okedai Khan.

'Which way shall it be, then?' asked Gotrek.

'That way,' said Felix and Tamascz together, their fingers pointing away to some shared, hidden point in the trees to the north.

Gotrek's eyes narrowed. 'What's over there?'

'I-I don't know,' stuttered Tamascz, paling.

The three of them let their eyes fall back to the axe, silent and grim in Gotrek's fists.

The dwarf chuckled coldly. 'Ha! I don't even care. Let the daemon lead us where it will. It wants the same thing as I do.'

Felix felt his skin crawl. He wasn't so sure.

A darting form caught Felix's eye. He spun round, sword drawn. He stared hard between the brooding trunks at where the thing had been, but now there was nothing. The snow was undisturbed, the hard leaves still. Again, the sound came from behind him, and again he spun. It was the sound of running feet. The strains of a woman's laughter crystallised from the air like ice.

'Gotrek,' he called, his voice seeming muffled and faint even to his own ears. 'Gotrek, help me.'

The movement came again, closer this time. He shifted his body just as something small and lithe but with tremendous strength carried him from his feet, and slammed him face down into the snow-blanketed earth.

He looked up into the face of a woman as beautiful as she was regal. Her hair was as pale as snow, her touch as cold as death. 'No...' he whispered. 'Not you.'

With tender affection, the pale woman caressed his cheek with an icy palm, uttering soothing noises, as if he were a tearful child. She smiled to see his fear, her soft red lips curling up to reveal dagger-like canines. 'Hush Felix, so fearful. Rest now. Live anew.'

She opened her small mouth wide. Felix felt the prick in his neck as one of her teeth snagged in his flesh.

'No! Ulrika!'

He fought, punching at the restraining strength with elbows and heels. He was rewarded with a grunt of pain and he felt the weight slide off him. He didn't allow himself a moment's hesitation, knowing he could not do what must be done if he did. He took up his blade and dived onto the vampire, holding aloft his sword to bury it in her heart.

'Felix! Stop, it's me.'

He looked down at Ulrika. She was beautiful, so beautiful.

He scrunched his eyes shut. Something was not right. That was not her voice.

She reached for him, her eyes beseeching.

'T-Tamascz?'

The woodsman suddenly relaxed, his head flopping down into the soft snow, sighing in relief as Felix hesitantly lowered his weapon. 'You cannot let yourself sleep,' he said. 'That is how the Everliving will trap you. Its evil finds your fears to use against you. Your mind is weakest when it dreams.'

Felix let out a shuddering breath, trying not to imagine the daemon inside his mind. He glanced around the circle of dark trees, the night lit only by the embers of their dying campfire. Then he looked across at Gotrek. The Slayer never seemed truly peaceful, but he slept soundly enough, undisturbed by daemons or nightmares or Felix's yelling.

'Why not him?' Felix asked, nodding in the dwarf's direction. 'Why doesn't it come for him, too?'

The woodsman shrugged.

'Fine,' Felix grumbled. He'd already gone one night without sleep. What was one more?

For most of the next day they trudged through knee-deep snow and unchanging forest. Felix had long ago lost any sense of direction, yet neither did he doubt that their path was true. Why that was, he couldn't say, and nor could Tamacsz, yet the burly Kislevite seemed to share his conviction. That in itself worried Felix, but his mind was too full of fog to treat such concerns with the severity that they were due. He would almost welcome death, the chance to lie down, and close his eyes...

'Look here, manling.'

Gotrek's granite-like voice roused him, pointing him in the direction of firelight. The glow threw long, shimmering shadows into the forest that danced to the beat of a distant drum.

They crept closer, lurking just beyond the tree line and peering out into a wide clearing that heaved with cavorting beastmen. Felix released a long breath. There must be over a hundred of the brutish creatures. If Ghrizzhtadt wanted the three of them dead, it seemed he was going to get his wish.

The herd was gathered around an immense brass gong twice the height of a man and suspended within a broad, triangular wooden frame. It practically thrummed with dormant power, rendering the clearing unseasonably warm. No snow settled here and flowers bloomed in the long grass, like some trick of fate to bestow this oasis of Kislevite springtime into the keeping of the Ruinous Powers. Beastmen stomped amidst the delicate blooms, sometimes pausing, seemingly at random, to pound the instrument with their claws or antlered heads. Some danced to the drums and pipes of others of their kin.

Others fought, stag-like horns intertwined, while others still rutted in a horrific blending of animal parts that Felix prayed he would live long enough to forget.

Gotrek smiled broadly. 'A glorious sight, eh? Ha!'

The Slayer roared in delight, charging from the tree line, the music snarling to a halt as all eyes turned on the demented dwarf bounding towards them.

'He's mad,' muttered Tamascz, notching a white-feathered arrow to his bow.

Felix smiled ruefully. 'You've no idea.'

Gotrek reached the nearest of the beastmen, a shaggy haired abomination with the head of a bull. As Gotrek swung his axe, Felix noticed the red mist trailing from it once more like a priest's censer. The cloud grew darker as it took on a greater solidity, wrapping around the Slayer's shoulder and pulling him down. The dwarf fell, rolling through the grass as he wrestled with the daemon mist. The bull-headed beastman blinked in surprise, its slow mind not quite keeping pace with events, before the dwarf leapt up and laid into the herd.

Crude weapons were drawn, and Tamascz loosed his bowstring, but the arrow flew high and wide. Evidently the woodsman was more accustomed to hunting rabbits than the beasts of Chaos.

Cursing the day he had met the doomed Slayer, Felix leapt from cover and sprinted after him. Gotrek seemed to be holding his own despite his struggles with the daemon mist. He acknowledged Felix with a grunt before spinning away to crush a beastman's ribcage with a sickening blow. Limbs, horns and sprays of gore flew around the rampaging dwarf as he carved a bloody ring into the crowding beastmen.

Felix tucked in behind the Slayer, shielding his companion's left side, focusing on fending off the herd of beastmen while letting Gotrek do the bulk of the killing. The Slayer cleaved a bloody path towards the great wooden pyramid in the centre of the clearing and Felix, keeping close, followed in the trail he left.

There they held, fighting back-to-back, using the frame to guard their flank. Up close, the metal of the gong was hellishly warm, its tremulous surface whispering its acknowledgment to the snorts and bellows of the raging herd.

With a roar of fury, Gotrek split a beastman's jaw in two with a savage upwards swing. The red mist quivered, seeming to grow ever more solid with each life the Slayer took. It flowed across his broad shoulders, trying to throttle his neck whilst also pulling on both arms. Emboldened by the Slayer's struggles, the beastmen were circling closer.

'How is it coming along?' Felix shouted. Gotrek shot him a confused look. 'Finding our angry friend a body, I mean! Don't be picky. Any one of these will do!'

'It's a daemon, manling, not a bloody crossbow. I can't just point and shoot!'

Lowing in blood-crazed hysteria, another beastman charged in, thrusting its spear up and into the Slayer's shoulder. Gotrek gritted his teeth against the pain, channelling it into a howl of pure outrage as he ripped the barbed point clear and brained his would-be attacker with the thick wood.

Gotrek flexed his massive muscles and bellowed at the rest of the cowardly beastmen. He bled from a dozen cuts, the one in his shoulder merely the worst of many. The daemon mist coiled about his many wounds like a swarm of hornets, shuddering and sparking with dark energies at the touch of blood. As the cloud swirled, a hollow chant began to ring from its formless depths, and it rose up from the battlefield like a crackling vortex.

Man and beast alike lowered their weapons to stare in horrified wonder as, trailing blood like a comet's tail, the daemon swooped down upon the nearest living thing.

The glaive-wielding beastman gagged as the cloud flooded its throat, its body jerking in violent spasms. The beast's fur stood on end, static discharges igniting the air, absorbing every last speck of daemon mist. Giving one final shudder, the beastman opened its eyes. Where once had been dull, black disks there now swirled pools of liquid gold.

Felix didn't know whether Gotrek's axe offered less protection to the evil beasts of Chaos, or whether their animal minds were simply more pliant hosts for the daemon, empowered by the blood of many new victims. Feeling his fears and woes known to the tremendous, undying intellect behind those eyes, Felix found himself certain of only one thing.

Ghrizzhtadt the Everliving had a new host.

Felix flinched as an arrow zipped by his cheek, embedding in Ghrizzhtadt's heart with a solid *thunk*. The daemon merely glanced down at the twelve inches of wood sticking from its chest, and snorted in some bestial facsimile of laughter. Felix noted that the arrow shaft had begun to burn. The tips of the daemon's fur fizzed like a thousand lit tapers.

'*Free. Free at last,*' whispered Ghrizzhtadt in the fractured, grunting speech of a beast. '*I should thank you, for bearing me from my prison. I could never have passed the wards alone.*'

Gotrek cackled madly. 'Come to me then, daemon. My axe misses you already!'

The daemon pumped its fists high above its head, clenched knuckles throbbing with power. It roared to a riot of hoots and barks from the gathered beastmen. 'Blood for the Blood God! Skulls for the throne of Ghrizzhtadt the Everliving!'

The beastmen surged around the pulsing daemon prince,

inspired by a sudden killing zeal. Gotrek met them with equal fervour, demonstrating his joy at reclaiming his beloved axe with the bountiful blood of his foes.

Felix kept in tight to the Slayer's back, fending off any beasts the dwarf missed. Still, things didn't look good. From the corner of his eye he saw Tamascz dragged from the trees. He struggled for a moment before a lumbering beastman gutted him with a swipe of its bull-like horns.

The man's screams were like a knife in Felix's side.

Felix was forced to ignore them as a heavy-bladed falchion stroked towards his skull. It gouged through empty air as Felix leapt back at the last moment, angling his sword into a guard position, and the brawny beastman wielding it followed after him. It lowed a challenge and stomped its hoofed feet, kicking up great clods of turf. Then, seemingly forgetting its weapon, it loped towards him, building to a gallop as it dropped its spiral-horned head and charged like a ram.

Hopelessly misjudging the creature's speed, Felix slapped the flat of his sword harmlessly off its flanks even as the horned head crunched into his chest. His mouth gaped in breathless agony as he was tossed back several feet, landing in a clattering heap of bruises and chainmail.

Through a film of tears, he watched the monster circle, wielding its falchion in two hands to finish him off with a thrust through the heart. Acting almost wholly on instinct, he kicked out, crunching his heel into the brute's shin. The beast-man fell to one knee and he ran his sword through its belly.

With a grunt of pain, Felix found his feet once more. He hunched to better cosset his injured ribs, and looked up to see Gotrek forging a path towards Ghrizzhtadt.

Snarling, the lumbering daemon-host barged aside the other beastmen to meet the Slayer head-on. It hefted its glaive and thrust at the charging dwarf, but Gotrek batted it aside on the haft of his axe. As he reversed his grip to slash at the thing's face, the daemon swung around the butt of its weapon shaft and smote it across the Slayer's chin. Gotrek staggered back, but only for the time it took to readjust his grip and lunge in again.

The Slayer's axe and Ghrizzhtadt's glaive became an inseparable blur of motion. For over a minute, the duel raged at that ferocious pace, only slowing when Gotrek sheared the glaive in two with a roar of triumph. The daemon's hands flew aside, each clutching half of the broken weapon. It smiled evilly, even as the Slayer's next strike rammed up through its ribs.

The daemon fell with a gurgled sigh of satisfaction.

'Foolish... dwarf... Do you still not see? You cannot kill... the Everliving.' Ghrizzhtadt looked past the body of its would-be slayer, its golden eyes meeting Felix's horrified stare. *'When this craven line of cowardly tzars lies buried under the ruins of Kislev, I will forge a new land, a* strong *land. These beasts of Chaos are fit to fight and to die, but only a* man *can rule...'*

The daemon's otherworldly chanting began again, the adopted body convulsing, blood bursting from its vessels in a grisly spray. The red cloud swept over the clearing, ignoring the beastmen that fled its path as it bore upon Felix.

The hideous words forced themselves into his ears like grasping claws, boring a path straight into his brain. His sword fell from his grip, and his mouth opened into a scream. He clamped his hands over his ears, but he could not block out the daemon's vile incantation.

Felix opened his eyes to see Gotrek lumbering away through the red mist, paying it no heed. He was charging towards the great gong in the middle of the clearing. The dwarf leapt into the air with his axe high over his head, powerful muscles bringing the magical blade down with all his might.

It crashed against the raised boss at the gong's centre, the titanic strength of Gotrek's blow releasing a shockwave of power from the ensorcelled metal which blasted him away through the air.

The bloom of force exploded outwards in all directions, striking beastmen from their feet and snapping branches from the trees at the edges of the clearing. Felix took the deafening blast like a hammerblow to the chest, which cracked a few of his already tender ribs and sent him skidding through the grass and trampled flowers.

He lay winded for a long moment, before he realised that he could hear nothing but a high-pitched ringing in his ears. Still stunned, he glanced around to see beastmen clutching their tufted ears and lunging around in pain, blood running thinly from their shattered eardrums. Gotrek too was grimacing and rubbing at the sides of his head, his axe lying on the ground nearby.

The dwarf's actions had deafened them all.

The pain in Felix's ears grew, and he shrieked wordlessly, no sound seeming to leave his throat. Finally, with blood trickling between his fingers, the ringing in his head dropped away to a faint, tinny squeal. He recalled Tamascz's words: *Deafness is the one defence against the Everliving.*

He tried to mouth his thanks as he saw Gotrek rise. The Slayer's face was bloody, his lips moving too fast for Felix to follow. He sat up, trying to shake the painful tinnitus from his ears, and looked again. Gotrek was still yelling, but now he was pointing too, gesturing wildly at something behind Felix's back.

Using one hand for support, Felix tottered to his feet and turned to see what had so excited his companion.

A curse tried to form on his lips, but the words would not come.

The thwarted daemon cloud fizzed and roiled before him, denied the new host it had sought. Instead it compressed under its own fury, becoming solid, sculpting itself into a massive, man-like shape. Clenching its coalescing fists, the daemon roared. It was near twice Felix's height and without a single scrap of flesh anywhere on its monstrous frame. Naked muscles pulled taut and proud between glistening ropes of sinew. Exposed arteries ran the length of the daemon's mighty form, blood haemorrhaging from them in impossible, seemingly limitless quantities. Its face was proportioned like that of a man, but with sharp, balefire-blackened horns thrusting from its flayed forehead either side of a single, vast eye – gold and lidless – that flickered with a fierce corona of light.

Felix felt his arms go weak, his courage seeming to plummet like a stone into a bottomless well. Every terror he could imagine was promised in that thousand-millennia stare. In a heartbeat, Felix felt as though he experienced every single one. He collapsed with a cry of horror.

Ghrizzhtadt ignored him completely, plucking the nearest beastman from its feet and hurling the yammering creature into the still trembling gong with daemonic strength. Felix felt, rather than heard, the impact which tore the instrument from its frame, and smashed the wood to splinters. The muffled sound still pained his ears, but it was nothing compared to the fury of the daemon itself.

'You think to thwart me so easily, dwarf? Think again! When I am done, the man will still be mine. No more weakness, no more games. Feel the wrath of a daemon prince of Khorne!'

Gotrek met the monster's gaze with his one good eye, undaunted. 'I'm still waiting, daemon.'

Ghrizzhtadt lifted its face and howled in the ecstasy of power. A serrated row of obsidian spines erupted from its arms in a shower of gore. It twisted its torso, throwing blood around like rain.

With startling speed, Ghrizzhtadt pounced, hammering down a fist. Gotrek dived beneath the daemon's blow as it smashed into the ground where he had been. Rolling between its trunk-like legs, he brought his axe down, aiming to sever the monster's hamstring.

Blood fountained from the torn muscle, forcing Gotrek to turn away. Gasping and sputtering for breath under the sickly torrent, the Slayer hacked blindly at the daemon's legs. He shortened his grip and pressed the attack, but the flow would not abate and Gotrek was forced to spend more effort shielding his eyes and mouth than actually swinging his axe. In just one moment of inattention, the daemon caught him a glancing blow to the temple with a cloven hoof, and he slipped to the ground in a blood-sodden heap.

Within a rout of panicked beastmen, Felix watched in a daze. The creatures fled from the daemon, requiring only the occasional lick of Felix's sword to encourage them on their way. His ears still ringing, he saw Gotrek fall, disappearing into the bloody mud as it began to pool at Ghrizzhtadt's feet. The Slayer's mouth was wide and gasping for air, even before the daemon stamped down on his struggling form, grinding him deeper into the slick.

'Drown, little dwarf. Drown in blood.'

Though fear still gripped his heart at the sight of the daemon, Felix knew he had to do something. From the corner of his eye, he spotted the broken body of Tamascz. The man's bruised face and bloodstained furs rendered him all but undistinguishable from the beastmen that lay beside him.

Felix's gaze shifted to the short bow that lay on the grass by his side.

Yes!

He scrambled across the field of corpses, weaving between stampeding beastmen to where the dead man lay. Snatching at the bow with one hand, he fumbled with the woodsman's quiver. He cursed as his fingers brushed against hard feathers – there was only one arrow left. It would have to do.

Spinning into a crouch, he turned to face the towering daemon. He nocked the arrow, taking a deep breath as he hauled back with two fingers on the string, squinting with one eye down the arrow's length. The daemon was oblivious to him, its baleful eye fixed on the Slayer that splashed and raged with impotent fury beneath its hoof.

Felix released his held breath and the taut string as one, leaping to his feet with an exultant shout as the shot struck home.

The daemon's head jerked back and it staggered drunkenly away, letting out a sky-shattering scream of agony. It raised a hand to its eye, an arrow shaft jutting between its fingers.

Felix cried out in relief as he saw Gotrek's massive axe flash from the bloody pool and bite into the daemon's groin. The daemon grunted and continued edging back, drawing the Slayer from the mud like some unlikely midwife delivering a particularly ugly, bearded newborn.

And, like most newborns, Gotrek was far from happy.

He pulled himself up one-handed on his axe, grabbing onto the great curved spines of the daemon's forearm. Before it could react, the Slayer wrenched his axe free, bringing it up in an overhanded swing, hewing into the tuberous, palpitating mass of Ghrizzhtadt's throat.

Ghrizzhtadt threw itself about in blinded fury. Gotrek held

on tightly as, more by chance than by design, he was clobbered by a monstrous fist, encircling his body with powerful, blood-dripping fingers that tried to wrench him free. He hacked again and again at the meat of the daemon's arm; blood ran in rivers, but Ghrizzhtadt seemed beyond caring.

At last, Gotrek's strength gave and the daemon prince pulled him clear, waving the cursing dwarf above his horned head like a trophy before turning and fixing Felix with its blind gaze.

Felix dropped the bow and took up his sword. He took a breath to steady himself, before letting it out in a nervous whistle. He felt a twinge of guilt that he might actually die before Gotrek. A strange thought, all things considered, but a promise was a promise. He raised his sword and broke into a run, a war cry rich with vengeance upon his lips.

He powered his runesword with all his might into Ghrizzhtadt's belly. The aftershock shuddered down Felix's arm, threatening to spring the sword from his grip. He cried out in alarm as he saw that his blade had barely scored the daemon's hide. He leapt clear of its enraged counter, dancing away from its clumsy blows. His ringing ears conspired to unbalance him and, even blind, the daemon struck with a frenzied, unnatural speed that took all his wits to evade. All the while, above his head, as though disconnected from his world, he heard Gotrek hacking into the daemon's arm, a slew of barely intelligible insults hurled after every stroke.

Felix jumped from the path of a ploughing fist, the killing spines shredding links from his chainmail and sending him stumbling over the body of a fallen beastman. Ghrizzhtadt took full advantage, bowling him from his feet and pinning him against the corpse with a massive, blood-soaked fist.

'Kislev will be mine. There is nothing to save you now.'

'That old tzar is long dead,' Felix shouted. 'The Great War is over.'

'*So naive. War is never ov–*'

Gotrek fell to earth with a cry of triumph, still gripped in Ghrizzhtadt's severed hand. The daemon stared dumbly at the gushing stump of its wrist as the dwarf squirmed free, trailing bloody vapour into the air.

Felix tried to focus on the daemon prince, but its form flickered and swam. He blinked, believing it to be some trick of his eyes, but the hazy outline of its body was beginning to blur into kaleidoscopic mist. The Slayer looked little better – his left arm hung limp at his side, the wound that the beastman spear had inflicted looking ugly and pale.

His face grim, the Slayer brandished his axe in his good hand and made ready for the final battle. He was ready to face his doom at last.

Felix took up his sword once more. If this was to be Gotrek's end, then he had to witness it. That had been his promise, as much as it pained him now that the moment was upon them. Every vile horror in the world would not make him abandon a friend.

Sniffing the air, Ghrizzhtadt cackled with glee and advanced with deliberate slowness. '*At last, Gotrek Gurnisson. I know what it is that you fear.*'

'I told you, daemon, this dwarf fears nothing! Come see for yourself.'

'*No. You fear that you will not die with honour. You fear that your crime will never be absolved. Drop your axe, dwarf. This is a fear you need never face...*'

To Felix's horror, Gotrek's axe actually lowered a fraction and the daemon sprang forwards, angling a blow to eviscerate the hesitating Slayer on the spines of its forearm.

But Gotrek hesitated for only a second, his face darkening with an anger Felix had seldom witnessed. With astounding speed and ferocity, he brought up his axe, catching the daemon's swipe on his blade. The starmetal wedged firmly between two long spines, its runes glowing brightly as inhuman strength measured itself against ungodly fury.

Ghrizzhtadt glared at the defiant dwarf with crimson rage. *'Foolish! You are mortal. You will die. You* wish *to die. Why not... just...* die!'

The daemon roared, power flaring in a glittering nimbus around its fading form as it forced its arm inexorably forwards. In the face of the losing battle, Gotrek let go, giving his axe one last twist to nudge the daemon's mad swing on its way as he ducked beneath it. Immediately, the Slayer bounced back up, giving the daemon no time to recover his arm as he swung his axe and, with every ounce of strength, hammered the ancestral weapon into its heart.

Ghrizzhtadt vomited blood as its legs separated from its body, dissolving before his eyes as the magic that kept it whole dispersed. Gotrek threw himself clear as the daemon fell, its jaw cracking hard as it landed.

It lay wheezing for a moment, its face pressed into the bloody mud.

'I... am... Everliving. I won't... go back... to him.' With that, Ghrizzhtadt once again took up its terrible chant, its spirit preparing to take flight once more.

Ghrizzhtadt's golden eye rolled sightlessly as the Slayer climbed onto its back, axe in hand. For the first time in its long existence, the Everliving knew for itself the cold taste of fear.

'None of that rubbish, daemon.'

Gotrek planted his boot into the back of the daemon's skull, crushing its face into the ground, stifling the unholy words before they could be uttered. Ghrizzhtadt began to thrash and jerk, writhing in panic as it fought to dislodge the Slayer from its shoulders, but it was already too far gone. Blood bubbled from a vanishing throat even as the daemon prince's body came apart, piece by piece.

Felix stood within an aurora of bursting and colliding stars as the remains of the Everliving were carved up by the Winds of Magic. As the last, it was as if it carried with it the faintest hint of a plea for mercy, an infinitesimal cry of anguish, before that too disappeared into oblivion.

'One thing's for sure – his bloody master's not awfully fond of magic,' Gotrek snorted, his face spread into a vicious grin. 'I'm thinking this Ghrizzhtadt has some explaining to do.'

Gotrek rose, presenting a battered golden circlet to his good eye for closer inspection. He frowned and bit into it before tossing it back onto the body of its former owner with a curse.

'Bah, typical Chaos beasts. Naught but gold leaf and copper.' The Slayer looked up at Felix with an expression that, on any other face, might have been considered kindly. 'We can head back to your Empire, manling. If you wish.'

'Truthfully?'

'You worry for your family. Nobody knows the importance of kin like a dwarf. And besides, who's to say we cannot meet our doom there, eh?'

Our doom, thought Felix, but dismissed the argument before it arose. He was too tired. He gazed wistfully in what, he fancied, was the direction of the Empire, of Altdorf, and home. He missed them, it was true... and yet his gaze turned northwards. It was all purely academic, of course. There was nothing to see in any direction but spindly, snow-capped trees. Not that he minded – with the Everliving gone, and its hold over him broken, he felt renewed.

Reborn, even?

'I wonder what's over there,' he murmured, gazing into the distance.

Gotrek grinned toothlessly. 'Our gold, I'll wager. The tomb of Okedai Khan.'

'Let's go and find it.'

Felix turned, just in time to see the heavy shape of Gotrek Gurnisson topple face-down into a bed of daisies. He lay, snoring raggedly; it appeared that the dwarf's exertions had finally caught up with him.

Chuckling, Felix cast his eyes over the clearing one last time. It was strewn with corpses – the scattered beastmen might return at any time and the brass gong, even broken, still veritably hummed with undimmed potency. At least it was warm, he thought. That was, after all, all he had really wanted.

ABOUT THE AUTHORS

David Guymer is no stranger to the worlds of Warhammer, with stories in *Gotrek and Felix: The Anthology* and *Hammer and Bolter*, and much more on the way. He is a freelance writer and occasional scientist based in the East Riding. When not writing, David can be found exorcising his disappointment at the gaming table and preparing for the ascension of the children of the Horned Rat.

Author of the novels *Knight of the Blazing Sun*, *Time of Legends: Neferata* and *Gotrek and Felix: Road of Skulls*, **Josh Reynolds** used to be a roadie for the Hong Kong Cavaliers, but now writes full time. His work has appeared in various anthologies, including *Age of Legend* and several issues of the electronic magazine *Hammer and Bolter*.

Frank Cavallo has written a number of short stories for Black Library, including 'Leechlord' and 'The Talon of Khorne'. He was born and raised in New Jersey, went to school in Boston and now lives in Cleveland, Ohio, where he works by day as a criminal defence attorney.

Jordan Ellinger is the author of the Gotrek and Felix novella *The Reckoning* as well as numerous short stories for Black Library. A first place winner in the Writers of the Future contest and a Clarion West graduate, his work can be seen in numerous anthologies across the science fiction and fantasy genres. When he is not writing, he is a freelance editor.